The Autobiography of Miss Jane Pittman

and Related Readings

Glencoe
McGraw-Hill

New York, New York   Columbus, Ohio   Woodland Hills, California   Peoria, Illinois

Acknowledgments

Grateful acknowledgment is given authors, publishers, photographers, museums, and agents for permission to reprint the following copyrighted material. Every effort has been made to determine copyright owners. In case of any omissions, the Publisher will be pleased to make suitable acknowledgments in future editions.

THE AUTOBIOGRAPHY OF MISS JANE PITTMAN by Ernest J. Gaines. Copyright © 1971 by Ernest J. Gaines. Published by arrangement with DOUBLEDAY, a division of Random House, Inc., New York, New York, U.S.A. All rights reserved.

Text excerpts, "I Want Women To Have Their Rights. . . . I Will Shake Every Place I Go To" by Sojourner Truth and "The Progress of Colored Women" by Mary Church Terrell from HISTORIC SPEECHES OF AFRICAN AMERICANS by Warren J. Halliburton, Ed., 1993, Franklin Watts.

"Ernest Gaines" by Tom Carter from *Essence*, July 1975. Reprinted by permission of *Essence*.

"1960: The Sit-ins" and "Martin Luther King, Jr.—The Power of Nonviolence" from EVERYBODY SAYS FREEDOM by Pete Seeger and Bob Reiser. Copyright © 1989 the Highlander Research and Education Center, New Market, TN. Reprinted by permission of the Highlander Center, Robert Reiser, and Pete Seeger.

Text excerpt, "The Trailblazer, Jackie Robinson" by Henry Aaron. Copyright © Time Inc. Reprinted by permission.

From I KNOW WHY THE CAGED BIRD SINGS by Maya Angelou. Copyright © 1969 and renewed 1997 by Maya Angelou. Reprinted by permission of Random House, Inc.

Cover art: Christie's Images/SuperStock

Glencoe/McGraw-Hill

A Division of The **McGraw·Hill** *Companies*

Send all inquiries to:
Glencoe/McGraw-Hill
8787 Orion Place
Columbus, OH 43240

ISBN 0-02-817971-4
Printed in the United States of America
3 4 5 6 7 8 9 026 04 03 02 01

Contents

The Autobiography of Miss Jane Pittman

Continued

Contents *Continued*

Related Readings 187

The Autobiography of Miss Jane Pittman

Ernest J. Gaines

Introduction

I HAD BEEN TRYING to get Miss Jane Pittman to tell me the story of her life for several years now, but each time I asked her she told me there was no story to tell. I told her she was over a hundred years old, she had been a slave in this country, so there had to be a story. When school closed for the summer in 1962 I went back to the plantation where she lived. I told her I wanted her story before school opened in September, and I would not take no for an answer.

"You won't?" she said.

"No, ma'am."

"Then I reckon I better say something," she said.

"You don't have to say a thing," Mary said.

Mary Hodges was a big brown-skin woman in her early sixties who lived in the same house that Miss Jane did and looked after Miss Jane.

"If I don't he go'n just worry me to death," Miss Jane said.

"What you want know about Miss Jane for?" Mary said.

"I teach history," I said. "I'm sure her life's story can help me explain things to my students."

"What's wrong with them books you already got?" Mary said.

"Miss Jane is not in them," I said.

"It's all right, Mary," Miss Jane said.

"You don't have to say nothing less you want," Mary said.

"He'll just keep on bothering me."

"Not if you tell him stay 'way from here," Mary said. "And I can always borrow Etienne's shotgun."

"When you want start?" Miss Jane said.

"You mean it's all right?" I said.

Now, they just look at me. I couldn't read Miss Jane's mind. When a person is over a hundred years old it's hard to tell what she is thinking. But Mary was only in her sixties, and I could read her mind well. She still wanted to borrow Etienne's shotgun.

"Is Monday all right?" I asked.

"Monday's good," Miss Jane said.

I had planned to record Miss Jane's story on tape that summer before school opened again. After the first two weeks I was sure I could do it. But during that third week everything slowed up to an almost complete halt. Miss Jane began to forget everything. I don't know whether she was doing this purposely or not, but suddenly she could not remember anything any more. The only thing that saved me was that there were other people at the house every day that I interviewed her, and they were glad to help in every way that they could. Miss Jane was constantly turning to one of them for the answer. An old man called Pap was her main source. Pap was in his mid-eighties, he had lived on that plantation all his life, and he could remember everything that had happened in the parish since the turn of the century. But even Pap's knowledge could not keep the interview within the schedule that I had planned. And after school opened for the new semester all plans were changed, because now I could only interview Miss Jane on weekends. I would talk to her and the other people at the house for several hours, then I would leave until the following Saturday or Sunday. (I should mention here that even though I have used only Miss Jane's voice throughout the narrative, there were times when others carried the story for her. When she was tired, or when she just did not feel like talking any more, or when she had forgotten certain things, someone else would always pick up the narration. Miss Jane would sit there listening until she got ready to talk again. If she agreed with what the other person was saying she might let him go on for quite a while. But if she did not agree, she would shake her head and say: "No, no, no, no, no." The other person would not contradict her, because, after all, this was her story.)

There were times when I thought the narrative was taking ridiculous directions. Miss Jane would talk about one thing one day and the next day she would talk about something else totally different. If I were bold enough to ask: "But what about such and such a thing?" she would look at me incredulously and say: "Well, what about it?" And Mary would back her up with: "What's wrong with that? You don't like that part?" I would say, "Yes, but—" Mary would say, "But what?" I would say, "I just want to tie up all the loose ends." Mary would say, "Well, you don't tie up all the loose ends all the time. And if you got to change her way of telling it, you tell it yourself. Or maybe you done heard enough already?" Then both of them would look at me as if I had come into the room without knocking. "Take what she say and be satisfied," Mary would say.

I could not possibly put down on paper everything that Miss Jane and the others said on the tape during those eight or nine months. Much of it was too repetitious and did not follow a single direction. What I have tried to do here was not to write everything, but in essence everything that was said. I have tried my best to retain Miss Jane's language. Her selection of words; the rhythm of her speech. When she spoke she used as few words as possible to make her point. Yet, there were times when she would repeat a word or phrase over and over when she thought it might add humor or drama to the situation.

Miss Jane died about eight months after the last interview. At her funeral I met many of the people whom she had talked about. I told them about the tape and asked could I talk to them sometime. Almost everyone, both black and white, said I could. Some of them wanted to hear the tape, or part of it, before they made any comments. After hearing the tape they refused to say anything. Others laughed and said not everything on the tape was absolutely correct. Still, others were glad to give information without listening to the tape at all, and in most cases much of what they said was pretty close to what Miss Jane had said before.

In closing I wish to thank all the wonderful people who were at Miss Jane's house through those long months of interviewing her, because this is not only Miss Jane's autobiography, it is theirs as well. This is what both Mary and Miss Jane meant when they said you could not tie all the ends together in one neat direction. Miss Jane's story is all their stories, and their stories are Miss Jane's.

the editor

BOOK I

The War Years

Soldiers

IT WAS A DAY something like right now, dry, hot, and dusty dusty. It might 'a' been July, I'm not too sure, but it was July or August. Burning up, I won't ever forget. The Secesh Army, they came by first. The Officers on their horses, the Troops walking, some of them dragging the guns in the dust they was so tired. The Officers rode up in the yard, and my mistress told them to get down and come in. The colonel said he couldn't come in, he was going somewhere in a hurry, but he would be glad to get down and stretch his legs if the good lady of the house would be so gracious to let him. My mistress said she most graciously did, and after the colonel had got down he told the others to get down too. The colonel was a little man with a gun and a sable. The sable was so long it almost dragged on the ground. Looked like the colonel was a little boy who had got somebody else's sable to play with. My mistress told me stop standing there gaping, go out there in the road and give the Troops some water. I had the water in a barrel under one of the chinaball trees. We knowed the soldiers was coming that way—we had heard the gun fire the day before, and somebody had already passed the house and told us if the soldiers came by be prepared to help in every way we could; so they had put me to hauling water. All morning long I hauled water to that barrel. Now I had to haul the water out the barrel to the Troops out in the road. Buckets after buckets after buckets. I can't remember how many buckets I hauled. The Troops was so tired and ragged they didn't even see me. They took the gourd from me when I handed it to them, and that was all. After they had drunk, they just let it hang there in their hands, and I had to reach and get it so I could serve another one. But they didn't even see little old black me. They couldn't tell if I was white or black, a boy or a girl. They didn't even care what I was. One was just griping. He didn't look too much older than me—face just as dirty as it could be. Just griping: "Just left to me I'll turn them niggers loose, just left to me." When I handed him the water he held the gourd a long time before he drank, then after he had drunk he let the gourd hang in his hand while he just sat there gazing down at the ground.

But these was the same ones, mind you, who had told their people they wouldn't be late for supper. That was before—when the war was just getting started—when they thought fighting a war was nothing but another day's work. "Don't put my food up," they said, "Don't put it up and don't give it away. I'm go'n kill me up a few Yankees and I'm coming right on back home. Who they think they is trying to destruck us way of living? We the nobles, not them. God put us here to live the way we want live, that's in the Bible." (I have asked people to find that in the Bible for me, but no one's found it yet.) "And He put niggers here to see us live that way—that's in the Bible, too. John, chapter so and so. Verse, right now I forget. Now, here them Yankees want come and destruck what the Good Lord done said we can have. Keep my supper warm, Mama, I'll be back before breakfast." These was the same ones griping out in the road right now.

Before all them had a chance to get some water, I looked up and saw another one coming down the road on a horse. He was hitting and kicking that horse fast as his arms and feet could move. Hollering far as you could hear him: "Colonel, Colonel, they coming. Colonel, Colonel, they coming." He went right by us, but the Troops was so tired some of them didn't even raise their head. Some of them even laid down on the ground when he went by. "How far?" the colonel asked him. "I don't know for sure," he said. "Maybe three, four miles back there. All I can see is that dust way up in the air." My mistress handed him two biscuits and a cup of water. He looked at that bread and water like he hadn't seen food or water in a long time and he kept bowing and saying, "Thank you, ma'am; thank you, ma'am; thank you, ma'am." The colonel hit his boots together and kissed my mistress on the hand, then he told the others to get on their horses. He hollered for them in the road to get to their feet, too. Some of them did like he said, but many of them just sat there gazing down at the ground. One of the Officers had to come out in the road and call them to attention. Even then they wasn't in any kind of hurry to get on their feet. They started down the road, and I could hear that same one that had been griping before: "Just left to me I'll turn them niggers loose, just left to me." One of the other Troops told him shut up before he got both of them shot. Him for complaining, and him for being his cousin. He told him shut up or cousin or no cousin he liable to shoot him himself. But till they got out hearing distance all I could hear was that little fellow griping: "Yankees want them, let the Yankees have them—just left to me."

After they had made the bend, I went back in the yard with the bucket and the gourd. My mistress was standing on the gallery watching the dust rising over the field, and just crying. "Sweet, precious blood of the South; sweet precious blood of the South." Just watching that dust, wringing her hands and crying. Then she saw me standing there looking up at her. "What you standing there for?" she said. "Go fill that barrel."

"What for, Mistress?" I said. "They gone now."

"Don't you think Yankees drink?" she said. "Go get that water."

"I got to haul water for old Yankees, too?" I said.

"Yes," she said. "You don't want them boiling you in oil and eating you, do you?"

"No, Mistress," I said.

"You better get that water then," she said. "A Yankee like nothing better than cooking a little nigger gal and chewing her up. Where the rest of them no 'count niggers at, I wonder?"

"They went hiding with Master in the swamps," I said, pointing toward the back.

"Stop that pointing," my mistress said. "You can't tell where a Yankee might be. And you watch your tongue when they get here, too. You say anything about your master and the silver, I'll have you skinned."

"Yes, Mistress," I said.

While I was standing there, one of the other slaves bust round the house and said: "Master say come ask that's all?"

"Where your master at?" my mistress asked him.

"Edge of the swamps there," he said. "Peeping round a tree."

"Go back and tell your master that ain't half of them yet," my mistress said.

The slave bust back round the house, running faster than he did coming there. My mistress told me stop standing there and go get that water.

The Yankees didn't show up till late that evening, so that little fellow who had spotted that dust in the air had a keen eye sight or a bad judge of distance. The Yankee Officers rode up in the yard just like the Secesh Officers did; the Yankee troops plopped down side the road just like the other Troops did. I got the bucket and the gourd and went out there to give them water.

"How many Rebs went by here?" one of the Troops asked me.

"I didn't see no Rebs, Master," I said.

"Come now," he said. "Who made all them tracks out there?"

"Just us niggers," I said.

"Wearing shoes?" he said. "Where your shoes?"

"I took mine off," I said. "They hurt my foot."

"Little girl, don't you know you not suppose to lie?" he said.

"I ain't lying, Master," I said.

"What's your name?" he asked me.

"Ticey, Master," I said.

"They ever beat you, Ticey?" he asked.

"No, Master," I said.

The Troop said, "I ain't a master, Ticey. You can be frank with me. They ever beat you?"

I looked back toward the house and I could see my mistress talking with the Officers on the gallery. I knowed she was too far to hear me and the Troop talking. I looked at him again. I waited for him to ask me the same question.

"They do beat you, don't they, Ticey?" he said.

I nodded.

"What they beat you with, Ticey?" he said.

"Cat-o'-nine-tails, Master," I said.

"We'll get them," the Troop said. "Ten'll die for every whipping you ever got."

"Ten houses will burn," another Troop said.

"Ten fields, too," another one said.

"One of y'all sitting there, take that bucket and go haul that water," the first Troop said.

"I better do it, Master," I said. "They whip me if I don't do my work."

"You rest," he said. "Troop Lewis, on your feet."

Troop Lewis got up real slow; he was tired just like all the rest. He was a little fellow and I felt sorry for him because he looked like the kind everybody was always picking on. He took the bucket from me and went in the yard talking to himself. The other Troop had to holler on him to get moving.

"What they whip you for, Ticey?" he asked me.

"I go to sleep when I look after Young Mistress children," I said.

"You nothing but a child yourself," he said. "How old is you right now?"

"I don't know, Master," I said.

"Would you say ten? 'leven?"

"Yes, Master," I said.

"I ain't a master, Ticey," he said. "I'm just a' old ordinary Yankee soldier come down here to beat them Rebs and set y'all free. You want to be free, don't you, Ticey?"

"Yes, Master," I said.

"And what you go'n do when you free?" he asked me.

"Just sleep, Master," I said.

"Ticey, you not the only one go'n just sleep," he said. "But stop calling me master. I'm Corporal Brown. Can you say corporal?"

"No, Master," I said.

"Try," he said.

I started grinning.

"Come on," he said. "Try."

"I can't say that, Master," I said.

"Can you say Brown?"

"Yes, Master."

"Well, just call me Mr. Brown," he said. "And I'm go'n call you something else 'sides Ticey. Ticey is a slave name, and I don't like slavery. I'm go'n call you Jane," he said. "That's right, I'll call you Jane. That's my girl name back there in Ohio. You like for me to call you that?"

I stood there grinning like a little fool. I rubbed my foot with my big toe and just stood there grinning. The other Troops was grinning at me, too.

"Yes," he said, "I think you do like that name. Well, from now on your name is Jane. Not Ticey no more. Jane. Jane Brown. Miss Jane Brown. When you get older you can change it to what else you want. But till then your name is Jane Brown."

I just stood there grinning, rubbing my foot with my big toe. It was the prettiest name I had ever heard.

"And if any of them ever hit you again, you catch up with me and let me know," he said. "I'll come back here and I'll burn down this place."

The Yankee Officers got on their horses and came out in the road and told the Troops let's go. They got to their feet and marched on. And soon as my mistress thought they couldn't hear her she started calling my name. I just stood there and watched the soldiers go down the road. One of them looked back and waved at me—not Troop Lewis: I reckoned he was still mad at me. I grinned and waved back. After they had made the bend, I stood there and watched the dust high over the field. I was still feeling good because of my new name. Then all of a sudden my mistress was out there and she had grabbed me by the shoulders.

"You little wench, didn't you hear me calling you?" she said. I raised my head high and looked her straight in the face and said: "You called me Ticey. My name ain't no Ticey no more, it's Miss Jane Brown. And Mr. Brown say catch him and tell him if you don't like it."

My mistress face got red, her eyes got wide, and for about half a minute she just stood there gaping at me. Then she gathered up her dress and started running for the house. That night when the master and the rest of them came in from the swamps she told my master I had sassed her in front of the Yankees. My master told two of the other slaves to hold me down. One took my arms, the other one took my legs. My master jecked up my dress and gived my mistress the whip and told her to teach me a lesson. Every time she hit me she asked me what I said my name as. I said Jane Brown. She hit me again: what I said my name was. I said Jane Brown.

My mistress got tired beating me and told my master to beat me some. He told her that was enough, I was already bleeding.

"Sell her," my mistress said.

"Who go'n buy her with them Yankees tramping all over the place?" my master said.

"Take her to the swamps and kill her," my mistress said. "Get her out of my sight."

"Kill her?" my master said. "Brown come back here asking 'bout her, then what? I'll put her in the field and bring another one up here to look after them children."

They put me in the field when I was ten or 'leven. A year after that the Freedom come.

Freedom

WE WAS IN THE FIELD chopping cotton when we heard the bell ringing. We was scared to stop work—the sun was too high in the sky for us to go in yet. But the bell went on ringing and ringing; just ringing and ringing. The driver, a great big old black, round, oily-face nigger kept on looking back over his shoulders toward the house. Every time the bell rang he looked back. He told us to keep on working, he was going in to see what all the ringing was about. I watched him go up to the house, then I saw him coming back waving his arm. We swung our hoes on our shoulders and went across the field. The driver told us the master wanted us all at the house. We didn't ask what he wanted us for, we had no idea, we just went up there. The master was standing on the gallery with a sheet of paper.

"This all y'all?" he asked, "All them children in the quarters, too? I want everybody here who can stand up."

The people said this was all us.

"All right, I got news for y'all," the master said. "Y'all free. Proclamation papers just come to me and they say y'all free as I am. Y'all can stay and work on shares—because I can't pay you nothing, because I ain't got nothing myself since them Yankees went by here last time. Y'all can stay or y'all can go. If y'all stay I promise I'll be fair as I always been with y'all."

Old Mistress and Young Mistress was standing in the door crying, and right behind them the house niggers crying, too. For a while after the master got through reading the Proclamation the people didn't make a sound. Just standing there looking up at him like they was still listening to his words.

"Well, that's that," he said.

Then all a sudden somebody hollered, and everybody started singing. Just singing and dancing and clapping. Old people you didn't think could even walk started hopping round there like game roosters. This what the people was singing:

> "We free, we free, we free
> We free, we free, we free
> We free, we free, we free
> Oh, Lordy, we free."

Just singing and clapping, just singing and clapping. Just talking to each other, just patting each other on the back.

The driver he never got in the celebration him. Everybody else singing and clapping, he just standing there looking up at the master. Then he moved closer to the gallery and said: "Master, if we free to go, where is we to go?"

Before the master could open his mouth, I said: "Where North at? Point to it. I'll show y'all where to go."

The driver said: "Shut up. You ain't nothing but trouble. I ain't had nothing but trouble out you since you come in that field."

"If I ain't nothing but trouble, you ain't nothing but Nothing," I said.

And the next thing I knowed, my mouth was numb and I was laying down there on the ground. The master looked at me down there, and said: "I can't do a thing about it. You free and don't belong to me no more. Got to fight your own battle best you can."

I jumped up from there and sunk my teeth in that nigger's hand. His hand was rough as 'cuda legs. He wrenched his hand out my mouth and numbed the side of my face. This time when I got up I grabbed that hoe I had brought out the field. An old man we all called Unc Isom stepped in front of me.

"Hold," he said.

"Hold nothing," I said. "Nigger, say your prayers. Maker, here you come."

"Didn't I say hold," Unc Isom said. "When I say hold, I mean just that: hold."

I eased the hoe to the ground, but I kept my eyes on the driver all the time. I touched my lips with my hand, but I couldn't feel a thing. Not bleeding, but numb as it could be.

When Unc Isom seen I wasn't go'n hit that nigger with that hoe, he turned to the master.

"The papers say we can go or we can stay, Master?" he asked him.

"No, they just say y'all free, Isom," the master said. "They don't care what y'all do, where y'all go. I'm the one who saying y'all can stay on if y'all want. If you stay, I got to work you on shares, and you work when you want. You don't have to work on Sundays less you want. Can go to church and stay there and sing all day if you want. You free as I am, Isom."

Unc Isom said, "Master, we can gather down the quarters and talk just between us?"

The master said, "What you go'n be talking 'bout down there, Isom?"

"Just if we ought to go or stay, Master," Unc Isom said.

"Sure, y'all free as I am," the master said. "Y'all can take all the time y'all want to decide. Long as you ain't deciding on burning down the place."

Unc Isom had to grin to himself. "Master, ain't nothing like that," he said.

"Give the children some apples before they go," the mistress said.

"And the men and women cider," the master said. "Celebrate y'all freedom."

"Hold," Unc Isom said. "Apples and cider later. Now, we go in the quarters and talk."

Unc Isom was a kind of advisor to us there in the quarters. Some people said he had been a witch doctor sometime back. I know he knowed a lot about roots and herbs, and the people was always going to him for something to cure colic or the bots or whatever they had. That's why they followed him when he spoke. The young people grumbled because they wanted the apples, but the old people followed him without a word. When we came up to his cabin he told everybody to kneel down and thank God for freedom. I didn't want kneel, I didn't know too much about the Lord then, but I knelt out of respect. When Unc Isom got through praying he stood up and looked at us again. He was an old man, black black, with long white hair. He could have been in his 80s, he could have been in his 90s—I have no idea how old he was.

"Now, I ask the question," he said. "What's we to do?"

"Slavery over, let's get moving," somebody said.

"Let's stay," somebody else said. "See if old Master go'n act different when it's freedom."

"Y'all do like y'all want," I said. "I'm headed North." I turned to leave, but I stopped. "Which way North?"

"Before y'all start out here heading anywhere, what y'all go'n eat?" Unc Isom said. "Where y'all go'n sleep? Who go'n protect you from the patrollers?"

"They got Yankees," I said.

"They got Yankees, they got Yankees," Unc Isom mocked me. I could see he didn't have a tooth in his mouth. "Yankees told you your name was Jane; soon as Old Mistress start beating on you, you can't find Yankee."

"They can't beat me no more," I said. "Them papers say I'm free, free like everybody else."

"They ain't go'n just beat you if they catch you, they kill you if they catch you now," Unc Isom said. "Before now they didn't kill you because you was somebody chattel. Now you ain't owned by nobody but fate. Nobody to protect you now, little Ticey."

"My name is Jane, Unc Isom," I said. "And I'm headed for Ohio. Soon as you point that way."

"I don't know too much 'bout Ohio," Unc Isom said, coming out in the road. "Where it at or where it s'pose to be, I ain't for sure." He turned toward the swamps, then he raised his hand and pointed. "North is that way. Sun on your right in the morning, your left in the evening. North Star point the way at night. If you stay in the swamps, the moss is on the north side of the tree root."

"I'm heading out," I said. "Soon as I get me few of them apples and my other dress. Anybody else going?"

The young people started moving out in the road, but the old people started crying and holding them back. I didn't have a mama or a daddy to cry and hold me back. My mama was killed when I was young and I had never knowed my daddy. He belong to another plantation. I never did know his name.

"Hold," Unc Isom said. He raised both of his hands like he was getting ready to wave us back. "This rejoicing time, not crying time. Ain't we done seen enough weeping? Ain't we done seen enough separation? Hold now."

"You telling us to stay here?" somebody young said.

"Them who want stay, stay," he said. "Then who must go, go. But this no time for weeping. Rejoice now."

"We leaving out," somebody young said. "If the old people want stay here, stay. We free, let's move."

"Amen," I said.

"You free from what?" Unc Isom said. "Free to do what—break more hearts?"

"Niggers hearts been broke ever since niggers been in this world," somebody young said. "I done seen babies jecked from mama titty. That was breaking hearts, too."

"That couldn't be helped," Unc Isom said. "This can be helped."

"This can't be helped," somebody young said. "They got blood on this place, and I done stepped all in it. I done waded in it to my waist. You can mend a broken heart, you can't wash blood off your body."

"Hold," Unc Isom said, raising his hands again. "When you talking 'bout mama and papa's heart, hold now."

"Mama and papa's heart can't be pained no more than they been pained already," somebody young said.

"Let's go," somebody else said. "All this arguing ain't putting us no closer North."

"Hold," Unc Isom said. "This wisdom I'm speaking from. Hold now."

"Give your wisdom to the ones staying here with you," somebody young said. "Rest of us moving out."

The boy who spoke to Unc Isom like that started up the quarters toward the big house. Unc Isom let him walk a little piece, then he hollered at him to stop. The boy wouldn't stop. Unc Isom hollered at him again. This time the boy looked back over his shoulder. Unc Isom didn't say a thing, he just stood there pointing his finger at the boy.

Me and some of the other people started toward the big house to get some apples, and one of the women said Unc Isom had put bad mark on the boy. Another woman said Unc Isom didn't have power to put bad mark on you no more, he was too old now. I didn't know how powerful Unc Isom was, so I just listened to the talking and didn't say nothing.

The master had put a barrel of potatoes side the barrel of apples, and he was sitting on the gallery watching the people coming back in the yard. He asked us what we had decided in the quarters. We told him some of us was going, some of us was staying. We asked him could the ones going take anything. He wanted to tell us no, but he nodded toward the barrel and told us to take what we needed and get out. We got all the apples and potatoes we could carry, then we went back to the quarters to get our clothes. In slavery you had two dresses and a pair of shoes and a coat. A man had an extra pair of pants and an extra shirt, a pair of shoes and a coat. We tied up the apples and potatoes in our extra clothes and started out.

Heading North

WE DIDN'T KNOW A THING. We didn't know where we was going, we didn't know what we was go'n eat when the apples and potatoes ran out, we didn't know where we was go'n sleep that night. If we reached the North, we didn't know if we was go'n stay together or separate. We had never thought about nothing like that, because we had never thought we was go'n ever be free. Yes, we had heard about freedom, we had even talked about freedom, but we never thought we was go'n ever see that day. Even when we knowed the Yankees had come in the State, even when we saw them marching by the gate we still didn't feel we was go'n ever be free. That's why we hadn't got ourself ready. When the word came down that we was free, we dropped everything and started out.

It was hot. Must have been May or June. Probably June—but I'm not sure. We went across the cotton patch toward the swamps. The young men and boys started breaking down cotton stalks just to show Old Master what they thought of him and his old slavery. Somebody hollered that they better use their strength to get some corn, and we all shot out for the corn patch across the field.

Now, when we came up to the swamps nobody wanted to take the lead. Nobody wanted to be the one blamed for getting everybody else lost. All us just standing there fumbling round, waiting for somebody else to take charge.

Then somebody in the back said, "Move out the way." I looked, and that was Big Laura. She was big just like her name say, and she was tough as any man I ever seen. She could plow, chop wood, cut and load much cane as any man on the place. She had two children. One in her arms, a little girl; and she was leading Ned by the hand. Don't worry, I'll come to Ned later. Yes, Lord, I'll come to him later. But even with them two children she had the biggest bundle out there balanced on her head.

Big Laura took the lead and we started walking again. Walking fast, but staying quiet. Somebody said we ought to get sticks just in case of snakes, so we all hunted for a good green stick. Now everybody had a stick but Big Laura. She leading the way with that little girl in her arms and Ned by the hand. She had found us a good clean path and it was cool under the trees, and everybody was happy. We walked and walked and walked. Almost sundown before we stopped the first time.

"We headed toward Ohio?" I asked.

"You got somebody waiting for you in Ohio?" they asked me.

"Mr. Brown told me look him up," I said.

Nobody believed Mr. Brown had told me that, but they didn't say nothing.

"I want go to Ohio," I said.

"Go on to Ohio," one of them said. "Nobody holding you back."

"I don't know the way," I said.

"Then shut up," one of them said.

"Y'all just sorry y'all ain't got nobody waiting for y'all nowhere," I said.

Nobody said nothing. I was little, and they didn't feel they needed to argue with me.

We was in a thicket of sycamore trees, and it was quiet and clean here, and we had a little breeze, because way up in the top of the trees I could see the limbs sagging just a little. Everybody was tired from the long walk and we just sat there quiet, not saying a thing for a good while. Then somebody said: "My new name Abe Washington. Don't call me Buck no more." We must have been two dozens of us there, and now everybody started changing names like you change hats. Nobody was keeping the same name Old Master had given them. This one would say, "My new name Cam Lincoln." That one would say, "My new name Ace Freeman." Another one, "My new name Sherman S. Sherman." "What that S for?" "My Title." Another one would say, "My new name Job." "Job what?" "Just Job." "Nigger, this ain't slavery no more. You got to have two names." "Job Lincoln, then." "Nigger, you ain't no kin to me. I'm Lincoln." "I don't care. I'm still Job Lincoln. Want fight?" Another one would say, "My name Neremiah King." Another one standing by a tree would say, "My new name Bill Moses. No more Rufus."

They went on and on like that. We had one slow-wit fellow there who kept on opening his mouth to say his new name, but before he could get it out somebody else had said a name. He was just opening and closing his mouth like a baby after his mama's titty. Then all a sudden when he had a little time to speak he said Brown. They had took all the other names from him, so he took Brown. I had been sitting there on the end of a log listening to them squabbling over new names, but I didn't have to get in the squabbling because I already had a new name. I had had mine for over a year now, and I had put up with a lot of trouble to hold on to it. But when I heard the slow-wit say his name was Brown I was ready to fight. I jumped up off that log and went for him.

"No, you don't," I said.

He said, "I, I, I, can be, be, be Brown if I want be, be, be Brown." He was picking on me because I was small and didn't have nobody there to stand up for me. "You not the on', on', only one ra, ra, round here that can be, be, be Brown," he said. "Me', me', mess round here wi', wi', with me, I ma', ma' make you, you, you change your name back to Ti', Ti', Ticey."

"I'll die first," I said.

"Go, go, go right on and di', di', die," he said. "Br', Br', Brown my name."

And I tried to crack his head open with that stick. But I didn't bit more hurt that loon than I would hurt that post at the end of my gallery. He came on me and I swung the stick and backed from him. He kept coming on me, and I kept hitting and backing back. Hitting and backing back. Then he jecked the stick out my hand and swung it away. I tried to get the stick, but I fell, and when I looked up, there he was right over me. He didn't look like a man now, he didn't even look like a loon, he looked more like a wild animal. Animal-like greed in his face. He grabbed me and started with me in the bushes. But we hadn't gone more than three, four steps when I started hearing this noise. *Whup, whup, whup.* I didn't know what the noise was. I was too busy trying to get away from that loon to think this noise had anything to do with me or him. I heard the noise again: *whup, whup, whup.* Every time it hit now I saw the hurt in the slow-wit's face. He was still heading with me in the bushes, but every time the noise hit I could see the hurt in his face. Then I saw the stick come down on his shoulder, and this time he swung around. Big Laura had the stick cocked back to hit him again.

"Drop her, you stud-dog," she said. "Drop her or I'll break your neck."

He let me slide out of his arms, just standing there looking at Big Laura like he was wondering why she had hit him. I tried to get the stick away from Big Laura so I could get another crack at him, but she pushed me to the side.

"Go back to that plantation," she said. "Go back there. That's where you do your stud-ing."

"No," he said.

"I say get out of here," she said, ready to hit him.

"No," he said. (Because he was a slow-wit, and he wouldn't know where to go by himself.)

Big Laura hit him in the side with the stick. She hit him twice in the side, but all he did was covered his head and cried. He was a slow-wit and couldn't look after himself. All he could do was do what you told him to do.

"You got just one more time to try your stud-ing round me," Big Laura told him. "Just one more time, and I'll kill you." She looked at everybody there. "That go for the rest of y'all," she said. "You free, then you go'n act like free men. If you want act like you did on that plantation, turn around now and go on back to that plantation."

Nobody said a thing. Most of them looked down at the ground. Big Laura went back to her children, and I went back and sat down on the log. The slow-wit stood over there crying and slobbering on himself.

The sun went down and we found the North Star. Big Laura put her bundle on her head, then she took that little girl in her arms and Ned by the hand and we started walking again. We walked and walked and walked and walked. Lord, we walked. I got so tired I wanted to drop. Some of the people started grumbling and hanging back, but they didn't know where else to turn and they soon caught up. Big Laura never stopped and never looked around to see who was following. That little girl clutched in her arms, Ned by the hand, she moved through them trees like she knowed exactly where she was going and wasn't go'n let nothing in the world get in her way.

We went on till way up in the night before we stopped to sleep. Big Laura dropped her bundle on the ground sat the children side it. She took everything out the bundle and spread the dress out so the children could have a pallet to lay down on. Then she dug a hole in the ground and filled it with leaves and dry moss. She stuck a little piece of lint cotton under the moss and leaves and started scraping a piece of flint and iron together near the cotton. Soon she had made fire, and she covered the fire with green moss to get smoke. She sat down by the pallet and waved her hand over the children in case mosquitoes broke through the screen. The rest of the people closed in but stayed quiet. And you heard nothing but the swamps. Crickets, frogs, an owl in a tree somewhere.

"You can go to sleep," I told Big Laura. "I'll keep mosquitoes off the children."

"Sleep yourself," she said. "You go'n need all the strength you have to reach Ohio."

That was all I needed to hear. The next minute I was snoring.

Massacre

THE NEXT THING I knowed the sun was shining bright and somebody was hollering, "Patrollers."

Everybody jumped up and made it for the bushes. Big Laura hollered at me to grab Ned and run. I had already passed Ned, but I leaned back and grabbed him and almost jecked him up off the ground. Half the time I was carrying him, half the time I was dragging him. We crawled under a bush and I pressed his face to the ground and told him to stay quiet quiet. From the bush I could still see the spot where we had been. The big slow-wit was still out there. He didn't know where to turn to or what to do. Like he wanted to go in every direction at the same time, but he didn't know where to go. I wanted to call him—but I was scared the patrollers might see him coming toward us. Then the patrollers came in on horses and mules. Patrollers was poor white trash that used to find the runaway slaves for the masters. Them and the soldiers from the Secesh Army was the ones who made up the Ku Klux Klans later on. Even that day they had Secesh soldiers mixed in there with them. I could tell the Secesh from the patrollers by the uniforms. The Secesh wore gray; the patrollers wore work clothes no better than what the slaves wore. They came in on horses and mules, and soon as they saw the slow-wit they surrounded him and started beating him with sticks of wood. Some of them had guns, but they would not waste a bullet. More satisfaction beating him with sticks. They beat him, he covered up, but they beat him till he was down. Then one of the patrollers slid off the mule, right cross his tail, and cracked the slow-wit in the head. I could hear his head crack like you hear dry wood break.

I wanted to jump up from there and run—but what about Ned? I couldn't leave him there—look what Big Laura had done for me just yesterday. I couldn't take him with me, either—they would see us. I stayed there, with my heart jumping, jumping, jumping.

The patrollers moved in the bushes to hunt for the rest of the people. They could tell from the camp there must have been lot of us there, and they knowed we was still close around. They moved in with sticks now to look for us. I could hear them hitting against the bushes and talking to each other. Then when they spotted somebody, a bunch of them would surround the person and beat him till they had knocked him unconscious or killed him. Then they would move somewhere else. First you would hear them hitting against the bushes lightly, then after they spotted somebody you would hear them hitting the bushes hard. Now, you heard screaming, begging; screaming, begging; screaming, begging—till it was quiet again.

I kept one hand on my bundle and one on the side of Ned's face holding him down. I was go'n stay there till I thought they had spotted me, then I was getting out of there fast. I told Ned be ready to run, but stay till I gived him the sign. I was pressing so hard on his face I doubt if he even heard me, but all my pressing he never made a sound. Small as he was he knowed death was only a few feet away.

After a while the patrollers left. They went right by us, and I could hear them talking. One was saying, "Goddamn, she was mean. Did you see her? Did you see her? Goddam, she could fight." Another one spit and said: "They ain't human. Gorilla, I say." The first one said: "Lord, did you see Gat's head? Made me sick." Another one: "Gat all right?" Another one: "Afraid not. Afraid he go'n die on us."

They passed right by us, and my heart jumping, jumping, jumping. I kept my hand on my bundle and I kept Ned quiet till the last one had passed. Then I relaxed a little bit. I took me a deep breath and looked up at the sky. It was quiet, quiet, not a sound. I mean you couldn't even hear a bird. Nothing but the sun—and the dust the men had raised thrashing in the bushes. I could see the sun streaking through the trees down to the ground like a long slide. Only one time, so they say, it refused to shine: when they nailed the Master to the cross.

I stood up and told Ned come on, and we went back to the place where we had camped. The slow-wit was dead, all right; his skull busted there like a coconut. One of his shirt sleeves was knocked clean off. I turned to Ned, but he was standing there just as calm as he could be.

I left the slow-wit, I wanted to find Big Laura and give Ned back to her. I saw somebody laying over in the bushes, but when I got closer I saw it was a man. He was dead like the slow-wit, and I went on looking for Big Laura. I had to give Ned back to her, and I needed her to show me how to reach Ohio.

I looked for her everywhere. Sometimes I made Ned stand side a tree while I went in the bushes looking for her. I saw people laying everywhere. All of them was dead or dying, or so broken up they wouldn't ever move on their own. I stood there a little while looking at them, but I didn't know what to do, and I moved back.

Then I saw Big Laura. She was laying on the ground with her baby still clutched in her arms. I made Ned stay back while I went closer. Even before I knelt down I saw that her and the baby was both dead.

I took the baby out her arms. I had to pull hard to get her free. I knowed I couldn't bury Big Laura—I didn't have a thing to dig with—but maybe I could bury her child. But when I looked back at Big Laura and saw how empty her arms was, I just laid the little baby right back down. I didn't cry, I couldn't cry. I had seen so much beating and suffering; I had heard about so much cruelty in those 'leven or twelve years of my life I hardly knowed how to cry. I went back to Ned and asked him if he wanted to go to Ohio with me. He nodded.

When I turned away I saw a patroller's cap laying on the ground covered with blood. I wondered if that was Gat's cap. Then I saw another one all busted up. So she had busted two of them in the head before they killed her and her baby.

Before we started out I thought we might as well take some of the grub that was left there. I got enough corn and potatoes to last us a week. I reckoned that in a week I ought to be in Ohio or close there. After I got the food, I got a few pieces of clothes for me and Ned to sleep on at night. Then I found the flint and iron Big Laura had used to light the fire with. Both of them looked like pieces of rock, so anytime anybody asked me what they was I just told them, "Two little rocks." I gived them to Ned and told him it was go'n be his job to see that they got to Ohio same time we did. After I had covered up Big Laura and the child with some clothes, I put the bundle on my head and we started out. Every now and then I asked Ned if he was tired. If he said no, we went on; if he said yes, we found a good place to sit down. Then I would take something out the bundle for us to eat. Ned would put the rocks on the ground while we ate. But soon as he was through eating he'd pick them up again.

We went on, staying in the bushes all the time. When Ned got tired, we stopped, nibbled on something, then after he had rested we started out again. When the sun went down and the stars came out we traveled by the North Star. We didn't stop that night till we came up to a river. But I could see it was too wide and too deep for us to cross, so we moved back in the swamps for the night. I dug a hole in the ground and built a little fire just like I saw Big Laura do the night before. While me and Ned sat there eating a raw potato, I put two more potatoes and two more yers of corn in the fire. When Ned got through eating, he went to sleep on the little pallet I had made for him on the ground.

I sat there looking at Ned, wondering what I was go'n do next. "I got this child to take care, I got that river to cross—and how many more rivers I got to cross before I reach Ohio?" I said to myself.

I looked at Ned laying there. He was snoring like he was in a little bed at home. I didn't hear any mosquitoes but I waved my hand over him like I saw Big Laura do the night before. After a while I laid down side him, and I didn't wake up till I felt the sun shining in my face.

The sky was more pretty and bluer than I had ever seen it before. I felt better than I had ever felt in my life. Birds was singing in every tree. I woke up Ned and told him look at the air and listen to the birds. But Ned wasn't much interested in this kind of stuff. He was probably thinking about his mama and his little sister. I was thinking about them, too; thinking about all the people; 'specially the slow-wit I had seen them kill; but I looked at it this way, we had to keep going. We couldn't let what happened yesterday stop us today.

I pulled the corn and potatoes out the hole. All of them good and done. We ate the potatoes for breakfast. I was go'n save the corn for me and Ned's dinner.

Heading South

I GOT MY BUNDLE TOGETHER and Ned picked up his two rocks, and we started for the river. It still looked too deep and too wide for us to cross, so I asked Ned what he thought we ought to do, go up or go down? He looked up, he looked down, then he looked up river again. He nodded that way and we started walking. The sun was on our backs now.

We walked all morning. Every now and then we stopped to nibble on something. We stuck to the bushes all the time, but we kept the river in sight. After going so far I would move closer to the river to see how deep it was. It was always the same—deep deep and wide.

That evening we heard voices. We was coming up to a bend in the river when we heard the people talking. I stopped and held my hand out so Ned would be quiet. Not that he had been making any noise, but I didn't want him to make any now for sure. We listened and listened. I thought I heard nigger, but I wasn't too sure, so I listened some more. When I was sure it was nigger I was hearing I nodded for Ned to come on.

When we came round the bend I saw niggers strung out all over the place just eating and resting. I had never seen so many happy black faces in all my life before. We done made it, we done made it to Ohio, I said. But if this was Ohio, how come I had made it here so fast? What was I doing carrying all this food on my head? Now, instead of me feeling good I felt letdown.

When the people saw me and Ned they all stopped talking and looked at us. Not far from where they was eating I saw two wagonful of furniture and bundles. Now, I didn't know what to think. Where would poor niggers get this kind of stuff from?

I dropped the bundle on the ground and asked the people if this was Ohio. It had been quiet till I opened my mouth. Now everybody started laughing. The air brimming full. One nigger had the cheeks to throw his pan of food up in the air and not even bother to catch it. Food scattered all over the place.

Then they got quiet. I didn't know why till I saw the white lady coming toward us. She had two girls about my size.

"What y'all want?" she asked me.

"We going to Ohio," I said. "This Ohio?"

"This Luzana," she said.

"Luzana?" I said. "We been doing all that walking and we still in Luzana? You sure, Misses?"

"I'm sure," she said. "And if I was you I'd head right straight on back where I come from."

"No, ma'am, we ain't going back there," I said.

Then a nigger stepped up and said: "Don't be telling my Misses what you ain't go'n do. She say y'all go back, you high-tail it on back there."

Ned stepped in front of me to hit him in the belly, but I made him get back.

The white lady said: "What you want to go Ohio for?"

"To freedom," I said.

"You free here," she said. "Ain't you heard about the Proclamation?"

"I done heard it," I said. "Don't mean I believe it."

Then I looked up at that nigger again. He was rolling his eyes at me like he wanted to slap me cross the face. He had a round greasy face and big white eyes, and he looked just like the driver we had left on the place. That kind was used to beating on poor black people who couldn't hit back.

"That's your child?" the white lady asked me.

"No, Misses, I'm just 'leven or twelve," I said. "He's for another lady the Secesh killed yesterday."

"There ain't no more Secesh," she said.

"They had some there yesterday," I said. "And they sure enough killed his mama and his little baby sister."

When I said that the rest of the niggers started looking a little scared.

"Y'all going North?" I asked the white lady.

"We coming in from Texas," the white lady said. "We going South."

"South?" I said. "Don't niggers know they don't have to go South no more?"

"We goes where us Misses tell us to go, little dried-up," the driver said. "She knows what she doing. Not you."

"Quiet, Nicodemus," the white lady told him. "We going back to our plantation," she said. "We left it when we heard the Yankees was coming through."

"My old master and them didn't go nowhere," I said. "Just hid out in the swamps with the goods till the Yankees packed up and left."

"Yankees do much ravishing to y'all place?" she asked me.

"Not much," I said. "Nothing the first time. Too busy running after Secesh. Next time, took stocks, something to eat, that's all."

"I hate to think what they did to Rogers Grove," she said. "It's been five long years, and I hate to think what I'm go'n find when I get home."

"Maybe they didn't touch a thing." I said.

"Oh, if I know Yankees I know they touched something," she said. "I just hope they left the house standing. Y'all children hungry?"

"We got food, Misses," I said.

"What y'all got?"

"Potatoes and corn, Misses," I said.

"Y'all want some cornbread and meat?" she asked.

I was hungry, but I made pretend I had to ask Ned if he wanted to eat. He said yes, and the white lady told somebody to bring us some food. Her and her two girls sat down on the ground in front of us.

"Lord, I ain't seen nothing but ravishing and more ravishing," she said. "Everywhere you look, nothing but ravishing. Ravishing, ravishing, ravishing. I been trying to cry, but I done already cried myself dry. Not another drop in me nowhere."

"No need to cry," I said. "Just got to keep going, that's all."

"Misses, just give me the word," the driver said.

The white lady didn't even look at him this time. I looked up at him, and he was standing there rubbing his fist. If that white lady had just nodded her head that nigger would have knocked mine off.

"Your mama in Ohio?" the white lady asked me.

"My mama been dead," I told her. "The overseer we had said he was go'n whip my mama because the driver said she wasn't hoeing right. My mama told the overseer, 'You might try and whip me, but nobody say you go'n succeed.' The overseer 'lowed, 'I ain't go'n just try, I'm go'n do it. Pull up that dress.' My mama said, 'You the big man, you pull it up.' And he hit her with the stick. She went on him to choke him, and he hit her again. She fell on the ground and he hit her and hit her and hit her. And they didn't get rid of him till he had killed two more people. They brought me to the house to see after the children because I didn't have nobody to stay with. But they used to beat me all the time for nothing."

"I never beat my people," the white lady said.

"Some people don't beat their niggers, but they sure used to beat us," I told her. "Old Master used to beat us with the cat-o'-nine-tails; Old Mistress beat us with the first thing her hands fell on. And had the nerve to cry when they said freedom had come. I ain't studying about her."

"You mind how you talk about white folks," the driver said.

"Quiet, Nicodemus," the white lady said. "You going to your daddy in Ohio?" she asked me.

"No, Misses, I ain't never seen my daddy," I said. "He didn't live on our place."

"Who you know in Ohio then?" she said.

"Just Mr. Brown," I said.

"Mr. Brown?" the white lady said. "Mr. Brown who?"

"A Yankee soldier," I said. "He said look him up when I get free."

"Oh, Lord, child," the white lady said. "A Yankee soldier? You going to Ohio looking for a Yankee soldier called Brown? A Yankee soldier who might 'a' been killed the day after he spoke to you?"

"No Secesh bullet can kill Mr. Brown," I said.

The driver cracked his knuckles when I said that. I didn't look up at him this time, but I heard his knuckles crack like dry wood.

The white lady said, "Oh, child, child."

"How far that river out there go?" I asked her. "Me and this little boy got to cross it before we head on."

The white lady said, "Oh, child, child, there ain't no Ohio. If there is, it ain't what you done made up in your mind. Y'all come back with me. Y'all come back. I'll treat you right."

"Me and this little boy started out for Ohio, and we going to Ohio," I said.

When we got through eating, I thanked her kindly, then I put my bundle on my head and stood up. Ned picked up his flint and iron, and we was ready to move on.

"They got a bridge for that river out there?" I asked her.

"A ferry," she said.

"What's a ferry?" I asked her.

The white lady said, "Oh, child, child, come back with me. There ain't no Ohio."

"What's a ferry?" I asked again.

"A boat," she said. "A boat that carry people and wagons. And you go'n need money to ride."

"We ain't got no money," I said. "Where we getting money from?"

"Come back with me," the white lady said.

"Thank you for the food, Misses, but we going," I said.

Just before we left I saw one of the girls patting her mama on the shoulder, and I knowed she was crying.

Shelter for a Night

WE WALKED AND WALKED; shadows getting longer and longer. I didn't ask the white lady how far up the river the ferry was, so we had to keep going till we saw it. The Secesh and the Yankees had been fighting on this side of the river. I could see how the big cannon balls had knocked limbs out of trees. I could see how they had knocked small trees completely out of the ground. I saw strips of cloth, buttons, sometimes a cap half buried under dry leaves and dirt. But we kept on going. We stayed in the bushes all the time, just enough in the open to keep the river in sight.

Late that evening I saw something like a big house floating on the river. I saw people and wagons on the other bank waiting for it to pick them up. I told Ned that's what we was go'n ride on. Ned didn't say a thing. Just following me with that flint and iron in his hands.

By the time we had reached the landing place on this side, the ferry was heading back. I felt so funny and weak standing there, I thought these little dried up legs was go'n buckle under me. Walking through the swamps all time of night didn't scare me nearly much as seeing this big old thing coming toward me now. I asked Ned if he was scared, too, but he shook his head. He wasn't much for talking. The ferry landed and the people and wagons got off. The people on this side got on, and we got on with them.

"And where y'all think y'all going?" the captain asked. Right off I could see he was nothing but white trash.

"Me and this little boy going to Ohio," I said.

"Ohio?" he said.

He didn't know no more about Ohio than I did. I told him Ohio was in the North.

"Who y'all for?" he said.

"We ain't for nobody," I said. "We free as you."

"All right, little free nigger, y'all got money?" he said. "It take a nickel to ride on here. Y'all got a nickel each?"

"No sir."

"Then get right straight off," he said.

"We got potatoes and corn," I said.

"And I got potatoes and corn at my house, too," he said. "None of them Beero people go'n come round here 'cusing me of stealing free niggers."

"We'll tell him you didn't steal us," I said.

"You ain't go'n tell him nothing, because you ain't going nowhere," he said. "Get off before I have one of my niggers throw you off. Oh, Lucas?"

A big nigger showed up. Me and Ned got off and sat down on the bank.

After everybody else had got on, the ferry left for the other side. I could see it drifting cross the river like a great big house. Looked like everything was go'n end right here on this side the river.

I looked back at Ned. He was just sitting there with that iron and flint in his hands. Watching the ferry, but not saying a word. I wondered if he was thinking about his mama and his little sister. I was doing everything to keep from thinking about anything but going to Ohio.

"You all right?" I asked Ned.

He nodded his head a little.

Almost sundown the ferry came back. The captain hollered at me and Ned to get moving. We moved back two or three steps and sat down again. The captain and that nigger he called Lucas was still watching us. I thought he was go'n make Lucas come out there and beat us up, but Lucas kept his distance.

The ferry stayed on this side till dark. They had hung lanterns on it now. Just as it was getting ready to leave for the other side, I heard somebody hollering, "Hold her up. Hold her up." I saw a man all in black riding toward the landing on a black horse. The man hopped off the horse and handed the reins to one of the niggers on the boat. Then he looked and saw us sitting there.

"Hoa there?" He said. He said it like he couldn't make us out too good.

I stood up so he could see I was a little girl. "Yes, sir?" I said.

"What y'all doing there?" he said.

"We want cross over," I said.

"Come along then," he said. "Pick it up, pick it up."

I already had my bundle in my hand, and Ned followed me with the flint and the iron. When I got on board I felt scared and funny. I thought these two little old legs was go'n buckle under me now for sure.

The ferry pushed away from the landing out on the river, and it looked like none of it was real, like I was dreaming all this. I felt all funny and giddy and tired as I was I wanted to laugh, but I didn't.

"Where y'all headed?" the man in the black suit asked me. He didn't sound like a Secesh at all. I had never heard nobody talk like him before.

"Ohio," I said.

He was smoking a pipe. He jecked it out his mouth quick. I could hear when it hit against his teeth.

"Ohio?" he said. "Y'all got people there? Ain't that a bit far for just two children? That one over there, that's you little bitty brother?"

"Just a little boy I know," I said. "We ain't got no people. My mama been dead. Overseer killed her. Secesh killed his mama yesterday."

"Oh, that gang," he said.

"You know them?" I asked him.

"Know of them," he said. "Well, you don't have to go to Ohio. I'll find you a place to stay till you find somebody'll take care of you. Where you from?"

I told him. I told him about Old Master reading the Proclamation to us and us starting out. Told him about the Secesh or patrollers who had killed the people. Even told him about Mr. Brown.

"Well, you don't have to go to Ohio, now," he said. "And your friend Brown might not even be there. I'll find you a place to stay till you find yourself a home. I still think the best thing for both of you is going back, though."

"We ain't going back there, Master," I said.

"Well, I'll find you a place to stay tonight," he said. He looked at Ned holding the flint and the piece of iron. "I say, Little Man, what them rocks for?" he asked.

"Fiyer," Ned said.

"I say," the man said, and smoked on the pipe.

It was pitch black on the river, but I could see lights on the other bank. Looked like even before we got on the ferry good it had landed again. The man in the black suit took my bundle and got on his horse and told me and Ned to come along. Now, I was on the ground again, and it looked like I had never been on a ferry.

"Ohio far from here, Master?" I asked.

"Afraid so," he said. "This Luzana you in."

"What?" I said. I stopped and looked up at him there in the dark. He held back on the reins and the horse stopped. "All the walking me and this little boy been doing, crossing a river on a ferry, you trying to say we still in Luzana?" I asked.

"Afraid so," he said.

"Luzana must be the whole wide world," I said.

"No, not exactly," he said.

"Then how come we still in it?"

"Nature more likely," he said.

I could hear him smoking the pipe. We started walking again.

"I want go to Ohio," I said.

"Afraid you'll have to change your mind," he said. "Ever hear-d tell the Freedom Beero?"

"No, Master."

"Well, 'cording to the Fedjal Gov'ment, they sending Yankees down here to help y'all out. See that y'all have something to eat, clothes, school. Everything Brown promised you, you go'n have right here in Luzana."

"You a Yankee?" I asked him.

"Afraid so," he said. "Call me a gov'ment invessagator. Hail from New York."

"That's farther than Ohio?" I asked.

" 'Pending on where you standing when you ask that question," he said. "Maine, no; Luzana, yes."

"I'm standing right here," I said. "Right here in Luzana where it look like I ain't go'n ever leave from."

He smoked on the pipe. I could hear it there in the dark. "Afraid so," he said.

We came up to a big house where children was playing in the yard. The invessagator got off the horse and told us to follow him. Another white man met us at the door. The two of them talked awhile, then the other white man called over his shoulder for somebody named Sarah. Sarah came in. She was a big black woman who looked after the children. The white man nodded toward us, and she told me and Ned to follow her. She took us up-stairs to another big room. They had pallets spread out all over the floor. Sarah told me that's where the girls slept, and she pointed out a pallet for me. Then we went to another room where the boys slept, and she pointed out a pallet for Ned. She asked us if we was hungry. I said yes but we had food. She told me we didn't have to eat that no more, I could leave my bun-dle side my pallet, or, better yet, dump it in the trash. She told Ned he could leave that flint and iron by the pallet or he could dump that in the trash, too. She had good food in the kitchen for both of us, she said; and she would find something else for Ned to play with. I told her we would eat her food, but we wanted to keep what we had. Where we went, they went. She looked at me a little while like she thought I was getting sassy with her, then she said suit yourself, follow me. We went downstairs to the kitchen and ate, then she told us we had to take a bath. I said I didn't want one. She said I had to take it if I wanted it or not, and she stuck me in a tub of soapy water and tried to wash my skin off. She even ducked my head under two or three times—and I'm sure she did it just because she thought I had sassed her up-stairs. After she had wiped me off, she stuck me in a little white gown made like a sack—it wasn't nothing but a sack—and she told me to go upstairs to my pallet. Little while later Ned came back upstairs in his little gown. He still had that flint and iron in his hands.

"Feel better?" I asked him.

He nodded his head.

"Get yourself a good night sleep," I told him. "Tomorrow morning when nobody looking, we getting out of here."

All Kinds of People

LITTLE WHILE AFTER I had laid down, the rest of the girls came in, making more noise than a pack of jay birds in a chinaball tree. But when the white man came in the room everything got quiet. "All right—knees," he said. Everybody knelt down side their pallet; I was the only one still laying there. "That go for you, too," he said. After I knelt down he said prayers, then he blowed out the lamp and went to the other room. "All right—knees," I could hear him saying. Then little bit later—"You with them rocks, that go for you, too." He prayed over them, then he blowed out the lamp and went back downstairs.

I was sleepy, but I felt too good to go to sleep. I just wanted to lay there and feel how good freedom was. I kept thinking to myself, "So this is freedom? This is freedom? Well, if this all I got to do, I don't mind putting up with that bathing a few more days."

While I was laying there thinking how quiet and peaceful everything was, somebody round the other side started hollering. I thought it was Ned and I jumped up and made it for the door. The white man got to the door same time I did and went in and lit the lamp. It wasn't Ned, it was the boy on the pallet next to Ned. Ned was laying on his pallet with the flint and iron in his hands.

"What happened?" the white man asked the boy crying.

The boy was crying too much to answer. He didn't even try to answer. Ned was still laying there with the iron and the flint. The rest of the children was sitting up looking.

"What happened?" the white man asked the boy again. "Don't you have a tongue?" The boy had his mouth wide open, but nothing was coming out; then it all came out. "What happened?" the white man asked Ned. Ned just laid there with the flint and the iron. "You, what happened?" the white man asked another boy.

The boy said, "Well, Claiborne there asked that little boy over there for one of them rocks and that little boy over there said no and Claiborne there said if that little boy over there didn't give him one of them rocks Claiborne there was go'n take it. Claiborne there reached and tried to get the rock out that little boy there hand and that's when that little boy over there konked Claiborne on the forrid. That's how come Claiborne got a knot coming on his forrid right now."

"You got to get rid of them rocks," the white man told Ned. Ned didn't answer him, just laying there with that flint and that iron in his hands. "You hear me?" the white man said.

"He don't have to get rid of nothing," I said, from the door. "He done brought them this far and we 'tend to keep on taking them. They for his mama. The Secesh killed his mama, and he can keep them if he want."

"You acting like you his mama," the white man said.

"I can't be his mama because I ain't no more than 'leven or twelve," I said. "But I ain't go'n let nobody mistreat him neither."

"Any more hitting with them rocks, I'm go'n take them from you myself," the white man told Ned.

"Tell that little old Claiborne boy go find his own rocks and Ned won't need to hit him," I said.

"And you, Claiborne, you leave him alone," the white man said. He blowed out the lamp and came to the door where I was. "And you, Miss Smarty, you better watch your tongue," he said. "And get back to that other room." When I walked away I heard him saying, "They told me not to leave, they told me not to come South. No, I want be friend to man. Now, they running me crazy."

I went back to my pallet, but I didn't go to sleep right away, I listened to see if they was go'n try to do Ned something round there. But nothing happened.

The next morning the children woke me up with their noises. We put on our clothes and went downstairs to eat. Sarah made us wash our face and hands first. The girls washed in one tub, the boys washed in another tub. then Sarah gave us our food—cush-cush and milk.

We wasn't through eating before I heard a bell ringing somewhere. I asked another girl what that was for, and she said the big children had to go to work and the little children had to learn ABC. In the evening the big children had to learn ABC and numbers. They had to learn them, too, or they couldn't go out and play.

I had been thinking I might stay here a couple of days, but now everything had changed. ABC and numbers was something I wasn't ready to start on yet. And the Lord knows I had heard enough bells in them 'leven or twelve years. I told Ned to have his flint and iron together by the time I went upstairs and got the bundle. The white man caught me coming out the room and asked me where I thought I was going.

"Ohio," I said.

"O what?" he said.

He followed me downstairs just fussing. But soon as he saw Ned with that flint and that iron he remembered Claiborne and left me alone. Him, Sarah and all the children stood on the gallery and watched us leave. They thought we was going little piece and we was go'n turn around and come back.

We headed for the river. Now, in daytime, I could see this was a little town where we had spent the night. They had had some fighting here between the Yankees and the Secesh—I could see how some of the houses had caught fire. The place where me and Ned had stayed that night was a big white house probably had been owned by some rich white folks. When the Yankees came in they took it over and made it a home for colored children. So many of the children didn't have nowhere to go, didn't have nobody to look after them.

Halfway to the river—now look what I see: two niggers in Yankee uniforms. I hadn't seen any colored soldiers before then, and I thought these two was just clowning round.

"Y'all real?" I asked.

"What you want?" one of them said.

"Y'all know a soldier called Mr. Brown?" I asked.

"You mean the colonel, don't you?" he said. "But I don't know where he would have knowed you. You pretty young, ain't you?"

"Old enough to know I don't care to know you," I said.

"Don't worry," he said.

"He from Ohio?" I asked.

"He can be," that nigger said. "When we play poker at night we talk about stakes, we don't talk about States."

He slapped the other soldier on the back and laughed.

"You don't look like you talk too good about nothing," I said. "I want to see Mr. Brown."

"You do, huh?" he said. "Well, you see that building setting over there? Go in there and tell that white soldier you want talk to the colonel. If he say the colonel talking to General Grant, tell him that's too bad, tell Grant wait."

Me and Ned started toward the house and they started laughing. When I looked back they was laughing so hard they had to hold on to each other to keep from falling down.

"Not all colored is niggers, but them niggers back there," I told Ned. "Yankee uniform or no Yankee uniform, they ain't nothing but common niggers."

Time I came in the house the white soldier said: "Down the road. Ask one of them colored soldiers out there to point the way."

"I know that way already," I said. "I'm headed from there. I like to see Mr. Brown."

"You mean Colonel Brown, don't you?" he said. "And may I be so bold and ask you why?"

"He know me," I said.

"Get out of here," the soldier said.

I took the bundle off my head and dropped it on the floor. The soldier looked at me a second and left the room. He was gone about an hour, then he came back. Ned was sitting down side the bundle, but I was still standing there.

"Y'all still here?" he said.

"I want to see Mr. Brown," I said.

"The colonel busy," he said. "Come back some other time."

"We going to Ohio," I said.

"Stop by on your way back," he said. "The colonel ought to be free by then."

He started outside and I headed for that room I saw him come out of. He must have seen me over his shoulder and he hollered at me to stop, but I had already opened the door. Now I was sorry I had wasted all that time. All I saw in the room was an old man with white hair and white whiskers. Sitting behind a table full of papers.

"Yes, private?" he said, raising his head. Then he saw me—and he almost jumped out of that chair. "What in the world? Who sent you here?" he asked.

The other soldier came in and said: "I'll get her out of here, colonel, sir. Get out of here, you," he said to me.

"No, let her speak," the colonel said.

"I thought you was Mr. Brown," I said.

"I'm Colonel Brown," he said.

"You ain't the right one," I said. "The other one was young and he was running Secesh. He gived me my name."

"Where you from, child?" the colonel asked.

"Master Bryant plantation," I said.

The colonel turned round in his chair and looked at a big map on the wall. All the time he was looking at the map he was going, "Hummmm, hummmm, hummmm." I pulled the door quietly and went out. I picked up my bundle and told Ned come on.

When we came up to the river we turned toward the sun. We was going so far this way, then we was go'n turn North again. If I had knowed anything about traveling we could 'a' headed North from where we had spent the night, but being so young and ignorant I thought I had to start back where I had come from the day before.

Soon as we lost sight of town we took to the bushes. You couldn't ever tell who you was go'n meet 'long the road, and we was too far from town to holler for help. We walked, we walked, we walked. The Yankees and Secesh had battled here, too. You could see how the Yankees had burned everything in sight. The ground was still black. The trees looked like black posts, no leaves, no moss, no limbs. When the sun got straight up in the sky we found a shady place in a ditch and sat down. I was so tired I felt like sitting there all day, but I knowed I had to keep going. Once I stopped moving that was go'n be the end for me and Ned. I looked at him sitting there and I asked him if he was all right. He nodded his head.

"Well, let's go some more," I said.

Late that evening I spotted a house setting cross the field. It wasn't in the direction we was going—it was in the West—but I wanted to know if we was headed right. We started for the house. Even before I reached the yard I could see poor white trash lived there. A little garden side the house, an old dress on the clothesline, a little scrawny woodpile in the back yard. A dog tied with a chain started barking at us when we came up to the gate. A woman in overalls looked out the door. She was poor and skinny, and she looked mean as she was poor.

"You can tell me if this the way to Ohio?" I asked her.

She looked at me, but she didn't say a thing.

"Please ma'am," I said.

"You don't get away from my gate, I'm go'n let that dog point the way to Ohio," she said. "Get away from my gate."

"I just want know if I'm headed right," I said.

"I don't know nothing 'bout no Ohio," she said. "And if you don't move from there like I done already told you I'm go'n turn that dog loose."

"We leaving," I said. "Can you tell me if y'all got a spring round here? Me and this little boy awful thirsty."

"You don't see no spring, do you?" she said.

"No ma'am."

She didn't say another word, she just stood in the door looking at us. I told Ned come on. She didn't say a thing till we got to the end of the fence, then she told us to stop. When I looked back toward the house I couldn't see her. But a few minutes later I saw her coming back with a cup of water. We met her at the gate. When I reached for the cup she pulled it back.

"You think I'm go'n let you put your black mouth on this cup?" she said. "Hold out your hands."

I cupped my hands together. The water was warm. I reckoned she had got it out a bucket or a tub setting in the sun. Ned didn't know how to hold his hands together, and I had to cup my hands again so he could drink. Long as we was standing there the woman was fussing at us.

"Don't think I love niggers just because I'm giving y'all water," she was saying. "I hate y'all. Hate y'all with all my heart. Doing it because I'm a God-fearing Christian. I hate niggers with all my heart. Y'all cause of all this trouble, all this ravishing. Yankee and nigger soldiers all over the place stealing my hogs and chickens. Y'all cause of it all. I hope the good white people round here kill all y'all off. Hope they kill y'all before the night over. I'm go'n tell them which way y'all went, and I'm go'n tell them go kill y'all. Now, get away from here. Get away from here before I kill y'all myself. If I wasn't a God-fearing Christian I'd kill y'all myself."

I thanked her for the water and told Ned come on. We went East till sundown, then we swung back North.

The Hunter

NIGHT CAUGHT US but we kept going, traveling by the North Star all the time. I reckoned it had been dark about three hours when we came in a thicket of pine trees, and I smelled food cooking. I stopped quickly and held out my arms so Ned would be quiet. I turned my head and turned my head, but I couldn't see the fire or the smoke. Now, I didn't know what to do—go back, go forward, or move to one side.

Then somebody spoke: "Now, don't this just beat everything."

I turned around so fast I dropped the bundle on the ground. But I felt much better when I saw another black face standing there looking down on us. He had a green stick about the size and link of a bean pole. He had come on us so quietly he could have killed both of us with that stick before we even saw him.

"What the world y'all doing way out here?" he said. "Y'all by y'all self?"

"Just me and this little boy," I said.

"Lord, have mercy," he said. He was one of the fussin'est people I had ever seen. "Y'all come on over here," he said.

I picked up my bundle and me and Ned followed him back to his camp. He had a rabbit cooking on the fire. He nodded for me and Ned to sit down. I saw a bow and arrows leaning against one of the trees. The man squatted by the fire and looked at us.

"Now, where the world y'all think y'all going?" he said.

"Ohio," I said.

"My Lord, my Lord," he said. "I done seen things these last few weeks, but if this don't beat everything, I don't know. Coming and going, coming and going, and they don't bit more know what they doing than that rabbit I got cooking on that fire there. I bet y'all hungry."

"We got something to eat," I said.

"What, potatoes and corn y'all done stole?" he said. "Don't have to tell me, I already know. I done met others just like y'all."

He took the rabbit off the fire and laid it on the leaves he had spread out on the ground. Then he took a knife from his belt and cut the rabbit up in three pieces. When it had cooled off good he handed me and Ned a piece.

He had seasoned it down good with wild onions that he had found out there in the swamps.

"You going North?" I asked him.

"No, I'm where I'm going right now," he said. "South."

I quit eating. "You got to be crazy," I said.

"I reckoned you got all the sense, dragging that child through the swamps all time of night," he said. "Good thing I'm a friend, not an enemy. I heard y'all long time before you stopped back there listening. I had been leaning on that pole so long I was fixing to fall asleep."

"We was quiet," I said.

"Quiet for you, not for me," he said. "A dog ain't got nothing on these yers. What you think keeping me going, potatoes and corn?"

I didn't answer him. The rabbit was good, but I didn't want show him how much I liked it. Just nibbling here and there like I was particular.

"Who you know in Ohio?" he asked me.

"Just Mr. Brown," I said.

"Mr. Brown who?"

"Mr. Brown, a Yankee soldier," I said.

"Lord, have mercy," the hunter said, shaking his head. "Now, I done heard everything."

"How come you going back South?" I said.

"What?" he said. He wasn't eating, he was thinking about me looking for Brown. "I'm looking for my pappy," he said. But looked like he was still thinking about me looking for Brown.

"Your mama dead?" I asked.

"What?" he said. He looked at me. "No, my mama ain't dead." He just looked at me a good while like he was thinking about me looking for Brown. "I know where she at," he said. "I want find him now."

"Y'all used to stay here in Luzana?" I asked.

"What?" he said.

"Your daddy and y'all?"

"When they sold him he was in Mi'sippi," the hunter said. "I don't know where he at now."

"Then how you know where to look for him?" I asked.

He got mad with me now. "I'm go'n do just what you doing with that child," he said. "Look everywhere. But I got little more sense."

"Well, if you was beat all the time you'd be running away, too," I said.

"I was beat," he said. "Don't go round here bragging like you got all the beating."

I ate and sucked on the bone. I didn't want argue with him no more.

"Who was them other people you seen?" I asked him. "Any of them going to Ohio?"

"They was going everywhere," he said. "Some say Ohio, some say Kansas—some say Canada. Some of them even said Luzana and Mi'sippi."

"Luzana and Mi'sippi ain't North," I said.

"That's right, it ain't North," the hunter said. "But they had left out just like you, a few potatoes and another old dress. No map, no guide, no nothing. Like freedom was a place coming to meet them half way. Well, it ain't coming to meet you. And it might not be there when you get there, either."

"We ain't giving up," I said. "We done gone this far."

"How far?" he asked me. "How long you been traveling?"

"Three days," I said.

"And how far you think you done got in three days?" he said. "You ain't even left that plantation yet. I ought to know. I been going and going and I ain't nowhere, yet, myself. Just searching and searching."

When he said this he looked like he wanted to cry, and I didn't look at him, I looked at Ned. Ned had laid down on the ground and gone to sleep. He still had the flint and iron in his hands.

I told the hunter about the Secesh who had killed Ned's mama and the other people. He told me he had seen some of the Secesh handywork, too. Earlier that same day he had cut a man down and buried him that the Secesh had hung. After hanging him they had gashed out his entrails.

"What they do all that for?" I asked.

"Lesson to other niggers," he said.

We sat there talking and talking. Both of us was glad we had somebody to talk to. I asked him about the bow and arrows. He told me he had made it to shoot rabbits and birds. Sometimes he even got a fish or two. I told him I bet I could use it. He said I didn't have the strength. He said it took a man to pull back on that bow. I asked him what he knowed about my strength. But he kept quiet. After a while he said: "Y'all want me lead y'all back where y'all come from?"

"We didn't come from Ohio," I said.

"You just a pig-headed little old nothing," he told me.

"I didn't ask you for your old rabbit," I said. Now I was full, I got smart. "I don't like no old rabbit nohow," I said.

"How come you ate the bones?" he said.

"I didn't eat no rabbit bones," I said.

"What I ought to do is knock y'all out and take y'all on back," he said.

"I bet you I holler round here and make them Secesh come and kill us, too," I said.

"How can you holler if you knocked out, dried-up nothing?" he said.

I had to think fast.

"I holler when I wake up," I said.

"I don't care about you, but I care about that little fellow there," the hunter said. "Just look at him. He might be dead already."

"He ain't dead, he sleeping," I said. "And I can take care him myself."

"You can't take care you, how can you take care somebody else?" the hunter said. "You can't kill a rabbit, you can't kill a bird. Do you know how to catch a fish?"

"That ain't all you got to eat in this world," I said.

He looked at Ned again.

"If I wasn't looking for my pappy I'd force y'all back," he said. "Or force y'all somewhere so somebody can look after y'all. Two children tramping round in the swamps by themself, I ain't never heard of nothing like this in all my born days."

"We done make it this far, we can make it," I said.

"You ain't go'n make nothing," he said. "Don't you know you ain't go'n make nothing, you little dried-up thing?"

"You should 'a' kept that old rabbit," I said. "I don't like old rabbit meat nohow."

He didn't want argue with me no more.

"Go on to sleep," he said. "I'll stand watch over y'all."

"No, you don't," I said. "You just want take us back."

"Go on to sleep, gnat," he said.

I shook Ned, and he woke up crying. I told him the Secesh was go'n catch him if he kept up the noise. I let him sit there till he had rubbed the sleep out his eyes, then we got up and left. All that time the hunter didn't say a word. We went a little piece, till we couldn't see the camp no more, then we turned around and came on back. I had made up my mind to stay wake all night.

"Well, how was Ohio?" the hunter said.

Ned laid down in the same place and went right back to sleep. I sat beside him watching the hunter. I felt my eyes getting heavy, but I did everything to keep them open. I dugged my heel in the ground, I hummed a song to myself, I poked in the fire with a stick. But nature catch up with you don't care what you do. When I woke up the sun was high in the sky. Something was cooked there for me and Ned—a crow, a hawk, an owl—I don't know what. But there it was, done and cold, and the hunter was gone.

An Old Man

WE ATE AND STARTED WALKING, going North all the time. I watched the ground getting blacker and more damp. With the sun straight up we came to the bayou that I knowed we had been headed toward for so long. Now, I had to carry Ned and the bundle, the bundle on my head, Ned on my hip. The water came up to my knees most the time, and sometimes it even got high as my waist. How I made it over only the Lord knows. But I made it and found a good place to sit down and rest. By the time I had rested, my dress had dried out, and we started walking again. We came in another thicket where they had had plenty fighting. You could see how cannon balls had knocked limbs and bark off the trees. It had a mound of dirt there about half the size of my gallery where they had buried many soldiers. They had put a cross at one end of the grave with a cap stuck on top of the cross. The weather had changed the color of the cap so much you couldn't tell if it belong to a Yankee or Secesh. We sat there and rested awhile and I told Ned not to be scared. He didn't look scared so I reckoned I was saying it for my own good. After a while we got up and went on. We came out of the swamps, and now far as I could see I saw nothing but briars stretched out in front of me. I didn't have time to stand there thinking which way to go— not with that sun coming down like that—I told Ned we was turning left. Not a tree in front of us nowhere. If we wanted shade at all we had to be back in the swamps or try to find a cool spot against the briars. One was just as bad as the other, so we kept on walking.

When we came to the end of the briars, it must have took us an hour to get there, we turned back right. Now I could see a little gray house way way cross the field. The field had nothing green, just weeds and dry corn stalks that could 'a' been there even before the war. We started toward that little house. We wasn't giving up, far far from giving up, but I knowed we had to take some chances. We needed water, and I had to find out if we was going the right way.

From way cross the field I could see smoke coming out the chimley. When I came up to the yard I saw an old white man standing on the gallery with a dog. The old man was short and fat with snow white hair just round the sides and the back of his head. Not a speck on top. His face was red red; not kind, but not mean either.

"This how I go to Ohio?" I asked him.

"That way," he said, pointing East.

"We ain't going that way, we going this way," I said pointing North.

"No, it's East," he said.

"We going North," I said. "We ain't going no East."

"You'll never get to Ohio that way," he said. "Iowa, maybe, but never Ohio. Ohio is East of Luzana."

"You trying to tell me I'm still in Luzana?" I said.

"Yes. Still Luzana," he said. "Lot more of it will be Luzana before you through. You and that boy out there hungry?"

"Yes sir," I said.

"Come in and eat," the old man said. "I have something ready for y'all."

We went in, and he made us sit down on a bench by the firehalf. It was nothing but a one-room cabin. He had a table in there, a bench that he had made himself, a chair he had made. He had a cot by the window. He had things on the wall—pots, jugs, pans and things like that. He had a big map on the wall at the head of his bed. He gave us some greens and cornbread and told us to eat. He didn't give us a spoon, we had to eat with our hands.

"Ohio is East," he said again.

"We been going the wrong way all this time?" I asked.

"I wouldn't say wrong. I wouldn't say exactly right, either," he said.

He got a pair eyeglasses of the mantelpiece and went to the map. I could see him moving his finger over the map and mumbling to himself.

"Yep. I was right," he said. "Yep. Ohio—38, 41 lat; 80, 84 longi. Iowa, let's see—where you at there, Iowa?—here you is you little rascal. Trying to hide from me and I ain't done you nothing, huh? Iowa—40, 44 lat; 90, 96 longi. Yep, that's where Iowa at, all right. While I'm standing here I might's well look up old Illy. Where you at there, fellow? Uh-huh, just what I expected—36, 43 lat; 88, 92 longi. Yep, yep, that's it, all right. Now, where you headed, you headed straight for 42 lat." He turned and looked over the rim of his glasses at me. "You don't want go to 42 lat, do you?"

Ned was almost through eating, but I had hardly touched my food. All a sudden it came to me how wrong I had been for not listening to people. Everybody, from Unc Isom to the hunter, had told me I was wrong. I wouldn't listen to none of them.

I felt like crying. But I asked myself what would happen to Ned. He was holding up only because I was holding up. If I broke down he had nobody to guide him. No, I wasn't go'n cry, I was go'n be strong. I looked at the old man standing at the map. How did I know he was telling me the truth? How did I know he wasn't just another old Secesh trying to get me woolgathered? What was all this lat and longi stuff he was talking about? How could Ohio be East when the Yankees come from the North?

I went on and ate, but I was keeping my eyes on him. Soon as I finished eating, me and Ned was getting out of there and we was heading North just like we had started.

"Come here," he said.

I went to the map with my pan of food.

"Look here," he said, tapping the map. "Now, this here is where you at now." I didn't see nothing but a bunch of odd colors, some crooked lines, and some writing. "That's Luzana," he said. "This thing running here, that's what they call Mi'sippi River. Course it ain't running on the paper, but that's how people say it—say it's running—running North and South."

"I ain't going no South," I said.

I had a mouthful of cornbread, and piece of it shot out my mouth on the map. The old man stopped talking awhile, but he didn't look at me, he looked at the crumb. Just kept looking at it like it was a bug and it might crawl off if he turned his head. When it didn't move he plucked it to the floor. "This one here, that's what they call the Red River," he said. "All this other stuff, river and roads. Up here—A-r—all this other spelling—that's Arkansas. Up here, that's Missouri. Spelt something like Mi'sippi, but not quite. Up here, that's Iowa. 40, 44 lat; 90, 96 longi. That's where you headed if you keep going North. Now, let's go back here and start all over. Mi'sippi River, Red River—all them other rivers and roads. (Throw few bayous in there, too—the bigger ones.) All right, now, you here, you going East to Ohio. You have to go through Mi'sippi first."

I hurried up and swallowed the food I had in my mouth. "I ain't going through nobody Mi'sippi first."

"No?" he said. He looked at me over the rim of his glasses. I looked straight back at him. He wasn't mad, he wasn't the kind who got mad quick, he believed in taking everything cool and slow. "All right, say you don't want go through Mi'sippi," he said, looking at the map again. "Say you want make it hard on yourself, you want go through Arkansas." Now he looked at me over the rim of his glasses. Maybe I didn't want go through Arkansas, either? "Because that's where you go'n have to go, less, of course, you planning on jumping over Mi'sippi," he said. "And I think that's a big order even for somebody smart as you." He waited for me to say something. I didn't. He looked at his map again. "All right, we in Arkansas now. Since Arkansas is North of Luzana, you go'n have to buck back East after you leave Arkansas—that's this way—and you end up in Tennessee. That's right here. All right, now you in Tennessee. You go till you hit Nashville—you done passed Memphis way back here near Arkansas: from Nashville you swing back North again and you ought to find you a good road to Louisville—that's in Kentucky. From Louisville you get to Cincinnati—and you in Ohio. Right there," he said, tapping the map. "Now, who you go'n look up in Ohio?"

"Mr. Brown. A Yankee soldier."

"Mr. Brown, a Yankee soldier," he said. "Yes, there ought to be a few Browns in Cincinnati—common enough name. But if he's not in

Cincinnati he might be in Cleveland. That's right here."

He kept on looking at the map. I looked at the map, too.

"I got to go through all them places and I'm still in Luzana?" I asked.

"Correct," he said.

"How I know you telling me the truth?" I said. "How I know you ain't a Secesh?"

The old man looked at me a long time before he said anything. His face wasn't kind, but it wasn't mean either.

"I might be a Secesh," he said. "Then I might be a friend of your race. Or maybe just an old man who is nothing. Or maybe an old man who is very wise. Maybe an old man who cries at night. Or an old man who might kill himself tomorrow. Maybe an old man who must go on living, just to give two more children a pan of meatless greens and cornbread. Maybe an old man who must warm another man at his fire, be he black or white. I can be anything, now, can't I?"

"How long it go'n take me to get there?" I asked him.

"Where?" he said.

"Ohio."

"Still going?"

"That's where I started for," I said.

"Well, now let me see," he said. He rubbed his chin and looked at me. He was so short I was nearly tall as he was—and you can see I'm no giant. "You weigh about what?" he said. "Seventy? Seventy-five pounds? Yes, I'll say seventy-five—give you a couple. That bundle, I'll say, about ten. Let's say you cover five miles a day—good weather and good road permitting. But the weather ain't go'n always be good, it might start raining anytime and rain from now on. Bad weather you'll cover only half the distance. That means two and a half miles instead of five. But weather ain't all you go'n have to worry about. You got rattlesnakes, copperheads, water moggasins— they got to be reckoned with, too. That means you got to by-pass all bayous and all weedy places, and in order to do that you go'n have to buck back South or go West, because if you go East you go'n be headed straight for Mi'sippi. So that'll knock that other half mile off, leaving you with just two per day. All right, that take care snakes and bad weather. But we have to consider at least one bad dog every other day. Now, since you and that boy'll have to clamb a tree and stay up there till somebody pull that dog away or till he just give up and wander off, that'll rob you of another half a mile. All right, that take care bad dog. Next come old Vet'rans from the Secesh Army still hating niggers for what happened, and since they can't take it out on the Yankees, wanting nothing better than to get two little niggers and tie them on a log full of red ants. So you duck round them and you lose another half a mile, leaving you with just one mile per day. That boy over there sooner or later will eat some green berries or some green 'simmons, and what they go'n do to his bowels will cause you to lose another half a mile, leaving you with just a half. Well, you done made it to Arkansas. But the people in Arkansas ain't heard the war is over, and soon as you and that boy land there they capture y'all and sell y'all to somebody in the hills. So, now, we forget traveling a few years—say, five, six—before they fully convinced Lee done surrendered and back at West Point teaching more gorilla tragedy. But let's get back to you and the boy—y'all free again. You bigger and stronger and you can go ten miles a day now instead of five. But you got another worry now—men; black and white. The white one to treat you like he done treated you and your race ever since he brought you here in chains, the black one to treat you not too much better. So you settle down with a black one. No, not to protect you from the white man; if the white man wanted you he'll take you from the black man even if he had to kill him to do so; you settle with one black man to protect you from another black man who might treat you even worse. But this one ain't no bargain either; he beats you from sunup to sundown. Not because he wants to, mind you; he has to. Because, you see, he's been so brutalized himself, he don't know better. But one day the boy there can't take your suffering no more, and while the man is sleeping, the boy sneaks in and bust him in the head with a stick. Y'all start out again—now, y'all running. Y'all find your way into Tennessee where y'all captured again. No, not by the law you been running from—you captured by the good citizens of Tennessee. These here good people of Tennessee even more backward than them good people you left in Arkansas—these still speaking Gaelic. Since you ain't got no Gaelic papers in this country, it's go'n take them ten more years to learn Lee done quit and probably even dead now. Some kind of way you and the boy get away and start asking about Ohio. But since both of y'all speaking Gaelic now the people don't know what the world y'all talking about, so they point toward Memphis just to get rid of you. In Memphis you meet another nigger you ask the way. He don't understand Gaelic either, but he's one of them slick niggers who feels that any nigger speaking Gaelic ought to be took for all he's worth, so he tells you and the boy to wait a minute and he'll take you where you want go. Y'all wait a minute, then y'all wait an hour, then a day, a year, five years—till that boy there got to bust this one in the head like he did the other one. Now, you and the boy steal horse and buggy and head out for Nashville—Nashville a straight shoot into Ohio. But in Nashville something else happens. Somebody there cracks the boy in the head. Since y'all been friends all these years you feel you ought to stay near his grave a year or two out of respect. But you finally get in Kentucky. In Kentucky you cook for white folks, you feed and nurse white children till you get enough money saved or till you fool another nigger to take you to Ohio. You know how to pick a man now and you pick a stupid one. Soon as you get there you drop him—you don't want nothing more to do with men ever in your life. Well, you land in Cincinnati and you start asking for Brown. But you got a hundred Browns in Cincinnati. Some white Browns, some black Browns, even some brown Browns. You go from Brown to Brown, but you never find the right Brown. It takes you another couple years before you realize Brown ain't here, so you head out for Cleveland. Cleveland got twice as many Browns. And the only white Brown people can remember that ever went to Luzana to fight in the war died of whiskey ten years ago. They don't think he was the same person you was looking for because this Brown wasn't kind to nobody. He was coarse and vulgar; he cussed man, God, and nature every day of his life."

"All right, now how long it's go'n take us to get there?" I asked him.

"I see, you still going," he said.

"That's where we started for."

The old man looked at me and shook his head. "The boy'll never make it," he said. "You? I figure it'll take you about thirty years. Give or take a couple."

"Well, we better head out," I said. "Thank you very much. I wonder if I couldn't bother you for a bottle of water?"

Ned was sound asleep, so I had to shake him to wake him up. I told him to get the flint and iron together. The old man gave me a jug of water and we left him standing out on the gallery.

I can tell you all the things we went through that week, but they don't matter. Because they wasn't no different from the things we went through them first three or four days. We stuck to the bushes most of the time. If we saw people, we hid till they had passed us. One day we had to run a dog back that was trying to follow us because we was scared the people might come looking for him. Another time I watched a house about an hour before I went and asked them for water. The people cussed us out first, then they broke down and gived us the water.

One day, with the sun straight up, we saw a man on a wagon. I went out in the road and waved him down and asked him where we was. He told me the parish. I asked him if that meant I was still in Luzana. He said close as he could speculate I was right in the middle of Luzana. I asked him could we ride with him. He said we could—if we was going the same way he was. But since it didn't look like we was, then he had to say no.

I had already throwed my bundle in the wagon; now I was helping Ned up on the wheel.

"Y'all look beat," the man said to me.

His name was Job; the people told us later.

"We was going to Ohio," I said. "My little friend here got tired."

"He look it," Job said.

Rednecks and Scalawags

JOB TOOK US TO HIS HOUSE. Soon as his wife saw us in that wagon she started fussing. Tall and skinny—nothing but a sack of bones. Looked like she ought to been too weak to even open her mouth; but that woman started fussing when we drove in that yard and didn't stop till we left there the next day.

"What you doing with them niggers?" she asked Job. "You ain't had no money to go and buy no niggers, and you sure ain't got nerve enough to steal none. If you brought them here to feed them you can turn around and take them right straight on back. Ain't got enough food here for me to eat."

"Let them stay here tonight," Job said.

"In my house?" the woman said. "Stink up my place?"

It was a cabin, not a house. Old—leaning to one side. Job had even propped it up with fence posts to keep it from falling all the way down.

"They can sleep in the crib," he said.

"That's right," his wife said. "Ain't got nothing else in there. No corn, no punkins, no cushaw, no 'tatoes. Look at this old ground." She stomped it with her foot. "Look at that garden. What garden? Where my turnips? Where my mustards? Look at them old dead mules. Look at this old ground." She stomped again.

Job told us to stay in the wagon, and he got down and started unhitching the mules.

"Old no count," his wife said. "That's why you didn't go to war like a man. Talking 'bout it ain't your war, it's their war. That's why I ain't got me no children. You no count. You just no count." Then she started laughing.

Job told me and Ned to stay in the wagon till he came back. We sat out there two, maybe three hours. All that time we could hear that woman in the house fussing. They had a bayou behind the house and you could hear crickets and frogs on the bayou, but over all that noise you could hear that woman. When Job came back outside it was so dark we could hardly see him. He told us to follow him to the crib. I had to wake up Ned and tell him come on. It was dark in the crib. The crib was hot and dry. I could feel dry grass under my feet, and the scent was strong. Job told us to go sit by the wall. I held my hand out till I touched the wall, then I sat down and pulled Ned down side me. Job was there now. I couldn't see him too good, but I could smell him. His scent was strong as the grass scent.

"Here," he said.

I reached my hand up in the dark and I touched his hand, then I took the piece of cornbread. It was wet on one end.

"Piece for him," he said.

I gived Ned the piece I already had, then I reached for the piece Job was holding. He told us we could sleep there tonight, and tomorrow he was taking us somewhere else. We sat there in the dark eating the soggy bread. It had been dipped in pot liquor. Pot liquor that had been round couple days.

When Ned got through eating he laid down and went back to sleep. I sat against the wall listening to that crazy woman till way up in the night. The war had done that to lot of them, drove them crazy like that. More than once I started to wake Ned up and tell him let's go. I even put my hand on his shoulder to shake him once. But he was so tired. And I was tired, too. I told myself I would just sit there and keep guard.

The next morning when Job woke us up I was still sitting there against the wall.

"Where we going?" I asked him.

"Y'all friend Bone," he said.

"I don't know nobody name no Bone," I said.

Job didn't say another word. We clambed in the wagon. The woman was standing in the door fussing. Looking the same way she looked the day before. Like she hadn't gone to bed, like she hadn't closed her eyes or closed her mouth a second. We could hear her saying "no count" and "niggers" till we got out of sight. When Job was sure she couldn't see us no more he reached in his pocket and brought out some pecans. That's what we had for breakfast and dinner that day—pecans.

I have seen some slow mules in my days, but the two pulling that wagon must have been the slowest yet. Two little brown mules not much bigger than Shetland ponies. You couldn't even see them from the back of the wagon. Like the wagon was moving there slow and creaky all by itself. I wanted to sit on the board with Job, but he told me to get back. And a good thing I did because later that day we met up with two Secesh on horses. Before they got to us Job told us to stay quiet and let him do all the talking. When they got a little closer he pulled back on the mules to make them stop. He didn't have to pull back hard.

"See you got some niggers there," one Secesh told him.

"Yes," Job said. "Can't say they much, but you got to start with something, a fellow poor like me."

"Feed them, they'll grow up," the Secesh told him.

"Will do," Job said.

"And y'all mind, y'all hear?" the Secesh told us.

"They better," Job said.

The Secesh rode off. Job shook the lines. Had to shake them twice to make them two little mules come up. He didn't tell us who the riders was, but I knowed all the time they was nothing but Secesh.

Job went on eating pecans and dropping the peels in the wagon. Looked like he didn't have strength enough to drop them out on the ground. And maybe he just didn't care—with that crazy woman back there fussing at him all the time. Them mules didn't care too much either; that wagon just creaked and creaked and wasn't getting nowhere.

Almost sundown that evening we stopped at a crossroad. Job told us to get down and walk half a mile and we was coming up to a big house. Go knock on the door, front or back, and tell the man there we needed a home. "But don't tell who brought you here," he said.

We started down the road, and the wagon moved on. The crop was down, and I kept looking back over my shoulder at Job. I could hear the wagon creaking, but it was moving so slow it looked like it wasn't moving at all. Now, all a sudden I remembered I hadn't told Job thank you. Now, I wanted to run and catch that wagon and tell him how much I appreciated what he had done for us. But my poor little legs was so tired they couldn't go nowhere. I wanted to holler, I wanted to wave, make some kind of sign, but I doubt if Job would have heard me or seen me. The way he was sitting there, gazing down at them two little brown mules, I doubt if he even seen or knowed where he was going.

We didn't see the house till we made the bend. A big white house with a gallery on the front and the side. To the right of the house you had fruit orchard—oh, maybe two or three acres—maybe more. On the other side, the left side of the house, you had horses and cows in a pasture. Farther down was the quarters.

Listening to Job, I went up to the front door and knocked. A nigger came there and looked down at me. Right off, I could see I had done the wrong thing.

"Job brought y'all here?" he said.

"Who?" I said.

"You see them steps?" he said, pointing behind me. "Go right on back down, march round that house and knock on that back door. That or catch up with Job."

I went round to the back but I didn't knock. I figured since he already knowed I was there, there was no need to knock. I stood there and stood there and stood there, but he never showed up. But soon as I knocked he opened the door and told me to come in.

"What you want?" he said.

"Mr. Bone live here?" I asked him.

He went up to the front. Little while later a white man came back in the kitchen. He was a big man with a red beard and blue eyes. And he had the biggest pair of hands I had ever seen.

"You too spare," he said, looking down at me and shaking his head. He looked at Ned standing behind me. "That one over there ain't weaned yet. I ain't running no nursery here, I'm running a plantation. Y'all can stay here tonight and I'll get somebody to take you to town in the morning. I can't use you."

"You mean work?" I said.

"That's what I mean," he said.

"I might be little and spare, but I can do any work them others can do," I said.

"I got women in that field eat more for breakfast than you and that boy weigh together," he said. "First thing y'all die on me and I have to answer to the beero."

"I don't mean to be disrespectful," I said. "But if we was ready to die we would have been dead long before we got here."

"You ain't been out there yet," he said.

"That's the only place I been," I said.

"Yes?" he said.

"Yes, sir," I said. "Me and this little fellow here ain't been doing nothing but walking and walking and walking ever since we heard of our freedom. Any of them out there can do more walking than that I like to see them."

"You got to do more than just walk out in that field," Bone said.

"I done pulled my share before," I said.

"Tell me about it," he said.

I told him.

"Your walking too," he said.

I told him.

"All right, I'll give you a try," he said. "But you still spare and I won't pay you more than six a month. Take it or leave it."

"I don't mean to be disrespectful again," I said. "What you paying them other women?"

Bone eyes opened just a little bit wider. Like he was ready to tell me, before he remembered I was nothing but a child, and a little black one at that. But if I was go'n work for him, maybe it was right for me to know.

"Ten," he said. "But they happen to be women."

"I'm a woman," I said.

"Prove it out there," Bone said. "Not in here. Fifty cents of that coming back to me to school that boy over there—if he wake up long enough. What he carrying them rocks for?"

"Secesh killed his mama. That's what's left."

"Fifty cents to school him," Bone said.

"If I keep up with the other women, I can get much as they get?" I asked him.

"Sure," he said.

He went in the front and came back with a feather and a sheet of paper. He handed me the feather and laid the sheet of paper on the table.

"Put a cross there," he said, pointing at the paper. "One time that way, one time that way."

"I know what a cross is," I said. "What it's for?"

Bone was still looking at the paper, but I knowed he wasn't reading it, because I was looking up at his eyes and I could see they wasn't moving. He was probably thinking he ought to take me by the neck and throw me outside. Then his eyes shifted from the paper to me. But he just looked at me like he was still thinking about something else.

"So I'll know you somewhere in my field even if I can't find you," he said. "You'll know I owe you five dollars and fifty cents."

"Six dollars, Mr. Bone," I said. "Then I give you back fifty cents."

"Sign that," Bone said. "Now."

I stuck the point of the feather in my mouth and leaned on the table to make my cross. After I made it it looked so correct I just stood there looking at it a long time. I started to add another little curve or a dot or something, but Bone took the feather and paper from me.

"I said a mark, not a book."

Bone called that nigger who had let us in the back door and told him to find somebody else to show us to the cabin. All we found in that cabin was two little beds and a firehalf. Beds was two wide boards nailed against the wall like a shelf. Mattress was dry grass sewed in ticking. We had no table, no chairs, no benches—you sat down on your bed or you sat down on the bare ground. After I had been there awhile I got the carpenter to make me a bench. Then I got him to make me a table. That was the only furniture I had for the next ten, twelve years.

We was clearing off the land. The land hadn't been 'tended since the war, and weeds and shrubs covered everything. The women used axes and hoes, the men did the plowing and hauling. After I had been there about a month, Bone came out there and told me he was paying me ten dollars a month like he was paying all the rest of the women because he didn't want me killing myself. I wasn't but 'leven or twelve, but I could do much work as any of them. And the ones who beat me had to do a lot of sweating to stay up there.

BOOK II

Reconstruction

A Flicker of Light; and Again Darkness

FOR A WHILE there looked like everything was go'n be good for us. We had a little school on the place, the first cabin on your left when you came in the quarters. All the small children went to school in the day, the big children and the grown people who had to go in the field went to school at night. The teacher was a young colored man from the North. A good-looking brown-skin man, very good manners. The grown people just like the children all loved him. One day a week we had a special Teacher's Day. When he went to somebody's house and took dinner with them. Everybody tried to out-do everybody else. I didn't have a chair in my house—the bench wasn't good enough for the teacher to sit on—so I sent Ned out to borrow me a chair. When he got back with the chair I sent him out to borrow a fork and a plate. I got the fork and plate from the woman who worked at the big house, and she told Ned to tell me don't be surprised if the teacher recognized them. Everybody else on the place had borrowed that same fork and that same plate before. Well, if he recognized them his manners kept him from saying he did. I didn't eat with him and Ned, I was too 'shame to do so. I pretended I had some work to do, but all the time he was eating I was looking at him to see how he liked the food. After they got through eating he asked Ned if he wanted to read something for me. He got the book out his pocket—the only book they had at school—and Ned had to stand side him. And while he pointed to the words Ned spoke them out. I stood there listening and smil-ing. Before then I doubt if I had ever looked at Ned like he was my own. I had always looked at him like he was a little boy that needed me. But listen-ing to him read I knowed if it wasn't for me Ned wouldn't be here now. And I felt I hadn't just kept Ned from getting killed, I felt like I had born him out my own body. After he went to bed that night, me and the teacher sat by the firehalf talking. He asked my why I didn't come to school like the rest of the people. I told him when I came out the field at night I was tired, and long as Ned was getting a learning I was satisfied. We talked and talked. He had very good manners and everybody liked him—'specially the ladies. I liked him, too, and I went to school couple times just to be near him. But I told myself I had no business thinking about somebody like that, and after I had gone there maybe three times I didn't go no more.

Then they had the colored politicians that used to come to the big house to hold meetings with Bone. They would come to the house once, maybe twice a week, stay couple hours and then leave. If they had anything important to tell us they would gather us at the school. This was church, too: school and church the same cabin. Most of the talk was about the Fedjal Gov'ment—'specially the Republican Party. It was the Republicans that had freed us, and it was the Republicans that had the Freedom Beero there to look after us. They wanted us to take interest in what was going on. They wanted us to vote—and vote Republican. The Democrat Party was for slavery, they said, and believe it or not, they said, there was niggers in the Democrat Party, too. You could always spot him, they said, because he had a white mouth and a tail. They told us they was go'n take us to Alexandria one day so we could see a nigger Democrat at work. The day came, they sent some colored troops to the plantation to bring us in town. The town square was full of people, white people and colored people. It was hot that day. People just standing there sweating and fanning. On the platform the people was giving their speeches. One after another, white and colored. Every now and then somebody would holler and call somebody else a damn liar, then the troops would have to step in to keep them apart. When a nigger Democrat got up on the platform, somebody hollered, "Pull his pants down, let's see his tail. We done already seen he got a white mouth." The nigger Democrat said, "I rather be a Democrat with a tail than be a Republican that ain't had no brains." The people on the Democrat side laughed and clapped. The Democrats talked awhile, then the Republicans got up there and talked. The Democrats wanted the Yankees to get out so we could build on our own. The Republicans wanted the Yankees to stay. The Democrats said we wouldn't have peace till the Yankees had gone. The Republicans said we didn't have peace before they came there. The Republicans said every free man ought to have forty acres and a mule. The Democrats said that was strange coming from a Republican when a dirty scalawag had one of the biggest plantations in the parish. The Republicans said Bone had the planta-tion there to give people work who couldn't go out and get work on their own.

It was burning up. The square packed. The arguing going on and on and on. Then somebody hauled back and hit somebody—and what he did that for? Looked like everybody was waiting for that one lick. I grabbed Ned and dragged him under the platform. I had to fight my way under there, because everybody who wasn't fighting on top the platform or round the platform was trying to get under there just like I was.

The fighting went on and on and on. Under the platform was burning up, but nobody moved out. Then after 'bout an hour, the troops got every-body quieted down again. They took the trouble-makers to jail and brought the rest of us back home.

We heard later it was the secret groups that had caused the trouble. Names like the Ku Klux Klans, the White Brotherhood, the Camellias o' Luzana—groups like that rode all over the State beating and killing. Would kill any black man who tried to stand up and would kill any white man who tried to help him. Just after the war many colored people tried to go out and start their own little farms. The secret groups would come out there and beat them just because their crops was cleaner than the white man's crop. Another time they would beat a man because he had some grass in his crop, "What you growing there, Hawk?" they would ask him. "Corn, Master," Hawk would say. "That look like grass out there to me, Hawk," they would say. "Well, maybe little bit, Master," Hawk would say. "But 'fore day in the morning I surely get it out—if the Lord spare." "No, you better start right now, Hawk," they would say. Then they would make you get down on your hands and knees and eat grass till you got sick. If they didn't get enough fun out of watching you throw up, they would tie you to a fence post or to a tree and beat you. "Tomorrow night we come back again, Hawk," they would say, "And you better not have no grass out there, you hear?" Or. "Tomorrow night we come back and you better have some grass in that field, hear, Charlie?" They was just after destroying any colored who tried to make it on his own. They didn't care what excuse they used.

But we seldom had trouble with the secret groups. Bone was important in the Republican Party and he always had soldiers out there guarding his place. Every time the colored politicians came they brought guards and stationed them at the gate and 'long the road. A mile or two away we would hear that somebody had got beaten up or killed, but we knowed it could never happen where we lived. People used to say, "Where y'all from?" We used to say, with our heads high, "Mr. Bone place." The people would say, "I hear that's a good place. They need any more people to work?" Sometimes we said yes; other times we had to say no.

Then one evening, right after we had come in from the field, Bone called us to the house. It was dark when we came in the yard, and Bone was standing on the gallery with two people holding lanterns on both sides of him. He said he didn't own the place no more, the Secesh did. We had heard that the Secesh was fighting for their land, we had even heard in places where they had got it back, but we never thought it could happen where we was. We had soldiers there all the time, colored politicians there all the time, how could the Secesh get the land? What was soldiers for? What was politicians for? What did they fight a war for if not to set us free? Bone said yes they had fought a war to set us free, but now they wanted to bring this country back together. They had to get it together no matter what. He said till that was done the Secesh was go'n beat and kill. We asked how come they couldn't send more troops in? He said the Yankees was already tired fighting for us. Some of them was sorry they had ever gone to war. Besides that the Yankees saw a chance to make money in the South now. The South needed money to get on her feet, and the Yankees had the money to lend. And that was the deal: the Secesh get their land, but the Yankees lend the money.

After he had paid us off we went down to the schoolhouse to talk. Some was for leaving, some was for staying. "But go where?" we asked. "Before, we knowed what we had to do. We had to leave the place where we was slaves. But where do we go now when Bone done already told us the Yankees don't care either?" "Let's stick it out," some of us said. "We not slaves no more. If we don't like it we can always move." We dismissed the meeting round midnight and went home. Half the people left anyhow. But this time I was one of them who stayed behind.

Couple days later the owner showed up. Bone had gone, the teacher and all the colored troops and colored politicians had gone. The few people left in the quarters went up to the house to hear what the owner had to say. He was standing on the gallery in almost the same place where Bone had stood couple days before. Tall, slim, narrow-face man. Still had on his Secesh uniform, even with the sable hanging on his side. His name, he said, was Colonel Eugene I. Dye.

"I hope I don't have no more nigger soldiers and no more nigger politicians round here," he said. He looked over the few of us left there. "That schoolhouse up there go'n be shut down till I can find y'all a competent teacher." He looked over us again to see what we had to say. "Wages still the same. Fifteen for the men, ten for the women. I can't pay y'all till the end of the year, but you can draw rations and clothing from the store. If that suit you, stay; if it don't, catch up with that coat-tail-flying scalawag and the rest of them hot-footing niggers who was here two days ago."

If Colonel Dye had told me that a week before I would have turned around then and left. But after what Bone had told us I had no more faith in heading North than I had staying South. I would stay right here and do what I could for me and Ned. If I heard of a place where I could live better, where Ned could get a better learning, I would go there to live. Till then I would stay where I was.

It was slavery again, all right. No such thing as colored troops, colored politicians, or a colored teacher anywhere near the place. The only teacher to come there was white; the only time he came was in the winter when the weather was so bad the children couldn't go in the field. You didn't need a pass to leave the place like you did in slavery time, but you had to give Colonel Dye's name if the secret group stopped you on the road. Just because the Yankee troops and the Freedom Beero had gone didn't mean they had stopped riding. They rode and killed more than ever now. The colored people wrote letters to Washington, sometimes a group would get up enough nerve to go there in person, but the troops never did come back. Yankee business came in—yes; Yankee money came in to help the South back on her feet—yes; but no Yankee troops. We was left there to root hog or die.

Exodus

THEN THE PEOPLE STARTED LEAVING. But the people had always left from here. All through slavery people was trying to get away from the South. The old masters and the patrollers used to go after the people with dogs. If you was a good slave, a good worker, they would bring you back home and beat you. Some of the masters would brand their slaves. If you was one of the troublemakers always trying to run away, then they would bring you back and sell you to a trader going to New Orleans. If you gived them any trouble in the swamps they would just kill you back there. I knowed a man who wouldn't come back and they had to shoot him. He told them he rather they shoot him down like a dog than go back, and he tored his shirt open to let them shoot at his heart. They shot him right where he was and left him back there for the buzzards. We had a bayou some five miles from where I lived that they called the Dirty Bayou. The people used to run in the bayou to throw the dogs off their scent, and that's how the patrollers used to catch them. The bayou was too wide and boggy and the slaves couldn't swim— they had to wade over   and that's how the patrollers would catch them. The patrollers would put the gun on them and holler for them to come back. If they didn't come back the patrollers would shoot them in the water or make them drown trying to get away. But many of them made it. Not trying to wade over—it was too wide and the mud too sticky—they used to build wharves. They would go in the swamps every night or every chance they got and they would work little by little till they had finished. Then they would edge the wharf in the water and head out. These was the smart ones. The dumb ones tried to wade over, and that's when they got caught. That bayou got more people in it than a graveyard.

Now, after the Yankee soldiers and the Freedom Beero left, the people started leaving again. Not right away—because Mr. Frederick Douglass said give the South a chance. But when the people saw they was treated just as bad now as before the war they said to heck with Mr. Frederick Douglass and started leaving. The old masters didn't think too much of it at first. They was glad the niggers was leaving. If they got rid of all the bad niggers— them the only ones leaving, anyhow—if all of them left there wouldn't be no more trouble. They didn't know it at first, but it wasn't just the bad ones leaving. Droves after droves of good and bad was leaving. If you went to town you would see whole families going by. Men in front with bundles on their backs, women following them with a child in their arm and holding another one by the hand. And now seeing this the old masters did start worrying. Who was go'n pick the cotton now? Who was go'n cut the cane?

They went to Washington. It was the North enticing the niggers for their votes. The Yankees pretended they wanted to help the South back on her feet, but all they want do is control the South. The people in Washington called the colored in and asked them if it was true the North was buying their vote. The colored said no, they was leaving because they couldn't get fair treatment in the South. Now, the old masters came back and tried to force the people to stay. They turned the Klans loose on them, the Camellias, the White Brotherhood loose on the people. The people still went. They slipped away at night, they took to the swamps, they still went.

Ned Leaves Home

SOME COLORED SOLDIERS from the war organized a committee to go round and see how the colored people was treated. They went all over the State checking on how the colored was living. Ned found out about the committee and joined it. He reported on the parish where we lived. He told the committee the work we did, how long we had to work, how much money we got for working, how much we had to pay for food and clothes, how the overseer treated us in the field. When the committee found out the colored was treated no better than they was treated in slavery they told them to leave for the North. Ned's job was to tell the people how to get to New Orleans. How to travel, where they could stop, where they could find help and food.

Ned was seventeen or eighteen then. I'm sure he wasn't twenty yet. Tall, slim, nothing but arms and legs. Very quiet—always serious. Too serious. I didn't like to see him serious like that. I used to always ask him, "Ned, what you thinking about?" He would say, "Nothing." But I knowed he was thinking about his mama. He never said it, he never talked about her (he used to call me mama) but I knowed he was thinking about her all the time. I would do anything so he could keep his mind off her. I would make him talk about school. He like his first teacher, the young colored man who was here when we first came to the place. And we used to talk about him long after he had gone. I would make him talk about the other children in the quarters. Make him talk about anything to keep him from thinking so much. But he was a serious child. Even if this terrible thing hadn't happened to his mama and little sister he still would 'a' been a serious person.

He had a pretty little smile though. He was real black, with dimples in his jaws, and he had the whitest teeth you ever saw. Real handsome when he wasn't serious. Tall, slim, handsome black child. He got heavy when he got older. He got to be two hundred pounds or better. But he was nothing but arms and legs when he was growing up.

He had changed his name now—Ned Douglass. Before, he was Ned Brown—after me. We didn't know his daddy's name, so he was Ned Brown. Then he changed it to Douglass, after Mr. Frederick Douglass. He was go'n be a great leader like Mr. Douglass was. He was Ned Douglass awhile, then he was Ned Stephen Douglass. Ned Stephen Douglass awhile, then he was Edward Stephen Douglass. All the rest of the young men round him was taking on names like that. Some Douglass, some Brown—after John Brown, not Jane Brown; some Turners, after Nat Turner; Sumners; some Sherman. Ask one his name, right off he would tell you John Brown. Ask him his daddy's name, he told you Ed Washington. The old people used to laugh and shake their heads, but these children was serious. I used to tell Ned all the time he was too serious. He had learned to read and he could write. He always had some kind of book round the house.

When the old masters came back from Washington to stop the colored people from leaving the South, they started watching people like Ned. They knowed about the committee, they knowed he was a member, and now they was watching him. Colonel Dye called me to the house one day and told me to make him stop. I told him I would talk to Ned. He told me don't just talk, make him stop or he was go'n get himself in a lot of trouble. I told Ned, but he said he wouldn't stop.

One night while he was out doing work for the committee, they came riding. My cabin was way down in the quarters, and they passed all the other cabins to come to mine. It was in the winter, and it was a full moon, and it had plenty stars, and they came on horses. Some eight or nine of them. I didn't know they was out there till they had kicked the door in. All had on their sheets. Three of them came in, the others stayed out. I could see them out there on the horses.

"Where's he at?" one of them asked me.

"Who?" I said.

He slapped me down with the back of his hand. Then they turned over everything in the house. Turned over my table, kicked the bench in the fire. The end of it got scorched and when they left I had to douse it out with water.

"You still don't know where he's at?" that same one asked me.

"No," I said, getting up.

He waited till I was up good, then he slapped me back down.

"Still don't?" he said.

"She don't know, Bo," another one said.

"She know," Bo said.

"Let her be, Bo," the other one said. "We'll get him some other time. Let's get out of here."

They got on their horses and went back up the quarters. They had to pass by the big house so the people at the house must 'a' heard them. I wouldn't 'a' been a bit surprised if Colonel Dye hadn't sent them himself.

Late that night Ned came back to the house. My face was swole and he asked me what had happened. I told him. He told me to pack, we was leaving now. We could take to the swamps till we got off the place, then we could take the road to New Orleans. In New Orleans we would get a boat for Kansas.

"I can't go with you," I said.

"You got to," he said. "They came here and beat you this time. They'll do worse when they come back."

"They won't do me nothing," I said.

"If I stop?" he said. "You want me to stop, too?"

"I want you to do what you think's right," I said.

"I'm doing what I think's right," he said.

"Then you have to go, or they'll kill you."

"You have to go with me."

"No," I said.

"You ain't married to this place," he said.

"In a way," I said.

"I can't stop, Mama," he said.

"Then you have to go," I said.

I sat on the bench in front of the firehalf and pulled Ned down side me. I looked in his face and he was already crying.

"This not my time," I said.

"After the war wasn't my time," he said. "But I went everywhere you wanted me to go."

"People don't keep moving, Ned."

"They move when they're slaves," he said.

"What's up there?" I asked him.

"Everybody else going," he said.

"Many going, but not everybody," I said. "I think you ought to go. But not me."

"Just leave you here to be a dog?" he said.

"I won't be a dog," I said.

"You'll be a dog," he said. "To eat the crumbs they throw on the floor."

"I won't eat crumbs, Ned, and I won't eat off the floor," I said. "You know better than that."

"I don't mean it like that," he said. "I mean they making us separate, and

I don't want us to separate."

"It had to happen one day," I told him. "I told you that when you first started."

"You want me to give it up?"

"Not less you want to," I said. "Things like this you got to make up your own mind."

He set there squeezing my hands and crying. I pulled him close and held him to my bosom.

"You ought to go," I said. "They might come back tonight."

"I ought to give it up," he said. "How you go'n live?"

"I'll make out," I said.

"I can't give it up," he said. "I ought to stay here and just let them kill me."

"I want you to go," I said. "They will kill you if you stay."

I had already cooked up his grub, and while he sat on the bench eating, I packed the rest for him to take. All the time I was packing his things I kept from looking at him. I knowed if I had looked at him he would 'a' seen how I felt and he wouldn't 'a' been able to go. I didn't want him to go—God knows I didn't want him to go—but I knowed he had to leave one day, so why not now. When I had packed his food and clothes I put the sack by the door.

Ned took a long time to finish eating. I did everything to keep from looking at him. When he got up to go, my heart jumped in my chest. But I forced myself to go up to him.

"We doing what we both think is best," I said.

He held me close. He was so tall and thin. I could feel him crying, but I held up till he was gone. I stood in the door and watched him till he had gone out the quarters, then I went back inside and laid down on the bed. And I cried all night.

Two Letters
from Kansas

I STAYED IN THE CABIN a long time by myself, then me and Joe Pittman started seeing each other. Joe Pittman had been married, but his wife was dead and left him with two children, two girls. We had knowed each other a long time before Ned left for Kansas, but we never looked at each other like we was interested. I had two reasons. Ned was by himself in this world, except for me, and I didn't want no man and no children spiting him just because he was an orphan. The other reason I never looked at a man, I was barren. An old woman on the place had told me that. I went to her one day and told her how my body act and didn't act. After we had sat down and talked awhile, she said one word: "Barren." I went to a doctor and he told me the same thing: "You barren, all right." He told me it had happened when I was nothing but a tot. Said I had got hit or whipped in a way that had hurt me inside. Said this might be one reason I didn't grow too much either. Asked me how my appetite was. I said, "Appetite? My appetite good as anybody else appetite." He said, "You all right. Go on back home."

When Joe Pittman asked me to be his wife I told him I wanted to think about it awhile. Because I didn't want to tell him I was barren. I liked him now and I was scared if I told him I was barren he would leave me for some-body else. He asked me again and I told him I wanted to think some more. He kept on asking me, and that's when I told him. We was sitting down in the house that day eating when I told him that. I told him if he didn't want me no more that was all right, I would understand. But all he said was, "Ain't we all been hurt by slavery? If you just say you'll help me raise my two girls, I'll be satisfied." He was a real man, Joe Pittman was.

We didn't get married. I didn't believe in the church then, and Joe never did. We just agreed to live together, like people did in the slavery time. Slaves didn't get married in churches, they jumped over the broom handle. Old Mistress and Young Mistress held the broom handle up off the floor, and Old Master told the slaves to hold hands and jump over. If they was old people, Old Mistress and Young Mistress would hold the broom down low and the old couple would step over sprightly. Old Master would say, "Step sprightly there, Jubal; step sprightly there, Minnie." They would step sprightly, and they was pronounced husband and wife. Me and Joe Pittman didn't think we needed the broom, we wasn't slaves no more. We would just live together long as we wanted each other. That was all.

Not long after we started living together Joe told me he wanted to leave

Colonel Dye's plantation. Joe was sharp with horses and he was sure he could find a place where he could get more money and get better treatment than what he was getting here. I told him if he wanted to leave I would go with him, but I didn't want to leave till I had heard from Ned. It was almost a year and I still hadn't gotten a word from Ned. I didn't want him to come back and I wasn't there or him to write me a letter and I didn't get it. Joe said he would wait till I heard but at the same time he would look around for a new place. Every chance he got he went out looking. If he heard of a place, no matter how far it was, if he could get there and get back before he had to go in the field he went and checked it out.

Ned wrote me a month after he left home, but I didn't get the letter for a year. He wrote the letter to somebody he met in New Orleans just before he got on the boat for Kansas. He didn't want send the letter directly to me because the people here would 'a' been suspicious. Anything that had Kansas or the North on it might 'a' been torn up and throwed away. He sent the letter to his friend and his friend was suppose to send it to the preacher on the plantation, and the preacher was suppose to read it to me. Instead of his friend sending the letter on to the preacher like he was suppose to do he put the letter somewhere and forgot it. When he found it again he could hardly read the address and he sent it to the wrong place. When it came back he had to get in touch with Ned in Kansas again. Ned was in Leavenworth when he first wrote the letter, but now he had gone to a place called Atchison. It was a year before everything got straightened out.

The letter told how people was coming into Kansas by the boat-load. At first how the white people in Kansas was helping them. How they collected money to give them. How they organized committees to go to Washington and places like that for money and clothes, money and food. Even from cross the sea they got money and clothes. The people at first was almost too nice. But that was the first letter. When I got the second letter things had changed already. The white people couldn't help all of them, and there wasn't any work for them to do. Now the white people didn't want them in town. Ned was on a committee that found new places for people to live. He traveled by boat up and down the river, but no matter where he went there was already too many people. His committee sent letters back to the South: not all the people to come to one place. There was other States where they could go and find comfort. But the people had heard of Kansas first. Like sheeps they had to go where everybody else had gone. Now the riots. When the letters and papers didn't keep them out, the white people drove them out with sticks and guns. When Ned went out in the country to see how they was living, he said some of them had died from the cold. Others was starving. Some was talking about coming back South. But most of them was going farther West or head North.

The only good news I got from Ned at this time—he was working for some white people who liked him. They saw how much he cared for his race, and they thought he could help them much more if he finished school. He told them he wanted to go on to school, but he thought he ought to help me. From the first letter on he always sent me three or four dollars every time he wrote. When I got the first money I wrote back and told him I didn't need it, I was making out just fine. He told me if I didn't need it, put it up, but keep it. He never told me he wanted to go back to school, he didn't tell me that till I wrote and told him me and Joe Pittman was married. We wasn't married, we was just living together, but Ned wouldn't 'a' liked that. But it wasn't till after I told him about me and Joe he told me he wanted to go back to school.

Ned was working on a farm in Kansas. He worked in the day, he rode a horse to school at night. This went on five, six years. When he finished, they gived him a job teaching there. He stayed there till that war started in Cuba, then he joined the army. After the war he came back here. He wanted to teach at home now.

Another Home

JOE PITTMAN FOUND A PLACE near the Luzana-Texas borderline where he could break horses. He knowed all about breaking horses and branding cattle—he had learned that on Colonel Dye's place—but now he wanted to go where he could make a better living. After we had talked it over, just me and him, he went up to the house to tell Colonel Dye he wanted to leave. Colonel Dye was old and wrinkled now, but onery still. Not just onery, he was losing his mind now. Once every year he used to put on his Secesh uniform and ride to Alexandria. Two or three days later he would come back. Looked like every time he went and came back he was more and more crazy. Sometimes he used to gather us all at his house just to look at us. After he had looked at us about a minute he would tell us to go back. One time he called us up there, and by the time we got there he had forgot he had sent for us. "What y'all doing here?" he asked. "You sent for them, Pa," one of his boys said. "Well, I'm sending them right on back," he said. "Get out of here. Go back to work." When Joe went up there that day and told him he wanted to leave, he said: "What's the matter, I ain't been treating you right?" Joe told him it wasn't that, he had been treated very good there, but he wanted to go out and do little sharecropping of his own. (He wouldn't dare tell the old colonel he wanted to go break horses for more money, he told him sharecropping.) Colonel Dye told Joe he would pay the family five dollars more a month if he stayed. Joe shook his head—no, he wanted to go out and do little sharecropping. The colonel said, "Listen, Joe, I'll turn over piece of that good bottom land to you, and you work it like you want." This was the first time Colonel Dye had offered anybody a piece of land on his place. He had said before that this was the last thing he would ever do. Joe knowed this before he went up there, that's why he went up there saying sharecropping. He said the old colonel looked at him like he was losing his best friend. "You a good man, Joe, and I need you here to mind my stock. My children round here too lazy to do a thing, and there ain't another nigger on this place that can tell you a cow from a hog." Joe shook his head. "I like to go sharecrop." Now, the old colonel got mad. Acting like he was losing his best friend one second, next second he was blazing mad. "All right, if you want go sharecrop, go sharecrop," he said. Joe thanked him and turned to go. "Just a minute," the colonel said. Joe stopped and looked at him. "Ain't you forgetting something?" "Sir?" Joe said. "My hundred and fifty dollars," the colonel said. "What hundred and what fifty dollars?" Joe said. "That hundred and that fifty to get you out of trouble when the Klux had you," the colonel said. "You forget that?"

It was true Joe Pittman had been mixed up in little politics just after the war, and everybody round there knowed about it. The Klux had got after him, and the colonel had spoke out. But at that time nothing was mentioned about money.

"I didn't know you paid," Joe said.

"Kluxes don't stop killing a nigger just because you say hold it," the colonel said. "Now you pay me my hundred and fifty dollars or get away from my door."

Joe came back and told me what had happened. We sat up all night trying to think what we ought to do next. Joe was set on leaving, no holding him back, but he couldn't leave and not pay Colonel Dye his money. He knowed he didn't owe Colonel Dye any money, but how could he prove it? The Freedom Beero once, but they wasn't there no more.

We stayed up all night. Then we both said that Joe ought to go see if he couldn't borrow the money from the new man he was go'n work for. 'Fore day the next morning Joe packed a lunch and started out. Started out on foot with a hundred miles to go. Somebody told Colonel Dye he was missing and Colonel Dye came out in the field and asked me where he was. "Gone look for your money," I said. The old colonel got mad at first, saying what he was go'n do to Joe when Joe got back. But then he started laughing. Where could a nigger get a hundred and fifty dollars from? He rode away laughing.

Couple weeks later Joe came back. Walked almost to Texas—rode a horse all the way back. He left the horse tied in the swamps, scared Colonel Dye might accuse him of stealing it, then he went up to the house and knocked. Colonel Dye came to the back door chewing. Had been sitting at the table eating.

"Where you been?" he said. "Don't you know them mules out there hungry? Want me come in that yard with my stick?"

Joe handed him the money. Colonel Dye wouldn't take it at first. Like it was confederate money. Then he took it—looked at it. Then he looked at Joe. Then at the money. Then he wiped his mouth and counted the money. "Look like it's all here—but the interest," he said. "Time lap' between loaner and loanee come to about thirty more dollars. Well?"

Joe came back and told me he owed Colonel Dye even more money. I had been getting money from Ned, and what I had saved from my wages came out to about twenty-five dollars. But we needed five more dollars. So here we go, up and down the quarters, selling the little furniture we had. I think we got about a dollar and a half for everything. Joe had a' old shotgun, he sold that: another dollar. We tried to sell our clothes, but nobody wanted them. We had a pig we was go'n take with us—but we needed the two dollars now. Joe stuck the pig in a sack and started up and down the quarters again. After he had sold the pig, he took the money to Colonel Dye. The colonel stood in the back door counting the money. When he saw it was all there, he started to shut the back door and go back inside, but he saw Joe still out there in the yard.

"Well?" he said.

"Mr. Clyde said be sure bring a receipt," Joe said. "He said he don't want have to come this far South for a piece of paper."

Colonel Dye went back inside and wrote that he had received one hundred and fifty dollars. He didn't say a thing about the extra thirty dollars. He came to the back door and throwed the piece of paper on the ground.

"Don't let the sun set on you anywhere near my place," he said.

Joe came back and told me and the girls to get ready. The two girls was called Ella and Clara. Ella the oldest one, and Clara the youngest one and looked just like Joe. After we had got everything we was go'n take with us, Joe led us back in the swamps. Ella and Clara got on the horse with the bundle, and me and Joe walked in front. I asked Joe how come he got the money so easy. He said it wasn't easy; some colored men he had met had to speak up for him. Then he had to prove to Mr. Clyde how good he was. Clyde picked one of the wildest horses he had. He broke the horse, true, but he was so stoved up he had to lay up awhile before he could start back home.

It took us about ten days to reach Clyde's place. We traveled the swamps all the time for fear the secret groups might see us and attack us for leaving Colonel Dye's place. We ran out of food four days out, and from then on we ate what we could find. Corn, potatoes. If Joe was lucky he might kill a possum, or if we came up to a bayou we might catch a fish or two. We ate anything we could get. We met people, black and white, but they saw us on the move and wouldn't have nothing to do with us.

We came up to Clyde's place about five one evening. Clyde and his men had been killing hogs, and when we came up, the men was standing in the yard talking. Clyde told Joe to take us to the back and tell the women in the kitchen to give us a good feeding. I could smell that good hogmeat from way cross the yard. The women was making hoghead cheeze and blood pudding. They handed us a big pan of food and we found a clean spot on the ground to sit down. When we got through, almost too full to move, we went back round the house. Mr. Clyde told Joe he wouldn't need him till Monday, so Joe could take us on home. The cabin wasn't much bigger than the one we had left, but we had made a new start and everything looked right smart better. After the children went to bed me and Joe sat at the firehalf talking. We was so proud we had moved, so happy for the good meal we got soon as we got here, every time we looked at each other we had to grin. Feet sore, back still hurting, but grinning there like two children courting for the first time. We tried to keep from looking at each other. I looked at the firehalf, Joe looked at the door; then I looked at the door, Joe looked at the firehalf. When we couldn't find nowhere else to look we looked at each other and grinned. No touching, no patting each other on the knee, just grinning.

Molly

WE GOT THERE ON A FRIDAY. Next day, Saturday, I heard that I was suppose to work in the big house. I hadn't worked in a house since I was a slave, but I work where they put me. What I couldn't figure out, why I got the job soon as I got there? How come some other woman didn't have it? Some people like house work. Make them feel more important. House niggers always thought they was better than field niggers. I asked Joe if he knowed why they had gived me the job. He said he didn't know, either.

'Fore day Monday morning when they called Joe for work I got up, too. After he ate and left, I went over to the house. It was pitch black, but I didn't know what they wanted me for, so I went on anyhow. At that time some of the kitchens used to set away from the house. I didn't know where I was go'n be working, so I went back to the kitchen and sat down on a barrel I saw in front of the door.

I sat there and sat there. I sat there over an hour. Just as the sun was coming up I saw a woman, a great big, brown-skin woman walking across the yard toward me. It had been a heavy dew the night before, and her legs and feet was shining wet. She came up to the kitchen and looked at me sitting there.

"Well?" she said.

"My name's Jane Pittman," I said.

"I didn't ask you that," she said. "What you want?"

"I'm working here," I said.

"No, you ain't," she said. "I don't need nobody spying on me."

"Spying?" I said.

"Get out my way 'fore I lam' you up side the head," she said.

She didn't give me time to move. She pushed me side the head and I fell on the ground. I brushed off my clothes and went in the kitchen where she was. She was lighting a fire in the firehalf. When she got through she looked at me standing there.

"You don't hear good, do you?" she said.

I was go'n tell her I didn't want be there in the first place, I rather be out in the field, but she grabbed me and pitched me back outside. I fell flat on my face, my hands covered with chicken and guinea stuff. I wiped my hands in the grass and went back in the kitchen. Molly was singing. She didn't even stop. She just grabbed me, still singing, and slammed me back out there. While I was sailing in the air I was hoping I hit a clean spot. That was like hoping I didn't hit the ground.

I wiped off my hands and clothes and went back in. Molly just stood there looking at me now. When she went back to the firehalf I got the broom and started sweeping. She jecked the broom out my hand and throwed it back in the corner. I kept out of her way after that, but I watched everything she did. After she got through cooking, she took the food to the house. I waited and waited for her to come back. When she didn't, I went over to the house too. The white people was sitting at the table eating. One white lady was just coming in the dining room. She was Mr. Clyde's daughter, Miss Clare.

"You must be Jane," she said.

"Yes ma'am," I said.

"You'll take care the children, Jane."

"I don't need nobody taking care them children," Molly said. "I can cook and take care them children."

Miss Clare didn't answer Molly. She looked at the side of my face and my forrid.

"You hurt anywhere else?" she asked me.

I touched my forrid, and I had a knot up there the size of a marble.

Miss Clare looked at the side of my face again. She was too much of a lady to tell me I had some guinea stuff there. I could see her mouth working like she wanted to say something, then she pressed her lips tight. Then her nose worked a little bit like she was smelling something. All this time she was looking straight in my eye. She wanted me to guess what she didn't want tell me.

One of the children at the table looked at me and pointed his finger. "Caw-caw," he said. Then everybody else at the table looked at me, and all of them bust out laughing. I touched the spot they was looking at, and it was there, all right.

Molly didn't want nobody else working in that house with her, scared the person would take her place. She had been with the Clyde family ever since she was a young lady. She had been the cook, she had been the nurse. But now she was in her sixties, and they thought she was getting old and needed help. Molly didn't think she needed help. She was scared if she got help the next thing the other person would be taking over. She had had it pretty easy all her life, and she wasn't go'n let nobody take it from her. The people tried to show Molly they didn't want nobody else to take her place. "We love you, that's why we want people here to help you," they told her. But Molly didn't see it that way. And she made everybody who came there to work pay for it. She would spill hot ashes on the floor and swear you was trying to burn the house down. If she heard one of the children crying she would swear you had done him something wrong. If you had to make a fire in the firehalf or you had to make up a bed she would find something wrong with it every time. She did everything to get rid of you; then after she had got you out she couldn't take care the work by herself.

Molly tried to get rid of me just like she had got rid of all the others. She had told lies on them till the white people had to let them go. When the white people found out she was telling lies and refused to fire the servants Molly vexed them and vexed them till they quit themself. When that didn't work on me she went to the white people crying. She was quitting because they didn't love her no more. She said she had wet nurse Miss Clare and now Miss Clare was the main one trying to put her out in the cold. They told Molly that wasn't true, they wanted her there, they wanted her there the rest of her life. Molly said they didn't want her, they wanted me.

One day she told them she was leaving. They told her she couldn't leave, she had been with them most of her life. She said me or her, one of us had to go. Miss Clare said I wasn't going, but she didn't want Molly to go either. She told me herself that she loved Molly much as she loved anybody and she wanted Molly to spend the rest of her life there with them. Molly said me or her, one had to go. I told them let me go in the field. No, they said.

Molly went to Deritter and got a job looking after an old lady there. I think for the first six months after Molly left, Miss Clare cried for Molly every day. She would go to Deritter every week to see Molly. If she didn't go to Molly, Molly came there to see her. They would sit in that front room and talk for hours. Molly would spend the night and go back the next day. I went to Miss Clare and told her I was quitting. She told me if I did, she just had to get somebody else. I told her I didn't care what she did, I was quitting. I went home and told Joe I had quit. Joe told me if I didn't get back up to that house he was go'n take a stick and run me back up there.

Molly died four or five years after that. The doctor said she died from old age, but Molly died from a broken heart. They brought her back to the place and buried her in the family plot. One of the things I'll always regret, me and Molly never got to be friends. Maybe in the Beyond we will meet again and I'll have a chance to tell her I never meant any harm. I think up there she will understand much better than she did down here.

A Dollar for Two

I STAYED THERE ABOUT TEN YEARS. All that time I worked in the house and Joe broke the horses. They used to get the horses out of Texas. We wasn't too far off the Luzana-Texas borderline, and they used to get the horses out of Texas and bring them home to break them, then sell them to a boat that went down the Sabine River. Joe was called Chief Breaker. Everybody called him Chief—Chief Pittman. He broke horses nobody else could ride. People used to come from all over just to see him. Bet on him like you bet on rodeo riders. Clyde made as much on his rodeo as he made selling the horses down the river.

I dreaded the days they went to Texas to get horses. Scared somebody was coming back and telling me Joe was dead. Scared they might bring him in the house all broken up. I had seen it happen. A young boy had been throwed against a fence. Laid in bed a week, suffering, screaming, before he died. Every time Joe went out now I thought about that boy. But when I told him how I felt, all he said was: "What else can I do? I got to make a living doing something. Maybe the Lord put me here to break horses." "And maybe He didn't," I said. "Well, till He come down here and tell me different, I reckoned I'll just go on breaking them," Joe said.

Together we was making a dollar a day. We didn't have to pay rent or buy food, so we could save most of what we made. After we had been there two, three years we had already paid back the hundred and fifty dollars Joe had borrowed. Couple more years, I thought we had enough and we ought to go out and find a little place of our own. Joe said it wasn't that easy. He was too valuable to just pack up and quit like that. And what would he do? Farm? He didn't want do no more farming. No, he wanted to ride horses. He was good at it and he liked it.

When I saw he wasn't go'n leave I started having dreams about his death. I saw him dead in every way you can think possible. Throwed on a fence, throwed against a tree, dragged through the swamps. Every way possible a cowboy could die, I dreamed it of Joe. Then one dream started coming back over and over, the one where he was throwed against the fence. When I told it to him, he said: "Now, little mama, man come here to die, didn't he? That's the contract he signed when he was born'—'I hereby degree that one of these days I'm go'n lay down these old bones.' Now, all he can do while he's here is do something and do that thing good. The best thing I can do in this world is ride horses. Maybe I can be a better farmer, but the way things is a colored man just can't get out there and start farming any time he want. He's go'n have to take orders from some white man. Breaking horses, I don't take orders from a soul on earth. That's why they calls me Chief. Maybe one day one of them'll come along and get me. Maybe I'll get too old and just have to step down. Maybe some little young buck'll come along and take over Chief from me and I won't have to ride the terrible ones no more. But till that day get here I got to keep going. That's what life's about, doing it good as you can. When the time come for them to lay you down in that long black hole, they can say one thing: 'He did it good as he could.' That's the best thing you can say for a man. Horse breaker or yard sweeper, let them say the poor boy did it good as he could."

Every time he left the house I thought that was the last time I was go'n see him alive. Then a month or two later they would show up with another drove. These was the good times, when the men came riding back. Everybody was happy, the white and the black. The men would put the horses in the corral a few days; then after the men had rested up, after the word was out they had new horses on the place, then they would go out to break them. The corral was between the house and the quarters, and I could see them riding the horses from the yard or from one of the windows at the house.

Seven or eight years after we had been living there it happened. It was cold that day when they came in with the horses. It was February, a Monday, almost freezing. Any time the men came back, 'specially with a good drove, they had a feast in the kitchen at the big house. Me and Joe went to the feast late that day. When we came up even with the coral, a black stallion ran long the fence whinnying and bobbing his head. I got so weak I almost fell. This was the same horse I had been seeing in my dreams. But when I told it to Joe, all he did was laugh.

Everybody was already in the kitchen when we got there. Joe sat down at the table and I served him. The women didn't sit at the table with the men on that day, they served their men. Clyde came back to the kitchen and had a drink, but he didn't sit down at the table. While he was back there Joe told him what I had said about the horse, and everybody bust out laughing.

"Well, if Joe don't ride him, reckoned I'll have to do it," Clyde said.

When he said that the rest of the men laughed even harder. Joe laughed so much he cried. He was Chief. Who was go'n ride something he was scared to ride?

When we was going back home, the stallion heard us coming or he smelt Joe's scent in the air, and he ran long the fence again. None of the other horses paid us any mind, just him. Tall, slick, and black, just running long the fence. We stopped there and looked at him awhile. He was the devil far as I was concerned, but Joe stood there grinning at him. Joe said he had given them more trouble than all the other horses put together. He was stronger and faster than any horse he had ever seen. Run for days and wouldn't get tired. Leap over a canal that a regular horse wouldn't even try. After they had been after him about a week some of the men started saying he was a ghost. Maybe even a haint. Clyde said he wasn't either. He was a horse and they was go'n catch him and take him home. They trailed him a week, night and day. They saw him here, they saw him over there: sometimes right on them; other times far, far away.

But they cornered him in the mountains. Joe said after they had caught him every last man there looked hurt. Hurt because the chase was over; hurt because they had to break him just like you break any other horse.

All the time we stood there looking at that horse he was pacing long the fence. After we walked away I looked back over my shoulder and I saw him standing there all tall, slick, and black. I told Joe that horse gived me the chills. Joe said it was just the weather.

Man's Way

I COULDN'T SLEEP THAT NIGHT for worrying over that horse. If I shut my eyes a second I saw him standing there in the corral. If I kept them shut any link of time I saw him throwing Joe against that fence. A cowboy to fall is no disgrace, but I had dreamed of this horse even before I saw him, and that did worry my mind.

The next day I made pretend I was sick and I asked them to let me go see the doctor. Joe wanted to drive me in town, but I told him it wasn't that bad. He told me to take Ella with me, but I told him I wanted to go by myself. Because it wasn't the doctor, it was the hoo-doo in town I wanted to see. I didn't believe in hoo-doo, I never have, but nobody else wanted to listen to me. I wanted to find out if I was dreaming this just because I wanted Joe to stop riding, or if I was dreaming this because it was go'n happen.

The hoo-doo lived in a narrow little street called Dettie Street, and the little town where she lived was called Grady. She had flower bushes all over the yard, but no flowers, because it was winter. She had bottles stuck upside down round all the flower bushes, and two rows of bottle side the walk from the gate up to the house. Bottles every color you can mention. She had scrubbed the gallery that morning, and she had sprinkled red brick over the gallery and the steps. She must 'a' heard me stop the wagon before the gate because she answered the door soon as I knocked. She was a big mulatto woman, and had come from New Orleans. At least, that was her story. She had left New Orleans because she was a rival of Marie Laveau. Marie Laveau was the Queen then, you know, and nobody dare rival Marie Laveau. Neither Marie Laveau mama, neither Marie Laveau daughter who followed her. Some people said the Maries was the same one, but, of course, that was people talk. Said the first Marie never died, she just turned younger in her later years. Well, from all I've heard, Marie Laveau was powerful, helped and hurt lot of people, but I don't think even she was that powerful.

This one name was Madame Gautier. Her name was Eloise Gautier, but everybody called her Madame Gautier. She wore a purple satin dress and a gold-color head rag. Two big earrings like the Creole people wear in her ears. She told me to come in. When she heard I had come there for special business she told me to follow her to another room. It was winter and it was cold and she had a fire in the firehalf. She had candles burning in every cor-ner of the room, and she had seven on the mantelpiece. She had another candle burning under a little statue on a little table by the window. She had Saint pictures hanging on the wall with crepe paper round each picture. She nodded for me to sit down. After she had put another piece of wood on the fire she sat down cross from me. I had felt a little scared of her till I saw her put the piece of wood in the fire. Then I told myself, "Well, she can get cold just like anybody else at least."

After I told her why I was there, she asked me why hadn't I stopped Joe in my dream from getting on that horse. I told her I couldn't stop him in real life, how could she expect me to stop him in a dream.

"You ever tried?" she asked.

I told her yes I had tried, but he never heard me. It was too dusty or too dark or too much noise was going on or he was too far away or too something else.

"Wait," she said, "before you go another step farther. How many children you done give to this man Joe Pittman?"

"I am barren," I said. And I told her what the doctor had said.

"Ah," she said. "Slavery has made you barren. But that is it."

"That's why he ride them horses?" I asked her.

"That's why you can't stop him," she said. "He probably rides for many reasons. That's man's way. To prove something. Day in, day out he must prove he is a man. Poor fool."

"Joe is good to me," I said.

"Sure he is, my dear," she said. "But man is foolish. And he's always proving how foolish he is. Some go after lions, some run after every woman he sees, some ride wild horses."

"That horse go'n kill him?" I asked her.

"Mon sha," she said.

I looked at her, waiting.

"You want the answer?" she said.

"If it's good," I said.

"There's just one answer," she said.

I looked in her face a long time to see what the answer was, but her face wouldn't show it. It was quiet, quiet in the room. So quiet you could almost hear them candles burning. Not quite, but almost. The fire popped so loud in the firehalf it made me jump. Now I was scared of the answer, and I was sorry I had come there.

"You can go if you want," she said.

"I want to know," I said.

"You brave, my dear?" she asked.

"That mean he go'n kill him?" I asked.

"I didn't say that," she said.

"But that's the answer?" I said.

"Oui," she said.

"And you absolutely sure?" I asked.

"I don't give nothing but sure answers," she said. "I am Madame Eloise Gautier, formerly of New Orleans, and that's why she got me out."

"Nothing can stop it?" I asked.

"Nothing can stop death, mon sha," she said. "Death comes. A black horse. Lightning. Guns. And you have grippe."

"Grippe?" I said. "What's grippe?"

"Grippe is grippe," she said. "Nothing like it."

"Can I kill that horse?" I said.

"Can you kill death?" Madame Gautier said. "Your Pittman will stand between you and death."

"When's it go'n happen?" I asked her.

"Mon sha," she said. "Don't you know too much already?"

"No," I said.

"When he falls three times," she said.

"He go'n fall three times?" I said. "How do you know that?"

"I am Madame Eloise Gautier, formerly of New Orleans," she said.

"If he don't get up after he fall the first time?" I said.

"He will," she said. "Chief—and don't get up? He will. Even if he must fall ninety times. Chief? he must."

"Can't you give me something to put in his food?" I asked her. She had a little cabinet against the wall, and she had all kinds of bottles and jars in the cabinet. "Some powder or something to make him sick?" I said. "If he's sick he can't ride."

"You go'n keep him sick?" she asked.

"Till somebody else break that horse," I said.

"Mon sha, mon sha, mon sha, mon sha," she said. "I have told you the horse is just one. If not the horse, then the lion, if not the lion, then the woman, if not the woman, then the war, then the politic, then the whisky. Man must always search somewhere to prove himself. He don't know everything is already inside him."

"Then he want die?" I asked her. "Because I can't give him the child?"

"No, he want to live," she said. "And not just because you barren. Many reasons. Many. Many. But it's in here, mon sha," she said, touching her bosom.

"But don't he know that horse can kill him?" I said.

"He don't know that," she said. "And he wouldn't believe any man on earth who told him so. He believes a horse is made to be broken. All horses made to be broken, true, but not every man can break every horse. This horse your Pittman will not break. Your Pittman has got old and fat now. Not the man he think he is."

"He's all right," I said.

"Ah, mon sha," she said.

"I know what I'm saying," I said. "And you can ask anybody else."

"We talking about breaking horses, mon sha," she said. "Your Pittman will not break this horse. Another man will have to do it. If he is true he will be destroyed by some other horse himself. If he's not true, then something else will take him. It could be grippe."

"Grippe again," I said.

"Grippe can do it," she said. "Mon sha, man is put here to die. From the day he is born him and death take off for that red string. But he never wins, he don't even tie. So the next best thing, do what you can with the little time the Lord spares you. Most men feel they ought to spend them few years proving they men. They choose the foolishes' ways to do it."

"Joe said he wouldn't mind farming if the white people let him farm in peace."

"I know, mon sha, I know," she said. "That'll be a dollar if you don't mind."

"I want some powder, too," I said. "I don't want nothing too strong—just to keep him off that horse."

"Give me a dollar and a quarter," she said.

While I was getting the money out of my handkerchief she went to the cabinet. I saw her opening one of the bottles and dumping the powder on a piece of paper. She looked at how much she already had on the paper, then she added a little bit more.

"When do they break the horses?" she asked me.

"Saturday," I said.

"Early or late?"

"Late. When the people get there."

"When the cock crow Saturday morning, get up and sprinkle some of this on the floor so Pittman will have to cross it," she said. "His side of the bed is best. Go to the corral gate and sprinkle some there while the cock is still crowing."

"And that'll keep him from riding the horse?" I asked.

"He will not ride him, my dear."

I paid her and left. My powder in my handkerchief, I felt good. All day I felt good. That night I didn't sleep, but it was just because I felt good. But the next day I felt shaky. How did I know that powder was go'n work? Maybe she had just gived it to me because I was worrying her so much. She didn't take time to pick a bottle, she just grabbed the first one she came to. Matter of fact I wanted some powder out of that little green bottle, not that red one. I got more and more shaky. Joe asked me if I was all right.

"Sure, I'm all right," I said. "What you got to be asking me that for?"

"Just asked you," he said.

At the house Miss Clare asked me the same thing.

"Something the matter with you, Jane?"

"Just tired," I said.

"Go home and come back tomorrow," Miss Clare said.

That was Thursday. Thursday night I didn't sleep at all. The next day I felt even worse.

"Go back home, Jane," Miss Clare said.

Joe went hunting that day, and I sat round the house by myself. If I laid down on the bed and shut my eyes a second time I saw that black devil standing in the corral. That night we went to bed early because the next day was Saturday, the day they broke the horses. Joe was tired from hunting and went right off to sleep. The two girls was asleep in their bed. I was the only one laying there awake. Probably the only one awake on that whole place.

I knowed I never would get any sleep that night, and I got up and put on some clothes. I was go'n sit at the firehalf, but the next thing I know I was outside. It was freezing out there, and the night clear as day. I didn't know why I had come out there. I knowed when I got up that was not in my mind. Now, out there, I found myself headed toward the corral.

All the other horses was standing together to stay warm, all but him. He walking round inside the corral like he was some kind of majesty. When he got a whiff of my scent he stopped walking and looked up. I stood there looking at him, my arms folded because it was near freezing. The next thing I knowed I had opened the gate and I was in the corral trying to get him out.

I was in the corral, waving my arms, going "Shoo, shoo, shoo," but he wouldn't go near that gate till Joe came there. Soon as he caught sight of Joe they started for the gate at the same time. He won by a foot and lit out cross the field. The ground was frozen and you could hear him pounding that hard ground a mile. Joe came in there and knocked me down, then he picked me up and threw me over the fence. I laid down there numb awhile, and when I got up I saw that he had swung upon his own horse and was going after the stallion. I started hollering and running after him. "Don't get back on him, don't get back on him, Joe." The people came out to see what was the matter. When they heard the stallion was loose they saddled their own horses and went after him. I ran after Joe till I came up to the swamps, then I turned around and come on back home. I sat by the firehalf all night waiting for them to come back.

Early the next morning they came back with the stallion and with Joe tied to his own horse. They said Joe had cornered and roped the stallion, but with no saddle to tie the rope on, the stallion had jecked him off his horse and had dragged him through the swamps. When they found him he was tangled in the rope, already dead. The horse still had the rope round his neck, eating leaves off a bush to the side.

They waked Joe Pittman that night and buried him that Sunday, and the rodeo went on that next Saturday. Before it started they toned the bell one minute for Joe Pittman. Every man took off his hat. The ladies bowed their heads. Soon as the minute was up a young boy called Gable got on the stallion. The stallion throwed him, but he got back on. The stallion throwed him again and he got back on him again. He kept getting back on till the stallion couldn't throw him no more. Not long after that him and Ella got married and moved to Texas. They took Clara with them.

When Joe Pittman was killed a part of me went with him to his grave. No man would ever take his place, and that's why I carry his name to this day. I have knowed two or three other men, but none took the place of Joe Pittman. I let them know that from the start.

A couple years after Joe Pittman was killed I met a man called Felton Burkes who was a fisherman on the seine boat. Felton and his crew was moving to the St. Charles River and I followed him here. That's how I got to this part of the State. Me and Felton lived together about three years, then one day he was gone. Didn't say a word. I didn't know he was gone for good till he didn't come back for a month. But that didn't bother me none; not long after he left, Ned showed up with his family.

Professor Douglass

NED USED TO WRITE ME, send me money all the time, but he never said anything about coming home. Not even he knowed he was coming back here till after he came from that war in Cuba. That war ended in 1898. He came here that next summer. And a year later, almost to the day, Albert Cluveau shot him down. Albert Cluveau and his gang patrolled the river from Johnville to Bayonne. Gustave Maurios and his bunch took over Johnville all the way to Creole Place. They used to get contracts to kill people just like you get contracts to cut wood.

I was fishing that day when the boy came down the river bank and told me some people was at my house. I asked him who they was. He said he didn't know; they had come there in a wagon. I pulled in my line and went up the bank.

I hadn't seen Ned in twenty years, but I knowed it was him the moment I saw him standing on the gallery. Not from the way he looked. He didn't look nothing like he did when he left here for Kansas. He was a great big man now. Powerfully built: broad shoulders, thick neck. I knowed it was him because I felt it was him.

Ned and his wife was standing on the gallery talking. I knowed it was about me because they was looking at me all the time. Ned still had on his Army uniform. He used to wear his uniform everywhere he went. When he was shot down he was in his Army uniform. His wife had on a red dress and a yellow straw hat. The three children was playing in the yard.

I don't know how I came in the yard because I don't remember pulling that gate open. But I remember walking up the walk saying, "I know that ain't nobody but you, Ned. You can't fool me. That ain't a soul but you." I couldn't stop saying that, and I couldn't say nothing else. That over and over: "I know that ain't a soul else in this world but you."

He met me in the yard and picked me up and swung me around. Me with that pole and bucket still in my hand. I could hear them children laughing.

"Put me down," I kept saying. But I was having much fun as the rest of them was having. "Put me down," I said.

He let me down slowly, and when my head stopped spinning I stood back and looked at him again. He still didn't look like the Ned I knowed. Even when he smiled he didn't look like the one I remembered. But I knowed it was him because I felt deep inside me it was him.

We went on the gallery and I met his wife. Her name was Vivian. A little brown-skin woman, very quiet. Then I met the children. Jane, Laura, and Tee Man. The girls was named after me and his mama; Tee Man was a junior.

We went inside and Ned gived me a package and told me to open it right away. I untied the ribbon and unwrapped the paper—and you never have seen such beautiful cloth. Of all colors. Lines, blocks, flowers in bloom; leaves. While I was admiring the cloth, Ned opened a wooden box and took out some dishes. He told Vivian about the time he had to go borrow a plate for the professor because I didn't want the professor to eat out a pan.

"You still remember that?" I asked him.

"It was me who had to walk up and down the quarters looking for that plate, I remember," he said.

I cooked supper, but I didn't eat with them. I stood back looking at Ned. Still didn't look like him. A boy had left here, a man had come back. Even his hair was turning gray. But when I looked at Tee Man I saw the resemblance. He was black just like Ned. Ned's teeth, Ned's grin, Ned's kinky hair. Looking at him was like looking at Ned when Ned was that size.

While Ned was drinking coffee he told me why he had come back to the South. He had come back to teach. We didn't have a school on the river then. The closest school was in Bayonne, and even then the children only went about three months out of the year. Ned asked me what was the people talking about. What was the preachers in church teaching the people? Was they teaching Mr. Booker T. Washington or was they teaching Mr. Frederick Douglass? Like I was suppose to know that. All I knowed was Mr. Booker T. Washington and Mr. Frederick Douglass was two great colored spokesmen. What they taught the people, I had no idea. Ned said Mr. Booker T. Washington taught that all colored ought to stay together, work together, and try to improve their own lot before they tried to mix with the white folks. Mr. Frederick Douglass taught that everybody ought to work together. Ned had always believed in Mr. Douglass's teaching, and after he went to that war in Cuba he believed in it even more. This place was much his as it was for the white man. That's what he had come here to teach.

I looked at Ned sitting there, at his wife sitting there with her head bowed, at his children listening to everything he was saying. In my heart I was so happy to see them. They was like my own, because Ned was like my own. But hearing Ned talking like that scared me.

Early the next morning he got on the horse and started traveling over the parish. The first day he went toward Bayonne; the next day toward Creole Place. But the people wasn't listening. Not that they didn't believe in what he was talking about, but they had already seen too much killing. And they knowed what he was preaching was go'n get him killed, and them too if they followed. The churches wouldn't help him either. They told him no when he asked them to let him use the church till he had built his school.

Ned bought a house on the road and started teaching in his house at night. At the same time he bought a piece of land on the river bank to build his school. Maybe when the people saw what he was willing to do by himself they would join him.

But the white people was already following Ned. They knowed everywhere he went; they knowed everything he did.

Albert Cluveau

ALBERT CLUVEAU HAD ALREADY killed more than a dozen people, black and white. Everybody knowed he had done it, and he wasn't hiding it either. Telling everybody: "Oh, yeah, yeah, I have killed. Killed a few there in my time I have." Hadn't he told me the same thing—and how many times?

I was taking in washing then, I wasn't cooking for nobody. I had my little horse, Pigeon, I used to ride to go pick up the laundry. Then I brought them to my house and washed them out there in the yard. To get water all I had to do was go draw it out the river. All the good water I needed, right across the road in front my house. After I had washed and ironed the clothes I would get back on Pigeon and go take them back to the people. Had that whole stretch of the river from where I lived clear into Bayonne.

In the evening when it was cool I would go down the river bank and fish. In the summer and when it was warm enough in the winter I fished practically every day. Fish I couldn't eat I used to give to other people. But I reckoned I done ate much fish round here as anybody. It's good for you—fish. Fish and work. Hard work can kill you, but plain steady work never killed nobody. Steady work and eating plenty fish never killed nobody. Greens good, too. Fish and greens and good steady work. Plenty walking, that's good. People don't walk no more. When you don't walk you don't drink enough water. Good clean water and greens clear out your system.

I used to go fishing just about every day the weather permitted. Turned my water pail upside down and sat on it till I got ready to go back home. Then I would put my string of fishes in the pail and go on up the bank. Albert Cluveau used to fish right there side me. If the water was shallow he would roll up his pants legs and wade out a piece. But most of the times he sat on the ground fishing right there side me. A short bowlegged Cajun. Face looked like somebody had been jobbing in it with an ice pick. Had that big patch of hair out the left side of his head, his head white where the hair had been. Sitting there telling me about the people he had killed. I wasn't a Christian then, I didn't join the church till I came to Samson, but I used to say to myself: "My Lord, my Lord, will you just listen to this? You hear this man talking about killing men like you talk about killing snakes?" But no matter how he talked I would sit there and listen to him. Sometimes he would follow me up to the house and sit on my gallery and talk. Sometimes he would go round the house and sit in the back door while I fried fish for supper. If I said, "Mr. Albert, chop me piece of wood," he would get out there and cut enough wood to last me a week. If I needed something from the store he would swing upon that mule and go get anything I needed. Sack of rice, flour, it didn't matter, he would bring it all back. After I had cooked, he would sit right there in the back door and eat. Then we had our coffee. He liked his coffee strong, sweet sweet and black.

Sometimes I got him off talking about killing. I would make him talk about fishing and raising crop. He could talk about anything. Because most of the people round here either fished or farmed for a living anyhow. But in the end killing always came back in Albert Cluveau's mind. He wasn't bragging about it, but he wasn't sorry either. It was just conversation. Like if you worked in the sawmill you talked about lumber more than you talked about cane. If you worked at the derrick, naturally, you talked about cane more than you talked about trees. Albert Cluveau had killed so many people he couldn't talk about nothing else but that.

One day while we was out there fishing, he said: "The people talking 'bout your boy, there, Jane. Just think I ought to tell you that."

We was fishing in shallow water that day, and both of us was standing out there in the river. It was hot and I could feel the hot river water on my legs. When Albert Cluveau said that about Ned my heart started beating so fast I thought I might fall. I held on tight to the fishing pole till I was steady, then I pulled in my line and went back home. I never did go in the house, I just sat down in my chair on the gallery. I'm sitting there only a minute and here he come. Leaned his fishing pole against the end of the gallery and sat down on the steps.

"Any coffee there, Jane?"

I didn't answer Albert Cluveau—what do you say to a fool? I sat there looking out at the river. After a while he forgot he had asked me for coffee; now he started talking about the people he had killed. He talked and talked; sundown before he left my house. I got on Pigeon that night and went to see Ned. Ned was staying farther up the road, closer to Bayonne. Just across the road from where he's buried now. I could see the horses and mules in the yard when I rode up there. The children had ridden from all over the parish to attend classes. Ned used one of the rooms in his house for his school. I sat in the sitting room with Vivian and the children, and we could hear Ned talking to his students in the other side. After Vivian had put the children to bed, me and her sat up there by ourself. She was never one to talk much, so we sat up there listening to Ned. 'Leven o'clock he dismissed class, but some of the children stayed there till mid-night. I sat there with Vivian till the last one had gone home, then I got up and went round the other side. Ned was sitting at the table with his head propped in his hands. He looked up when I came in. He thought I was Vivian.

"I didn't know you was here, Mama," he said.

"Just dropped by."

I had come in there to tell him what Albert Cluveau said, but I could see how tired he was. I didn't want add a burden to his mind.

"Something the matter?" he asked me.

"Nothing the matter," I said. "I got here early. I just didn't want to disturb you."

"I'll ride back home with you," he said.

"Pigeon know his way home," I said.

He rubbed his hand hard over his face. I stood there looking at him. I still wanted to tell him about Albert Cluveau.

"It's been a long day," he said.

"I'm leaving," I said.

"You ought to stay here tonight," he said.

"I'm going to my own house," I said.

He went outside with me and led Pigeon up to the gallery so I could get on. Next Sunday Albert Cluveau came to my house and sat on the steps. I gived him some coffee. Strong, sweet sweet and black. He sipped and sipped at that coffee, then he said: "They talk 'bout your boy there, Jane. They don't want him build that school there, no. They say he just stood to stir trouble munks niggers. They want him go back. Back where he come from. They don't know Albert tell you this."

Week or so later I was in the yard heating water when I saw him getting off the mule. He came up to me and spoke, then he just stood there looking at the water steaming in the pot.

"They want me to stop him, Jane," he said.

"You mean kill my boy?" I said.

"If they say do it I must do it, Jane."

"Raise your head, Mr. Albert," I said.

He wouldn't.

"Mr. Albert?" I said.

He raised his head slowly and looked at me. Great killer he was and scared of me. I didn't say a thing, I just looked at Albert Cluveau. Gray beard all over his old wrinkled face. Watery old blue eyes. That old felt hat, sweat-stink, torn at the top. An old man who ought to be sitting in the sun—here talking about killing.

"Speak, Mr. Albert," I said.

"I tell them me, you, we all time fish there in the St. Charles River," he said. "I tell them I eat at your house. I tell them you make Albert good Creole coffee. I tell them, I say: 'Jane good nigger woman just like you see me there.' I say. 'If he must stop, let Maurios stop him. Not Albert. Albert and Jane, side by side, fish there in the St. Charles River.' They say: 'Albert Cluveau, this your patrol. Maurios patrol farther down the river. If we say, Albert, stop that nigger, Albert, you stop him. If you don't, Albert—.'"

"Can you kill my boy?" I asked him.

"I must do what they tell me," he said.

"Can you kill my boy?" I asked him.

"Yes," he said.

I looked at Albert Cluveau a moment, then I felt my head spinning. I made one step toward the house, then I was down on the ground. I heard somebody way off saying, "Jane, Jane, what's the matter, Jane?" I opened my eyes and I saw Albert Cluveau with his ugly face kneeling over me. And I thought I was in hell, and he was the devil. I started screaming: "Get away from me, devil. Get away from me, devil. Get away from me, devil." But all my screaming was inside, and not a sound was coming out. I heard from way off: "You sick, Jane? You sick?" I was screaming, but I wasn't making any noise. I was struggling to get up, but I couldn't move.

"Get away," I said. "Get away from me."

I could hear myself, so I knowed he could hear me too. I saw him standing up, looking funny, like I shouldn't be talking to him like that. Looked like he wanted to say, "Jane, what I said to make you act like that?" I pushed myself up off the ground and started toward the house.

"You need a doctor, Jane?" he said. "Jane?"

I went in and laid down on the bed. That evening I went to Ned. I didn't tell him I had fell, but I told him to beware of Albert Cluveau. All he said was, "I will build my school. I will teach till they kill me."

I went to Vivian.

"They'll kill him if he keep on," I said. "Why don't you take them children back to Kansas. He'll have to follow you if you go."

"He told me when he was coming here he could get killed," she said. "But I came with him anyhow. I have to stay now."

The Sermon at the River

TWO WEEKS BEFORE Ned was killed he gathered us at the river. It was on a Sunday, a beautiful, blue-sky day. No, you had a few clouds, way up high, paper thin. A little breeze stirred on and off. You could see it moving the willow leaves down near the water.

The people was at the river when I got there, but Ned hadn't started his talk yet. He was sitting on the grass with Vivian and the children. When he saw me he told me to come down there and sit with them. One of his students took my arm and helped me down the hill. The bank wasn't that steep, I had gone down them steeper than that, but he wanted to help me and I couldn't tell him no.

I had my head rag on under my straw hat, and I took the head rag off to sit on. I used my straw hat to fan with. Ned was there in his Army uniform looking serious serious. I asked him what was the matter. He told me nothing. But Jane, the oldest girl, told me that white people had been passing by there ever since they came down to the river. She pointed at two men fishing in a boat now. They was close enough for me to see who they was—two of the LeCox brothers from Bayonne. They made their living on seine boats running up and down St. Charles River.

"Maybe you ought to not talk today," I said.

"That's what they want," he said.

When everybody had come there Ned got up and turned his back to the river and to the men out there in the boat. He told us to kneel while he prayed. After the prayer he told us to sit down. I looked back at the people who was there. Mostly children. The old people had stayed home.

I can't remember everything Ned said to us that day, I can't even remember half of what he said, but I can remember some. I can remember it because Ned believed in it so much—and his talk at the river that day definitely hurried him to his grave.

"This earth is yours and don't let that man out there take it from you," he said. "It's yours because your people's bones lays in it; it's yours because their sweat and their blood done drenched this earth. The white man will use every trick in the trade to take it from you. He will use every way he know how to get you wool-gathered. He'll turn you 'gainst each other. But remember this," he said. "Your people's bones and their dust make this place yours more than anything else.

"I'm not telling y'all men own the earth," he said. "Man is just a little bitty part of this earth. When he die he go back in the earth just like a tree go back in the earth when it fall, just like iron go back in the earth when it rust. You don't own this earth, you're just here for a little while, but while you're here don't let no man tell you the best is for him and you take the scrap. No, your people plowed this earth, your people chopped down the trees, your people built the roads and built the levees. These same people is now buried in this earth, and their bones's fertilizing this earth."

I was listening to Ned, but I was keeping my eyes on the LeCox brothers out there in the boat. They pretend they wasn't listening, but they was listening. Each time they whipped out the lines they was looking over where we was.

"You got some black men," Ned was saying, "that'll tell you the white man is the worst thing on earth. Nothing horrible he wouldn't do. But let me tell you this," he said. "If it wasn't for some white men, none of us would be alive here today. I myself probably'll be killed by a white man. I know they following me everywhere I go."

When he said this everybody looked at the men out in the boat.

"Look at me," Ned said. "Not at them." When the people turned their heads toward him he went on. "But even when he raise the gun or the axe or anything else he might use I won't blame all white men. I'll blame ignorance. Because it was ignorance that put us here in the first place. Ignorance on the part of the black man and the white man. Because the white man didn't have to go in Africa with guns to get us. The white man came with rum and beads. And why? Because we was already waiting for him when he came there in his ships. Our own black people had put us up in pens like hogs, waiting to sell us into slavery. He didn't tell the white man how to treat us after he got us on his ship, the white man made up them rules himself. It was just his job to hand us over, and he did that. And that he did."

Ned went on: "I wish I could stand here and tell y'all our African people fought and fought the white man. And there was war and war and war. But that's not true. Our people fought each other, and the white man bought the captives for a barrel of rum and a string of beads. I'm telling y'all this," he said, "to show y'all the only way you can be strong is stand together. The white man never would have brought us here if we was together. He never would have separated a nation. But little tribes beat each other, and all the white man had to do was wait."

Ned was sweating, standing there in the sun, and Vivian got up to wipe his face. He told her to sit down, not to come close to him. If the people in the boat shot at him now, he didn't want her to get hit.

"I don't know how old I am right now," he said. "I can be thirty-nine, I can be forty or forty-one. But I've seen a lot in this world, and I know this: I'm much American as any man; I'm more American than most. And what is this American? I'll tell you what he is. Because they didn't have no such thing as American till we got here. The Indians was the first ones here and they never called themself Americans. Matter of fact they didn't even call themself Indians till Columbus came here and started that. After him, then here come Vespucci with his stuff."

When Ned said Vespucci the children looked at each other and started giggling. Ned had to smile at that too. The funniest name any of us had ever heard—Vespucci.

After the children had quieted down, Ned went on: "Columbus had a black man with him when he came here and called these red men Indians. By the time Vespucci came here and called this place America you had black people running every which a' way. America is for red, white, and black men. The red man roamed all over this land long before we got here. The black man cultivated this land from ocean to ocean with his back. The white man brought tools and guns. America is for all of us." he said. "and all of America is for all of us.

"I left from here when I was a young man, but most people thought that was the best thing to do then. But I say to you now, don't run and do fight. Fight white and black for all of this place. You got black people here saying go back to Africa, some saying go to Canada, some saying go to France. Now, who munks y'all sitting here right now want be a Frenchman and talk like they do? Let me see his hand in the air."

The children started laughing. Ned had said that to make them laugh.

"Be Americans," he told the children. "But first be men. Look inside yourself. Say, 'What am I? What else beside this black skin that the white man call nigger?' Do you know what a nigger is?" he asked us. "First, a nigger feels below anybody else on earth. He's been beaten so much by the white man, he don't care for himself, for nobody else, and for nothing else. He talks a lot, but his words don't mean nothing. He'll never be American, and he'll never be a citizen of any other nation. But there's a big difference between a nigger and a black American. A black American cares, and will always struggle. Every day that he get up he hopes that this day will be better. The nigger knows it won't. That's another thing about a nigger: he knows everything. There ain't a thing on earth he don't know—till somebody with brains come along.

"I'm telling you all this because I want my children to be men," Ned told us. "I want my children to fight. Fight for all—not just for a corner. The black man or white man who tell you to stay in a corner want to keep your mind in a corner too. I'm building that school so you'll have a chance to get from out of that corner."

One of the children raised his hand, and Ned told him to stand up. The boy was way in the back and we couldn't hear him too good and Ned told him to speak louder. Ned told him not to pay any mind to the people out in the boat because if we had anything to hide we wouldn't be out there in the first place. The boy came closer to the water.

"Professor Douglass," he said. "You keep saying we ought to not listen to Mr. Washington, but ain't Mr. Washington saying that to keep the race from getting slaughtered? Mr. Washington growed up round these white people. He know a man'll shoot a black man down just for standing on two feet. This something maybe the people in the North don't know yet. And another thing, Professor Douglass," the boy said, "ain't he saying learn a trade because a trade is the thing that's go'n carry this country?"

The boy stood there with his hands to his side till Ned told him to sit down. The boy sat down quickly, but looking at Ned all the time. I felt very proud, seeing how well Ned had trained them. Ned smiled and nodded his head. He was proud that one of his students had asked him a question like that. He was always harping on Mr. Washington, and here was another chance to harp on him again.

"I agree with Mr. Washington on trade," he said. "But trade is not all. I want to see some of my children become lawyers. I want to see some of my children become ministers of the Bible; some write books; some to represent their people in the law. So trade is not all. Working with your hands while the white man write all the rules and laws will not better your lot.

"Now, that other thing—don't mess with the white man and he won't slaughter you. Well, let me tell you a little story. My own mother was killed by white men, not because she was messing in their business, she was trying to leave the South after she heard of her freedom. Her head and my little sister's head was bashed in with sticks.

"But other people was killed on that day," he said. "And many, many have been killed since. I agree many of them have been killed because they stood up on their two feet. But if you must die, let me ask you this: wouldn't you rather die saying I'm a man than to die saying I'm a contented slave? Mr. Washington might have had the safety of our race in mind—I think Mr. Washington did—but since he made that statement over five years ago over a thousand men have been lynched. And for no other reason but their black skin."

Ned took out his handkerchief and wiped his face, then he folded it carefully and put it back in his pocket.

"Maybe one day the white man will tell you to leave this country or die in it," he said. "There's talk that this can happen. Well, let me tell you this, warriors. He's got no idea how many of us here. All of us look alike to him anyhow, so he'll count ten, get tired, and not count the other five. And that's on our side. So this is what you do. (I might not be with you—and I hope it never come to happen. But if it come to happen, this is what you do.) Let everybody go except one young man in each family. Let that young man hide in the swamps, hide in the field, anywhere he can hide hide. When the rest are safe, let these young men set fire. As many fields, as many woods, as many houses and barns and cribs he can. Let him run, run, run till his black legs refuse to move, till his black arms hang to the ground. Show them, warriors, the difference between black men and niggers."

Ned got quiet and looked at us for a long time. His eyes was sad again now. Behind him the river was blue and calm: nothing to disturb the water—but that boat over to the right there.

"Let us pray, warriors, this day never come," Ned went on. "If it do, it'll be the worst day of your life."

When Ned got through talking his shirt was soaking wet. He came back where we was and laid down side his wife. Everybody was quiet, thinking 'bout what he had said. I felt Ned looking at me. For a while I kept from looking back at him, but keeping my eyes on the people out there in the boat. But the longer I looked at them the more I could feel him looking at me. Then I looked in his face. His eyes said, "I'm go'n die, Mama." But I knowed he had no fear of death.

Assassination

A MONTH PASSED—no Albert Cluveau. I didn't think he was worrying about stopping Ned, I didn't think he had enough sense to worry; I just thought he was sick and couldn't get around. I wanted to ask about him— not that I cared about Albert Cluveau—but I wanted to know what he was doing. Why all this quiet all of a sudden? Don't tell me conscience was catching up with him. It never bothered him before. But no matter who I asked, nobody had seen Albert Cluveau. When I went to Bayonne on Pigeon I had to go by the lane where he lived, but I always found excuse not to go to his house. Coming back home, the same thing: I would look down the lane but I would never lead Pigeon that way. I could have gone to his house in five minutes, but, no, never.

But I used to see Ned all the time. He used to live just across the road from where he is buried now. He is buried side the place where he was building his school. The people finished the school after his death, but it was destroyed during the second high water. That was back in '27 when we had a very bad high water. We had one in '12, but the one in '27 was much worse. Ned used to live on the field side of the road; his school was on the river bank side of the road. Another house is built in the place where his house stood, but we kept the place where his school was and where he is buried. It will never be sold. We collect from people to pay the taxes and keep up the land, but it is ours. It is for the children of this parish and this State. Black and white, we don't care. We want them to know a black man died many many years ago for them. He died at the end of the other century and the beginning of this century. He shed his precious blood for them. I remember my old mistress, when she saw the young Secesh soldiers, saying: "The precious blood of the South, the precious blood of the South," Well, there on that river bank is the precious dust of this South. And he is there for all to see. We have a marker there for people to stop by and see if they want to. No, it is not a tall and showy thing. It's nothing but a flat piece of concrete, but it's there for all to see if they just get out the car and look.

I used to go by all the time when he was alive. He had already cleaned up that acre of land, and now he was laying down the foundation for the school. The children used to help him in the evenings and on the weekends when they didn't have to work. Sometimes I used to stop by and instead of finding them working I would see them out in the river swimming. I was so scared for Ned's life, I was scared the white people might pay some of them bigger children to drown him. He would always come out the water when he saw me sitting there on Pigeon. "You call that building a school?" I would say. "Me, I call that playing." "I have to teach everything," he said. "Swimming is good to learn." Looking at Ned, now, you could see how big he was, how powerfully he was built in the chest and shoulders. If he was standing close to me I would put my hand on his shoulder.

"You worry too much, Mama," he would say.

"Do I, Ned?" I would say. Because both of us knowed that day was coming. When and where we didn't know.

Two nights before he was killed I had a dream where a bunch of Cajuns had lynched him in the swamps. The next morning I got on Pigeon and went up to his house. When I told him about my dream he brushed it aside like it was nothing. While I was up there he told me he was going to Bayonne to get some lumber for his school. He was taking two boys with him and he was go'n spend the night in Bayonne with a friend. He told me to stop worrying; this was making Vivian worry, too. She was already getting nervous, he said. I stayed up there till he left that evening, then I got on Pigeon and went on back home. The next evening when he was on his way home with the second load, Albert Cluveau shot him down. Alcee Price and Bam Franklin, the two boys he took with him, told us how it happened. They had spent the night in Bayonne with Ned's friend talking about the school. Nobody went to bed before mid-night even when everybody had to get up early the next morning and go to work. They got up around five because they wanted to pick up the lumber and get it back here before the weather got too hot. They got back to the school around eight-thirty. That evening when it got cool again they went back to Bayonne for the second load. After they had loaded up it was around five. They didn't have far to go, three, four miles, but they had to travel slow because of the road. The road was dirt and full of ruts and the lumber was heavy. Bam said every half mile they had to stop to give the mules a rest. They always stopped in the open. At that time you had cane fields and houses on one side of the road; trees on the river bank side. They always stopped near a house or a yard. After resting the mules a few minutes they would start out again. Bam said they had just driven off after the second or third stop when they looked up and saw Albert Cluveau. He was on his mule at the end of a cane row with the gun already sighted at Ned. He told Ned to get down. Ned stopped the wagon, but nobody moved.

"What do you want?" Ned asked him.

"Get down," Cluveau said.

"You don't scare me, Cluveau," Ned said.

"Get down," Cluveau said.

"First let me talk to the children," Ned said.

"Get down now," Cluveau said.

Ned handed Bam the lines, Bam pushed them back.

"Let me go," Bam said. "I don't care about me."

"But I care about you, Bam," Ned told him. "That's what I've been teaching all the time—I care about you. When will you ever hear me, Bam?"

"I won't let you die," Bam said. "He ain't got nothing but a double barrel there; he'll need both of them to bring me down."

"Stay here," Ned said. "Take the lumber home. Finish the school. Talk to my wife. Talk to Mama."

"No," Bam said.

"I order you to do that," Ned said. "You must listen to me sometime, Bam."

Bam and Alcee both said Ned looked at them a second, then he looked all round him, even glancing at the sky, like he wanted to see everything for a moment. Then he jumped from the wagon and started running toward Cluveau. Cluveau hollered for him to stop and get down on his knees, but he kept running on Cluveau with nothing but his fist. Cluveau shot him in the leg—the white people had told Cluveau to make Ned crawl before killing him. When Cluveau shot him, he fell to one knee, then got back up. Cluveau shot again. This time he tored off half his chest.

Albert Cluveau swung the mule around and rode away. Bam and Alcee didn't go after Cluveau, they picked up Ned and laid him on top the lumber. The lumber was red when they got home. Blood dripped through the lumber on the ground. A trail of blood all the way from where Ned was shot clear up to his house. Even the rain couldn't wash the blood away. For years and years, even after they had graveled the road, you could still see little black spots where the blood had dripped.

The People

WHEN THE PEOPLE heard the news they started crying. The ones living side the road followed the wagon to the house. When the others came in from the field and heard what had happened they knelt down right there and cried. They didn't want go near him when he was living, but when they heard he was dead they cried like children. They ran up to the wagon when it stopped at the gate. They wanted to touch his body, they wanted to help take it inside. The road was full, people coming from everywhere. They wanted to touch his body. When they couldn't touch his body they took lumber from the wagon. They wanted a piece of lumber with his blood on it.

I knowed he was dead before Frank Nelson's boy came there and told me. I was laying down on my bed when I heard this sweeping noise passing through the house. "Now what?" I said. I sat up and looked, and it wasn't sweeping at all, it was a light on the floor. Like a flashlight, but not shaking like a flashlight would shake, moving smooth, going from the front to the back. "They done killed him," I said. And I got on Pigeon and started for his house. I met Nelson's boy coming to tell me. But he could see I already knowed, and he turned around and ran back long side the horse. When I got there they had already took his body inside and had laid it on the bed. Vivian was sitting in the chair just looking at the body. People all round her crying, but she wasn't hearing a thing. Just looking at the body. I put my arms round her shoulders and I could feel her trembling. It was hot as it could be, but she was trembling like she had chill. I tried to say something to her, but she didn't hear me. I doubt if she even knowed I was there—just looking at the boy. I told the people to get out. Making all that noise wasn't doing a bit of good—get out. I kept a couple women in there to help me with Ned and Vivian, but I wanted the rest of them out. After we had put Vivian to bed round the other side, I came back in and told the people let me be by myself with Ned awhile. They didn't want leave me alone, but I told them I was all right, and they went out. I sat down side Ned and held him close and started talking to him like he was still alive. I can't recall what I said to him—just little talk; I can't recall when I fell on him, but I remember people pulling me off the bed and my clothes soaking wet with his blood. They took me to the children's room and made me lay down. Somebody stayed in the room with me, but I can't recall who it was.

The sheriff came and examined the body and asked Bam and Alcee some questions. They told him it was Albert Cluveau—like they needed to tell him anything, like he didn't already know it was Albert Cluveau, like everybody round there didn't already know it was Albert Cluveau—but he told them he wanted them to come to Bayonne the next day and make a full statement. From what he could see there now everybody was too excited to make sense. The next day Bam and Alcee went to his office. The first thing he asked them, even before they had a chance to say good morning, if they had been to the wake last night. They said yes. He asked them if they had had anything to drink there, coffee or maybe little wine? They said yes, little homemade wine; blackberry. He said, "Uh-hum, now tell me what happened." They told him the only thing they could tell him was that Mr. Cluveau shot Professor Douglass when Professor Douglass wouldn't get on his knees and crawl. He asked them if they was sure it was Mr. Cluveau. They said yes they was sure. He asked them if it was a cane field or a corn field. They had already told him it was a cane field, so they said cane again. He told them with cane so high that time of year (July) how could they see a man? They said Mr. Cluveau came out of the cane on the headland. He said he thought they told him Mr. Cluveau shot Ned *from* the cane field. He said just like they was changing their story from cane field to headland, maybe they would change that story from headland to corn field. And maybe they would change that story from corn field to pecan tree. He said if memory served him right there was a pecan tree close to where Ned was shot. He said was he right or wrong. They said right. He said, "You sure the person didn't shoot from round the pecan tree?" They said they was sure he didn't, he shot from the headland of the cane field. He asked them if they had anything to drink the night they stayed in Bayonne. They said they didn't. He asked them how come. They said they was too young and Professor Douglass would 'a' frowned on that. He said what they meant they was too young. He said didn't they just tell him they had drunk exactly one night later at the wake. He said do one night age niggers that fast. Or is it the sight of seeing a dead man that put the gray in their head. Bam and Alcee told him they had the drink because some older men had the bottle. One of the older men said, "Here. Drink. Rejoice when somebody leave this wicked world. Do not weep." He said, "Rejoice, huh? Do not weep, huh? And maybe y'all did some rejoicing in Bayonne the night before. And maybe y'all was still rejoicing when y'all was coming home yesterday. And with all that rejoicing going on, maybe y'all mistook one man for another." He said he had heard that had often happened when niggers started rejoicing. Half the time they don't know what they see. And he said how did he know the two of them hadn't gotten together and killed the professor. He said from what he had been hearing around there that professor was getting on a lot of people nerve trying to make them vote and go to school. He said how did he know some of these people hadn't paid them to shoot that drunk professor to make him leave them alone. He said just to show you it couldn't have been Mr. Cluveau, he had talked to Mr. Cluveau the night before and Mr. Cluveau had told him with his own mouth, mind you, that he had spent all day yesterday and all night the night before gigging frogs on Grosse Tete Bayou. He said to prove it, old man Cluveau had showed him the mosquito bites—his poor old body was just full of welts. He told them he was sure they didn't want call a nice old man like old man Cluveau a liar, now, did they? They said they could just tell him what they saw. He said he didn't ask them that. He said he asked them if they wanted to call a God-fearing man like Mr. Albert Cluveau a liar. They said no. He told them to go on back home and he didn't want hear that kind of talk out of them no more.

Vivian stayed here till we finished building the school, then she went back to Kansas. She wanted to stay here and do Ned's work, but we was scared she could get herself killed just like Ned was killed. We made her go and we hired a teacher by the name of Jones. Professor Jones didn't look nothing like Ned. A little light-skin man about half Ned's size. Didn't teach what Ned wanted to teach either. Taught just what them in Bayonne told him to teach—reading and writing and 'rithmetic—and we had to take that or get nothing. He stayed there till the high water destroyed the school in '27.

The Chariot of Hell

I WAITED TILL WE HAD PUT Ned in the ground, then I went out looking for Albert Cluveau. But no matter when I came up to his house, Adeline, the oldest girl, said he had just left. "What you want?" she said. "I want talk to him," I said. "Daddy just left," she said. I would turn Pigeon around and go on back home, but that evening or the next day I would go back to his house again. Every time I thought about Ned I would head back to that house. Adeline would be standing on the gallery waiting for me. "I want speak to your daddy." "Daddy just left." "Just left again, huh?" "Yes, Jane." One day I made pretend I was going back home. I went a little piece and came right back. I saw him sitting on that mule back there in the yard. He was just getting ready to get down when he looked up and saw me. He swung that mule around and shot out cross the yard, headed for the swamps. Another time when I went there he didn't have time to get on the mule. Headed for the swamps and left the mule.

"Where your daddy?" I asked Adeline.

"Gone."

"Where?"

"Bayonne."

"What George doing back there in the yard?" I said. "You know Albert Cluveau ain't never went to the toilet if he wasn't on George's back."

"He walked this time," Adeline said.

"I'll catch him," I said, and left.

But I knowed then I would never catch Albert Cluveau at that house. Him or one of them children would see me long before I ever got there. I would have to catch him somewhere else.

Not to kill Albert Cluveau. That wasn't it. What would I look like killing Albert Cluveau? Let God kill him; let the devil take him. I just wanted to speak to him. But he did everything to stay out of my way. He kept one of them children looking out for me at his house. If I was fishing or getting water out the river, he wouldn't even pass on the main road, he would go use the back road. If he knowed it was the time of day I like to sit on my gallery, he would go down the river bank to pass my house. Sometimes I would see him laying down far as he could on that mule to keep me from seeing him. I knowed if I had run out of the yard or if I had jumped on Pigeon he would 'a' been too far for me to catch him. So I just waited. I bid my time.

One day the devil fooled Albert Cluveau. Guy Collier was fishing in front of my house. Me and Aunt Guy Collier was about the same size and color and he thought it was me down there. So he turned around and headed for the back road. I was back there on Pigeon, on my way to see Dune White at Grosse Tete. The crop was high and we didn't see each other till we made the bend and Pigeon almost butt George in the head. Now Albert Cluveau wanted to turn and run. But I had already seen him, and he had no place to go. So he turned his head. I let him turn his head good, but I told him what I had been waiting to tell him for a long time. "Mr. Albert Cluveau, when the Chariot of Hell come rattling for you, the people will hear you screaming all over this parish. Now, you just ride on."

The people wanted to say I went to a hoo-doo for Albert Cluveau. But I didn't go to no hoo-doo, because I don't believe in no hoo-doo. I went to just one hoo-doo in my life—that was for Joe Pittman and that horse— but even then I didn't believe in her the way you suppose to. I went to her because nobody else would listen to me. But after I had gone I still didn't take her advice. Anyhow, the word got back to Albert Cluveau that I had gone to a hoo-doo, and, he, so simple minded, he started to believe it.

A year or so later he came down sick and thought he was go'n die, and now he jumped in bed with his two daughters, Adeline and Christine. His wife had been dead and him and his sons had done so much dirt together he was scared to sleep in the same room with them. Adeline and Christine begged and begged Albert Cluveau to get out their bed. It wasn't nice. What would people think. Albert Cluveau said he didn't care what people thought, he heard the Chariot of Hell in that other room with his sons. Adeline told him there wasn't no such thing. Albert Cluveau said he knowed better, he heard it. He dared them to get out the bed and sleep on the floor; they had to sleep on both sides of him and protect him from the Chariot of Hell.

By and by he started hearing the Chariot of Hell even in this room with the girls. But he heard it in just one ear, the ear that was pointed toward Adeline. So he reckoned Adeline hated him. She had always been ashamed of him, so now she must hate him, too. Besides that he was sure she was messing round with men when he wasn't at the house. And he didn't want his daughters to be rotten like him and his sons. He wanted them to stay pure. That's why he always made them go to church—to keep them pure. But either Adeline wasn't pure or she hated him. Cluveau: "Adeline, you hate your pap?" Adeline: "No, Papa." Cluveau: "Adeline, you pure?" Adeline: "I swear by the Holy Mother I'm pure, Papa." Albert Cluveau would turn over, but still the Chariot of Hell would come from Adeline's side of the bed. Cluveau: "Adeline, if you so pure; Adeline, if you don't have no hate in your heart for your pap who never do you no wrong; Adeline, how come that Chariot of Hell he just run over there, huh?" Adeline told him, "Papa, there ain't no Chariot of Hell." Cluveau told her she was a damn liar and he jumped out of the bed and started beating her with the strap. The boys had to come round there and pull him off. After a while he would get back in bed, but the chariot would start all over. Poor Adeline would lay on her side of the bed crying in the sheet.

This went on for days, for weeks. Then one day Adeline came to my house. She would do anything if I took the hoo-doo off her papa. I told Adeline I had no more hoo-doo on Albert Cluveau than I had on my own self. It was just his sinning ways catching up with him. Adeline pulled her dress down over her shoulders and showed me the welt marks where Albert Cluveau had beat her. She told me to please help a little Cajun gal who had done nobody no harm in all her life. I told her I couldn't do a thing because I had no hoo-doo on Cluveau. I asked her if she wanted some coffee and tea cakes. She said yes. She was a big fine gal, big pretty legs. She was already old enough to be married, but they kept her there to cook for them. I gived her some coffee and tea cakes and we sat right there on my gallery.

"It's not me," she said. "I'm not bad. I'm a true virgin, I believe in my Catholic faith. But Christine—ah, she's no virgin. No virgin her. She went bad at 'leven. But she is the baby and they like her. None care for poor Adeline. And the chariot, even the chariot, can find no place to run but on my side. Every night he run, every night Papa jump out of the bed and whip me. I want to leave, but where can poor Adeline go? I change sides with Christine. I say, 'Christine, dearie, sleep here. Let your poor sister Adeline get one night peace.' Christine's got a pure soul, poor dear. She says, 'All right, my dear.' We change sides—but do that stop the chariot? Christine went bad at 'leven, but that chariot runs right where I sleep. That hoo-doo is against me more than it is against my papa. You must take it off, Jane."

"I ain't got no hoo-doo on your papa," I told her. "I told him when the Chariot of Hell come for him we will hear him all over this parish. That we will. That I will, less the Lord take me first. Other men who did the dirt your papa done have screamed at that last moment. He will scream, too. Yes, Adeline, he will scream. But that has nothing to do with hoo-doo. It's hell beckoning."

"He's poor and foolish, Jane."

"He shouldn't 'a' killed my boy."

"Do you hate me, Jane?"

"I don't hate you," I said. "I don't even hate him. But he will pay."

"I'm the one paying," she said. "I'm the one suffering."

"You don't know what suffering is, Adeline," I told her.

"I showed you the marks on my back," she said.

"I wish I could show you the ones on my heart," I told her.

"Poor Jane," she said.

Cluveau didn't come to die for ten more years. Died just before the high water there of '12. Christine had been gone. Had fooled around with every man on that river—black and white. Had gotten more buckets of figs, pecans, muscadines from them black boys on that river than you'd care to name. The one day she got on a wagon with a drummer from St. Francisville. The drummer used to sell pots and pans and sharpen knives and scissors. Him and Christine left here one Sunday evening. But poor Adeline was still at the house Albert Cluveau wasn't sleeping in the same bed with her now, she told him when Christine ran off with the drummer he had to go back round the other side. If he didn't, she was go'n run off too. He went back round the other side and she stayed there to look after him. Just the two of them there now. The boys had run off just like Christine did.

The weekend Albert Cluveau died, poor Adeline lived in a madhouse. People could hear Cluveau screaming half a mile. He died on a Sunday. Jules Patin passed by my house and told me Cluveau was at the point of death. I asked him how he knowed. He said he had heard him screaming and when he asked a Cajun what was the matter the Cajun told him Cluveau was at the point of death. I had always thought I wanted to hear Cluveau scream. I had told myself that ever since he killed Ned. But that had happened so long ago, and now I couldn't help but feel sorry for Cluveau—'specially Adeline there. But everybody else heard him screaming. People went by that house all time of day and night just to hear him scream. The doctor came, the doctor went, and still he screamed. Adeline sat on the side of the bed wiping his face with a damp towel, but Cluveau screamed. Just before he came to die he pushed Adeline away and got out of bed. Nobody thought he had that kind of strength left. He had his hands up the way you hold a gun. "I'll kill him," he said. "I'll kill him. I'll kill him." He made two steps and fell. He covered his head and screamed and screamed for Adeline to stop the horses. She knelt down on the floor side him. And he died there in her arms.

BOOK III

The Plantation

Samson

I KNOWED AUNT HATTIE JORDAN a long time before I came to Samson. She was the cook here then. Had been cooking for the Samsons even before the war between Secesh and North. When she got old—I'm sure she was already in her seventies when I met her—they gave her a horse and buggy to travel round in. Once or twice a week she passed by my house when I was living on the river. When Albert Cluveau died I told her I was ready to move off the river. She asked me why didn't I come to Samson. I told her that wasn't too much of a move, seven or eight miles. I told her I wanted to go farther than that, so I wouldn't be reminded of these memories. She told me even if I moved a hundred miles I would still be near memories, because memories wasn't a place, memories was in the mind. And she told me she knowed, too, that I wanted to be close to Ned's grave so I could always put flowers there. After thinking about it I told her she was right—and that's how I came to Samson. I came here one night and asked Paul Samson for the house. Paul Samson was the daddy of Robert Samson who's running the place now. "You kinda spare, ain't you?" he said. "How do I know you can carry your load?" I told him I had been doing it for more than fifty years now. "And you can be a little tired," he said. "I think I'll be around fifty more," I said. "You can have that room side Unc Gilly and Aunt Sara," he said. "But you go'n have to get here by yourself." "I'll get here," I said.

I borrowed a wagon from off the river and moved here by myself. It took me two trips, but I did it all by myself. It was spring, because the people was plowing and hoeing in the field. Buzz Johnson was the water boy; Diamond was his mule. Used to carry the water in a great big barrel with a hyphen stuck at one end. One day he lost the hyphen and wasted all the water, and the people in the field almost wanted to kill him coming back there with nothing in that barrel. He made three trips to the field every day. He came in the morning round nine-thirty, he came at dinner time, and he came again in the evening. On the twelve o'clock run, the middle run, he brought your dinner buckets. Most of the people had the little dime buckets, and Buzz Johnson looked like a junk man coming back there with them shiny little buckets all over the cart. When he was running late he would have Diamond loping, and you could hear them dime buckets hitting against that water cart from way cross the field. Thirty or forty dime buckets on that cart. Had so many of them he had to put some of them in a crocker sack and hang the sack on diamond's back. The people used to mark their buckets with little pieces of cloth—red, yellow, blue. Some put their 'nitials on the top. Toby Lewis put a hog ring on the handle of his bucket. From then on they called him Hog Ring Toby. They was calling Toby Lewis that when I came here: Hog Ring Toby. But he was the best man you had working out there. Could cut and load more cane than any other man ever lived on this place. Every year somebody was crazy enough to challenge him, and every year Toby broke him down. Hawk Brown wanted to cut cane with him; Toby nearly killed Hawk. Joe Simon wanted to load cane with him; when Toby got through with Joe Simon he could hardly pick up enough cane to chew. Now he had to work long side the women. In the spring instead of him getting a plow, now he had to get a hoe.

The worse thing happened in the field while I was out there was that thing with Black Harriet. Her name was Harriet Black, but she was so black (she was one of them Singalee people) and the people called her Black Harriet. She didn't have all her faculties, but still she was queen of the field. She was tall, straight, tough, and blue-black. Could pick more cotton, chop more cotton than anybody out there. Cut more cane than anybody out there, man or women, except for Toby Lewis. She was queen long before I came here and she probably would have been queen long after if Katie Nelson hadn't showed up. Katie Nelson was a little tight-butt woman from Bayonne. No kin at all to the Nelsons on the St. Charles River. They wouldn't own her. What sent Katie to Samson with that little red nigger she called a husband, only God knows. He looked about much a husband as one of them fence posts. Soon as she got in the field she started running off at the mouth. "I'm go'n beat her. Queen, huh? Well, she ain't go'n be no queen for long. You wait, I'm go'n queen her."

Black Harriet would never say a thing. Would stay to herself all the time—because she lacked all her faculties. Working and singing—singing one of them Singalee songs—but never bothering a soul.

Every morning Katie Nelson would say: "I'm go'n get her. I'm go'n get her." One morning she came out there and said: "This the morning. That man I got gived me so much loving last night I'm just rarrying to go. Y'all ever seen a wild horse just rarrying to go? Well, y'all ain't seen nothing yet. Watch out there, queen of spade, here I come."

We was all for it. I got to say it now, we was all for it. That's how it was in the field. You wanted that race. That made the day go. Work, work, you had to do something to make the day go. We all wanted it. We all knowed Katie couldn't beat Harriet, but we thought the race would be fun. So the morning soon as Katie said this was the day, we all said, "Go get her, Katie. Go get her." Katie said, "Here I come, queen of spade, ready or not."

Katie trying to catch Harriet was like me trying to fight Liston. But Katie kept after her all morning. She knowed she couldn't beat Harriet, but if she kept on talking she could work on Harriet's mind. Twelve o'clock, everybody got their buckets and sat down in the shade. Harriet sat under a little tree by herself and ate her fish and rice. When she got through eating she filed her hoe, and then just sat there waiting for one o'clock. I looked over there at her singing her Singalee song to herself, but she never paid me no mind. Katie was somewhere else with that little red thing she called a husband. About as much a husband as a dry blood weed. Soon as dinner was over she came back and started running off at the mouth again. "I didn't get you this morning, queen of spade, but I'll get you this evening. I'm go'n run all that black off you. When I get through with you you go'n be white as snowman."

This world is so strange. Now, why a Katie Nelson? What good is one? Why here with that little red nigger she called a husband? Why not Baton Rouge? New Orleans? Why not the North? Huh? Tell me.

Tom Joe was out there that evening. He always rode that big red horse. Always had on a cowboy hat and cowboy boots. Had been a cowboy in Texas once—according to his story. But he was overseer here now, and he got as much fun out of a race as anybody did. This always made the rest of the people work faster.

The first set of rows, nothing happened. But the next set, Harriet caught a row of wire grass. Wire grass is not hard to cut, but you have to get the roots or it'll spring back in a couple of days. The grass slowed Harriet so much Katie came up almost even with her. Now, to stay ahead of Katie, Harriet started leaving grass behind. Grace Turner was on the next row. At first she caught all the grass that Harriet left behind. But the longer the race went on the more grass Harriet left behind. Now everybody saw it. Tom Joe hollered at her from down the field, but she acted like she didn't even hear him. He hollered at her again, she still didn't hear him. She was chopping faster now and talking to herself in that Singalee tongue. Chopping as much cotton down as she was chopping grass. Sometimes she was chopping cotton instead of chopping grass.

We had all stopped and was just watching her now. Watching that hoe go up and down, up and down, digging up as much cotton as it was cutting grass. We just stood there watching, not saying a word. Not one of us moved till Tom Joe went down there and started beating her 'cross the back. He didn't try to take the hoe from her, he just rode down there and started beating her with the bridle reins. But the more he beat her, the more cotton she was digging up. Grace Turner was the first one to run down there. She pushed Harriet down and laid on top of her. Now Tom Joe started beating Grace just because she was trying to protect Harriet. Bessie Hebert ran down there with the hoe and threatened to chop his head off, and now Grace jumped up off Harriet and grabbed Bessie. We was all down there now. Some of us pleading with Tom Joe, the rest of us trying to help Harriet. Harriet was just laying there laughing and talking in that Singalee tongue. Looking at us with her eyes all big and white one second, then say something in that Singalee tongue the next second, then all of a sudden just bust out laughing.

When we got her quieted down, me and Grace brought her to the front and cleaned her up, and that night they drove her to Jackson. The Samsons didn't do a thing to Tom Joe, but they fired Katie. And they told Bessie she had to leave the place. Bessie had a house full of children, but still she had to go. They told her if she didn't have so many children they would 'a' put her in jail for threatening Tom Joe.

The Travels of Miss Jane Pittman

NOT TOO LONG AFTER HARRIET went to Jackson, I joined the church. She went to Jackson that spring, I joined the church that summer.

I had been fighting with my conscience ever since Ned was killed. I had been brought up 'round church people all my life, ever since I was a slave, but I doubt if I had ever thought too much about joining the church. Sometimes I would think of myself, yes, I ought to join; serve Him. Other times I didn't see no sense joining at all. But after Ned was killed I knowed I had nothing else in the world but the Lord. Still, I didn't go to Him with all my heart till I moved to Samson. That was twelve, thirteen years after Ned's death.

When I first moved to Samson I was living side Unc Gilly and Aunt Sara, 'cross the road from Grace Turner. Grace was married to Lawrence Hebert at that time and she was staying over there with his people. Me and Grace used to sit out on the gallery every night and listen to the singing up the quarters. We didn't have a church then, the church wasn't built till much later. The people used to hold services 'cross the road from where the church is now. Me and Grace used to sit out there every night and listen to the singing and praying. Sometimes she would come over to my place and sit there with me, but more often we would just talk to each other from 'cross the road. It would be so dark sometimes we couldn't even see each other, but that never stopped us from having a long conversation. One day Grace came up to me and said, "Jane, I'm go'n join church." I said, "Grace, I'm so happy for you." she said, "Jane, why don't you join with me? Nobody can't say you ain't a nice, decent person. You belong up there." I said, "Grace, you don't know the times I been thinking about doing just that." I said, "Give me a week or two, time to think."

Nancy Williams was praying for religion, too. Me, Nancy, Grace, Peter July. Who else? Lobo. How can I ever forget that? Lobo's travel, he saw Mannie Hall running Lizzy Aaron up a tree. If that wasn't the craziest travel anybody ever had. Everybody laughing, coughing, wiping their eyes. Everybody but Lizzy. Lizzy mad as she can be. Right there in church she called Lobo a lying dog. "You nothing but a lying old dog, you ain't seen nobody running me up no tree. I don't even know how to clamb no tree." Lobo standing up there, sweating. "I know what the Lord showed me," he said. "Mannie was throwing clods at you. Them children was saying, 'Look. Yonder. She on that limb over yonder.' And you went hopping from limb to limb like a cat."

The people laughed so much at Lobo, the pastor had to hold up service. While he was trying to get the people settled down, Lobo leaned against the pulpit railing, sweating like he was standing in the sun.

"That nigger drunk," Lizzy said.

The people started laughing all over. It was near mid-night before we left church.

Nancy Williams came through out there in the field—picking cotton. She was picking cotton way down the field by herself, and when we heard her hollering we knowed she had come through. We ran down there where she was. "I got it," she said. "I got it. I got it at last. He done lift my feet out the mirey clay." We told her to go home and get herself ready to talk that night. She dropped her cotton sack and took off for the quarters, just running and whooping.

Tom Joe came out there to weigh up, and he asked us where Nancy was. We told him she had gone home because she had found religion that day. Tom said: "What I care 'bout her and her find 'ligion there? Find that 'ligion at night; find them cotton in the day. And that go for the rest of y'all hunting 'ligion round here, too."

When Grace heard that she broke away from the headland and took off down the field. Tom said, "There go another one there finding her 'ligion." I went after Grace and I found her kneeling in one of the rows. "You done come through, Grace?" I said. "Come through, nothing," she said. "I'm praying to God to keep me from killing Tom Joe. The no good dog." I said, "Grace, now you praying for religion and you can't think evil." "I know," she said. "But times like these I wish I had let Bessie chop his head off with that hoe. They couldn't do no more than hang her." "Grace," I said. "What's the Lord go'n think hearing you talk like that? Don't you know Tom Joe was put here by the devil?"

We went back to the headland where Tom Joe was weighing cotton. He said: "Well, you find Him down there?"

I could see Grace getting mad again. "Grace," I said.

A week or so later Grace did find religion. It looked like everybody was finding it but me. I said so to Grace. She said, "Just pray harder, Jane." I said, "I'm praying hard as I can now. Maybe I ain't fit for Glory." She said, "That's nonsense. You just keep praying."

I used to pray all day and half the night. Long as I was up I was praying. Sometimes I used to go in the field so tired and so sleepy I couldn't hardly keep my eyes opened. Then one Thursday morning—I won't ever forget it long as I live—I was on my way in the field when it hit me. Looked like a big load just fell off my shoulders.

"Grace," I said. She was walking little bit ahead of me. "Grace, I got it."

"At last," she said. "At last. Jane, how do you feel? You feel light?"

"I feel light," I said. "Look like I can fly."

"That's it," Grace said. "If you feel light, that's it. It always makes you feel light." she said, "Go back home. Don't go out in the field at all. Go back home and get yourself ready for tonight."

That night I told my travels.

I had a load of bricks on my shoulders and I wanted to drop it but I couldn't. It was weighing me down and weighing me down, but I couldn't let go of the sack. Then a White Man with long yellow hair—hair shining like the sun—came up to me. (He had on a long white robe, too.) He came up to me and said, "Jane, you want get rid of that load?" I said, "Indeed, indeed. But how come you know me? Can you be the Lord?" He said, "To get rid of that load and be rid of it always, you must take it 'cross yon river."

I looked where He was pointing, and yes, there was a river. I turned back to Him, but He was gone. I started toward the river with the sack of bricks on my back. And briars sprung up in front of me where briars had not been, and snakes crawled round my bare feet where snakes had not been, and wide ditches and bayous with green water stood before me where they was not before. And a man, jet black and shiny, with cuckleburrs for hair, stood before me and told me he would take the sack. I told him no. I told him the White Man told me to cross yon river with the sack, and I was go'n cross yon river with it. And just like that this man turned into Ned. "Give me the sack, Mama," he said. I said, "Ned that's you? That's you, Ned?" "Give me the sack, Mama," he said. I said, "I don't believe that's you, Ned. I believe that's nobody but the devil trying to fool poor Jane." I said, "If that's you, Ned, tell me what you carried all them days when your mama was killed." I peered into this devil face playing Ned and I saw him straining and straining trying to think what Ned had carried, but he couldn't remember. And I knowed for sure it wasn't Ned, because Ned would never forget this, and I went on. It was hard to go on, because the warmth he had brought to my heart, but I knowed I had to keep going. And when I came to the river I looked, and there was Joe Pittman, and he wasn't old like me, he was still young. "Give me the sack, Jane," he said. "I must cross that river, Joe." I said. "Give me the sack, Jane," he said. "No, Joe, I must cross the river, I said. And when I didn't give it to him on the third time he asked for it he disappeared. And I moved down into the water, and all round me alligators snapped at my legs. I looked and—snakes—hundreds and hundreds of them swimming toward me. But I kept moving with the sack on my back, and with every step the water got deeper. When it came up to my neck I looked up to see how far I had to go—and there was Albert Cluveau. He was sitting on the horse that had killed Joe Pittman, he was holding the gun that had killed Ned. I looked back over my shoulder, and there was Joe and Ned on the other bank beckoning for me to come back to them. But I would not turn back. I would go on, because the load I was carrying on my back was heavier than the weight of death. When I got near the bank Albert Cluveau raised the gun to shoot me. But when he saw I was 'termined to finish crossing he disappeared, too. And soon as I put my feet on solid ground the Savior was there. He smiled down at me and raised the load off my shoulder. I wanted to bow to His feet, but He told me rise I had been born again. I rose and I felt light and clean and good.

That was my travel. That's how I got over. And that's what the church sang that night.

> Tone the bell
> > Done got over
> Tone the bell
> > Done got over
> Tone the bell
> > Done got over
> > Done got over at last.
>
> Plucked my soul from the gate of Hell
> > Done got over
> From the gate of Hell
> > Done got over
> From the gate of Hell
> > Done got over
> > Done got over at last.
>
> My Jesus glad, old Satan mad
> > Done got over
> Old Satan mad
> > Done got over
> Old Satan mad
> > Done got over
> > Done got over at last.

Two Brothers of the South

TIMMY AND TEE BOB WAS BROTHERS—half brothers; Timmy was nigger, Tee Bob was white. Everybody on the plantation, everybody on the river, everybody on that house, including Tee Bob and Miss Amma Dean, knowed Timmy was Robert Samson's boy. And Robert never tried to hide it, and couldn't even if he wanted to, because Timmy was more like him than poor Tee Bob ever would be. When he was nothing but a child Timmy liked to ride and hunt just like Robert always did. Had all of Robert's mischief ways. You stayed on your guard 'round either one of them. Robert didn't care what he did to white or black. Timmy didn't care what he did to men or women long as they was black. Built just like Robert, tall and skinny. But Robert was white—red—and Timmy was brown. Robert had brown hair and gray eyes; Timmy had reddish-brown hair and brown eyes. Nose hooked just alike. Now, Tee Bob was small and delicate all his life. The only reason they gived him the name little Robert, the doctor told Miss Amma Dean she couldn't have any more children. But any other name would 'a' fit Tee Bob better.

When Tee Bob got big enough to ride, Robert came in the quarters and told Verda he wanted Timmy to ride with him. Called Verda to the gate, like coming to that house was something new to him. Like he hadn't tied that horse at that gate a hundred times and walked in that house and stayed there till he himself got ready to leave.

"I don't want him up there," Verda told him.

"He'll be treated right," Robert said.

"I don't want him waiting on nobody's table," Verda said.

"He'll just ride with Tee Bob," Robert said.

"Tee Bob's butler?" Verda said. "His brother's butler?"

"I expect him up there tomorrow," Robert said.

"Not if he go'n wait on table," Verda said.

"Tomorrow," Robert said, and rode away.

Timmy came up to the front to work. He was about twelve then, because he was six or seven years older than Tee Bob. When Tee Bob was at school, Timmy looked after the horses. When Tee Bob came home, Timmy saddled up the horses and they rode out in the field together. Tee Bob on his little Shetland pony, Johnnie; Timmy on that half-broke thing called Hurricane. Soon as they hit the field Tee Bob would come over where I was. No matter what I was doing—picking cotton, cutting cane—here he would come. If my sack was full he would take it to the end for me. If we was cutting cane and it was cold he would tell me to go stand by the fire. He took a liking to me soon as I came here. So when Aunt Hattie died—Unc Buddy wasn't far behind—I was the one he told the people at the house to bring up there. I didn't want go up there, I loved the outside too much. Then, even cold I didn't mind. Then, I looked at cold and heat like everything else. But them at the house thought I was slowing up in the field and I could do better at the front. Paul Samson was the one who come out there and asked me what I knowed about cooking. (We was cutting cane. December. Almost freezing out there.) I said I had been doing it over sixty years. I hadn't answered soon enough for him, and now he just sat there on that horse looking down at me. He said he meant cooking for white people. I said I ain't poisoned none yet. He sat on that horse looking down at me awhile, then he said: "Be at that house six o'clock tomorrow. Show me if you can make biscuits smart as you can talk." I said, "I like it right where I am, if you don't mind." He sat there looking down at me awhile, then he said: "You do?" (Real cold that day. Joe Ambrose way down the row, just cutting cane and singing.) Paul Samson said: "Maybe you ain't heard it yet? On Samson you like what Paul Samson like. Or maybe you have heard it and you just don't mind borrowing that wagon again. Well, which is it?"

That's how I got up there. But after I was up there awhile I didn't mind it at all. I had other people to help me do the work, and I had all the free time I wanted to fish and work in my garden. Sometimes I would get Timmy to get Rags out of the pasture for me and I would ride out in the field. One day I was crazy enough to ride out there with Timmy and Tee Bob.

I should 'a' knowed Timmy had some rascality up his sleeves when I first got on that horse. Everything felt too good to be true. The saddle was just right—he had drawed up the stirrups so my feet could fit in them. He had put on a good bridle, good strong reins. The girt tied well—everything just right. I'm thinking: "Something he want me to do for him. He ain't doing all this for nothing." All the way back in the field I'm trying to figure out what Timmy wants. Probably money, I think. Then I try to figure what he wants the money for. I don't ask him, I just look at him out the corner of my eyes. Looking at Timmy, you looking at nobody but Robert Samson himself. Them shoulders up, them elbows in, riding there just like Robert. That straw hat cocked a little over his eyes, just like Robert for the world. But them eyes wasn't saying a thing, just looking straight ahead like nothing was going on. I looked down at Tee Bob. He ain't saying nothing either. But him and Timmy had worked this all out together.

When we got in the field we went over where Grace and the rest of the people was cutting cane. Grace looked at me and said—"Well, if it ain't the high class." "Just my little evening stroll," I said. "That's when you the high class," Grace said. "Me, I got to work for a living."

I followed Grace down the cane field, just talking. All that time Tee Bob and Timmy wasn't too far away. Then after I had been out there a while I began to feel chilly, and I told Grace I thought I'd be heading back to the front. Soon as I said that, Tee Bob went over a few rows and shot out for the headland. Little Johnnie was running so fast, his mouth almost touching the ground. "What's the matter with him?" I said. "Gone crazy all a sudden?" Then Grace hollered: "Jane, hold on." But Timmy had already hit Rags with the stalk of cane, and the horse almost shot out from under me.

Now, it was nobody but me, Rags, and that cane field. I was holding pump, mane, and bridle. All over the field, people was hollering at me: "Hold him, Miss Jane, hold him. Hold him, Miss Jane, hold him."

Rags hit that headland and leaned way to the right like he might tip over, but he held to his feet. A few more strides he hit that back road and leaned way to the left, but he kept to his feet again. Now, it wasn't nobody but me, Rags, and that back road, because I had passed Tee Bob way back there, and there wasn't nothing ahead of me now and nothing likely to catch me till Rags got to that front gate and stopped. Of course, Timmy could have caught me on Hurricane. That time, Hurricane could beat any horse in the parish running, probably any horse in the state running. But Timmy never could leave Tee Bob behind him. No matter what happened Tee Bob rode ahead, if just by a nose, but not ever behind him. So I had nothing to stop Rags now but that gate at the front. Of course, I wanted to fall off, but fall where? It was grinding, and that ground hard as a rock, and I was in my sixties, and if I had hit that ground raveling a hundred miles an hour I would have busted open like a watermelon. So I didn't fall; I held on tight.

Unc Gilly and Aunt Sara was sitting out on the gallery, and Aunt Sara heard the horse running off. She said she knowed the horse was running off because a horse makes a different sound than he makes when he's just running for the fun of it. His hooves make a louder sound and they don't keep rhythm like they do when the horse is just racing. She said she had to holler at Unc Gilly three or four times before she could make him hear her. "Horse running off," she said loud. "Horse. Jane. Gilly? Horse. Jane." She said she knowed it was me because Timmy could handle Hurricane with ease, and Tee Bob's horse Johnnie couldn't make that kind of noise. "Horse. Jane," she said loud. "Gilly? Gilly?" When he caught on to what she was trying to tell him he came out in the road with his walking stick. From way down the quarters I could see him waving the stick up and down. Not right and left like he should 'a' been waving it, but up and down. The closer I got the faster Unc Gilly waved the stick. Now he was waving it with both hands and backing up at the same time. Waving and backing up, waving and backing up. Then I didn't see him. When and how Rags went by Unc Gilly or over Unc Gilly I don't know. I know one second I was seeing him waving that stick, the next second I was passing the churchhouse.

When Rags came up to the big gate he stopped so quick I almost went over his head. Miss Amma Dean was already there with the spy glasses. She had watched the whole thing from the back gallery. In grinding, when most of the cane was down, you could see couple miles back in the field. She said she had seen Rags turn off the headland onto the back road, and she had seen him coming straight for the big house, straight toward her like a train on a railroad track. She said she could see Tee Bob, too, on Johnnie, his little elbows sticking way out, kicking Johnnie to make him go faster, like, if kicking a horse the size of Johnnie could ever make him catch a whirlwind. She could see Timmy, too, riding a little behind Tee Bob. Both of them laughing. No, she couldn't see their mouths with the spy glasses, just like she couldn't see my eyes with the spy glasses, but she could see how tight I was holding on, and she could guess how scared I was; and seeing how loose and free Timmy and Tee Bob was riding, she could tell they was laughing even when she couldn't see it. By the time Rags got to the gate she had closed up the spy glasses and run 'cross the yard.

"It was Timmy?" she said.

"I don't know," I said. "It might 'a' been a wahs."

Rags was breathing hard. I was breathing hard. Both of us sweating. Almost freezing now, but both of us sweating.

"Wahs?" Miss Amma Dean said, and looked at me a long time. She knowed it was Timmy, because Timmy was Robert's son, and Robert would 'a' done the same thing. No, not would 'a', did it. To one of her cousins. Had put one of her own cousins on a half-broke horse, and the horse had throwed him 'cross the fence.

Timmy and Tee Bob came up there still laughing. Little Johnnie was so tired his mouth hung about an inch off the ground.

"Wahs?" Miss Amma Dean said, still looking at me with the spy glasses in her hand. Then she looked at Timmy. At first she was mad enough to hit him with the spy glasses, but the longer she looked at him the more she saw Robert. Robert would have done the same thing; no, he had done it. But Timmy wasn't Robert, even if he was Robert's son. He had to remember he was still a nigger.

"Robert, you know better," she told Tee Bob.

"Jane can ride," Tee Bob said.

"Best I ever seen," Timmy said.

"Shut up," Miss Amma Dean said. "Nobody told you to open your mouth." She waited for him to say something else. He was Robert's son, and Robert definitely would 'a' answered back. "Mr. Robert will hear about this," she said.

He was looking 'cross the yard at the big house. From the way he was sitting in that saddle, not slumped over like a nigger ought to be, but with them shoulders up, with that straw hat cocked a little over his eyes, he was telling us Robert wasn't go'n do him a thing. But he didn't have to tell it to me. I knowed all the time Robert wouldn't do him nothing. But Miss Amma Dean still didn't know. Had been married to Robert ten, twelve years, and still didn't know what he would do.

"Take that hat off, Timmy," she said.

He took it off, but he still didn't look at her.

"Well?" she said.

"Yes ma'am," he said, hardly loud enough even for me to hear him, and I was up there on the horse.

When Robert came in that evening, Miss Amma Dean told him what had happened. Robert started laughing. He wished he had been there. He didn't know Rags still had that spunk. Did my eyes get big and white, did they go up and down in my head? Could Miss Amma Dean hear my teeth hitting together through the spy glasses? He wasn't ever at home when all the good things happened.

"And Timmy?" Miss Amma Dean said.

"Jane's not hurt," Robert said.

"She could 'a' been hurt."

"Well, she's not."

"Well, he can take his hat off," Miss Amma Dean said.

"I'll talk to him," Robert said. "But I wish I had seen it. When you going for another ride, Jane?"

"Not with them ever," I said.

"That's too bad," he said.

He didn't say a word to Timmy. He knowed Timmy respected Miss Amma Dean. He knowed Timmy had to respect Miss Amma Dean just like he had to respect every white lady or white man. The other thing didn't matter.

Not long after that happened Timmy had his run-in with Tom Joe and had to leave home. Timmy and Tee Bob was riding in the field when the horse throwed Tee Bob and broke his arm. Tom Joe was walking 'cross the yard when Timmy brought Tee Bob home. He carried Tee Bob in the house himself, then he came back outside and asked Timmy what had happened. Timmy told him; he knocked Timmy down.

He hated Timmy with all his might. Timmy got away with too much from that house up there. He knowed that Timmy was Robert Samson's boy, and he hated the Samson in Timmy much as he hated the nigger in him. More, because it was the Samson blood in Timmy that made him so uppity. No, he didn't hit Timmy for what had happened to Tee Bob. He hated Tee Bob much as he hated the rest of the Samsons. He knocked Timmy down because he knowed no white man in his right mind would 'a' said he had done the wrong thing.

Albert Walker and Cleon Simon was picking moss in the yard, and they stopped to see what was happening. They said when Timmy got up he said, "That's enough, Tom Joe." Tom said, "Call me Mister, nigger." Timmy said, "I wouldn't call white trash Mister if I was dying." Tom swung at him again, and Timmy moved back. Tom swung again, and Timmy moved back again, and now he was grinning at Tom Joe because Tom Joe couldn't hit him. Tom ran on him to throw him down, but Timmy brushed him to the side, and Tom Joe was the one who fell. When he got up he grabbed the pole out of Albert's hand. He didn't have to grab it, Albert was so scared of Tom Joe he practically handed him the pole. The people used to get moss out the trees with those long poles they used for thrashing pecan trees. You would stick the pole in a pile of moss up in the tree, then wind it round good, then pull it down. Tom Joe grabbed the pole out of Albert's hand and struck Timmy with it. Instead of Albert and Cleon trying to help Timmy, Cleon started hollering for Miss Amma Dean to come out there and stop Tom Joe. Miss Amma Dean left me in there to look after Tee Bob and she ran out in the yard. I could hear her screaming at Tom Joe the moment she came out on the back gallery. She would have him run off the place, she would have him put in jail, put in the pen even. But her screaming at Tom Joe, threatening Tom Joe meant no more than threatening a fence post. That hatred for Timmy was too deep in him to stop now. And what white man would put him in jail or keep him in jail after what Timmy had let happen to Tee Bob? By the time Miss Amma Dean got out in the yard Timmy was bloody and unconscious. Tom Joe throwed the pole to the side and walked away. Miss Amma Dean had Albert to bring Timmy inside. And when the doctor came there to see after Tee Bob he had to look after both of them.

Robert came home later that night and Miss Amma Dean told him what had happened. Tom Joe ought to be run off the place; no, put in jail. Robert told her he wasn't go'n do either. You pinned medals on a white man when he beat a nigger for drawing back his hand. "Even a half nigger?" Miss Amma Dean said. "There ain't no such thing as a half nigger," Robert said.

A few days later Robert called Timmy to the house to give him some money and send him away. Timmy wanted to see Tee Bob before he left. Robert said Tee Bob was asleep. Timmy asked could he come back when he woke up. Robert told him no.

When Tee Bob was able to ride again they got Claudee Ferdinand to ride with him. But it wasn't the same. Tee Bob wanted Timmy. Timmy was his brother, and he wanted his brother there with him. He used to come back there in that kitchen every day and talk about Timmy. He could understand why Timmy had to saddle his horse, he could understand why Timmy had to ride behind him, but he couldn't understand why Timmy had to leave home after a white man had beat him with a stick. I told him Timmy had to leave for his own safety. But he didn't understand what I was saying. I told Miss

Amma Dean to try to explain it to him. Then his uncle Clarence tried. After Clarence, his parrain, Jules Raynard, in Bayonne, tried to explain it to him. All of us tried except Robert. Robert thought he didn't have to tell Tee Bob about these things. They was part of life, like the sun and the rain was part of life, and Tee Bob would learn them for himself when he got older. But Tee Bob never did. He killed himself before he learned how he was supposed to live in this world.

Of Men and Rivers

TIMMY LEFT HERE WHEN? Let me think now, let me think. 1925 or '26— because he was gone before the high water, and the high water was in '27.

When did Long come in? Long came in when? After the high water— yes. Before the high water we didn't have school here at Samson. The children went to school in the Bottom or at Ned's school up the road. Long came in after the high water and gived us free books for the first time. And that's when they started teaching in the church here on the place. They had just built the church. They hadn't even painted it, yet.

The damage from that high water was caused by man, because man wanted to control the rivers, and you cannot control water. The old people, the Indians, used to worship the rivers till the white people came here and conquered them and tried to conquer the rivers, too. Now, when I say they used to worship the river I don't mean they used to call the river God. There's just one God and He's above us. But they thought the river had extra strength, and I find no fault in that. Because I find that in some things, too. There's an old oak tree up the quarters where Aunt Lou Bolin and them used to stay. That tree has been here, I'm sure, since this place been here, and it has seen much much, and it knows much much. And I'm not ashamed to say I have talked to it, and I'm not crazy either. It's not necessary craziness when you talk to trees and rivers. But a different thing when you talk to ditches and bayous. A ditch ain't nothing, and a bayou ain't too much either. But rivers and trees—less, of course, it's a chinaball tree. Anybody caught talking to a chinaball tree or a thorn tree got to be crazy. But when you talk to an oak tree that's been here all these years, and knows more than you'll ever know, it's not craziness; it's just the nobility you respect.

So they tell me the Indians used to respect the rivers that same way. They used to catch fish out the river and eat the fish and put the bones back. They used to say, "Go back and be fish again." And when they caught another fish they thought it was one of the same ones they had already ate. But when the white man came here, so they say, he conquered the Indians and told them that no such thing as bone can become fish again. The Indians didn't believe what he said so he killed them off. After he had killed them he tried to conquer the same river they had believed in, and that's when the trouble really started.

I don't know when the first levee was built—probably in slavery time; but from what I heard from the old people the water destroyed the levee soon as it was put there. Now, if the white men had taken heed to what the river was trying to say to him then, it would have saved a lot of pain later. But instead of him listening—no, he built another levee. The river tored that one down just like the first one. Built another one; river tored that one down. Here, the river been running for hundreds and hundreds of years, taking little earth, maybe few trees, maybe a cabin here and there when the water got too high, maybe a cow, horse, but never, never a whole parish—till the white man came here and tried to conquer it. They say he was French. And that's why, up to this day, I don't have too much faith in any Frenchman. Now, what possessed him to come from way 'cross the sea to come here and mess with our rivers. They tell me he said, "This here water got to be confined." But he said it in French—he was a Frenchman. "We can't let the rivers run wild like this, taking our trees like that." Our trees, mind you, like he planted a tree here. He didn't know the river had been taking a tree here and there for a hundred years or more. "We got to get that water to running where it's suppose to run. Suppose to run in the river and we got to keep it there." Like you can tell water where to go. "Now, what we got to do is fill these here sacks full of sand and stack them all long the river where we think it might flood over. When we do that we got her licked." Well, they stacked sacks and stacked sacks, and every time the river got ready to break through it went right on and broke through that Frenchman's little levee like it was made of matchsticks.

I remember the high water of '12 well enough, but the high water of '27 I won't ever forget. Because in '26 it rained and rained and rained. And that same winter we had a big freeze. Early next spring we got more rain, and the water couldn't seep in the ground because the ground was already full from the year before, and the water had to go to the rivers. The Mi'sippi, the Red River, the 'Chafalaya River. But after so much rain that spring even the rivers couldn't take all the water. And the water had to find somewhere else to go.

The people said when the levee first broke—it broke at McCrea they could hear that water coming for miles. Coming like a whirlwind, coming like a rain, like thunder, like guns roaring. Taking everything up in its way—showing that little Frenchman who had lived long before who was still boss. Taking up big trees by the roots, taking houses with the people still in them. Nothing to see mules, cows, dogs, pigs floating on the water. Nothing to see people in trees, people on top of houses waiting for boats to pick them up. Days and days, I don't know quite how long, before it stopped. But it hadn't really stopped. The force had just gone out of the water. The water was still there. It was just flowing now smooth and quiet. Like a snake in the grass, like a shadow, like a cloud. The sun was out, the sky was blue, and you said to yourself: "Thank the Lord; over at last." But that was before you looked over your shoulders. You turned. What's that? A sea. A whole sea creeping up on you.

The water covered the swamps and the fields here at Samson, but it never got in the quarters. Because Robert Samson had the men build a dike 'long the railroad tracks from one end of Samson to the other. The men worked day and night to keep the water back, and the women had to keep hot food and coffee going to the men. The old men and the children who couldn't work on the railroad tracks had to take sticks and guns and keep back the wild animals that was trying to reach higher ground at the front. The animals that couldn't swim or climb trees had to seek higher ground, and the only high ground was at the front. Robert Samson's orders was: not one stray animal, not even a tadpole, was to cross them tracks. He told every man, the old men, to take his own gun, and he, himself, supplied the bullets. He told them to shoot anything and everything on four legs coming toward them. And all times of day and night we, here in the quarters, could hear the guns firing.

The birds left the swamps just like the rest of the animals did. The water, quiet as it was, just by sweeping up the leaves, scared the birds. We could hear their little cries long before we saw them, and when they flew overhead it was like a black cloud passing over the sun. For days and days, and even at night, we could hear their shrill little cries. Olive Jarreau said it was Judgment Day. It wasn't Judgment Day. Man had just gone a little too far.

Now he's built his concrete spillways to control the water. But one day the water will break down his spillways just like it broke through the levee. That little Frenchman was long dead when the water broke his levee in '27, and these that built the spillways will be long dead, too, but the water will never die. That same water the Indians used to believe in will run free again. You just wait and see.

Huey P. Long

HUEY LONG CAME IN THE YEAR after the high water. Nothing better could 'a' happened to the poor black man or the poor white man no matter what they say.

Oh, they got all kinds of stories about him now. He was a this, he was a that. Nothing but a dictator who did this and that to the people. When I hear them talk like that I think, "Ha. You ought to been here twenty-five, thirty years ago. You ought to been here when poor people had nothing. You wouldn't be running off at the mouth so. Ha."

Even them children going round here saying what they got to respect Long for—didn't he used to call our people nigger? I agree he did call the colored people nigger. But when he said nigger he said, "Here a book, nigger. Go read your name." When the other ones said nigger they said, "Here a sack, nigger. Go pick that cotton."

They don't know what the poor people went through. They think they always had a school bus, they always had a school. I can tell you when poor people didn't get two months of school a year. And to even get that little bit they had to walk five and six miles.

What they think the rich people killed Long for? Because he called the colored people nigger? They killed him for helping the poor, the poor black and the poor white. Because you're not suppose to help the poor. Let the poor work, let the poor fight in your wars, then let them die. But you're not suppose to help the poor.

Now, they want say Dr. Weiss killed Long. Well, they ain't go'n make me believe that. Want say he killed Long because Long said Dr. Weiss wife's granddaddy had nigger blood in his vein. Well, they got white people round here'll kill you for saying much less than that, but they ain't go'n make me believe that's why Long died. I know them rich people got them guards to kill Long. All the poor know that. Telling the poor he was killed because he said the old judge had nigger blood in his veins. They said that because they thought the poor might rise. They knowed how much the poor loved him, and they said that to keep them from rising up. Well, they didn't fool the poor people, and they don't need to think they did.

I remember the night they shot him, remember it well. I was down the quarters sitting up with Grace Turner. She wasn't feeling too good, and me, Olive Jarreau and Lena Washington was sitting up with her. We was inside talking when Etienne Bouie came by and knocked on the end of the gallery. I went to the door to see what he wanted and he told me what had happened. He said, "Jane, guess what? They done shot Long." I said, "Don't tell me that,

Etienne. Don't tell me that, no. Don't tell me that, now." He said, "Yes, they shot him. He's not dead, but they fear for his life." He said he had just seen Manuel Ruffin and Manuel had heard it over the radio in Bayonne. Manuel had got in his car and come home because he was scared the white people might start war over this. Etienne and Manuel was going through the quarters telling the people what had happened. They tried to get Just Thomas, the head deacon, to go ring the church bell, but Just told them he wasn't getting in white folks' business. Grace told Etienne to come in and have some coffee, and before you knowed it the house was full of people. Unc Gilly got down on his knees and told us to pray for Long. But do you think they was go'n let him go on living? Not after what he had done for the poor.

Now, you mean to tell me out of all the doctors you got in a hospital, not one of these doctors know what he's suppose to do—if to go in the front or the back of a man to keep him from bleeding to death? You trying to tell me that? What you got them there for if they don't know how to operate? No, they didn't want stop the bleeding. They had paid them guards to kill him, and now they sure wasn't go'n save his life in no hospital. I wouldn't be a bit surprise if one day they don't find out them doctors didn't help kill him in that place.

Look like every man that pick up the cross for the poor must end that way.

Miss Lilly

AFTER LONG CAME IN OFFICE and gived us free books we got our first teacher here on the place—Miss Lilly. Miss Lilly stayed up the quarters with me all the time she was here. When they made me cook I had to moved up the quarters because they wanted the cook to live closer to the front. Since I didn't need all of the house for myself I let the teacher have one half and I kept the other half. Every teacher that ever taught here, long as I was the cook, stayed up there with me.

Miss Lilly was a little bowlegged mulatto woman from Opelousas. A big pile of black hair, she used to pin in a roll on top her head. The people used to go up to the church and look through the window at her teaching the children. Half of the people on the place had never been in a school, and for a while everybody wanted to know what Miss Lilly was like. Sometimes you would find somebody standing at every window up there looking inside at her. After they got used to her up there, though, they stopped going. The children was about ready to stop, too. Miss Lilly was too tough on everybody.

She didn't just want lesson, she wanted the girls to come there with their dresses ironed, she wanted ribbons in their hair. The boys had to wear ties, had to shine their shoes. Brogans or no brogans, she wanted them shined.

The children put up with that a couple months, then they stopped going to school. Everybody got sick. If it wasn't cold, it was headache; if it wasn't headache, it was belly ache. Miss Lilly started taking medicine to school. A little brown bottle of asafetida, a little clear bottle of castor oil. When she called roll and missed somebody she went out looking for him. She wouldn't teach the children who was already there, she had to go out looking for the lost lamb. When the children saw her coming, they let out cross the field. Sometimes they headed the other way, toward the river. I would see them from the big house. The boy first, then a little while later Miss Lilly. She could really run for being bowlegged like she was. Poor thing.

Now the next thing she wanted, she wanted everybody to have a tooth-brush. People didn't have money to buy bread with, but Miss Lilly wanted them to have toothbrushes. She gived everybody a week. The end of the week, nobody had a toothbrush. Some of the children had been rubbing soda over their teeth; some of them rubbed charcoal over their teeth; but none of this was good enough for Miss Lilly. She wanted them brushed. She went to the store and asked for two dozen toothbrushes. She was go'n pay for them herself and the children could pay her back when they got the money. Clarence Samson, the brother who used to run the store, told her he didn't have no toothbrushes and he wasn't ordering none. People found out he was ordering toothbrushes for niggers they would tar and feather him and run him out of the parish on a rail. Miss Lilly asked him what if he said he was ordering the toothbrushes for white folks. Clarence said they would laugh at him so hard he would pack up and leave of his own. Miss Lilly didn't argue with him, she walked out of the store, and that weekend she went to Bayonne and got a brush for every child.

Poor Miss Lilly.

One evening Miss Lilly was coming from down the quarters when she heard Oscar Haynes' two boys, Tee Bo and Tee Lo, crying up there in the tree. It was getting dark, she couldn't see them, but she could hear them plain as day. One cry a little while and stop, then the other one start off. This one a little while, then the other one. Miss Lilly stood at the gate looking in the yard. Oscar had green moss burning under the tree. People used to keep a smoke like that in the summer to keep away mosquitoes, but tonight it wasn't mosquitoes. Miss Lilly stood at the gate awhile, then she came in the yard. Oscar and Viney and them sitting out there on the gallery. Nobody saying a word. Just sitting there in the dark. Up in the tree Tee Bo and Tee Lo crying. One a little while, then the other. One a little while, then the other. When Miss Lilly got closer to the tree she saw the two sacks up there.

"What's going on up there?" she asked.

"That's you, Miss Lilly?" Tee Bo said. Miss Lilly could hardly understand him with his mouth pressed up against the sack.

"That's me," Miss Lilly said. "What's going on up there?"

"Daddy smoking us," Tee Bo said.

"Come out of that tree," Miss Lilly said.

"These sacks tied," Tee Bo said.

"Stop fooling with me," Miss Lilly said. "Come down from there."

Nobody on the gallery said a thing. Just sitting there in the dark. Not even looking at Miss Lilly out there in the yard.

"Do I have to come up there?" Miss Lilly said. "Come out of there."

"These sacks tied, Miss Lilly," Tee Bo said.

Miss Lilly made two little jumps to reach the sacks, but didn't come nowhere near reaching them. Then she went up to the gallery and looked at Oscar and them sitting there in the dark. She wouldn't say a thing. They didn't say a thing. Acting like she wasn't even there.

"All y'all crazy?" she asked.

Nobody answered.

"I asked is all y'all crazy?" she said again.

"No business sassing old people," Aunt Julie said. Aunt Julie was Oscar's mama.

"No business sassing old people?" Miss Lilly said. "You whip children when they sassy old people, you don't smoke them. Get them children down."

Nobody answer.

"You hear me?" she said to Oscar.

"I'm hearing everything you saying," Oscar said.

"Well?" Miss Lilly said.

"You better go on up the quarters to Miss Jane," Oscar said. "Teacher or no teacher."

"I leave when them children come down," Miss Lilly said.

Oscar didn't say another word. When he got up, Viney said: "Oscar be careful. The law on her side." He didn't say nothing to her, either. He came on down the steps, picked up Miss Lilly with one hand and started with her toward the gate. Miss Lilly screaming and kicking now. "What you doing to me? Put me down. Animal, animal. Put me down. Help. Help." Oscar pushed the gate open and set her on the ground, then he gave her a big whack on the behind and went on back in the yard. Just before he went on the gallery he throwed another piece of green moss on the fire to keep the smoke going up the tree.

Miss Lilly went from house to house, trying to find somebody to go down there and make Oscar stop smoking his children. When she couldn't find nobody down there she came up to the house and asked me to come go with her to see Robert Samson. I told her the same thing Robert Samson was go'n tell her—leave it alone. She asked me if I knowed what I was saying. I told her I knowed what I was saying—leave it alone. She said she still wanted to talk to Robert. I took her over there. Robert told her to stick to her teaching and let people raise their children the way they wanted to. We came back home. Miss Lilly taught the rest of the year, then she went home to Opelousas and never came back.

After Miss Lilly, then came Hardy. Joe Hardy was one of the worst human beings I've ever met. A little short, oily-face black man with a' open crown gold tooth right in front. Telling poor people the government wasn't paying him much, so he would 'preciate it if they could help him out some. Poor people selling all their little gardening to give Joe Hardy money; selling eggs, selling chickens, killing hogs and selling the meat, to give Joe Hardy money. This wasn't enough for him, he had people raising onions and potatoes for him. Used to take the children out in the field in the evening to hoe and plow his onions and potatoes. Telling the children that one of the lessons our great leader Mr. Booker T. Washington taught was for children to learn good honest labor.

But that wasn't enough for Hardy either. Now he had to start messing with the young ladies at the school. Every time you looked around he had one of the young ladies staying at school helping him correct papers. One day he kept Marshall Bouie's daughter, Francine, up there. Marshall and two of his boys came looking for Hardy. They found him and Francine sitting at the table talking. Night already. Lamp burning. Papers stacked to the side—him and Francine sitting at the table talking. When Marshall walked in, both Hardy and Francine jumped up. Marshall told Francine to go on home, he would deal with her later. Then he told Hardy to blow out the lamp and close up the school, because he wanted Hardy to come go somewhere with him and his boys. After Hardy had propped that post behind the door, Marshall marched him through the quarters back to the graveyard. The two boys tied Hardy to one of them little pecan trees, and Marshall took a stalk of jobo cane, and every time he hit Hardy you could hear Hardy from one end of the plantations to the other. Manual Ruffin cut Hardy loose round mid-night. He said he just got tired listening to Hardy moaning over there. He said he knowed he wasn't go'n get any sleep, so he got a butcher knife out the kitchen and went over to the graveyard and chopped him loose. Soon as Hardy got loose, instead of him going on where he came from, no, he want go to Bayonne and tell the law on Marshall. Sam Guidry sleep, now—Hardy woke him up. "A man tried to beat me to death." Guidry: "Look like he did a halfway job." Then Guidry told Hardy he knowed all about him, and as a matter of fact he was thinking about talking to him one day himself. He told Hardy he had no intention of 'resting Marshall; on the other hand he was giving Hardy about one minute to get out *his* parish. He told Hardy he was going back inside and wash the sleep out his eyes; he was go'n put on his gun belt, then he was coming back with that four-batt'ry flashlight to look for him.

Nobody down here know if Guidry found Hardy that night. Maybe he just told him that to scare him out the parish. But after that night nobody round here ever seen or heard of Hardy again.

For a year and a half we didn't have a school on the place at all. Going into the second year we got that LeFabre girl.

The LaFabre Family

MARY AGNES LEFABRE COME FROM a long line of Creoles back there in New Orleans. Her grandmother was one drop from being white herself. Her grandmother had been one of those ladies for white men. They used to give these great balls before the war, and the white men used to go there to choose their colored women. They didn't marry these women, but sometime they kept them the rest of their life. The one who took this girl's grandmother was called LeFabre.

She named all her children after him. Some of them didn't want these children to carry their name, but old man LeFabre didn't mind. When he died he left them money and property—even slaves. And for the rest of her life, Mary Agnes was trying to make up for this: for what her own people had done her own people. Trying to make up for the past—and that you cannot do. 'Specially somebody pretty like she was. She was medium height, but a little thin. She reminded you of some of these dagoes round here who call themself Sicilians. But she wasn't fat like most of them get. She had long black hair, black as any hair I have ever seen, and it used to come way down her back. Sometimes at night when she got ready to comb it I used to ask her let me help. She would sit on the floor in front of me—that same Mary Agnes LeFabre.

After the war, the family moved from New Orleans to Creole Place. What brought them to Creole Place, I don't know; maybe they had people there already. You had always had some mulattoes there, since long before the war, and now it got to be a settlement for them.

The people at Creole Place did everything for themself. Did their own farming, raised their own hogs, their own cattles, did their own butchering. Had their own church—Catholic; built their own school and got their own teacher. The teacher had to come from there just like the priest had to come from there. Gived their own dances, their own parties, and people like them was the only ones invited. No matter how white you was if you didn't have Creole background they didn't want you there. Same for them who left. Some went North and passed for white; others joined the colored race. But no matter what they did, once they left they couldn't go back.

I want tell you a little story just to show how these people looked at things, and this story is true. People here at Samson right now who can back me up. Etienne, Pap, either one of them can back me up on this. Sappho Brown rode through Creole Place and saw the mulattoes hanging lanterns and crepe paper up in the trees. That was Friday. He figured they was go'n have a dance that Saturday night so he told Claudee—Claudee Ferdinand— let's go there. Now Sappho and Claudee white as any white man in this parish, but they knowed good and good well they didn't have no business going there messing round with them Creoles. Both Sappho and Claudee's daddy was white, but not Creole white. Poor white—no quality. Everybody telling them not to go. "Please don't go down there messing round with them people. You know how them Creole mulattoes act." But telling this to Sappho and Claudee was like talking to a block of wood. "We just as white as them. Whiter than lot of them. Anyhow, they go'n have so many people there they won't even see us." They get on Joe Sipp horse and head out. Creole Place five, six miles from Samson, going toward Baton Rouge. Just before they come up to the dance they tie the horse under a tree and walk the rest of the way. Nothing for them to do soon as they get there but start messing round with these girls. They don't know five words of Creole between them, but the girls speak some English, so they start messing with these girls. By and by the mulattoes get them surrounded. A tall, skinny mulatto in a white cowboy hat did all the talking. "Who you know here?" Sappho said before he could say we don't know nobody here, we just stumbled in, we don't mean no harm, and we don't mind leaving—Claudee said: "Jacques. Us know Jacques." If you're at a Creole dance you got to have somebody there called Jacques. "Us know Jacques." The tall mulatto in the white cowboy hat said: "Fetch me Jacques." Jacques come up—white shirt, khaki pants. Tall mulatto in the white cowboy hat said: "Jacques, you know theses common niggers?" Jacques. "Non. Can't say I do, Raphael." Claudee said: "I didn't mean Jacques, I meant Jean." Sappho said he started to tell Claudee to please shut his mouth and let's get out of here while they was still able to, but, no, now he know Jean. Tall mulatto in the white cowboy hat said: "Jean what?" Claudee said: "Jean— oh—er—Jean LeFabre. Jean LeFabre. Yeah, that's the Jean. Jean LeFabre. But he might not be here tonight. When he told me 'bout the fair he told me he wasn't feeling too good. Headache." The tall mulatto in the white cowboy hat said: "But yes. He got the headache over. Fetch me Jean." Now Jean come up.

A little bowlegged mulatto—thick glasses. Jean: "What now, Raphael?" Tall mulatto in the white cowboy hat: "Them two niggers, Jean?" Jean: "Kee?" Tall mulatto: "Know them?" Jean went up to Sappho and looked at him a while, then he went up to Claudee. He looked at Claudee longer, and everybody, even Sappho, was getting the feeling that maybe he did know Claudee. Then he backed away, shaking his head. "Non." Claudee: "Come on, Jean, you know you know me. Stop fooling the people. You told me 'bout this dance in Bayonne." Jean: "Bayonne? Bayonne? Alcee Bayonne. He live yet? Tell me about Alcee Bayonne and Ad-de-line." Claudee: "Who? What? What you talking 'bout, Jean? Town. No man, Jean. Town. Town. Way up the river. Buy meat. Rice. Many people live." Jean: "Bayonne? Town? Meat? No copron." Tall mulatto in the white cowboy hat said: "'Nough of this. Langlois, fetch two plow lines off that wagon."

Sappho said he was running before the tall mulatto mentioned the plow lines, he just started running faster when he heard it. He said the first person he knocked down coming in the gate was a lady and a fat one at that. She was soft soft and smelled sweet sweet and powder flew up in his face when he hit her. The other person he knocked down was a man—short and hard because the man gave him a jolt right in the pit of his stomach. Claudee didn't wait for the gate to clear up, he went over the fence. When he hit the other side he had left a chunk of his leg on that barb wire the size of his thumb. Now, they was on that road for Samson. Sappho said he was already passing Joe Sipp horse when Claudee hollered at him to untie the horse. He said he said to himself: "You untie him. You the one walking back there."

Behind them the mulattoes had got on their own horses, and Sappho and Claudee could hear them hollering and shooting pistols in the air. Sappho said even before Claudee said field he was already heading that way, he just picked up more speed now because he knowed Claudee was following him. He said he heard Claudee say: "Oh, I'm losing blood. Lord, I'm losing blood." Sappho said he thought to himself: "Just don't lose time and expect company, brother."

The cane was high, and that was the only thing that saved them. They hid in the cane, and for two or three hours they could hear the mulattos riding their horses up and down the rows. Mid-night, the mulattoes gived up and went back home. They untied the horse Sappho and Claudee had left and headed him toward Samson. The horse got here before Sappho and Claudee did. They took Claudee to the doctor early the next morning, and the doctor said the only thing that kept him alive was packing dirt in that cut. He would have bled to death if he hadn't.

Mary Agnes was going to school in New Orleans when this happened. She told me that some of her own people was in this, and she knowed they would have lynched Sappho and Claudee if they had caught them. The law wouldn't 'a' done a thing. Creole Place was for the mulattoes there; everybody else keep out.

When Mary Agnes came here to teach school, the people at Creole Place told her never come back home again. But that was after they had tried to get her back and she wouldn't go. The first time they came to get her, the old man brought his sons with him. All of them threatened to beat her, the old man even slapped her. But she wasn't going back. One night the old man came back by himself. I could hear him round the other side begging her to come back home. They forgived her if she came back now. She told him she couldn't go back, and he left here crying.

A Flower in Winter

TEE BOB SAW Mary Agnes the first time when she brought the children up there to look at his uncle. In the old days all the people had to go up to the house and look at the master in the coffin. If he was a good master you went; if he was a bad master you still had to go. When Clarence Samson died, Robert said everybody on the place was coming up there and pay last respects to his brother. They had to bathe and they had to wear their best clothes. The children in the morning, the grown people in the evening. They had to march in quietly, view the body a moment, then leave. He didn't want no whooping and hollering in the room. If they had to cry, cry after they had gone back outside.

Tee Bob wasn't in the house when Mary Agnes came there with the children, he was standing in the shop door with Etienne Bouie. Etienne was the yardman then. Kept all the tools cleaned and sharpened. Fixed everything that broke. Him and Mr. Isaiah Gunn fixed all the firehalfs and chimleys you see on this place. Mr. Isaiah was probably the best carpenter this state has ever seen. He fixed that house up there anytime something was wrong with it. When that gallery started sagging he rebuilt that gallery and them steps. But he's dead now. Etienne and Tee Bob was standing in the shop door when the girl came in the yard with the children. Etienne said Tee Bob said, "I don't like this. Them children didn't love Uncle Clarence. They was scared of him, and they hated him."

I was standing on the back gallery watching them, because I had to let them in the house. They marched cross the yard like little soldiers. The smallest ones holding hands in front, the biggest ones following, with Mary Agnes following them all. Everybody had on their best clothes. It was

October or November, and they had on the best coat or sweater they had at home. Mary Agnes was dressed in black. A black veil over her face—and that's why I know Tee Bob couldn't see her face that day. She was Catholic, like I have said, and she carried her beads in her hands. I opened the kitchen door for them and waited till they had all come inside, then I led them up to the parlor. Just the coffin and a dozen or more chairs was in the parlor, but they wasn't there for the niggers. Put there for the white people to sit on later that night when they came to the wake. The children marched round the coffin and looked in and went back in the kitchen to wait for the teacher. Some of the bigger girls cried quietly, and I saw that girl, Mary Agnes, wiping her eyes, too. I stood at the door and watched them go back cross the yard. I saw Tee Bob and Etienne looking at the girl, but Tee Bob still didn't see her face. They marched back down the quarters quiet as they had come up to the house. They didn't have school that day, they wouldn't have school till Clarence was laid in his tomb. The people wouldn't even let the children play in the yard—fear Robert might ride by there and see them out there having fun.

Tee Bob didn't see Mary Agnes's face till she came up to the house a few days later. She wanted to ask Robert for a load of wood for the school, but Robert wasn't there. Tee Bob was in the kitchen with me drinking coffee. He asked me who I was talking to at the door, and I told him that the teacher from down the quarters had come to ask for a load of firewood. Tee Bob said tell her she could get the wood, but before he had finished talking he was already at the door. He had come there with his coffee cup, but he never raised it again. When he saw the girl he almost dropped the cup on the floor. His face got so red I thought he was go'n faint right there in the kitchen. After he had been standing there a while, doing nothing but looking at the girl, she nodded her head and went back down the steps. He stood at the door watching her till she had gone cross the yard.

Tee Bob stayed in the kitchen the rest of the day. Sometimes I had to tell him move out of my way so I could do my work. That evening when I got ready to go home he said, "That girl almost white, ain't she?"

"What girl you're talking about, Tee Bob?" I said.

"The teacher," he said.

"Almost, but not quite," I said.

"How long she been here?" he asked me.

"Going on two years," I said. "How come you asking me all these questions?"

Tee Bob was going to school at LSU there in Baton Rouge. He went back that Sunday evening, but couple days later he was back home again. Robert and Miss Amma Dean didn't know why, but I knowed all the time. I just didn't know how far it would go. And even if I did know, who was Jane

Pittman to tell Robert Samson Junior what he ought to do or what he ought to not do when anytime he wanted to he could tell me to shut up my black mouth? Tell Robert? Say what? Hadn't Robert done the same thing? Go to Miss Amma Dean? Say what there? "Miss Amma Dean, Tee Bob want mess with that teacher"? And suppose she told me to mind my own business? I know Robert would have said exactly that.

Tee Bob hung around the kitchen all day. He wouldn't ask me nothing till late that evening. Then he wanted to know if Mary Agnes stayed on the place or left each day. I told him she stayed at the house with me, round the other side. He left again. That weekend he was back. Everybody was glad to see him, but they wondered what brought him back here so much now. Sometimes he stayed away from the house two and three weeks. A boy that rich had friends everywhere who was always inviting him to their place.

He went through the quarters looking for Mary Agnes. That was Friday. Saturday again, Sunday again he went by looking for her. Then he asked me where she was. I told him she stayed here during the week but she left every Friday evening. She had friends in New Orleans where she stayed till Monday morning, then she came back here again. I said: "How come you asking me all these questions, Tee Bob? You never did tell me."

He went back to Baton Rouge that Sunday night, but Tuesday he was home again. Now he pretended he was sick. Sick for about an hour, then he got on that horse and went riding through the quarters. He didn't stop by the church this time, he went all the way back in the field where the people was cutting cane. Stayed back there a while, then came back up to the derrick where he stayed there a few minutes talking to Billy Red. When he came back in the quarters the children was outside playing.

Strut Hawkin's gal, Ethel, said Miss LeFabre had kept her inside to put some 'rithmetic problems on the board, and both of them was standing at the blackboard when Tee Bob came in. She said at first it scared her to see him in there because she had never seen a white man at the school before. So she asked Miss LeFabre could she be excused. She had said it very low and Miss LeFabre didn't hear her. Or if Miss LeFabre did, she didn't under-stand what she had said. And maybe she did and just didn't want to be in there by herself with Tee Bob.

Miss LeFabre said, "Can I help you, Mr. Samson?" But Miss LeFabre had said "Mister" the way white people say "Mister" when a nigger was there. Not like she felt she ought to call somebody like Tee Bob Mister, but you always said Mister or Miss in front of somebody like her.

Tee Bob told her he had been riding through the quarters and he had just stopped by to see if she had got the load of firewood. Ethel said he picked up one of the books and went through it till he came to a place where a page was missing. He asked Miss Agnes if many of the books was like that. She told him yes, but she always made the children read out somebody else's book. Ethel said after Tee Bob had put the book down he looked at the hats and coats hanging on the spools against the wall.

"Nice and warm in here," he said.

"The heater gives off good heat," Mary Agnes said.

She asked Tee Bob if he would like to hear the children recite. They was already practicing for their little Christmas play, and some of the children had already learned their parts. He told her no, not today, but maybe some other time.

Now he just stood there looking at Mary Agnes like some little boy, Ethel said. She said at first she was scared to be in there, but now she felt like laughing at Tee Bob. If he was a man she would 'a' knowed this was no place for her and she would 'a' begged Miss LeFabre to let her be excused. But Tee Bob was not a man. His mouth was too red and soft, his eyes was too big and sorrowful. His skin wasn't rough enough. He didn't have a mustache. He had never shaved in his life, and he never would shave.

Tee Bob went back to LSU the next day, but he came back to Samson Friday evening before Mary Agnes left for New Orleans. He had already figured out the buses. She couldn't get the one at two-thirty because she didn't let out school till three; so that meant she had to catch the one at seven o'clock. That meant she had to come to the road between six-thirty and quarter to seven. Six-thirty he went by in the car; Clamp Brown was out there and saw him. Clamp was courting Louise Ricard at the time and he was on his way to Baton Rouge to see her. He said Tee Bob went to the Three Star Club and turned around and came on back. Mary Agnes still wasn't out there, and he went up the road a piece. Not too far—he didn't want meet that bus. A few minutes later he was back. Mary Agnes was out there now; her and Clamp was standing there talking. When the car stopped and Clamp saw who it was he moved to one side.

Tee Bob didn't get out of the car, he just opened the door. Clamp said he couldn't hear everything Tee Bob was saying, but from what he could hear he knowed Tee Bob wasn't talking about how he felt about Mary Agnes. Clamp said he heard him saying something about Christmas play, something about firewood, something about heater, but nothing about how he felt about her.

When the bus came up, Clamp had to pass by Tee Bob to get on the bus. He said he wasn't too sure, but he do believe he heard Tee Bob call the girl's name just before the driver closed the door.

Confession

TEE BOB KEPT IT TO HIMSELF long as he could, then he had to tell it to somebody, and he told it to that redhead boy there of Clarence Caya, Jimmy Caya. Clarence Caya and his brothers owned a plantation on the other side of Bayonne, not far from Tainville. The place was no more than a small farm but they called it a plantation—just so people would think they was in the upper class. Tee Bob met Jimmy Caya at the university there in Baton Rouge, and they used to come home together on the weekends. Jimmy Caya would put Tee Bob off here at Samson, then he would go on to Bayonne to his people. Tee Bob told him 'bout the girl, Mary Agnes, couple weeks after Clamp saw them talking at the road. But he had seen her many more times since then. He was coming back here just about every day now, and every time he came home he went riding through the quarters. He would go all the way back in the field, then he would come back through the quarters just when she was letting out school. If she stayed in there awhile after all the children had gone home, Tee Bob would talk to somebody in the quarters till she came out. If she was already walking up the quarters when he came in from the field, he would run the horse to catch up with her. Then they would come up the quarters together. Him on the horse, her walking with the books and papers in her arms.

Everybody knowed about it now. The ones here in the quarters, the ones at the house up there, the ones on that river. From Bayonne to Baton Rouge they talked about it. "Reason he don't show more interest in Frank Major's daughter, Judy, there, he ain't sowed all his wild oats yet. From what I hear, he found something on his daddy's place. One of them high yellow from New Orleans almost white there." The talk went on from Bayonne to Baton Rouge, both sides of the river.

One day I came up on them standing at my gate. Tee Bob up there on the horse, Mary Agnes on the ground with them books and papers.

"How you feel, Jane?" Tee Bob said.

"Just like I felt a' hour ago, Tee Bob," I said.

He just sat there on that horse. He didn't want me standing there looking up at him.

"Thought you was in the field?" I said.

"I was," he said.

"Judy at that house," I said. She wasn't there, but I thought he had more business at his own house than he had in front of my gate.

He turned the horse away from the gate. He didn't say a thing to the girl. He wasn't supposed to tell her good-bye in front of me, just like he wasn't supposed to carry them papers and books through the quarters.

"What's going on, Mary Agnes?" I said. "Now, you can tell me it ain't none of my business if you want."

"Nothing's going on," she said.

"You sure?" I said. "Now, it ain't none of my business."

"Nothing's going on, Miss Jane," she said.

"I believe you," I said. "But I wanted to hear it from you."

"He ain't nothing but a child," she said. "A lonely boy."

"He's a man, Mary Agnes," I said. "And he's a Samson."

"I can't help it if he want ride through the quarters side me," she said. "I can't make him leave his own gate."

"What y'all talk about, Mary Agnes?" I said.

"Nothing much," she said. "School. Children. Wood. Christmas play."

"Don't y'all ever talk about you and him?" I asked her.

"No, ma'am," she said.

"Don't you know that's what he want talk about?" I said.

"I have no interest in that boy," she said.

"I believe you, but he got interest in you," I said.

"That's his fault," she said. "But I got no interest in men, black or white. I'm for these children here. That's why I left home."

"It's coming a time when he go'n tell you what he's interested in," I told her.

"I can handle Robert," she said.

"That's what you call him? Robert?"

"Yes, ma'am."

"And he don't say nothing?"

"He want me to call him Robert," she said. "I never thought about calling him nothing else."

"Never Mister?"

"In front of them children; never by myself. No, ma'am; never. I reckoned I would break down laughing first."

"And you think you can handle him?" I said.

"More than anything else in this world, Robert is decent," she said.

"Is this world decent, Mary Agnes?" I said.

"Robert is more human being than he is white man, Miss Jane," she said.

"And how long you think this world go'n let him stay like that?"

"Robert is good," she said. "That's why I don't fear walking with him. The day he get out of line I'll tell him he's too decent for that."

"And you think he'll listen?"

"Yes, ma'am, because he's decent," she said. "Some people do make it, Miss Jane."

"Some do, yes," I said. "But they happen to be the strong ones. And Tee

Bob is not one of them."

One day Miss Amma Dean asked me: "Jane, what's going on between Robert and that girl down there?"

"Nothing, Miss Amma Dean," I said.

"I can see them through my glasses," she said.

"I talked to her," I said. "Nothing's going on."

"I don't want him to think he can do that," Miss Amma Dean said.

Robert heard us talking and came back there in the kitchen where we was. "Do what?" he said.

Miss Amma Dean looked straight at him. "Hurt people," she said.

"Maybe she's leading him," Robert said. "You ever thought about that?"

"She don't go to Baton Rouge and pick him up every day," Miss Amma Dean said. "She don't come up here and saddle that horse."

"She don't have to," Robert said.

"You ought to know," Miss Amma Dean said.

"A few things," Robert said.

"I'm go'n talk to him again," Miss Amma Dean said.

"Leave him alone," Robert said.

"I don't want it," Miss Amma Dean said.

"You don't want what?" Robert said.

"No more Timmy Hendersons," Miss Amma Dean said.

"Whoa, Eve, don't touch that apple," Robert said.

"Eve or no Eve, he's my only child," Miss Amma Dean said.

"But not mine?" Robert said.

"No," Miss Amma Dean said, looking straight at him.

The next day she was on the back gallery watching Tee Bob through the spy glasses. She watched a little bit, then she let me watch some. I could see Tee Bob going back in the field. She took the glasses and kept them awhile, then she handed them back to me. I saw Tee Bob coming back, loping the horse. Miss Amma Dean took the glasses and I saw her working them. Tee Bob was in the quarters now, and she had to work them for the quarters because the quarters was so much closer than the fields. When she handed them to me I saw Mary Agnes and Tee Bob together; Tee Bob on the horse, Mary Agnes on the ground with them books and papers. I couldn't see them all the time—the houses was blocking them out; I had to see them when they was between the houses. Miss Amma Dean took the glasses and told me to go down there and tell Tee Bob Judy Major was here. When I came in the quarters they was standing in front of my gate.

"Judy at that house," I said.

"I don't care," Tee Bob said.

"What?" I said. "You want me to go back and tell your mama you sassed me, Tee Bob?"

"Yes," he said.

"You getting smart with me, Tee Bob?" I asked him.

He didn't say another word, he just turned his head and looked down at Mary Agnes. She told him good day and went in the yard. I was looking up there at him, and I could see how much he wanted her to stay out there. He watched her till she had gone in that house, and he didn't look at her the way you think a white man look at a nigger woman, either. He looked at her with love, and I mean the kind that's way deep inside of you. I have not seen too many men, of any color, look at women that way. After she had closed the door he looked down at me again. His face scared me. I saw in his face he was ready to go against his family, this whole world, for Mary Agnes.

When Miss Amma Dean asked me about them again the next day, I told her I thought Tee Bob loved that girl, but I was sure she didn't love him and she wasn't enticing him. And I thought the best thing was for them to get her away from here, and get her away from here quick as possible. Miss Amma Dean just stood there gazing at me. Then she patted her bosom. Then she drawed breath. Then she asked me how could I say such a thing. I should be ashamed of myself to even think Tee Bob could love a woman like that when I knowed all the time he was marrying Judy Major in the spring. To show how wrong I was she was giving a party—that Friday evening—for Tee Bob and Judy Major, and she was inviting all their friends.

The same day that she gived the party, Tee Bob told Jimmy Caya about Mary Agnes. They was coming from school that day, and Jimmy Caya was driving his family's car. He said he was driving fast because he had to go all the way to Bayonne before he came back to the party. It was raining that day. Had been raining steady for a couple days now. That kind you get in the grinding that can go on and on and on. He said Tee Bob had been sitting in the car fifteen, twenty minutes, and hadn't said a word all that time. He didn't say nothing either, because he thought Tee Bob had his mind on the party. Then all a sudden Tee Bob wanted him to stop the car because he had something to say. He asked Tee Bob couldn't they talk while he drove. Tee Bob said no. He asked Tee Bob didn't he want to hurry up and get home so he could change clothes for the party, it wasn't for him, it was for his mother.

He found a good place and pulled to the side, and that's when Tee Bob told him about the girl. Right there in front of him, in his own car, and that rain falling outside, Tee Bob told him he loved a nigger woman more than he loved his own life. He said at first he didn't think he had heard him right. He couldn't believe what he had heard. He knowed Tee Bob was seeing that woman every time he came home, but he thought just like everybody else did: Tee Bob was sowing his wild oats before he married Judy Major. He had never thought it went any further than that. So he told Tee Bob to repeat what he had said, and this time take it slow.

Tee Bob said: "I never told this to nobody else. Not even her. I'm telling it to you because you're my friend."

"I'm not that good a friend," he told him.

"Who else can I turn to?" Tee Bob said. "Who else will understand?"

"Nobody," Jimmy Caya said. "Me neither."

"Then who?" Tee Bob said.

Jimmy Caya said he couldn't control himself no longer, and he grabbed Tee Bob's coat and started shaking him. "Robert, Robert, Robert," he said. "Don't you know who you are? Don't you know what she is? Don't you know these things yet? At the university, and you don't know these things yet?

"That woman is a nigger, Robert. A nigger. She just look white. But Africa is in her veins, and that make her nigger, Robert."

But with all his shaking and screaming at him, he said Tee Bob acted like he wasn't hearing him.

"Robert," he told him. "Don't you listen in class? Ain't you heard him" (I forget that teacher's name, but I think he said Gamby) "over and over and over? You think she changed since then? She's the same woman, Robert. She know her duty, and all she expect from you is ride the horse down there. But that's far as she expect you to go. The rest is her duty, Robert. She knows that. He" (I'm almost sure he called that teacher Gamby) "told you it was like that then, and it's the same way now."

But he could see Tee Bob wasn't hearing him.

"Robert, you're my friend, and I won't allow it," he said. "I'll have her run off the place. I'll see to it they run her out of the State."

Tee Bob just sat there like he was not listening, or like he was thinking about something else.

"Listen, Robert," Jimmy Caya said. And that's when he told Tee Bob what everybody had always told him. From his daddy to his teacher had told him. "If you want her you go to that house and take her. If you want her at that school, make them children go out in the yard and wait. Take her in that ditch if you can't wait to get her home. But she's there for that and nothing else."

Jimmy Caya said he didn't see the lick coming. He didn't see it, because it came even before Tee Bob's face had time to change. He said Tee Bob couldn't 'a' stayed mad more than a second, because the next thing he saw Tee Bob was gazing down at his hand. The way a man will look at a gun after he's shot somebody. Like he wants to say, "Where did this come from? Who put it in my hand? How could I ever do that?" Tee Bob gazed at his hand like somebody or something else had raised it.

I was at the house when they got there. Miss Amma Dean had brought Ethel up there to serve the drinks and the sandwiches, and she had asked me to stay there to make coffee. I was back in the kitchen when Tee Bob and Jimmy Caya came in. They spoke to some of the people who had got there already, then they went in the library. Robert had a bottle of whiskey in there; Tee Bob and Jimmy Caya poured up something to drink. Jimmy Caya stayed in there half an hour, then he left for Bayonne. He was going home and change clothes, then he was coming back. He said just before he walked out of the library, Tee Bob raised his glass to him. He said he thought Tee Bob was just apologizing for hitting him in the ear. He didn't know Tee Bob was telling him good-bye.

Robert and Mary

WHEN TEE BOB HEARD Judy Major and her people coming in the house, he came out of the library and headed for the door. Miss Amma Dean asked him where he thought he was going, didn't he see Judy there taking off her coat? But he was outside even before she got through talking.

Mary Agnes was packing her suitcase when she heard him knock at the door. She didn't know who it was; she wasn't even sure somebody had knocked. Then she heard it again. She thought it was Clamp, so she went to the door to tell him she'd be ready in a second. But when she opened the door she saw Tee Bob standing there. His face red and swole—his eyes wild, strange. She said he scared her for a second. Not because she thought he would do her anything. She thought he was sick or had done something wrong and had come to her for help. She asked him what's the matter. He said he had to talk to her. She asked him if he was sick. He told her he just had to talk to her. Then he pushed his way in the house. When he passed her she could tell he had been drinking.

She turned from the door, but she left the door wide open. In case somebody passed and saw that car out there, she wanted them to see that door open, too. Tee Bob went to the bed and sat down. Mary Agnes still thought he was in some kind of trouble and had come to her for help.

"Tell me what's the matter," she said. "I have to hurry and leave."

He just sat there looking at her. His face all red and swole. She could tell he wanted to say something, but he didn't know how she was go'n answer.

"Something the matter?" she asked him.

She talked to him like she talked to a brother or a first cousin. She had always looked at him like that: like he was more like her; not like he was a white man. She thought he looked at her that same way. That's why she never worried about him riding there side her. She never thought he would try anything; and if he did, she always thought she would be able to make him understand.

Now he told her why he had come there. He said it quick, looking straight at her. He wouldn't stop for breath. He said it all before she had a chance to answer.

She didn't say nothing, but she started shaking her head from the moment he started talking. But he wouldn't stop. He swore to God he meant every word. He would give her the Samson name tonight. They could go to New Orleans and get married. Nobody there could tell she was colored.

"You can't give me something you don't own yourself, Robert," she told him.

"I own my own name," he said.

"You don't even own that," she said. "They gived you that, they can take that from you."

"Come here and sit down," he said.

"I want you to leave, and I want you to leave now," she said.

"Come here and sit down, Mary Agnes," he said.

The door was still open; she went to the bed where he was. He took her hands and pulled her down side him. His face was red and swole; his hands burning up. She could tell he had drank too much. She knowed he wouldn't be doing this if he hadn't. He told her he had talked to Jimmy Caya about her; had told him how much he loved her. She started shaking her head again.

"I had to tell somebody," he said.

She shook her head.

"He said you was a nigger," he said. "I was suppose to look at you like you look at a nigger. Do to you what you suppose to do to a nigger. You're not a nigger, are you, Mary Agnes?"

She said she could tell he had drank too much. Now she thought he was losing his mind.

"Jimmy is right," she said to him. But she said it quiet. The way you talk to a child.

"Don't say that," he screamed at her. But the next second he was quiet, too quiet. "Don't say that. Don't say that."

"Go home, Robert," she told him. She said it quiet, too. Like you talk to a child.

"I want you in the car," he said.

"I can't get in that car, Robert," she said. "Don't you know that?" She was talking to him like you talk to a child. "That's why you never asked me to get in there before, Robert. That's why you never asked me to get on the horse with you."

"I want you in the car now," he said.

"I want you to leave, Robert," she said, quiet. Just like you talk to a child.

"You don't understand," he said. "I don't have no place to go. That's why

I hit him. That's why I left that house. I don't have no where to go—but to your bosom. That's what I'm trying to say."

"We can't have nothing together, Robert," she told him.

"If you say yes," he said. "That's all you got to say."

"I can't say that," she said.

She got up and started packing her suitcase. He just sat there watching her—his mind, she said, far, far off. Then he noticed her.

"Where you think you're going, Mary Agnes?" he asked.

"New Orleans," she said.

"You're not leaving from here, Mary Agnes," he said. "I don't have nothing if you go."

She went on packing. When she got through she picked up the suitcase and turned toward the door. He was standing there now. She came toward the door. Still didn't think he could do her anything—too decent for that.

Clamp Brown was headed to the front in his black raincoat and his rubber boots. Going to Baton Rouge to see that Ricard girl. But he wasn't thinking about her right now, he was thinking about Miss LeFabre. He liked to be with Miss LeFabre even if he didn't feel too comfortable with her all the time. She was a quiet, beautiful lady. She had a good quiet smile; a smile, like she didn't want to smile, but she had to at the crazy things that went on round her all the time. She talked nice and quiet and talked to anybody. He liked to travel on the bus far as Baton Rouge with her. He didn't feel too good sitting right there side her all the time, but she always made you feel just a little bit better than you thought you could feel 'round a teacher. He had told her about Louise Ricard and she had even written couple letters for him. That's why he looked for her every Friday evening.

Clamp said he saw Tee Bob running out my yard. Running and stumbling. He had seen the car from way down the quarters, but he thought it was just somebody visiting me. That's why he didn't recognize Tee Bob at first. That's why he thought it was Joe Scott's boy, Lester. He knowed Lester had tried to court the girl and I had run him way from there before. He hollered: "Lester? Hey, boy, Miss Jane after you?" Tee Bob kept running and stumbling. Then he clambed through the fence and ran 'cross Samson yard. Now Clamp knowed it wasn't Lester. He recognized the car now, and he knowed it was Tee Bob. But what was Tee Bob running from? Even if he had killed somebody, and he had done it here at Samson, he wouldn't need to run. Clamp went by the car to get a better look. He wanted to make sure it was Tee Bob. Not that he was go'n ever say nothing 'bout it. He just wanted to make sure it was Tee Bob, because he still couldn't see no reason for Tee Bob to run from nothing here on the place. After Tee Bob had gone behind the trees in Samson yard, Clamp looked toward my house again. Mary Agnes door was still wide open.

Clamp started calling Mary Agnes from out there in the road. Not loud. Even if she was standing in the door and wasn't looking straight at him she wouldn't 'a' heard a word he was saying. He was standing out there in the road calling her the way you call somebody in a dark room when you know you scared.

When she didn't answer him, he came in the yard. He told her he knowed he had no business in that yard, with that Samson car parked before the gate and Tee Bob running away from that house. Not just in the yard, but he had no business even passing by here this time of day. If he had to see Louise Ricard he should 'a' took that back road or walked that railroad track till he got to Morgan and waved that bus down from back there.

He came up on the gallery, looking at her door; but he went to my door and knocked, calling my name. Her he wanted, her door wide open, mine shut tight, but he knocked on my door, calling my name. "Miss Jane? Miss Jane? You in there, Miss Jane?" Calling me like somebody in a dark room knowing all the time he was scared.

When I didn't answer him, he looked toward her door, but he knocked on my door again. This time he called her name. No louder than he had called it out there in the road, no louder than he had called my name; but her name, now; knocking on my door. She didn't answer him. Now he went toward the door, knocking quiet long the wall, calling her name. When he got to the door it was so dark in the room he had time to call her name two more times before he saw her laying there on the floor.

He turned and screamed, "Ida? Ida? Ida?" He fell when he jumped off the gallery. He got up running toward Joe Simon's house still calling Ida. Joe said he heard Clamp calling his wife's name before Clamp reached the gate, so he was already on the gallery when Clamp ran in the yard. He said Clamp slipped and almost fell just before he reached the gallery, and he said to himself, "That fool go'n break his neck before he tell me what he's running from."

"Tell Ida run," Clamp said.

"For what?" Joe Simon said.

"That girl been ravished," he said.

"Bea in here," Joe said. "What girl?"

"Not Bea," Clamp said. "The teacher. I think it was—"

Joe Simon said he had seen that car parked in front of my door while Clamp was still running in the yard, so now he stopped him.

"And Ida go'n get in that?" he said. "Get away from here. I don't even know you said it. And if I was you I'd go on to Baton Rouge and play like I didn't say it, either."

"I'm going," Ida said, behind him.

"You ain't going nowhere," Joe said. "I'm the man of this house. If he hadn't done it, somebody else had to do it. Playing like she Miss high-class."

"Come on, Clamp," Ida said.

"You don't hear good?" Joe Simon said. "I told you to stay here."

"Go tell that house," Ida said.

"Not me," Clamp said. "I done told enough people."

"Tell Miss Jane," Ida said. "Knock on that back door, she sitting back there in the kitchen. Let her tell them."

"Can't one of them children go?" Clamp said. "Put a raincoat on Jocko. He can use mine. Here, Jocko. Run."

"You going," Ida said, "She ain't never wrote no love letter for Jocko."

"And I'll skin him if she do," Joe Simon said.

"Come on here, Clamp," Ida said.

Ida said when she got back to my house she had to stand in the door till her eyes got used to the dark. Then she saw the girl on the floor. She wasn't moving or making a sound, and Ida thought she might be dead. But after she went in and knelt down side her she saw her crying. Ida called her, but she wouldn't answer. Ida said she called again; she still wouldn't answer. Just laying there crying quiet—her head turned toward the wall. Ida put her arms round the girl and helped her to the bed. She said after she had pulled the covers up over her, something made her look toward the door again. Clamp was still there. That raincoat dripping water just inside the room.

"You been already?" she asked him.

"I want Jocko to go with me."

That's when Ida screamed. She said she knowed she had no business screaming, with that girl laying there hurt. But what else could she do, when she was doing all she could, and still couldn't get men like Clamp and her husband to understand.

"Just once," she screamed. Then she said it quiet—pleading with him. "Just once. Lord, just once before I die."

He moved back—scared of her now. But still he didn't leave. Just out of the door so she couldn't see him—but she knowed he was still out there. Out there in that wind and rain, looking up and down the quarters for somebody to go with him to Samson house.

Samson House

I WAS SITTING IN THE KITCHEN having a cup of coffee with Jules Raynard when Tee Bob came back to that house. Like I have said, Jules Raynard was Tee Bob's parrain. Big man with snow-white hair and a red red face. Breathe loud all the time. Since I knowed him, and that had been years and years, always had that problem breathing. Me and Jules Raynard talked every time he came to that house. Sometimes just the two of us at that house, sitting back there in the kitchen drinking coffee and talking. No, not sitting at the table at the same time. He always let me sit at the table and he sat in a chair by the door. Or if it was cold I might sit in a chair by the stove and he would sit at the table. That day I was sitting at the table with my coffee, he was over by the icebox with his cup.

Ethel came back there and told me Tee Bob had run in the house wet and locked himself up in the library. After she went back to the front I felt Jules Raynard looking at me. He had been talking about Tee Bob and the girl just a few minutes before that. He said about a week ago he had spoke to Tee Bob about Mary Agnes. Like everybody else 'round there he knowed Tee Bob had been seeing the girl a lot, and he asked him what it meant. Tee Bob wouldn't answer him. He said he told Tee Bob from looks the girl could easily pass for white. She was beautiful, and any man in his right mind could fall in love with her, and many of them probably was. But the girl wasn't white, he told Tee Bob, and love for her, at least in the open, was impossible. Jules Raynard said that to me just minutes before Ethel came back in the kitchen. After she went back to the front I could feel him looking at me again.

"Did that car come back?" he said.

"I didn't hear it."

He probably would 'a' got up and looked out the door, but every move Jules Raynard made was an effort on his part. He sat there and sipped from his coffee.

Ethel came back a little while later.

"Still in there," she said. "Knock, knock. But he won't answer."

"What's the rest of them doing up there?" Jules asked her.

"Making like nothing's going on," Ethel said.

"Anything going on?" Jules asked her.

"I ain't got nothing do with it," Ethel said. "Just say he come here wet and locked himself up."

She filled up the glasses and took them back to the front. Jules watched her till she had gone in the other room, then he looked at me. But neither of us had anything to say.

Ethel came back again. Looking at me, shaking her head. Because she was looking at me, not at Jules, he wasn't suppose to be able to see her. "Won't answer," she whispered.

She took a tray of sandwiches to the front. Soon as everybody had got one she came back.

"I don't like this," she said. She wasn't talking to me, now, she was talking to herself.

"Go home then," Jules said.

"Raining too hard out there," she said.

"Then shut up," he said.

She went back to the front. But I knowed she hadn't gone all the way. She was standing in the hall between the kitchen and the parlor.

Jules looked toward the screen door and raised his head like he was listening to something. Then he turned his head toward the hall.

"Say there, gal?" he said.

Ethel came back in the kitchen. "Yes, sir?"

"Peep out that door there."

Ethel went to the door and cracked it open, and I could feel the chill come in.

"Clamp out there hollering," she said. She hollered back: "What you want?"

With that door open, I could hear him now. "Hoa, Miss Jane? Hoa, Miss Jane?"

"What you want, Clamp?" Ethel hollered.

"Hoa, Miss Jane?" he hollered. "Hoa, Miss Jane?"

"Talking to that loon like talking to that rain," Ethel said. "What you want, Clamp?"

"Tell Miss Jane come see."

"Tell him come in here," Jules said.

"Miss Jane say you must think she crazy coming out there in all that rain. Say you come in here."

I heard him coming up the steps and I heard him scraping his boots on the back gallery and kicking the mud on the ground. He knocked.

"Now, what you knocking for, loon?" Ethel said. "Can't you see I'm holding this door open?"

"Miss Jane in there?" he asked.

"Sitting at that table."

"Tell her come see."

"Boy, come on in here," Ethel said.

He came in with that rubber hat in his hand. His raincoat and them boots shining wet. He looked at Jules sitting over there by the icebox and I could see he was scared. He turned to me with his back to Jules, but he still didn't say nothing.

"Speak, boy," Jules said.

"That girl," Clamp said to me. "Been ravished."

"What girl?" Jules said. "Speak, boy."

But we all knowed what girl before Clamp said it. Ethel screamed. Jules told her to be quiet. I got up. I was coming home to look after the girl, but Jules told me to find Miss Amma Dean and be careful what I said.

When I came to the front, they was all standing there with them glasses and sandwiches. Trying to act like nothing was going on—but you felt it the moment you came in that room. Miss Amma Dean was standing near the library. Maybe she had just knocked, maybe she was just getting ready to knock again. When I spoke to her she jecked around like she expected bad news.

"Kitchen," I said.

Any other time she would 'a' said, "Kitchen for what?" but she didn't say a word. She moved so fast I couldn't keep up with her.

I heard Jules saying: "That door still locked?"

I don't think she answered him. I know she was looking at Clamp when I got back there. Clamp was standing there with that water dripping off that raincoat down on the floor. He was trying to hide the water behind him, but no matter where he moved it dripped some more. She didn't ask Clamp why he was there, she knowed he was the one who had brought word. She turned to go back to the front, but Robert was already headed back that way. They looked at each other, then he moved to the door and looked at Clamp. Clamp wanted to hide that water now for sure.

"Get him out of there," Jules said to Robert.

Robert didn't look at Jules, he was still looking at Clamp. But he didn't say a word. Looking like he was trying to get things together for himself. Then he whirled—Miss Amma Dean no more than a step behind him. Even in the hall, before she even got to the parlor, she was calling Tee Bob: "Robert? Robert? Robert?"

I went go get my coat, but Jules stopped me again.

"Nothing you can do down there," he said. "Somebody see you leaving and figure what happen, this whole thing can blow up."

"Anybody down there with her?" I asked Clamp

"Ida," he said.

"Anybody else know?"

"Joe and them children," he said.

"Nobody else?"

"No, ma'am."

We could hear Robert beating on the library door and calling Tee Bob. Then we could hear him beating louder and cussing. Then it would get quiet a second while he listened. In the time he was listening, we could hear Miss Amma Dean calling quietly.

"Go find that axe," Jules said to Clamp. "And you stay here," he said to Ethel. "Run out of here screaming and this whole thing blow up. And you, too," he said to me. "Go find that axe," he said to Clamp. "Go get in a corner somewhere," he said to Ethel. "Just don't run out of here."

He went out of the kitchen breathing hard. He hadn't got half way up the hall before Ethel and Clamp shot out of there, headed for home. I started to follow them, because I thought that girl might need me. But Clamp said Ida was there, and I figured she could do anything I could do and could probably do it better.

I went outside to get the axe. It was still raining, and when I came back in the house my dress and scarf was good and wet. Coming up the hall I could hear Robert slamming his shoulder against that door. When Jules saw me with the axe he figured out what had happened, and he took the axe from me and handed it to Robert. All the people moved back when Robert started swinging the axe at the door. He was swinging it blade first. He wasn't aiming to break the door in, he wanted to chop it down now. Every time he hit the door the water from the axe sprayed the people in front and they had to move further back. The sound of the axe against the door went like thunder through that old house. Pictures of the old people shook on every wall. A looking-glass fell and scattered all over the floor. Women screamed. That gal, Judy Major, almost knocked her daddy over getting in his arms. But Robert went on. Miss Amma Dean over to the side, tapping the wall and calling Tee Bob's name so quiet I doubt if even she could hear it. But Robert went on. His face wasn't sad, scared, worried—just plain hard. I kept thinking, "Lord, Lord, Lord, what will it take to change this man? Don't he know that's his boy in there? Do he know at all what he go'n find when he open that door?"

After he had chopped a hole big enough for his hand to go through, he unlatched the door from inside; then he had to throw his shoulder against it to clear away the things Tee Bob had stack there. Tee Bob was sitting in the high back chair facing the window. He was sitting there like he was just looking out of the window. Then somebody screamed. I looked down and saw the dirk on the floor. No, not a dirk, a letter opener. The one Paul Samson had used at the capital there in Baton Rouge.

Robert hollered for the women to get out, but the people didn't go out, they went in, and I went in with them. And that's how I saw when Jules Raynard snatched the letter up off the table and put it in his pocket. Everywhere he turned from then on I had my eyes on him. I figured if it was something bad he was go'n tear it up. But he didn't tear it up, he waited till most of the people had gone, then he called Miss Amma Dean to another room. After she read the letter she sent for Robert. Everybody else was gone now. They left quietly, not saying a word. When they asked for their coat and umbrellas, they asked for them in a whisper. The cars even left the yard quietly. Half hour after Robert got that door opened, nobody was left but him and Miss Amma Dean, me and Jules Raynard. They was in another room, I was in the library with Tee Bob. We had covered him over with a sheet. The sheet had a red spot in the middle the size of a saucer. Everything else was just like we found them. Even the dirk—the letter opener—was still on the floor.

Jules Raynard came out the other room, and I heard him telephoning the sheriff's office. Then he came in the library where I was.

"What was in that letter, Mr. Raynard?" I asked him.

"What letter?" he said.

"The one you snatched off that table over there."

"You saw then?" he said.

"I saw."

"To his mother," Jules Raynard said, looking down at the sheet. "He had to find peace. He couldn't find it here."

"And the girl?" I said.

"Innocent," Jules Raynard said, looking down at the sheet—not at me.

"Who go'n believe that?" I asked him.

"I believe it," he said, looking at the sheet all the time.

Robert and Miss Amma Dean came in the library. Miss Amma Dean pulled the sheet from Tee Bob's face and looked down at him. She stood there so long Jules Raynard had to pull her away and lead her to a chair against the wall. I covered Tee Bob's face again. Robert hadn't moved. He didn't know what to do, or what to say. He wasn't looking at Miss Amma Dean or Tee Bob; just standing there like he was still trying to figure out something.

Me and Jules Raynard was standing in the parlor when we heard the car come in the yard. It came in too fast and stopped too quick, so we knowed it wasn't the sheriff. The person ran up on the gallery and knocked on the door loud and quick. By the time Jules got to the door he had knocked two or three more times.

"What do you want?" Jules asked, when he opened the door.

Jimmy Caya didn't answer Jules. He pushed right by him and came inside. He saw me standing there, but he went right by me. When he got to the library door he saw Robert and Miss Amma Dean, then he stopped. Now he went in quietly.

Jules Raynard came back toward the library. I could tell from the way he looked he didn't like Jimmy Caya there. He never did like the Cayas. They was just rednecks who had come up. He had even warned Tee Bob against Jimmy Caya. I could see in his face now how he didn't want him there.

"Is that my friend?" Jimmy said in the library. "Is that Robert?"

Miss Amma Dean was sitting in the chair and Robert was standing by the chair, but neither of them answered Jimmy Caya. Maybe they didn't even hear him at first. Miss Amma Dean just gazed at that sheet like she couldn't look nowhere else. Robert was standing side her like he was still waiting for something to happen.

"I warned him," Jimmy Caya said. "I warned him 'bout her."

Jules Raynard stood in the library door looking straight at Jimmy Caya. I could see in his face how much he hated him.

"He told me she wouldn't let him alone," Jimmy Caya said. "He told me that no later than today. Poor Robert. Now look at him."

Jules Raynard turned red just standing there. But he didn't say a thing till Robert looked at the boy. Then he knowed he had to move. But even before he got in the room, Robert had turned. Jules moved back in the door. His frame almost took up the whole door.

"Get out the way," Robert said.

"No, you don't," Jules said.

"Do I have to walk over you?" Robert said.

"Yes," Jules said. "And soon as Guidry get here I'll accuse you of murder. Trash will be trash anywhere, anytime, but me and you, we know better."

"Only thing I know, I should 'a' done it before now," Robert said.

"I ain't lying to you," Jules said. "I'll tell sure as I'm standing here."

"Do you know who's in that chair?" Robert said.

"I know who's in that chair," Jules Raynard said. "And I know he did it himself. And I know why he did it."

"She did it," Jimmy Caya said. "That nigger wench did it."

"Shut up," Jules told him.

"What?" he said.

"You killed him," Jules said.

"What?" Jimmy Caya said. "Robert was my best friend."

"But he wrote a letter," Jules said, looking at Robert, not at Jimmy Caya.

"What letter?" Jimmy Caya said. "What you trying to say, old man?"

"And we know that letter is true, don't we, Robert?" Jules Raynard said. "Because we know what everybody else know in this parish, and that's he loved her. And because she couldn't love him back, because she knowed better, he killed himself. We know that, don't we, Robert?"

"What's going on here?" Jimmy Caya said.

"Something your kind could never understand," Jules Raynard told him.

Jimmy Caya turned to Robert. "Mr. Robert?" he said. "Mr. Robert? Robert was my friend—my best friend. I loved Robert."

"Well?" Jules Raynard said.

"Nobody pay?" Robert said.

"Yes, you and Amma Dean," Jules Raynard said. "And everybody else who loved him."

"And that woman?" Robert said.

"Kill her because she wouldn't run away with him?" Jules Raynard said. "That's what you want kill her for? That's what you want put her in the pen for?"

"I said nothing 'bout no pen," Robert said.

"Then walk over me and do it, Robert," Jules Raynard said. "And I'll accuse you of murder sure as I'm born to die. Yes, I stood next to you when you married Amma Dean; yes, I christened Robert. Yes, I carried one handle of

Mr. Paul's coffin; one handle of Clarence's. But don't think for a moment I won't tell Guidry this was plain cold-blooded murder. And if Guidry won't do nothing 'bout it I'll go somewhere else. I'll tell what was in that letter, Robert."

Robert knowed Jules meant what he said. For a moment he just stood there facing him. No, not to tell him to get out. Robert wouldn't 'a' dared tell Jules Raynard to leave that house. Jules Raynard was not a kin, but he was like a second father there. He had been coming to that house all his life. Robert knowed this. Even when he felt he ought to do something about Tee Bob's death, he knowed he couldn't walk over Jules Raynard to do it. He looked at Miss Amma Dean. Whatever she said, that's what he was go'n do. But she was just sitting there with her head bowed. Like she hadn't even heard them talking. Robert turned around quickly and went toward the window. Now, he just stood there looking out at the rain.

Jules Raynard looked at Jimmy Caya. "Come out here," he said. "You foul the air in there."

Jimmy Caya looked at Robert. "Mr. Robert?" he said. Robert looked out of the window. Jimmy Caya looked at Miss Amma Dean. "Miss Amma Dean?" he said. She kept her head bowed. "Miss Amma Dean, I loved Robert. The Lord knows I loved Robert." But she didn't look up. He looked at Robert again. But Robert still looked out of the window. He looked at the sheet that covered Tee Bob. He put his hand on Tee Bob's shoulder, then he came toward the door. Jules Raynard grabbed him in the collar and jecked him out in the parlor.

"You go'n tell me what went on today or you go'n tell Guidry," he said.

He held him with one hand and slapped him hard cross the face. Then he pushed him down in a chair. Jimmy Caya sat there covering his face and crying.

"Bring me a chair," Jules said to me.

I brought him the chair. He sat in it facing Jimmy Caya.

"Well?" he said.

"I didn't tell him nothing," Jimmy Caya said, crying.

"No?" Jules said.

Jimmy Caya cried, but didn't say nothing else. Jules grabbed him again.

"No more than the rules," he said, flinching back from Jules's hand that was already in the air.

Jules turned him loose. "Explain them rules to me," he said.

"She's there for his pleasure, for nothing else," Jimmy Caya said.

"You told him more than that," Jules said. "Lot more. And you go'n tell it to me or you go'n tell it to Guidry. Well?"

"I didn't kill him by myself," Jimmy Caya said. "We all killed him."

"You getting warm," Jules said.

"Robert was my friend," Jimmy Caya said. "I loved Robert. I loved him."

He looked at Jules, crying. "I loved Robert. Can't you understand nothing? I loved Robert."

"Me or Guidry?" Jules said.

"I didn't tell him no more than what my daddy told me," Jimmy Caya said. "What my daddy's daddy told him. What Mr. Paul told Mr. Robert. What Mr. Paul's daddy told him. What your daddy told you. No more than the rules we been living by ever since we been here."

"That's all well and good," Jules said. "But what did you tell Robert today, or are you waiting for Guidry? Guidry don't play, remember. And right now he owe me a big big favor."

"Robert was my best, my only friend," Jimmy Caya said.

"Well, I guess you want to talk to Guidry," Jules said. "And I warn you, that letter got your name everywhere."

Robert came out the library and nodded for me to go in there. When I came in, Miss Amma Dean got up from her chair and went to look at Tee Bob again. Then she knelt down on the floor by his chair. I got down on my knees side her, and I said my prayers quietly to myself.

Sam Guidry showed up not too long after that. A tall, slim man. Dressed in a blue serge suit and a raincoat. The coat was wet, and it shined in the light. Guidry came in very quiet, with his hat in his hand. Miss Amma Dean was sitting in a chair when he came in; I was sitting in another chair 'cross from her. After Guidry spoke to her, he raised the sheet and looked at Tee Bob. Not more than a few seconds, then he pulled the sheet back over his face. When he saw the letter opener on the floor, he looked at me. He had a hard and brutal face. He didn't ask you for information, he told you he wanted it. I just glanced down at the floor. He got a piece of paper and picked up the letter opener, then he wrapped it up in a handkerchief and put it in his pocket. He went back out, and I heard him and Jules talking. Next thing I heard him say was, "Well?"

Sam Guidry looked at black people and white people in two different ways, but he must 'a' looked at Jimmy Caya the way he looked at black people, because Jimmy Caya started talking and wouldn't stop. After they heard his story, they told him to go on home. Then Jules and Sam Guidry came on down the quarters to talk to the girl. Ida was still there. They told Ida to go in my side of the house while they asked the girl some questions. Ida said with them big cracks in the wall, they might as well had let her stay in there because she could hear everything anyhow. She said when she heard that Tee Bob had took his life she had to hurry and cover her mouth to keep from screaming. But the girl didn't make a sound. If she did, it wasn't loud enough for Ida to hear. Ida said even when Sam Guidry told her her life depended on what she had to say, she still wouldn't say anything to him. He told her he wasn't go'n beg her, he had ways to make her talk. She still didn't say a word. Ida said it got quiet in there, and she wondered what they was doing. She didn't hear any scuffling, so they couldn't be hurting the girl. Maybe they was just waiting for her to start. Ida waited too. Then she heard a slap. She heard Jules Raynard say: "That won't help." Sam Guidry said: "It worked before." It was quiet again. Then Jules Raynard's voice, gentle, like a father talking to his child. He told the girl about the letter and she wasn't accused of nothing. Tee Bob had said over and over she was innocent of everything. And it was this, nothing else, that made her tell them what had happened. Ida heard it all from the other side. She had squatted down on the floor, with her ear to the wall, and she heard every word the girl said. She said when Mary Agnes got through talking, Guidry said: "I want know one thing—and this better be the true. Did he rape you?"

"No, sir," the girl said. "When I started by him, he grabbed me and swung me back 'cross the room. I struck my back against the wall and fell. I was almost out, and I saw him standing there over me. He looked scared. Then he turned and ran out the house. I heard Clamp calling me, and I tried to answer him, but I couldn't. Next thing I knowed, Ida was helping me to bed. But, no, sir, he didn't do that. Robert was too decent for that."

"Then what he had to go and do a fool thing like that for?" Guidry said.

Ida said it was quiet in there a moment, then she heard Jules Raynard telling the girl not to ever say a word about this ever again. And they wanted her to get away from here tonight. He asked her if she had any money. She said she had some. He told her he wanted her to leave for New Orleans tonight, and he wanted her to leave New Orleans soon as she could. He told her not to tell nobody where she was going, not even him. Then he called Ida back 'round the other side. He told Ida to go find somebody with a car and tell him—he didn't care who—to take this girl to New Orleans, and take her there now.

Jules Raynard and Sam Guidry came back to the house and talked to Robert and Miss Amma Dean. I didn't hear what they had to say, but the next day the newspapers said they had no idea why young Robert Samson of Samson, Luzana had taken his own life. The newspapers said everybody thought he was so happy, knowing in a few weeks that he was go'n be the husband of the beautiful and cultured Judy Major of Bayonne, Luzana. Sheriff Sam Guidry was invessagating the matter, the newspapers said.

The coroner came and took Tee Bob away while I was still at the house. Then Jules Raynard brought me on home. When he stopped before my gate I started to get out the car, but I looked at him again.

"You a good man, Mr. Raynard," I told him.

"Because I didn't let them kill her?" he said, over his shoulder.

"Yes, sir."

"We caused one death already this evening," he said. I sat in the back seat looking at him; he was looking out at the rain. "Jimmy was right," he said.

"We all killed him. We tried to make him follow a set of rules our people gived us long ago. But these rules just ain't old enough, Jane."

"I don't understand you, Mr. Raynard," I said.

"Somewhere in the past, Jane," he said. "Way, way back, men like Robert could love women like Mary Agnes. But somewhere along the way somebody wrote a new set of rules condemning all that. I had to live by them, Robert at that house now had to live by them, and Clarence Caya had to live by them. Clarence Caya told Jimmy to live by them, and Jimmy obeyed. But Tee Bob couldn't obey. That's why we got rid of him. All us. Me, you, the girl—all us."

"Wait," I said. "Me?"

He looked back over his shoulder.

"You, Jane," he said.

"All right, lets say I'm in there," I said. "Where I fit in, I don't know, but let's say I'm in there. But the girl: you mean she was leading him on all this time, then at the end she backed down?"

"It wasn't nothing like that," he said. "She led him on for just a second. And maybe not that long. And even then she didn't have control over herself."

"Who told you this?"

"Nobody," he said. "If she had said it, Guidry would 'a' put her in jail for the rest of her life. If Tee Bob had put it in that letter, Robert wouldn't 'a' waited for Guidry to put her in jail; he would 'a' broke her neck with his bare hands. Nobody told me—but it happened. Sure as I'm sitting here, it happened.

"When he came to the house, he poured his soul out to her. He wanted to put her in that car, take her away from here, and never see none of us again. She was the only thing that meant a thing in this world to him. But instead of her falling in his arms, she told him the same thing Jimmy Caya had told him earlier. She was a nigger, he was white, and they couldn't have nothing together. He couldn't understand that, he thought love was much stronger than that one drop of African blood. But she knowed better. She knowed the rules. She was just a few years older than him in age, but hundreds of years wiser.

"But no matter what she said, he kept telling her love was everything. She gave up trying to talk to him; she got her suitcase and started for the door. That's when he grabbed her and swung her back. The weight of the suitcase slammed her 'gainst the wall. Now he was standing over her. To carry her to that car? To choke her? To rape her?—I don't know. But he was standing close enough to see something in her face. (No, he didn't say it, because Robert would 'a' come down here and killed her if he had. And if she had said it, Guidry would 'a' slammed her in jail for the rest of her life.) While he was standing there over her she invited him down there on the floor. Because—"

"But ain't this specalatin?" I said.

"It would be specalatin if two white people was sitting here talking," Jules Raynard said, looking round. But he couldn't look round too far; his weight didn't allow that.

"But it's us?" I said.

"And that makes it gospel truth," he said.

"Then what happened?" I said, sitting back there in the back seat.

"In the flash when her head and back hit the wall, something happened to her," he said. "The past and the present got all mixed up. That stiff proudness left. Making up for the past left. She *was* the past now. She was grandma now, and he was that Creole gentleman. She was Verda now, and he was Robert. It showed in her face. It showed in the way she laid down there on the floor. Helpless; waiting. She knowed how she looked to him, but she couldn't do nothing about it. But when he saw it he ran away from there. Because now he thought maybe the white man was God—like Jimmy Caya had said. Maybe the white man did have power that he, himself, didn't know before now. He ran and ran, stumbling and falling: like a hurt animal. Then he was home. Home. Home. Home. Now he tried to forget what he had seen on the floor back there. But nothing in that library was go'n let him forget. Too many books on slavery in that room; too many books on history in there. The sound of his grandfather talking to his daddy and his uncle come out every wall; the sound of all of them talking to him come from everywhere at once. Then there was Jimmy Caya's voice still fresh in his ear.

"He saw grandpa's letter opener. He picked it up. He laid it back down—but close enough to reach any time he needed it. He got paper and started writing. He wanted to run away from here. That was his first thought—get away from here. 'Mama, I don't know what to do. I must go somewhere where I can find peace. Then maybe later.'

"Then he heard Robert beating on the door and hollering at him. 'When you come to me, Mama, I won't be here. Forgive me. I love you.'"

Jules Raynard pulled out his pocket handkerchief and wiped his face and neck.

"But seeing her on the floor like that just hurried it up," he said.

"He was bound to kill himself anyhow?"

"One day. He had to. For our sins."

"Poor Tee Bob."

"No. Poor us," Jules Raynard said.

I opened the car door and got out.

"Good night, Mr. Raynard," I said.

"Good night, Jane."

BOOK IV

The Quarters

PEOPLE'S ALWAYS LOOKING for somebody to come lead them. Go to the Old Testament; go to the New. They did it in slavery; after the war they did it; they did it in the hard times that people want call Reconstruction; they did it in the Depression—another hard times; and they doing it now. They have always done it—and the Lord has always obliged in some way or another.

Anytime a child is born, the old people look in his face and ask him if he's the One. No, they don't say it out loud like I'm saying it to you now. Maybe they don't say it at all; maybe they just feel it—but feel it they do. "You the One?" I'm sure Lena asked Jimmy that when she first held him in her arms. "You the One, Jimmy? You the One?"

He was born a little bit farther down the quarters. Shirley Aaron was his mama's name—but I don't need to tell you who his daddy was. That don't matter—and, yes, it do. Because if his daddy had been there the cross wouldn't 'a' been nearly so heavy. Oh, heavy it would 'a' been—it had to be—because we needed him to carry part our cross; but the daddy, if he had been there, would 'a' been able to give him some help. But he didn't have a daddy to help him. The daddy had done what they told him a hundred years before to do, and he had forgot it just like a hundred years ago they had told him to forget. So it don't matter who his daddy was, because you got some out there right now who will tell you his daddy was somebody else. Oh, sure, they all know who he was, but still they'll argue and say he was somebody else.

Lena Washington was his aunt, his great aunt, his mama's daddy sister; and it was Lena who sent Sappho up the quarters to get me because it wasn't time to go get Selina from Morgan. It was in the winter—grinding—and it was me, Jane Pittman, who helped him into this world. When I took him 'round the other side and handed him to Lena she was sitting at the fire crying. That's why I'm sure she asked him if he was the One. No daddy, and soon will be no mama, because mama was go'n leave for the city to work like all the other young people was doing—I'm sure Lena asked him if he was the One.

Lena was the first one to ask him if he was the One, then we all started wondering if he was the One. That was long long before he had any idea what we wanted out of him. Because, you see, we started wondering about him when he was five or six. I ought to say everybody except Lena. Lena started wondering about him soon as she saw him that first morning. I probably would 'a' done so myself, but I didn't have time then, I was too busy looking after his mom on that bed. But I did later. We all did later. When he was five or six we all did. Why did we pick him? Well, why do you pick any-body? We picked him because we needed somebody. We could 'a' picked one of Strut Hawkins's boys or one of Joe Simon's boys. We could 'a' picked one of Aunt Lou Bolin's boys—but we picked him. It was back there in the thirties. Joe had just tanned S'mellin'. We all knowed Joe was from Alabama, and we said if Alabama could give One that good, Samson, Luzana could do the same. Oh, no, no, no, we didn't say it exactly like that. We felt it more. In here, in here. People never say things like that. They feel it in the heart.

In the forties, during the war, we started watching him. I had moved down the quarters. I wanted to move out of the house soon after Tee Bob killed himself, but Robert kept me up there to be with Miss Amma Dean. I stayed five years more and I told them I wanted to get out. Robert told me I got out when he said I got out. I told him at my age I did what I wanted to do. Miss Amma Dean told me she wanted me up there because I needed looking after much more than she did, but, she said, if I wanted to go, go. I told them I wanted to go, I wanted to move down in the quarters. They said why move in the quarters when I already had a nice little house at the front. "Don't you have a hyphen?" they said. I said, "Yes ma'am." "Don't you have lectwicity?" they said. I said, "Yes, sir." "Then what you want go down there for?" they said. "There ain't no hyphen down there and no lectwicity. Not even a pump in every yard. Just that well side the road. You got anything against good light and drinking good water?" "Nothing at all," I said. "But the house I'm staying in now been the cook's house even since I been here and probably long as Samson been here. Since I'm not y'all cook no more I don't feel I have the right to be there." "Maybe you don't know it," Robert said, "but you ain't been doing too much cooking 'round here in about ten, 'leven years. But you been doing your share of eating." "I hope I have not deprived you of a meal, Mr. Robert," I said. "My hand is quicker than your eyes," he said. "That's why I want to go down the quarters and raise a garden and some chickens," I said. "I hate to see a grown man snatching food off his own table." "Go if you want go," Miss Amma Dean said. "How you plan to get down the quarters, and where will you stay? Is the house clean? How far you go'n have to haul water? The Lord knows I see no point in you leaving." "I must leave," I said. "Mr. Robert, is it all right with you if I moved in that house side Mary?" "You asking me?" he said. "I didn't know I was still running Samson. I thought you was. I thought it was up to you to tell me when you wanted to move and where. And it was my duty to go down there and clean up the place for you. To run a special pipe down there so you can have hyphen water. To run a special line of lectwicity down there so you wouldn't have to run out to the store for coal oil every day. I thought that was my duty at Samson. Is I done missed out on a duty? Oh, yes, I think I have missed one. I'm suppose to cut all them blood weeds down and run all them blue runner over in Hawk yard so they won't come upon your gallery at night and keep you company. If it ain't slipped my mind, you scared of snakes—or have you changed since about yesterday this time?" "Go if you want go," Miss Amma Dean said. "Find Bea and Mae and tell them clean up that place for you. I'll get Etienne to take them things down the quarters."

It was in the war I moved down the quarters. He was five or six then. Maybe four because he wasn't in school yet. He didn't start school till that Richard girl came here and started teaching. That was after Lillian. Lillian was between Mary Agnes and Vivian Richard.

Shirley went to New Orleans soon after she weaned him, and now it was just him and Lena in the house down there. After I moved down the quarters I spent many days over there on Lena's gallery and at her firehalf. But not just me; looked like all the people met there. Lena had that willow tree in the yard and it kept shade on the gallery on the hottest days. There was always somebody down there talking to her, and Jimmy sitting right there listening to all we had to say. I think that's how we started watching him. Seeing him sitting there all the time, we started wondering if he was the One. No, we never said nothing to him about it, we never said nothing to each other about it—but we felt it. When we found out he count to a hundred by ones, twos, fives, tens, and we found out he knowed all his ABCs, we used to make him recite for us any time we went down there. "Y'all hear that?" Lena used to say, with that big grin on her face. "No more than six now, and y'all hear that?" It made her feel good and sad. Good because he could do it; sad because if he was the One he was go'n have to leave sooner or later.

We used to watch him passing by in the road on his way to school. If it was cold and we saw that sweater not buttoned, we would say, "Get that thing buttoned there, Jimmy." If we saw him trying to break ice in that ditch with the toe of his shoe, we would tell him to cut that out before he caught a death of cold. In summer we used to tell him, "You better stay out them weeds before snake bite you, boy." If we saw him fighting we chastized him no matter who was wrong. He wasn't suppose to fight these here in the quarters, he was suppose to stand up for them. You see, we had already made him the One.

When he learned how to read we made him the reader in the quarters. And by the time he was nine he could read good as anybody down here except the schoolteacher. He used to read and write our letters for us, and he used to read the newspapers, too. Miss Amma Dean used to send me the newspapers every evening and I used to get him to read the sports to me. I didn't care for nothing in the papers side the sports and the funnies. I used to make tea cakes, and I used to give him tea cakes and clabber, and he used to sit right there and read me the funnies. And could go just like Jiggs and Maggie. Go just like Dagwood. "See what devilment they in this time," I used to say; and he used to sit right there and read it all to me. Then he used to read the sports to me and tell me what Jackie had done. Jackie and the Dodgers was for the colored people; the Yankees was for the white folks. Like in the Depression, Joe Louis was for the colored. When times get really hard, really tough, He always send you somebody. In the Depression it was tough on everybody, but twice as hard on the colored, and He sent us Joe. Joe was to lift the colored people's heart. Of course S'mellin' beat him the first time. But that was just to teach us a lesson. To show us Joe was just a man, not a superman. And to show us we could take just a little bit more hardship than we thought we could take at first. Now the second fight was different. We prayed and prayed, and He heard our prayers, and at the same time He wanted to punish them for thinking they was something super. I heard every lick of that fight on the radio, and what Joe didn't put on S'mellin' that night just couldn't go on a man. You could look a week and you could still see the niggers grinning about that fight. Unc Gilly used to come up to my house and lay down on the floor on his back and kick his heels up in the air to show me how S'mellin' had fall. Up till Unc Gilly died he was showing people how S'mellin' fell when Joe hit him.

Now, after the war He sent us Jackie. The colored soldiers coming back from the war said we could fight together we could play ball together. Not till then would they hire Jackie. And when they got him he showed them a trick or two. Homeruns, steal bases—eh, Lord. It made my day just to hear what Jackie had done. Miss Amma Dean would send me the papers when they got through with it at the front, and soon as I got it I would send for Jimmy to come read me the sports and the funnies. If the Dodgers had won, if Jackie had done good, my day was made. If they had lost or if Jackie hadn't hit, I suffered till they played again.

Then I found out Jimmy was telling me lies. He knowed how much I liked Jackie and the Dodgers and on them days I wasn't feeling too good he would tell me Jackie had stole two bases when Jackie hadn't stole a one. Would tell me Jackie had got three or four hits when Jackie hadn't got near the first base. Then on them days when Jackie got a bunch of hits and stole a bunch of bases he would take couple of them back to make up for the others he had gived him earlier. (He wasn't nothing but a child, and he didn't know we had already made him the One, but he was already doing things the One is supposed to do.) Side reading the newspapers, he used to read the Bible for us, too; and he used to read and write our letters. Knowed how to say just what you wanted to say. All you had to do was get him started and he could write the best two-page letter you ever read. He would write about your garden, about the church, the people, the weather. And he would get it down just like you felt it inside. I used to sit there and look at him sitting on my steps writing and water would come in my eyes. You see, we had already made him the One, and I was already scared something was go'n happen to him or he would be taken from us.

One summer he stayed in New Orleans with his mama, and we got that ugly boy there of Coon to read and write for us. That boy was ugly as a monkey and had ways twice as bad. He had a little ugly brown dog that used to follow him everywhere, and the children here in the quarters used to call the dog Monkey Boy Dog. The dog's name was Dirt, but the children wouldn't call him Dirt; called him Monkey Boy Dog.

But that boy was something else. What was in that paper, that's what he read. He didn't care how bad you felt. He came to your house to read what was in the paper, he didn't come there to up lift your spirits. If Jackie stole a base, he read that. If Jackie didn't steal a base, he read that, too. The people used to tell him that old people like me needed her spirit up-lifted every now and then. "Can't you make up a little story at times?" they used to tell him. He used to say, "I ain't no preacher. Let preachers tell them lies." Oh, he was evil, that boy. Same when it came to writing your letters. Wrote what you told him and nothing else. When you stopped talking, he stopped writing. "I don't know your business if you don't know it," he used to say. "I come here to write your letter, not think myself crazy." One time I told him: "Can't you say something about my garden?" He said: "Say what about it? Say it out there? I can say that if you want me to. You want me to say, 'My garden still here?'" "Can't you say, 'Beans dry' or something," I said. (I always like to fill both sides of the page when I write a letter, you know.) He said: "If you want people in New Orleans to know your beans dry, I'll go on and write your beans dry. Don't make me no never mind."

It was pretty clear to everybody in the quarters that he wasn't the One.

Jimmy was born after Tee Bob killed himself, so that mean Robert had already turned the place over to sharecroppers. Tee Bob was to inherit the place, but when he died and they didn't have another son to give the place to, Robert chopped the place up in small patches and called in the people. First, he called in the Cajuns off the river and gived them what they wanted. Then he called in the colored out the quarters and gived them what was left. Some of them got a good piece of land to work, but most of them got land near the swamps, and it growed nothing but weeds, and sometimes not even that. So the colored people gived up and started moving away. That and the war took most of the young men and women from here. After they left, the old people and the children tried to work the land, but they got even less from it. The Cajuns, on the other hand, was getting more and more all the time. And the more they got, the better plows and tractors they got. And the better the plows and tractors, the more they got. After a while they wanted more land. That's when Robert started taking acre by acre from the colored and giving it to them. He took and took till there wasn't enough to support a family, so the people had to give up and leave or give up and work for the Cajuns. If they left a house that was rotten, Robert boarded up the windows and doors awhile, then he had somebody on the place tear it down, and he let the Cajuns plow up the land where the house used to be. That's why coming down here now you see cane and corn where houses was twelve, fifteen years back. But they've had a many babies born here, and many old people have died here, you hear me. Sappho and them right over there; Claudee and them little farther down. Then Grace, then Elvira and them. On this side Lettie and her brood. (Corine drowned one of Lettie's children in that well down the quarters way back there in the twenties.) On the other side of Lettie, Just Thomas and Elsie; then Coon and her drove. Hawk Brown, Gerry and their children right over here. Little farther up, Phillip, Unc Octave and Aunt Nane. Strut Hawkins and his bunch. Then go on the other side and start where I used to live. Little farther down Joe Simon and Ida. Harriet. Little farther, Oscar, Rosa, their children. Manuel, his family. Toby, his bunch. Bessie and hers. Aunt 'Phine Jackson and them. Aunt Lou Bolin and her hungry bunch. Billy Red, his mama and daddy. (He went to New Orleans and called himself Red Billé—a Frenchman.) Little farther down, Unc Gilly and Aunt Sara. Timmy and Verda. And many many more I can't think of right at the moment. But now just a few of us left. Now nothing but fields, fields, and more fields. They don't have nerve enough to kick the rest of us off, so they just wait for us to move away or die. Well, I got news for them: these old bones is tired, and that's true, but they ain't about ready to lay down for good, yet. I done seen a hundred and ten or more years, and I don't mind seeing a few more. The Master will let me know when He wants His servant Up High. Till then I will have some of them children read me the Bible, read me the papers, and I'll do all the walking I can. And I will eat vanilla ice cream which I loves and enjoys.

Jimmy saw this place changing, and he saw all the people moving away. He saw the young men going to war, and he saw the young women going to the city. His own mom was in that crowd. He saw the tractors come and tear down the old houses and plow up the land, and he saw us all standing there watching the tractors. He saw all that. Now he heard this: heard us on that gallery talking about slavery, talking about the high water, talking about Long. He heard me talk about Cluveau and Ned. He heard us all talk about Black Harriet and Katie; Tom Joe and Timmy. And when the young men came back to visit the old people he heard them talking about the war. The japs wasn't like the white people said they was. They was colored just like us, and they didn't want kill us, they just wanted to kill the white soldiers. If the colored soldiers was marching in front, the japs would shoot over the colored soldiers head just to get to the white boys. If the colored soldiers was marching in the back, the japs would drop the bombs shorter. It was this that made them integrate that Army and nothing else.

Jimmy heard all this before he was twelve; by the time he was twelve he was definitely the One. We watched him every move he made. We made sure he made just the right ones. If he tried to go afoul—and he did at times—we told him what he had heard and what he had seen. No, no, no, we never told it to him like I'm telling it to you now; we just looked at him hard. But it was in that look. Sometimes that look can tell you more than words ever can.

He tried first there with Strut's gal, Eva, or she tried it with him, because they was both about that age now, and from what people had been saying she had already tried it with a few others. So now he thought it was his time to try it, or be enticed by it. It was spring, it was the year he was twelve. It was April, it had just rained. Evening—just getting dark. Lena sent him to the store to get a gallon of coal oil. We had lectwicity down here now, but the old people still kept some coal oil for the lamps just in case something happened to the 'lectric wires. And side that they used coal oil to light fire. Lena sent him to the store that evening to get coal oil. Nobody know who said what to who, but next thing—Aunt 'Phine saw it when she came out on the gallery— that coal oil can was hanging on that gate and he was on Strut's gallery trying to throw Strut's gal down. Yes, Aunt 'Phine said, that's the noise she had heard in the house. She said she was sitting in the front room eating supper when she kept hearing this booming noise over there on Strut's gallery. It kept going, *boom*. Then little bit later, *boom*. Then little bit later, *boom* again. She went out on the gallery to see what was making the noise. It was almost dark, but she could see somebody trying to throw somebody down. Instead of pushing her down like it was clear she wanted him to do—no, he was trying to throw her down. Picking her up and swinging her over his shoulder. But each time he swung her, her feet, her heels, hit the floor before her back did. If he had pushed her down like she wanted him to do Aunt 'Phine wouldn't 'a' heard the noise and he wouldn't 'a' got whipped, but, no, he wanted to pick her up and slam her down. And each time he tried it, she made sure her heels hit first. (Teasing him.) Aunt 'Phine said before she recognized him, she recognized that coal oil can hanging on Strut's gate. No, she didn't recognize the coal oil can, it was too dark: she had talked to Lena earlier that day and Lena had mentioned something about getting a gallon of coal oil from the store soon as Jimmy came home. Now since that person on Strut's gallery was about Jimmy's size and age, the age to be thinking about doing what this one here was trying to do, she hollered: "Get away from there, Jimmy." Instead of him moving, he picked that gal up and slammed her back on her heels again. "Boy, you hear me?" Aunt 'Phine said. He picked her up and slammed her back down. "Wait," Aunt 'Phine said. She sat her pan of food on the gallery and started out the yard. She said she heard *boom* again, then again *boom*. But by the time she got to Strut's gate, the coal oil can was gone, and nothing but a black streak was headed up the quarters. Aunt 'Phine came on down to Lena. When Jimmy got back home, Lena sent him out in the yard to get her a good switch. And that was the first time.

Now he tried it in the loft. He knowed what had happened to him for trying it on the gallery even when he had failed—so now he tried it in the loft. All the children in the quarters playing hide-go-seek that day. Twenty, thirty of them running all over the place. Everybody got found, everybody but him and Eva. They up there in Strut's loft. The rest of the children got tired playing hide-go-seek, they start playing something else. But him and Eva still up there in the loft. I'll never forget, it was hot hot that day. Dead in the summer, and we was all sitting on Lena's gallery stitching a quilt. By and by here come one of the children running in the yard to tell Lena they had found Jimmy and Eva. Where? The loft. Little bit later, here he come.

"I hope you got what you went after," Lena said. "Now, you got something else to get."

He didn't ask what, he knowed what, he went and got the switch.

"You go'n whip me in front of them?" he said.

The yard was full of children now. The gallery was full of old people. Etienne was there, too, sitting with his back against the post.

"You go'n whip me in front of them?" he asked her.

"You wasn't thinking about them in that loft," she said.

"You go'n whip Eva?" he asked her.

"No," Lena said. "Eva will get her belly full soon enough."

We all looked at him standing there with the switch in his hand. It was hot—sweat running down his face. We all wanted him to get the whipping. We didn't care if Eva got it or not. What did any of us care about Eva? We all knowed what Eva was go'n turn out to be. And we knowed what we wanted out of him. We didn't say it to him, we didn't say it to each other; maybe we didn't say it to ourself—but we felt it.

"Only natural," Etienne told Lena in Creole. Etienne was always taking up for boys—and 'specially for Jimmy.

"I don't care how natural it is," Lena said, back in Creole.

"I did it," Etienne said. "All boys do it."

"Look where it got you," Lena said in Creole. "You want him there?"

"No," Etienne said.

"You think I like this?" Lena said in Creole.

"I know you don't," Etienne said.

While they was talking they was looking at him, not at each other. He knowed they was talking about him, he knowed Etienne was taking up for him, but he didn't understand Creole and he didn't know what they was saying.

"You want it now or tonight before you go to bed?" Lena asked him.

"Can you whip me in the kitchen?" he said.

"Yes. Come on," Lena said.

They went in the back. We heard the licks, and her talking to him, and we could hear him crying. We wanted him to get the whipping, but after it was over I'm sure we all wanted to put our arms round him. I know for the rest of the week we got him to do things for us just so we could give him something. A nickel, a dime; tea cakes, pralines.

We wanted him to get religion that year, too, the year he made twelve years old. The Master started when He was twelve, if you will remember. We knowed if he was to be the One—no, not if no more, he was already the One—we knowed he had to find religion. The colored has suffered in this world, and that is true, but we know still the Lord's been good to us. Look at me: I'm more than a hundred and ten. If it's not the Lord keeping me going, what is? I can sit in the sun, I can walk—no, not like I used to, but I can still move around a little bit. On days when I'm feeling real good, I can go all the way to the road and look at the river. But generally I just go up the quarters a piece and sit under my old tree. The people done fixed me a clean little spot there, and I can go up there and sit and talk to my tree, talk to myself, talk to my God till I get tired. Sometimes I stay there an hour thanking Him for His blessings, then I come on back home.

We wanted him to get religion that summer he was twelve. Lena made him go to prayer meeting every night, and every night he went and sat up on the mourners bench with the rest of the children, and every night they prayed over him. Elder Banks prayed over him more than he prayed over any the others because it was known all around now that he was the One. But all this praying didn't do no good that year. Lena thought he still had his mind on Strut's gal, and she thought the best medicine was a switch every now and then, but I told her no. I told her he would come around. She said when. Then she would start crying. "When?" Because, you see, the rest of the children his age was getting religion, and he wasn't. And he was the One, and the One had to lead in everything. "When?" she would say. "The Lord knows how we feel. He won't let us down," I would tell her.

But the summer he was twelve passed and he was still a sinner.

The next year we started on him early. Prayer meeting starts in the summer, but we started on him in the spring. He was thirteen now, and we meant for him to put away his sinful ways. So every time he wrote a letter for us now, we had him say something about the church and something about all the little children who had joined the church last summer.

We didn't allow him to play cards for fun or pecans. We didn't want him to play marbles or ball like all the other children did. If we saw him trying to steal off and do these things we called him in and sent him to the store. Or we sent him to somebody else's house to borrow some tobacco or some sugar. Or maybe borrow a hoe or an axe. No matter if we needed it or not—

go borrow it. We didn't want him to go to the fair on Saturday nights. They had music and dancing at these fairs, and that was sinful. We didn't like for him to listen to the radio, either; 'less he was listening to gospel music on Sundays.

When summer got here and the people started prayer meeting at the church, we asked him if he was praying for religion. He said yes. We told him we was all praying for him. When we went to church now and prayed for the sinners we kept him in mind. We didn't call his name—that wasn't right to the rest of the sinners—but we did it on the sly. We used to say things like: "Lord, go with them who don't have a daddy and whose mama's gone off to the city. Go with the old people who's left to look after the children. Lord, make them obedient to the old people and let them seek thy kingdom for their salvation. In that way both him and the Lord knowed who we was talking about, and we didn't even have to mention his name.

He got religion the first week of August—that was back in 1951. He came to me that day—I was sitting out there on my gallery—and he said, "I got religion, Miss Jane."

Me and Etienne was sitting out there on the gallery, and I said: "You sure?"

He said: "I believe so."

I said: "No believing. You got to be sure."

He said: "I'm sure."

I said: "I will hear you talk tonight."

He went to all the old people that day and told them he had religion. That's what you did in them time. You went to all the old people and told them you had religion. If they couldn't show up at the church that night to hear you talk, you would tell them your travels then. You would tell it right out there on the gallery, or maybe in the room where you wouldn't be disturbed by noise.

(When Mack Jenkins got religion he came here and told me he had religion, and now he wanted to kneel down and kiss my foot because I had been a slave and he wanted to humble himself to me. I said, "Jenkins, if you don't get away from here, I'm go'n haul back and kick you in the mouth. Religion raises the heart, makes you noble, it don't make you crazy." I said: "If I was you I would check again to see what I really got." Lord, that Jenkins was one more, you hear me.)

"I hope they didn't push him too fast," Etienne said, after Jimmy went out of the yard.

"Thirteen ain't too young," I said.

"Not if you ready," Etienne said. "But I don't know if he's through with Strut's gal yet. It's cool under them Palm-o'-Christians this time of year, and from what they say about her that was her favorite laying down place."

I said, "Etienne, if you don't quit that kind of talk round here, I'm going in that house and find that stick. Come back out here and knock the fool out you."

That night he told his travels. Lena sat there crying, and I wept, too. But when I got back home I felt better than I had felt in a long long time.

After he got baptized we wanted him to preach. Listening to his travels we knowed he was close to God, and now we wanted him to pick up the gospel. He told us he was not a preacher. He would work in the church, but he was not a preacher. Now the people started looking at each other. They said, "He talked that good and now he don't want preach?" Some of them started having doubts about his religion. But I did not. I knowed, if anybody had religion, he did. I just wondered when he got it. Maybe he had it long long before he knowed he had it or any of us knowed he had it. "If he don't want preach let him serve in some other way," I said. I was the oldest in the church and they called me the church mother. But I like baseball so much they had to take it from me and give it to Em-ma. But I was the church mother then, and I said, "Let him do something else." They said, "The One ought to be in front of everything." (They didn't say it like that—but that's what was in their faces.) I said, "Let's give him some time. Let's not push him. Not everybody is sent to preach. Some are sent to pray, some are sent to sing. Some are sent to ring bells, some are sent to build altars, and others are sent to cut the grass in church yards. Just because we made him the One, don't let's try to make him a preacher, too."

When the people saw he didn't want preach, they wanted to make him a deacon. But he didn't want that either. He wanted to sit back in the congregation like the rest of us. If a lady shouted he would help the ushers hold her down. If they had to take her outside to catch fresh air he would help the ushers take her to the door. Sometimes he would ring the bell if Just wasn't there. Sometimes he would open the service by reading from the Bible.

One time he put on a little play at the church—not a religious play, a funny play—and the people here in the quarters won't ever forget it. He got some black shoe polish and some white shoe polish and put this on the children face and put them up there on the pulpit saying crazy things. Lord, if the people didn't laugh. People laughed till they cried. Children up there talking like people over there on Morgan talk: "Yassuh." "Nawsuh." "I's be going now, bossman, suh." "Man, you better take yo' hand off ma 'oman, yeah. Don't you know that's ma 'oman you handlin' there?" Lord, if the people didn't laugh.

But the people wanted him to preach, and he didn't want preach. Sometimes me and Jimmy would be sitting there on the gallery talking, and all a sudden he would stop listening to what I was saying and start gazing out in the road like he was listening to something else. One day he was back there in the kitchen with me while I was cooking. I won't ever forget it—I was cooking Irish potatoes and cabbage that day. He said, "Miss Jane, I got something like a tiger in my chest, just gnawing and gnawing and want come out. I want rip my chest open and let it free. I pray to God to take it out, but look like the Lord don't hear me. This thing gnaw and gnaw at me and I want scream. I want run in the woods and beat my head against the trees. I want go down in the bottom of that river and stay there and stay there. Something in me want come out, Miss Jane, but I don't know how to get it out. Nobody helps me, not even the Lord."

Jimmy told me that exactly a year before that desegregating bill passed there in Washington. Maybe we didn't know at first why we had made him the One, but that was the reason.

But the people here at Samson wasn't the only ones wanted Jimmy to be the One. Colored all over this parish wanted him to be the One. By the time he was twelve he had traveled all over this parish with Olivia Antoine. Olivia is the lady here in the quarters who sell garden seeds and the cologne stuff. And she cash the checks and do all the shopping for the old people here on the place. When our welfare checks come in we sign them and give them to her to cash for us and do our little shopping. Jimmy used to write down on a tablet what we wanted. Sometimes Olivia had many as six, seven people to make grocery for. Her and Jimmy going from house to house. Her in front, Jimmy walking behind with that pencil and tablet.

After they had got everybody's list they would head out for Bayonne. But since Olivia had customers long the road, she had to stop to see if they needed anything. She had been selling garden seeds and cologne and things like that for many many years, so she knowed everybody. She knowed the mulattoes and she knowed all the Creoles. The Creole gals love that sweet stuff on them when they go out. You got lot of them up the road, 'round Bayonne, and on the Island, there. Jimmy used to listen to Olivia talk to them. Nobody on earth can talk like the old Creole people can talk. For hours and hours they can go on like that. She said even they used to look at him and say things about him. "He is very bright." "He will make some girl happy." "He will be a credit to his family." "He will be a credit to his race." "But he must be careful or the white people will kill him, sure." She said many times she wished he was her own son. Sometimes when she went out and didn't take him with her the people would say: "Where's your boy there, 'Livia?" "He'll be with me next time," she would tell them. And she said she was always lonely when he wasn't there.

Olivia said she tried to show him sales talk, but he never was interested. He was more interested in the people they visited. Even when they talked in Creole and he couldn't understand what they was saying, he was interested in the way the words sounded. Olivia said sometimes when they was by themself he would ask her: "Miss 'Livia, what do *takalapala* mean?" She would say: "Not for a little boy to know." Other times, if it wasn't too serious, she would tell him.

And it was this, going round with Olivia, listening to people talk, listening to us talk here on the place, what was gnawing in his chest. This was the thing he wanted to let out. No, not out. To let this out he had to both blind himself and defend himself. No, what he wanted was to help. But he didn't know how.

Jimmy left from here the same year they passed that law in Washington. Went to New Orleans to stay with his mama and go to school. They passed that law in the spring, he left here in the summer. We all went out to the road with him to catch the bus. Lena, Olivia, myself—others. It was a Sunday. A Sunday evening. We gived him a little party the night before, but we still had him loaded down with food. Cake, fried chicken, oranges. Going right there to New Orleans—he had enough food to last him a week. We stayed out there with him till he got on the bus, then we came on back down the quarters.

Jimmy came back home every two weeks when he first left here. Then he started coming back home about once a month. After a while just on holidays—Easter and Christmas—then we wouldn't see him again till summer. But anytime he came back the people got him to write letters. Sure, we had somebody else writing for us now, but they didn't write like he did. They couldn't think up things to say, and even when they did, it didn't sound the way he made it sound. We used to give him a quarter for writing one letter, fifty cents for writing two. We didn't have to pay him, mind you. When you make somebody the One you don't have to pay them with money. You help them when they needs it. Books if they can't buy their books. Give them money if they need to get somewhere. If you don't have it yourself, you go to church, you go to the white people, but you do everything in your power to help him. That you owe him who you make the One.

But the first thing people noticed after he had been away awhile, he no longer cared for the church. I'm not saying he didn't go to church, I'm not saying he spoke against it. No, he never spoke against the church, and when he first started coming back he used to go up there with Lena all the time. But you could tell he didn't have the right interest no more. If he prayed it didn't have that fire now like it used to have. It was too dry now, too educated. Old people sitting in church didn't feel the spirit. They never helped him on. They just sat there quiet, waiting for him to hurry up and finish so somebody else could pray. I used to try to help him, but you can feel a cold church. Quite likely he didn't feel his prayers either, just did it because his aunt wanted him to do it. After it was over he would just sit there dreaming about something else.

One time when he got up to tell his 'Termination he tried to say something about the new school law. But the people wasn't interested with what he had to say. They nodded, you know, but they didn't know what he was talking about. When he went back to his seat and sat down I saw him gazing out the window. Sitting there like he was all by himself.

The first three or four years after he left here was the beginning of all that Civil Rights trouble. These white people had been living like this for hundreds and hundreds of years and they wasn't about to give up without a fight. Look what they did that young lady at that Alabama school. Look what they did them little children there in Tennessee and there in Arkansas. What about that thing they had to kick out the Catholic church there in New Orleans? Suppose to be great leaders—but who was the bravest? Tell me. Dogs in a pack can fight—but who was the bravest? Answer me that. Any of them braver than Miss Lucy? What a charming young lady. What a beautiful face. What lovely eyes. And them little children? I still remember the little faces looking through the car windows at the dogs standing on two feet barking at them. Oh, my God. I'll never forget the one with the ribbon in her hair. What a sweet little face—don't you remember? I'll take the memory of it to my grave just like I will take this scar on my back to my grave. Cussed them little children and still they went. Throwed rocks and bricks at them and still they stood up.

And look how they treated Reverend King—how they bombed his house and jailed him. Suppose to be leaders of state and look at them. Leaders my foot. I will and I do call them a pack of vicious dogs. Look how they bombed Mr. Shuttleworth's home—and on Christmas at that. I was sitting at the firehalf when I heard the news. I said a very mean thing about all white people, but then I fell on my knees and asked God to forgive me. No matter what happens, He's not asleep. He sees what we does; it's all written down.

The ones at the front never thought the demonstrations could get this far. Everything that was going on was going on somewhere else. Alabama, Mi'sippi, New Orleans—but not Samson. The niggers here was contented. I heard Robert saying that with my own ears. Miss Amma Dean had gotten him to take me to the doctor in Bayonne. That bus with the Freedom Riders had just been destroyed—and Robert and one of them laws was standing side the car talking about it. I'm sitting in the car listening. "That's what you get, what you ought to get when you poke your nose in other people business," the law said. "Well, my niggers know better," Robert said. "Heard that, granny?" the law said. I didn't even look at him. "Over a hundred," Robert said. "She know what'll happen if they ever try it."

But not too long after that he called us up to the front. Hot just like it is today. Brady asked me if I wanted to ride, but I told him I would walk with all the other people. Me and Yoko, poor soul, walked up there together. I had on my sun glasses because that dust out there hurt my eyes. They call me Miss Movie Star anytime I put my sun glasses on—'specially Yoko. "Hey, there, Miss Movie Star. How you feel?" When I went by my tree up there, I said: "Well, Sis Oak, look like another one of them crazy meetings." Yoko said: "One of these days that tree go'n answer you back and you go'n break your neck running down them quarters." I told Yoko, I said: "I got news for you, Yoko, she talks back to me all the time." Yoko, dead and gone now, said: "Now, I know you crazy." And me and Yoko just killed ourself laughing.

When we came up to the yard, Miss Amma Dean came out on the back gallery and told us Robert wasn't there but he had something important to tell us and he wanted us to wait. She told me to come sit down in the kitchen, but I told her I would stay out there in the yard with Yoko and them. It was cool under the trees and it wasn't so bad at first, but after we had been there a while it got tiring. The children began to fret, and some of the grown people started grumbling. But no Robert. He didn't show up till almost sundown. We went up there at three o'clock and he didn't show up till almost sundown. "What's going on here?" he asked. "Everybody leaving?" Etienne said: "You sent for us, Mr. Robert." He said: "Did I? Oh, yes, I had almost forgot." Then he hollered for Bertha to bring him something cold to drink. He didn't say another word to us till Bertha had brought the glass and left.

"Now, let's see," he said. "Oh, yes, now I know. I just want remind every last one of y'all y'all living on this place for free. You pay me no rent, you pay me no water bill. You don't give me a turnip out your garden, you don't give me one egg out your hen house. You pick all the pecans you can find on the place and all I ask for is half, what I never get. I ask you for half the berries you pick, you bring me a pocketful so dirty I wouldn't feed them to a hog I *don't* like. All right, I'll let all that go. But this I will not let go: there ain't go'n be no demonstrating on my place. Anybody 'round here think he needs more freedom than he already got is free to pack up leave now. That go for the oldest one, that go for the youngest one. Jane to—who the last one had a baby down there?"

Somebody said Eva. A little boy—Peter.

"That go for Jane, that go for Eva's boy Peter," Robert said.

He went inside the house, and we turned around and went back down the quarters.

Not a month later, Batlo got mixed up in some kind of demonstrations in Baton Rouge, and some kind of way the word got back to Samson. Robert came down here and told Yoko she had to move in twenty-four hours. Yoko started crying. She said she couldn't control Batlo, nobody could control children these days. She said she had been working here ever since his daddy, Mr. Paul, was alive, and one time Mr. Paul said himself she was one of the best workers he had on his place. Robert told her she had twenty-three hours and fifty-nine minutes and not a second more to get off his place.

When he went back up the quarters, Yoko sent one of Strut's children to tell me to see Miss Amma Dean. When I got up there Bertha told me Miss Amma Dean had a headache and was laying down 'cross the bed.

"When she took her headache?" I asked Bertha.

"She got it when she looked out in the road with them spy glasses and saw you headed this way," Bertha said.

"Think I ought to wait?" I asked Bertha.

"No use," Bertha said. "I'm sure it won't pass till Yoko leave."

"She talked to Robert at all?" I asked Bertha.

"She talked to him," Bertha said. "But his mind made up, Yoko got to move off the place."

I started back down the quarters. Brady caught up with me in the car and drove me back to Yoko's house. Yoko had already started packing. She already knowed what the answer was go'n be. That night everybody showed up to give a hand. When they got through packing, the people sat there talking till way up in the night.

The next day she moved. Brady wanted to borrow a truck off the river and move her, but Batlo said he wanted to use wagons. He wanted to go slow long the road and show everybody what Robert Samson had done. He had even made signs to hang on the wagons. AFTER FIFTY YEARS, ROBERT SAMSON KICKED US OFF. BLACK PEOPLE FATE. He had the signs on both sides and on the back of the wagons.

The first wagon had most of the heavy furnitures—bed, chairs, stove, dresser—and it had that chifforobe. Yoko hadn't covered that chifforobe glass and the glass was flashing all over the place. From the time they brought it out the house till they left the quarters it flashed all over the place. All over the empty places where houses used to be and where the Cajuns got their fields now. It flashed on all these old houses and all these old fences. It flashed on you, too, if you didn't get out the way. The wagon stopped out there in front my gate, and that glass stayed on my gallery all that time.

Yoko was on the back wagon. She was sitting way up high. Batlo wanted her way up there to show the people what Robert Samson had done. We was scared Yoko might fall off, but Batlo wanted her to stay up there.

That was one more day, you hear me? Yoko up there crying; we down here on the ground crying. Yoko waving from the wagon, we waving from the gate and waving from the gallery. Waving like you wave to people already dead. When somebody die and you don't follow the hearse to the graveyard, you stand up and wave them good-bye. Best to wave with a piece of white rag or a pocket handkerchief. A man, of course, he take off his hat and holds it in a respectful manner over his heart. Ladies, they wave. All us waving: "Good-bye, Yoko, good-bye." Yoko, way up there: "Good-bye, Etienne; good-bye, Lena; good-bye, Jane." We down here on the ground: "Good-bye, Yoko, good-bye."

Not a year later—poor Yoko was dead. Staying there with her daughter in Port Allen, and not a year she was dead. The children wanted to bury her at Sun Rise where she got people, but we knowed Yoko wanted to be here with Walter, and we forced them to change their mind. Robert said he didn't care one way or the other long as she didn't carry on no demonstrating in that graveyard. The children brought Yoko back there, and she's there side Walter right now. Just go to that last oak, closest one to the fence; you'll find both of them side by side right there.

Not long after Yoko moved away from here, Jimmy showed up at the church. I hadn't seen Jimmy in over two years. He had been back here to see Lena, but I hadn't seen him. I was surprised to see how tall he had got. Tall and skinny now and eyes very very serious. He came up to me and spoke. He said he had just been down to see Lena and she wasn't coming to church that day because she wasn't feeling too good. I told him I knowed it because I had talked to Lena myself just yesterday. I held his hand and looked up at him and I could see how serious his eyes was. He was standing there with me, but his mind was somewhere else.

It was 'Termination Sunday. 'Termination Sunday is when you tell the church you still carrying the cross and you want meet them 'cross the River Jordan when you die. You start out singing your song. Soon as you have sung a little bit, no more than a chorus, the church joins and sings with you. You can keep your song going long as you want, if it's a good spirity song, and the church will follow. Yoko used to sing and sing and sing: "Father, I stretch my hand to Thee, no other help I know." Then after you get through singing, you talk to the church little bit—tell them you still on your way—then you shake hand with everybody—you can just wave to them sitting way back there in the back if you don't feel like walking back there—then you got sit down. Then somebody else get up and they do the same. But he sing a different song. Everybody got his own song. You better not sing somebody else's song before he do or sing it better even after he do, because you might have trouble on your hand. Sometimes when I don't feel well enough to go to church, or I want stay home and listen to the ball game, I can sit on my gallery and tell who is telling their 'Termination just listening to the song. And in the years I've been living on this place I've heard a many songs, I tell you.

Jimmy was the last one to go up to the front that day. He waited so long I didn't think he was getting up at all. But when he was sure everybody else had spoke, he got up and came to the front. No singing, he just walked up there. He spoke to Elder Banks first, then to the deacons, to us sitting over there on the side bench, then he faced the front and spoke to the rest of the people. He told us he had come there for our help. He said we knowed what was happening all over the South, and it ought to be happening here, too. We was surely no better off than the people in Alabama and Mi'sippi was. He had been to Alabama and Mi'sippi; he had even been to Georgia. He had met Reverend King, he had gone to his house, he had gone to his church, he had even gone to jail with him. Reverend King and the Freedom Riders was winning the battle in Alabama and Mi'sippi, but us here in Luzana hadn't even started the fight.

"And end up like Yoko?" Just Thomas said.

"That's why I'm here now," Jimmy said. "Because what they did to Miss Yoko. I had been telling myself over and over it wasn't time for us to start here yet. Over and over I had been telling myself that. But when I heard what happened to Miss Yoko I knowed it was time."

"Time for what?" Just said. "For the same thing to happen to us?"

"I don't want nothing to happen to you," Jimmy said. "The place where you live, that's what I want."

"This place go'n be here," Just Thomas said. "Where we going after they put us off?"

"Don't you have children?" Jimmy said.

"That's the trouble with y'all now," Just Thomas said. "Y'all come round here telling people to follow y'all, then y'all want know if they got children to take them in."

"Just Thomas not the only person in this church," I said. "What you asking us for, Jimmy?"

"I'm head deacon here," Just said.

"Then you better ask him what I just asked him," I said.

Elder Banks stood up behind the altar and told me and Just don't argue.

"That's what happen when the devil walk in," Just said. "Good Christians fight."

"He can't defeat nobody but the weak," I said.

Elder Banks cut his eyes at me to make me shut up. He told Jimmy: "You don't come to our church no more, Jimmy. But now you come because you want us to help you. A cause we don't even understand."

"I don't go to church no more," Jimmy said, "because I lost faith in God. And even now I don't feel worthy standing here before y'all. I don't feel worthy because I'm so weak. And I'm here because you are strong. I need you because my body is not strong enough to stand out there all by myself. Some people carry flags, but we don't have a flag. Some carry guns, but we know it would be nonsense to even think about that. Some have money, but we don't have a cent. We have just the strength of our people, our Christian people. That's why I'm here. I left the church, but that don't mean I left my people. I care much for you now as I ever did—and every last one of you in here know me. Do you think I'll hurt you? My aunt's down the quarters sick right now, do you think I want to hurt her? But we have to fight. We have to fight. I'm not the only one doing this. They doing it everywhere. They told me to come here because this is my home, and they feel I can talk to you better than anybody else can. You don't have to worry about the Samsons pushing you off. If it was just here they would do it, but it's everywhere now. And to push everybody off would cripple this state. They'll change things before they let that happen."

"That's what you saying," Just said. "And how you know the rest of the people go'n listen to this craziness?"

"Because they listened to the craziness Martin Luther King was teaching in Alabama," Jimmy said.

"Now, he getting smart," Just said. "Y'all hear that, don't you? Don't come here but once a year, but now he getting smart."

"Oh, shut up, Just," I said.

"What?" Just said. "Who said that? That's right, that's you." He always kept a pocket handkerchief with him to wipe his bald head—keep it from shining all over the place. Now he started shaking that wet, dirty handkerchief at me. "That's why they took the mother from you," he said. "If you ain't arguing about something you don't know nothing bout, you at that house listening to them sinful baseball games."

"I don't need the mother to serve my Master," I said.

"Left to me you'll never get it back," he said.

"That's all right with me," I said. "I don't need to sit where Em-ma sitting to get on my bending knees."

"When the last time you got down on them bending knees?" Just said.

"I ain't been feeling too good lately," I said.

"That ain't it," Just said. "You got your mind on baseball. I bet you ain't been feeling too bad to turn that radio on."

Elder Banks waited till me and Just had shut up, then he turned to Jimmy.

"I know how you feel, Jimmy," he said. "I was young myself once and I know how the young feel. But we old now, Jimmy. This church is old. Look at the people here. Where are the children? Where are the young people, Jimmy? Count the ones in here. We got thirty-seven people in here today—but where are the young ones? All we want to do is live our life quietly as we can and die peacefully as the Lord will allow us. We would like to die in our homes, have our funerals in our church, be buried in that graveyard where all our people and love ones are. The man up there owns that graveyard, Jimmy. He owns the house we live in, he owns the little garden where we grow our food. The church where we at right now, he owns this; he even owns the bell that calls our people to meeting. And the day he tells us to leave, we got to go, and we got to leave bell and church. Reverend King and his people owned things in Georgia and Alabama. We don't own a thing. Some of us don't even own the furniture in our house. The store in Bayonne own it, and they can take the bed or the stove from us tomorrow."

Elder Banks looked at Jimmy awhile, then he went on. "I'm sure you mean good, Jimmy," he said. "But I can't tell my church to go with you. If they want go, that's up to them; but I won't tell them go and they have no place to come back to. You don't have a place for them, Jimmy, and they don't have money to buy nothing. What happened in Birmingham, what happened in Atlanta, can't happen here. Maybe something else; maybe when all of us in here are gone; but I can't see nothing happening here now, Jimmy."

"I can't promise you a thing," Jimmy said. "But we must go in, and the ones already working will go on. Some of us might be killed, some of us definitely going to jail, and some of us might be crippled the rest of our life. But death and jail don't scare us—and we feel that we crippled now, and been crippled a long time, and every day we put up with the white man insults they cripple us just a little bit more.

"You mentioned you have an old church," Jimmy said. "Because you want me to see your way of life. Now, I mentioned what we have, because I want you to see our way of life. And that's the kind of life the young will feel from now on. Not your way, not no more. But still we need your strength, we need your prayers, we need you to stand by us, because we have no other roots. I doubt if I expected you to understand me this time. But I'm coming back. I know we can't do a thing in this world without you—and I'm coming back."

He told us he was sorry he had disturbed our church, and he walked out.

"Another dead one," Just said.

"Not if some people keep their mouth shut," I said.

"Sis Pittman, stand up right now and apologize to this church," Elder Banks said.

I got up and said I was sorry and sat back down. I looked at Just Thomas all the time I was at church that day, but he didn't have the nerve to look back at me. I wasn't thinking bout being sorry for what I had said.

That evening I was sitting on my gallery when Jimmy and another boy came in the yard. I have a bad habit not liking some people on first sight. I have begged the Lord and begged Him to wipe this from my heart, but it's still there. This one of my worse habits, probably the worst I have, but I can't get rid of it. Maybe the Lord is waiting till that final hour to clear it away. But I didn't like that boy from the start. He was a little fellow with a big mouth; a long head, a raggedy beard. Steel-rim eye glasses like the old people wear. To beat all that he had on overalls and a jumper—even wearing clodhoppers. Now, what's all that for? I ask you. It surely didn't make him look no better than he did before he put it on. And if he was trying to dress like the people here in the quarters he was absolutely mistaking. People here don't dress like that on Sunday, and if you do they sure go'n laugh at you. Just like them children passing out there in the road laughed at him sitting there on the steps.

Jimmy came by to tell me he 'preciated what I had said at the church. I told him I could understand what he was trying to do because my boy had tried to do the same thing long long before he was born. I asked him if he wanted some lemonade. Mary had made up a big pitcher of lemonade and had gone down the quarters. Soon as I mentioned lemonade, that long head boy said, "Oh, good country lemonade." Jimmy went back in the kitchen and poured us all up a glassful. That long head boy sat on the steps in them overalls and smacked his lips

"Jimmy, Jimmy, Jimmy," I said. He was sitting in a chair against the wall where Mary had been sitting earlier that evening. The piece of cloth that Mary used to fan at flies was still hanging on the back of the chair. "The people here ain't ready for nothing yet, Jimmy," I said. "Something got to get in the air first. Something got to start floating out there and they got to feel it. It got to seep all through their flesh, and all through their bones. But it's not out there yet. Nothing out there now but white hate and nigger fear. And fear they feel is the only way to keep going. One day they must realize fear is worse than any death. When that time come they will be ready to move with you."

"That's our job," that long head boy said.

"People and time bring forth leaders, Jimmy," I said. I didn't look at that long head boy, I wasn't talking to him, I was talking to our Jimmy. "People and time bring forth leaders," I said. "Leaders don't bring forth people. The people and the time brought King; King didn't bring the people. What Miss Rosa Parks did, everybody wanted to do. They just needed one person to do it first because they all couldn't do it at the same time; then they needed King to show them what to do next. But King couldn't do a thing before Miss Rosa Parks refused to give that white man her seat."

"We have our Miss Rosa Parks," that long head boy said; then he sipped some lemonade.

"They sleeping out there, Jimmy," I said.

"But what can I do?" he said. "It's burning up in here, Miss Jane," he said, touching his chest. "I got to do something."

"Talk, Jimmy," I said. "Talk to them."

"You mean go slow?" that long head boy in them overalls said.

"Jimmy," I said. "I have a scar on my back I got when I was a slave. I'll carry it to my grave. You got people out there with this scar on their brains, and they will carry that scar to their grave. The mark of fear, Jimmy, is not easily removed. Talk with them, Jimmy. Talk and talk and talk. But don't be mad if they don't listen. Some of them won't ever listen. Many won't even hear you."

"We don't have that kind of time, Miss Jane," he told me.

"What else you got, Jimmy?" I asked him.

He didn't know what to say.

"First, you got to wake them up, Jimmy," I said. "They sleeping out there. Look around you, Jimmy; look at this place. Travel over this parish. Do you hear anything rumbling? No. Things must rumble before they move. The nigger, Jimmy, must one day wake up and push that black quilt off his back. Must tell himself I had it on too long. But I won't be here when that happen, I'm afraid."

"You can help us now, Miss Jane."

Before I could say "how?", that long head boy in them overalls said, "Your mere presence will bring forth multitudes."

I was listening to that boy but I was looking at Jimmy. "Me help? How?" I said.

"Going with us."

"Going with y'all where? When?"

"When we get ready to move," he said.

"I'm a hundred and eight or a hundred and nine," I said. "What can I do but get in the way?"

"You can inspire the others," Jimmy said.

"Somebody a hundred and eight or a hundred and nine inspire people?"

"Yes ma'am," he said.

"I never heard of nothing like this before," I said. "But if you say so—and if I'm able to move."

"Now there will be multitudes," that long head boy said.

I was getting fed-up with that boy. "Boy, who you for?" I asked him.

"Joe and Lena Butcher," he said.

"They teach you to talk like that?" I said.

"Ma'am?"

I just looked at him.

"That's retrick," he said.

"Well, I can do without your retrick here," I said. "If you can't say nothing sensible, don't say nothing."

He looked at me awhile—feeling hurt now—then he sipped from that lemonade. He looked at me again—still feeling hurt—then he looked at Jimmy. Want Jimmy to speak up for him. But Jimmy didn't offer him any help.

Jimmy told me what they had in mind. He told me just six of them knowed right now, and I made seven. He didn't want me to tell nobody else, not even Lena. No, she wouldn't speak at the wrong time, but she might start worrying and try to stop him.

Do you know Bayonne at all? You done drank from that fountain in the courthouse, used that bathroom in there? Well, up to a year ago they didn't have a fountain there for colored at all. They didn't have a bathroom inside, either. White, yes; but nothing for colored. Colored had to go outside, rain or shine and go down in the basement. Half the time the bathroom was so filthy you couldn't get inside the door. The water on the floor come almost to the top of your shoes. You could smell the toilets soon as you started downstairs. Very seldom a lady would go down there because it was so filthy. They would go back of town and use a bathroom at one of the cafés; other times they would go to Madame Orsini and ask her could they use her bathroom. Madame Orsini and her husband owned a little grocery store there in Bayonne. They was very nice people, and I think they called themself Sicilians. Everyday dagoes far as I'm concerned, but they said Sicilians, and they was very nice to colored. She would let a lady come in—never a man— and the lady could bring in her child. And that was the only place uptown you could go, side the basement at the courthouse. No gas station, and no department store uptown would let you use the bathroom. You think a store would let you use a bathroom when they wouldn't even let you try on clothes there? You gived them the number, they gived you the clothes. If they fit— good; if they didn't, that was too bad, you wore them anyhow. Lord, have mercy, the poor nigger done gone through plenty, you hear me there? Unc Gilly got Brady to bring him a pair of overalls from Bayonne. Brady came back here with a pair of overalls big enough for two people Unc Gilly's size. Unc Gilly got mad at Brady, and since Brady couldn't take them back, he want make Brady buy them now. If the people didn't carry Unc Gilly a dog's life in these quarters. Robert Samson teased him much as the colored did. Every time he saw Unc Gilly in them big overalls he started laughing. When Unc Gilly died, Matt Jefferson mentioned them overalls at the wake. Unc Gilly laying up there in his coffin, and the people thinking about foolish things like that. I reckoned when I'm gone they will say crazy things about me, too. The Lord knows I've done some strange things in my time.

The bathroom was to be just one thing they wanted to demonstrate against, the hyphen was to be the other thing. The white people had a fountain, one of them white fountains you have in most places. A shiny little thing to drink from, a shiny little knob to turn. Round the corner from the fountain, the colored had a hyphen with a cup on a nail. Everybody was suppose to drink out the same cup if you didn't bring your own. Lot of the people used to carry round them little 'luminum cups that you can pull open and shut. If you didn't have that or a glass, you drank out that one cup hanging on the nail.

They had a bucket under the hyphen to catch the water because the hyphen used to drip all the time. A loon called a guard had to make sure the bucket never run over. He was one of the Bush. The looney one— Edgar. They made him a guard after that desegregating bill passed there in Washington. His job, to keep the niggers out the courthouse from bothering people for rights. Time he saw a colored person he broke up there and asked you what you wanted. You better hurry up and tell him or he pushed you right straight out. He broke up there and bellowed at me once. I told him he could bellow and slobber all he wanted, he put his hand on me and I was go'n crack his skull with that stick. He looked at me like I was the looney one there, then he went and bellowed at somebody else. Now, one of his jobs was to see that that bucket never run over. Twice a day he got a nigger prisoner out the cell and made him dump the water out. You had to dump it out in the white men toilet, and that was just 'cross the hall from the hyphen. Soon as the prisoner dumped it out, the loon made him go back in his cell. He used to stand by the front door just to scare the niggers when they came up there seeking rights. Always chewing gum, always slobbering. A loon if you ever saw one. Everybody knowed he should have been in Jackson, but they kept him there to scare away the colored. Bertha went up there one day with Miss Amma Dean and that thing got behind Bertha and had her scampering all over that courthouse. In and out them people office; up and down them narrow halls. Bertha said when she got back to the car she locked all the doors and laid down on the seat. She didn't look up till Miss Amma Dean came there and tapped on the glass.

Now, this what Jimmy and them had in mind. They had picked out a girl to drink from the white people's fountain. (This was their Miss Rosa Parks.) She was one of the Hebert girls, a Catholic, up there in Bayonne. The Catholics and mulattoes don't generally get mixed up in things like this, but this girl wanted to do it. Her own people didn't know nothing about it till after it happened. Jimmy and them had it set for a week after they told it to me. That Friday when everybody was getting off work. He wanted it on a Friday because he wanted to use that weekend to spread the news. Wanted to use the churches, wanted to use the saloons. Two girls would be at the courthouse. When they saw the people coming toward them, one girl was go'n drink from the fountain. Somebody was go'n cuss the girl or push her out the way, and the girl was go'n fight back. She was go'n be arrested—no doubt about that—and the other girl was go'n bring the news. The reason they didn't choose a boy, they was afraid that loon up there might beat the boy and not arrest him. They wanted somebody in jail because they wanted to march on the courthouse the next Monday. They wanted to show the world what the South would do to a nigger—not even half nigger in this girls' case—just because she wanted a drink of water.

I was sitting out here on the gallery the day it happened. Me, Etienne, Mary—Strut was here. Look like somebody else was here, too. No, not Lena. She was home. Who? Yes. Fa-Fa. That's right—Fa-Fa. Because she had been fishing out there in the river and she had brought me a mess of perches. Now it was getting late in the evening and she didn't feel like walking all the way to Chiney, and she had sent one of Strut's children down the quarters to see when Brady was coming back. The boy had just come from down the quarters to tell her Jessie didn't know when Brady was coming home, then somebody looked up and saw the dust coming down the quarters. Etienne said, "That's him now." Fa-Fa told the boy run out there and wave him down. But the car had stopped before the gate before the boy got out there. Jimmy and that boy in them overalls came in the yard. It was getting dark and I didn't know who it was till they had come up to the steps. Jimmy spoke and I recognized his voice. First thing I thought was something had happened to that girl.

After Jimmy spoke to everybody he came up on the gallery and kissed me.
"How you feel?" he said.
"Fine," I said. "Yourself?"
"I'm all right, Miss Jane," he said.
I looked up at him there in the dark. This old heart was jumping in this old chest, I tell you.
Then he told us: "They throwed a girl in jail today for drinking from that fountain inside the courthouse. We will meet in front of the courthouse Monday morning at nine o'clock. We want every black man, woman, and child to be there."
"Well, y'all done finally done it," Fa-Fa said. "Let me get on to Chiney where I belong."
"Ain't you waiting on Brady?" Mary asked her.
"Brady might get back here *after* them Cajuns burn this place down," Fa-Fa said. "I'm leaving right now."
Fa-Fa had been sitting there on the end of the gallery. Had her two fishing poles and her bucket of fish there side her. Next thing you knowed she was walking out the yard, headed for Chiney.
"I just wanted to come down and tell you, Miss Jane," Jimmy said. "I have to be moving on. We have a lot of work to do between now and Monday morning." He looked at me there in the dark. We had had a secret, but now it was out. "You'll be there?" he asked me.
"If the Lord say the same."
"No, she won't, either," Mary said.

"Yes, I will, Mary," I said.

"I'm here to look after you," Mary said. "I can't stand by and let you kill yourself."

"I will go," I said.

"And who go'n pick you up when they knock you down and tramp all over you?" she said.

"The Lord will help me to my feet."

"See what you done started?" Mary said to Jimmy.

"They started it long time ago," Jimmy said.

"With her leading us on, multitudes will follow," that long head boy in them overalls said.

I didn't look at that boy, I looked up at Jimmy. Jimmy, Jimmy, Jimmy, I thought. The people, Jimmy? You listening to that thing that boy call retrick and counting on the people?

"You hungry, Jimmy?" I asked him.

"I'm going home," he said. "I have to tell Aunt Lena."

"Be careful with Lena, Jimmy," I said. "She ain't too strong, you know."

"I'll be careful," he said. "And I'll see you Monday, Miss Jane. Nine o'clock Monday morning. How you getting there?"

"I'll find a way, the Lord say the same."

"Miss Det still gives her fairs on Saturday nights?" he asked me.

"Every Saturday night God send."

"I'll come by tomorrow night," he said. "And I'll be in church on Sunday."

I looked up at him in the dark. Jimmy, Jimmy, Jimmy, I thought. Don't listen to that long head boy's retrick bout the people, Jimmy. The people, Jimmy? The people?

He kissed me good night and left. The dust followed the car down the quarters. You could feel the dust in your skin when it drifted from the road and settled on the gallery.

"Well, there go Lena," Strut said. "And you, too, Miss Jane, you go to Bayonne Monday."

"I'm going if the Lord spare me," I said.

"Why?" Mary said. "To die in Bayonne?"

"I will die in Bayonne only if the Lord wills it," I said. "If not, I'll die in my bed. I hope."

"Over a hundred and eight," Mary said. "How come they don't pick on somebody eighteen?"

"The girl is fifteen," I said.

"Oh, I see," Mary said. "You knowed about it all the time. Y'all had it all worked out. Where I was when all this was going on?"

"Down the quarters," I said.

"Well, me, I got a ditch bank to cut Monday morning," Strut said. "And

I'm sure it go'n take me all day."

"Reckoned lot of ditch banks'll be cut Monday morning," Etienne said.

"You got one to cut?" Strut said.

"Not yet," Etienne said.

Jimmy, Jimmy, Jimmy, I thought there in the dark. The people, Jimmy? The people?

Brady was at Det's house when Jimmy and that long head boy came there Saturday night. But the people there was more interested in eating gumbo and drinking beer than they was in what Jimmy had to say. After that other boy had passed out a sheet of paper with that girl's picture on it, they left out for Chiney to visit another fair. Fa-Fa youngest boy, Henry, was at the fair. He said the people at the fair listened to what Jimmy and the other boy had to say, and some of them even promised to come to Bayonne that Monday morning, but soon as Jimmy and the boy left the house the people at the fair changed their minds, too.

By the time he came to church Sunday the whole place had heard about it. Just Thomas was against even letting him come in the church, but Elder Banks told him nobody would ever be kept out of church long as he came there in peace. When Jimmy got up to talk some of the people went outside. Many of the ones who stayed didn't show interest or respect. I sat there looking at Jimmy, thinking: Jimmy, Jimmy, Jimmy, Jimmy, Jimmy. It's not that they don't love you, Jimmy; it's not that they don't want believe in you; but they don't know what you talking about. You talk of freedom, Jimmy. Freedom here is able to make a little living and have the white folks say you good. Black curtains hang at their windows, Jimmy, black quilts cover their body at night; a black veil cover their eyes, Jimmy; and the buzzing, buzzing, buzzing in their ears keep them from 'ciphering what you got to say. Oh, Jimmy, didn't they ask for you? And didn't He send you, and when they saw you, didn't they want you? They want you, Jimmy, but now you here they don't understand nothing you telling them. You see, Jimmy, they want you to cure the ache, but they want you to do it and don't give them pain. And the worse pain, Jimmy, you can inflict is what you doing now—that's trying to make them see they good as the other man. You see, Jimmy, they been told from the cradle they wasn't—that they wasn't much better than the mule. You keep telling them this over and over, for hundreds and hundreds of years, they start thinking that way. The curtain, Jimmy, the quilt, the veil, the buzzing, buzzing, buzzing—two days, a few hours, to clear all this away, Jimmy, is not enough time. How long will it take? How could I know? He works in mysterious ways; wonders to perform.

But look at me acting high and mighty. Don't the black curtain hang over my window; don't the veil cover my face? And maybe, now, because my arms too weak to push the quilt down the bed I tell myself I'm brave enough to go to Bayonne. But do what in Bayonne when the least little breeze will blow me down?

That night after the Ed Sullivan show I told Mary I was going to bed. Her and Albert was sitting out there on the gallery talking. I told her I was going to bed but I wasn't going to sleep because I wanted to see Brady when he came home. I went to my side and knelt down at the bed to say my prayers. I prayed ever so long. Most of my praying was for Jimmy, for his protection. I asked the Lord to give us enough courage to follow him. Because it was us who wanted him long before he knowed anything about it.

After I got through praying I pulled down the bar and went to bed. Summer and winter I always sleep under my bar. Summer to keep out mosquitoes; winter to help keep out draft. Laying there, I looked at all the old furnitures in the room. The light was off, so I could barely make out the shape of the furniture. I looked at my old rocking chair just setting there. "You can set there like you don't know what's happening, but tomorrow this time you might be headed away from here." I thought about Yoko and that looking glass, and I looked at the glass on my washstand. "You too," I said. "You ain't so high class you can't get packed on a wagon." I looked at my old sewing machine, my armoire. Looked like they was just as live as y'all is now. After you been round things so many years you get to be like them or they get to be like you. Exactly which way it works I ain't figured it out yet. Probably never will.

I laid there on my side waiting for Brady to show up. Then I heard Albert saying, "Light just turned down the quarters." He went to the gate to flag Brady down. A minute later, Brady was knocking on the door. When he came in I could smell he had been drinking. I told him to turn the light on.

"No, ma'am," he said.

"I like to see people when I'm talking to them" I said.

"Yes'm," he said.

"Well?"

"No ma'am," he said.

"You been drinking, ain't you, Brady?" I said.

"Yes ma'am," he said. "And Miss Jane, I can't take you there tomorrow."

"Take me where tomorrow, Brady?" I said.

"I know you promised him, Miss Jane," he said.

"That's why you went out and got drunk, Brady?"

He didn't answer. I looked at him standing there in the dark.

"Snap that light on, Brady," I said.

"No ma'am," he said. And he started crying. "I can't take you there, Miss Jane."

"He did many things for you, Brady," I said. "Used to write for your mama and daddy all the time, you forget that?"

"I'm scared, Miss Jane," he said, crying, "They'll kick me off this place and I know it. I see how Tee Sho and them look at my house every time they go by the gate. They ready to knock it over now—and I'm still in there. Mr. Robert just waiting for a good reason to give it to Tee Sho and them."

"Brady, Brady, Brady," I said.

"I'm sorry, Miss Jane," he said. "You know how I like doing things for you. Anytime you want go to the doctor—things like that."

"Brady, Brady, Brady," I said.

"I know I ain't no man, Miss Jane," he said.

"Brady, Brady, Brady," I said.

"I know I ain't," he said. "I know it ought to be me, not him. I know all that."

"Go home, Brady," I said. "Go to your wife and children."

He didn't move, just standing there in the dark, looking down at me.

"Miss Jane?" he said. I didn't answer him. "Miss Jane?" he said.

"Yes, Brady?" I said.

"I swear to God, Miss Jane, I'm go'n to make it up to you one day. I swear. I swear to God."

"You don't have to swear, Brady, I understand."

He stood there crying now, crying and calling on God.

"Go home, Brady," I said.

He went out crying.

Not long after Brady left the house, Lena came up on the gallery. I still hadn't shut my eyes. Laying there thinking who to turn to next. The only other person on the place with a car running was Olivia Antoine. I was wondering if I ought to ask Albert to go up there and ask her to take me. Then I heard Lena asking Mary about me. Mary told her I was in bed.

"I'm not sleep," I said.

Lena didn't hear me because she knocked on the door and said, "Jane, you wake in there?"

"Come in, Lena," I said.

She pushed the door open and I told her to turn the light on. She was a big woman, but not well. Her health had been failing her now four, five years. I watched her pulling the rocking chair closer to the bed. I knowed she had come there to talk about Jimmy. I wondered what I could say to give her courage.

"You talked to Brady, too?" she said.

"Yes."

"Won't take you either?"

"You going?" I asked.

"I have to go," she said. "I don't want go; I don't want see them kill him in front of me, but I have to go."

"Nothing's go'n happen, Lena," I said.

"They go'n kill him," she said. "I held him to my breast longer than his mom ever done, and I know when something go'n happen."

She was holding her hand and looking down at the floor like she was praying.

"I don't care if I ever use that toilet up there," she said. "What I care about water? I drink before I go to Bayonne; I drink when I come back home. That's what I been doing all my life anyhow."

I looked at her. I didn't know what to say.

"Why he got to be the One?" she said. "All the others want it, why him?"

"He wrote the letters for us, Lena," I said. "He read the newspapers and the Bible for us. And we never chastized nobody else like we chastized him."

"We didn't do that for this," she said.

"Did we know what we was doing it for?" I asked her.

"I knowed what I was doing it for," she said. "I wanted him to be a teacher or something."

"He is a teacher," I said.

"You can't teach from the grave," she said.

"Jimmy's not dead, Lena," I said.

"Not dead yet, you mean," she said. "I'm almost forced to go out there and tell Robert to stop this thing from happening."

"That won't stop Jimmy," I said.

"It'll stop him from getting killed tomorrow," she said.

"Look at them other children," I said. "They didn't get killed."

"You mean all of them didn't get killed," she said. "And they wasn't in Bayonne either. The likes of Albert Cluveau has not vanished from this earth."

We didn't say nothing for a long time. She just sat there holding her hand, looking down at the floor. I reckoned she had already cried all she could cry.

"How you going?" I asked.

"Going up and see Olivia," she said. "If not her, reckoned I'll catch the bus."

"I'll go with you," I said.

"Get your rest," Lena said. "I'll let you know what she say."

Albert was getting ready to leave, too, and Lena got Albert to walk up the quarters with her. About an hour later she came back and told me Olivia said she would take us.

"She don't mind if they put her off the place?" I asked.

"She done saved up a few dollars," Lena said.

Mary got up the next morning just after sun-up and told me if I was going to Bayonne with her I better get up and get myself ready. I asked her when did she make up her mind to go. She said she made up her mind when she saw nothing was go'n keep me from going. Who was go'n look after me when they knocked me down. I said the Lord. She said the Lord might be busy helping somebody else, and it wouldn't look right for Him just to drop that person and come help me. I got up and said my prayers. After I had pushed back my bar and made up my bed I went in the kitchen to have my coffee.

"You better eat something solid," Mary said. "You might have to do some fast shuffling."

"You can give me a bisquit with my coffee," I said.

"I mean grits and eggs," Mary said. "When you fall I want to make sure it's a billy club, not hungriness."

"Don't give me too much," I said.

Mary had opened the back door and cool air came in. I looked out at the sun, orange color on the grass. Usually I liked this time of day, the freshness, but today I felt something funny in the air. My heart was jumping too much. I wasn't scared I might get hurt—when you get to be a hundred and eight or a hundred and nine you forget what scared is: I felt something funny in the air, but I didn't know what it was. I just sat there looking out at the grass, and I could remember the times when I used to bend over and run my hands in the dew. But of course that was long long ago. Now, all I can do is walk in it sometime, and I got to be careful doing even that.

"Air feels funny," I said.

"How do funny air feel?" Mary said.

"Just feel funny," I said.

Mary brought the food to the table and she sat down across from me.

"I know I cause you trouble," I said.

"Don't start that," Mary said. "You don't cause me no trouble."

"You don't have to go, Mary," I said.

"Staying on this place don't mean that much to me," she said.

"Where you going if they put you off?" I asked her.

"I don't know," she said. "Probably be somewhere close 'round you."

"Everything I own is yours when I die," I said.

"Don't try to pay me, Miss Jane," she said. "I was brought up too good for that."

"I'm not trying to pay you," I said. "But I love you much as you love me, and that's all I have to give. I want you to have my all."

"I have your love and your respect, and that's enough," she said.

"I want you to have my rocking chair and my sewing machine," I said.

"All right," Mary said. "But they'll have to kill me first. Then somebody else can get everything."

"I didn't mean today," I said.

"That's right, today we secured," Mary said. "I wonder what we go'n do to turn them back—sing?"

"And maybe little clapping," I said.

"Well, I got a feeling them things in Bayonne go'n want more than just spirituals today," Mary said. "Lot lot more."

"You feel death in the air, too, Mary?" I said.

Mary felt death just like I felt it, but she didn't want answer. She got up and washed the dishes, then she swept out the kitchen.

Lena called for us 'round eight thirty. Mary helped me on with my sweater and I found my walking stick and we went out on the gallery. The place was quiet the way it is on Sunday nights when you don't have church. I leaned on Mary till I reached the ground. When we came out in the road, there was Etienne standing there in his best clothes.

"Well, Etienne?" I said.

"Miss Jane," he said, tipping his hat.

I looked at him and nodded, and I was very proud of Etienne.

Just the four of us started up the quarters to Olivia's. It was still cool, and the dust in the road was cool and soft. The sun hadn't come above the trees, yet, and the shadows from the trees and the crop was on the road. I could see where drops of water had dripped from the weeds hanging over the rim of the road.

We had been walking quietly all the while, but just before we came up to Strut's house, Etienne looked back and said it looked like somebody else was coming that way. The person was too far for me to make out who it was; all I could see was a dark form in the white dust. We hadn't gone too much farther when Etienne said it looked like two or three more people was coming that way. I looked back again. I still couldn't recognize them, just dark forms in that white dust. Before we got to Joe Simon's house I looked back, and this time I stopped and leaned on my walking stick. This time it was not one or two, it was many. They was not marching, they was not hurrying; it didn't look like they was even talking to each other. They was walking like every last one of them was by himself and any little noise could turn him around. But the longer I stood there looking, the more I saw coming toward me. Men, women, children. I couldn't recognize who they was way down there, but I could tell dresses from pants, and I could tell grown people from children. No, not everybody in the quarters was headed that way—Brady's car was still down there. Probably half of the people was still down there. But the number of people I saw coming toward me was something I never would 'a' dreamed of. I wouldn't 'a' believed nobody if he had told me this could happen. I stood there watching them, thinking: Jimmy, Jimmy, Jimmy, Jimmy, Jimmy. Look what you've done. Look what you've done. Look what you've done, Jimmy.

They came up and stood all 'round us. Most of them was scared and they wasn't shame to show it. But they was standing there, and that's what mattered. And I felt like telling each one of them thank you, thank you, thank you. I told myself when I got to the courthouse I was going up to Jimmy and say, "Jimmy, look at your army from Samson. Did you think they was go'n show up?" And he was go'n look at me in that sad-sweet way and say, "Sure, I knowed they wasn't go'n let me down."

I looked at them all there and I was so happy I started crying. Mary and them saw me crying, but they didn't say nothing to me because they knowed it was from joy, not sorrow.

Olivia came out the house and saw us all there and said she was sorry, she wouldn't be able to take nearly half that many. The people said they would catch the bus, and said tell Jimmy don't start till they got there. Olivia asked them if they all had money. They had forgot about money. Olivia told them wait—she was going back in the house to get her pocketbook—but just as she turned to go back inside, Robert Samson drove his car down the quarters.

I heard Lena scream, and I saw her running heavy heavy straight toward the car. Mary and Olivia and Merle Anne went after her and pulled her out the way. She screamed and screamed and tried to get away from them. Robert got out of the car and looked at all us standing there.

"Go back home," he said.

"What happened to my boy?" Lena asked him. "What happened to my boy?"

"Go back home," Robert said.

"What happened, Mr. Robert?" Etienne asked.

Robert was looking at Lena, and I could tell something bad had happened.

"No," Lena started screaming. "No. Lord, no."

"Take her home," Robert said.

"We got a right to know, Mr. Robert," Etienne said.

"Where's my boy?" Lena asked Robert. "I want to see my boy."

"You'll see him tomorrow," Robert said. "I'll take you there tomorrow."

"Is he dead?" Etienne asked.

"They shot him eight o'clock this morning," Robert said.

Then she fell. Even with Mary and them holding her up she fell. They picked her up and took her inside the house.

"Who shot him?" Etienne asked.

"Who knows?" Robert said.

"Somebody knows," Etienne said. "Somebody knows, Mr. Robert."

"Well, I didn't shoot him," Robert said. "I didn't know nothing about it till they called the house."

He stood by the car looking at all us standing there.

"Go back home," he said.

"You mean get off, don't you?" I said.

"I mean go on back home," he said.

"I'm going to Bayonne, me," Strut's boy said.

"I'll follow Alex," I said.

"Them who want go to Bayonne, let's go to Bayonne," Alex said. "Let's go to Bayonne even if we got to come back here to nothing."

"What you think you go'n find in Bayonne, boy?" Robert said.

"Jimmy," Alex said.

"Jimmy is dead," Robert said. "Didn't you hear me say Jimmy was killed at eight o'clock?"

"He ain't dead nothing," Alex said.

"You know better," Robert said to me.

"Just a little piece of him is dead," I said. "The rest of him is waiting for us in Bayonne. And I will go with Alex."

Some of the people backed away from me when I said this, but the braver ones started for the road. They had forgot about bus fare again, and since I didn't have enough money for everybody I sent one of the children in the house to Olivia. He came back with a ten dollar bill and said Olivia said she would be up there later. I stuck the money in my pocketbook. Me and Robert looked at each other there a long time, then I went by him.

Related Readings

Sojourner Truth

I Want Women to Have Their Rights. . . . I Will Shake Every Place I Go To

Sojourner Truth, a former enslaved person, was renowned as a rousing public speaker on the subject of equal rights. Mary Church Terrell was the cofounder and first president of the National Association of Colored Women. At a time when many people in the United States were trying to establish that "all men are created equal," both women delivered speeches on equal rights for African American women.

MY FRIENDS, I am rejoiced that you are glad, but I don't know how you will feel when I get through.

I come from another field—the country of the slave. They have got their rights—so much good luck. Now what is to be done about it? I feel that I have got as much responsibility as anybody else. I have as good rights as anybody.

There is a great stir about colored men getting their rights, but not a word about the colored women; and if colored men get their rights, and not colored women get theirs, there will be a bad time about it. So I am for keeping the thing going while things are stirring; because if we wait till it is still, it will take a great while to get it going again. White women are a great deal smarter, and know more than colored women, while colored women do not know scarcely anything. They go out washing, which is about as high as a colored woman gets, and their men go about idle, strutting up and down; and when the women come home, they ask for their money and take it all, and then scold because there is no food. I want you to consider on that, chil'n.[1] I want women to have their rights.

In the courts women have no right, no voice; nobody speaks for them. I wish woman to have her voice there among the pettifoggers.[2] If it is not a fit place for women, it is unfit for men to be there. I am above eighty years old; it is about time for me to be going. But I suppose I am kept here because something remains for me to do; I suppose I am yet to help break the chain. I have done a great deal of work—as much as a man, but did not get so much pay. I used to work in the field and bind grain, keeping up with the cradler;[3] but men never doing no more, got twice as much pay. So with the German women. They work in the field and do as much work, but do not get the pay. We do as much, we eat as much, we want as much.

I suppose I am about the only colored woman that goes about to speak for the rights of the colored woman, I want to keep the thing stirring, now that the ice is broken. What we want is a little money. You men know that you get as much again as women when you write, or for what you do. When we get our rights, we shall not have to come to you for money, for then we shall have money enough of our own. It is a good consolation to know that when we have got this we shall not be coming to you anymore.

You have been having our right so long, that you think, like a slaveholder, that you own us. I know that it is hard for one who has held the reins for so long to give up; it cuts like a knife. It will feel all better when it closes up again. I have been in Washington about three years, seeing about those colored people. Now colored men have a right to vote; and what I want is to have colored women have the right to vote. There ought to be equal rights more than ever, since colored people have got their freedom.

I know that it is hard for men to give up entirely. They must run in the old track. I was amused how men speak up for one another. They cannot bear that a woman should say anything about the man, but they will stand here and take up the time in man's cause. But we are going, tremble or no tremble. Men are trying to help us. I know that all—the spirit they have got; and they cannot help us much until some of the spirit is taken out of them that belongs among the women. Men have got their rights, and women has not got their rights. That is the trouble. When woman gets her rights man will be right. How beautiful that will be. Then it will be peace on earth and good will to men. . . .

And now when the waters is troubled, and now is the time to step into the pool. There is a great deal now with the minds, and now is the time to

---

1. **chil'n** contraction of the word *children*
2. **pettifoggers** dishonest lawyers
3. **cradler** a person who cuts grain with a scythe

start forth. . . . The great fight was to keep the rights of the poor colored people. That made a great battle. And now I hope that this will be that last battle that will be in the world. Let us finish up so that there be no more fighting. I have faith in God and there is truth in humanity. Be strong women! Blush not! Tremble not! I want you to keep a good faith and good courage. And I am going round after I get my business settled and get more equality. People in the North, I am going round to lecture on human rights. I will shake every place I go to.

Mary Church Terrell

The Progress of Colored Women

WHEN ONE CONSIDERS the obstacles encountered by colored women in their effort to educate and cultivate themselves, since they became free, the work they have accomplished and the progress they have made will bear favorable comparison, at least with that of their more fortunate sisters, from whom the opportunity of acquiring knowledge and the means of self-culture have never been entirely withheld. Not only are colored women with ambition and aspiration handicapped on account of their sex, but they are almost everywhere baffled and mocked because of their race. Not only because they are women, but because they are colored women are discouragement and disappointment meeting them at every turn.

But in spite of the obstacles encountered, the progress made by colored women along many lines appears like a veritable[1] miracle of modern times. Forty years ago for the great masses of colored women there was no such thing as home. Today in each and every section of the country there are hundreds of homes among colored people, the mental and moral tone of which is as high and as pure as can be found among the best people of any land.

To the women of the race may be attributed in large measure the refinement and purity of the colored home. The immorality of colored women is a theme upon which those who know little about them or those who maliciously misrepresent them love to descant.[2] Foul aspersions[3] upon the character of colored women are assiduously[4] circulated by the press of certain sections and especially by the direct descendants of those who in years past were responsible for the moral degradation[5] of their female slaves.

And yet, in spite of the fateful heritage of slavery, even though the safeguards usually thrown around maidenly youth and innocence are in some

---

1. **veritable** real
2. **descant** comment on
3. **aspersions** misrepresentations
4. **assiduously** persistently
5. **degradation** humiliation

sections entirely withheld from colored girls, statistics compiled by men not inclined to falsify in favor of my race show that immorality among the colored women of the United States is not so great as among women with similar environment and temptations in Italy, Germany, Sweden, and France.

Scandals in the best colored society are exceedingly rare, while the progressive game of divorce and remarriage is practically unknown.

The intellectual progress of colored women has been marvelous. So great has been their thirst for knowledge and so Herculean[6] their efforts to acquire it that there are few colleges, universities, high and normal schools in the North, East and West from which colored girls have not graduated with honor. In Wellesley, Vassar, Ann Arbor, Cornell and in Oberlin, my dear alma mater, whose name will always be loved and whose praise will always be sung as the first college in the country broad, just and generous enough to extend a cordial welcome to the Negro and to open its doors to women on an equal footing with the men, colored girls by their splendid records have forever settled the question of their capacity and worth. The instructors in these and other institutions cheerfully bear testimony to their intelligence, their diligence and their success.

As the brains of colored women expanded, their hearts began to grow. No sooner had the heads of a favored few been filled with knowledge than their hearts yearned to dispense blessings to the less fortunate of their race. With tireless energy and eager zeal, colored women have worked in every conceivable way to elevate their race. Of the colored teachers engaged in instructing our youth it is probably no exaggeration to say that fully eighty percent are women. In the backwoods, remote from the civilization and comforts of the city and town colored women may be found courageously battling with those evils which such conditions always entail. Many a heroine of whom the world will never hear has thus sacrificed her life to her race amid surroundings and in the face of privations[7] which only martyrs can bear. . . .

It is almost impossible to ascertain exactly what the Negro is doing in any field, for the records are so poorly kept. This is particularly true in the case of the women of the race. During the past forty years there is no doubt that colored women in their poverty have contributed large sums of money to charitable and educational institutions as well as to the foreign and home missionary work. Within the twenty-five years in which the educational work of the African Methodist Episcopal Church has been systematized, the women of that organization have contributed at least five hundred thousand

---

6. **Herculean** like the mythical Hercules in strength or courage
7. **privations** hardships

dollars to the cause of education. Dotted all over the country are charitable institutions for the aged, orphaned and poor which have been established by colored women. Just how many it is difficult to state, owing to the lack of statistics bearing on the progress, possessions and prowess[8] of colored women. . . .

Up to date, politics have been religiously eschewed[9] by colored women, although questions affecting our legal status as a race are sometimes agitated by the most progressive class. In Louisiana and Tennessee colored women have several times petitioned the legislatures of their respective states to repel the obnoxious Jim-Crow-car laws.[10] Against the convict-lease system,[11] whose atrocities[12] have been so frequently exposed of late, colored women here and there in the South are waging a ceaseless war. So long as hundreds of their brothers and sisters, many of whom have committed no crime or misdemeanor whatever, are thrown into cells whose cubic contents are less than those of a goodsize grave, to be overworked, underfed and only partially covered with vermin-infested rags, and so long as children are born to the women in these camps who breathe the polluted atmosphere of these dens of horror and vice from the time they utter their first cry in the world till they are released from their suffering by death, colored women who are working for the emancipation and elevation of their race know where their duty lies. By constant agitation of this painful and hideous subject they hope to touch the conscience of the country, so that this stain upon its escutcheon[13] shall be forever wiped away.

Alarmed at the rapidity with which the Negro is losing ground in the world of trade, some of the farsighted women are trying to solve the labor question, so far as it concerns the women at least, by urging the establishment of schools of domestic science wherever means therefor can be secured. Those who are interested in this particular work hope and believe that if colored women and girls are thoroughly trained in domestic service, the boycott which has undoubtedly been placed upon them in many sections of the country will be removed. With so few vocations open to the Negro and with the labor organizations increasingly hostile to him, the future of the boys and girls of the race appears to some of our women very foreboding and dark.

---

8. **prowess** great ability or skill
9. **eschewed** avoided
10. **Jim-Crow-car laws** state laws requiring separation by race in public transportation
11. **convict-lease system** state laws that allowed prisons to lease out prisoners as laborers for large companies
12. **atrocities** crimes
13. **escutcheon** shield

The cause of the temperance[14] has been eloquently espoused[15] by two women, each of whom has been appointed national superintendent of work among colored people by the Woman's Christian Temperance Union. In business, colored women have had signal success. There is in Alabama a large milling and cotton business belonging to and controlled by a colored woman, who has sometimes as many as seventy-five men in her employ. Until a few years ago the principal ice plant of Nova Scotia was owned and managed by a colored woman, who sold it for a large amount. In the professions there are dentists and doctors whose practice is lucrative and large. Ever since a book was published in 1773 entitled "Poems on Various Subjects, Religious and Moral by Phillis Wheatley, Negro Servant of Mr. John Wheatley," of Boston, colored women have given abundant evidence of literary ability. In sculpture we are represented by a woman upon whose chisel Italy has set her seal of approval; in painting by one of Bouguereau's pupils and in music by young women holding diplomas from the best conservatories in the land.

In short, to use a thought of the illustrious Frederick Douglass,[16] if judged by the depths from which they have come, rather than by the heights to which those blessed with centuries of opportunities have attained, colored women need not hang their heads in shame. They are slowly but surely making their way up to the heights, wherever they can be scaled. In spite of handicaps and discouragements they are not losing heart. In a variety of ways they are rendering valiant service to their race. Lifting as they climb, onward and upward they go struggling and striving and hoping that the buds and blossoms of their desires may burst into glorious fruition ere long. Seeking no favors because of their color nor charity because of their needs they knock at the door of Justice and ask for an equal chance.

---

14. **temperance** moderation in the use of something, especially alcohol
15. **espoused** embraced
16. **Frederick Douglass** (1817–1895) former enslaved person and leader of the abolition movement

Tom Carter

Ernest Gaines

This interview with Ernest Gaines provides insight into the life of the author of The Autobiography of Miss Jane Pittman.

AFTER 15 threadbare, relatively obscure years of writing, Ernest Gaines scored with *The Autobiography of Miss Jane Pittman*. The timing of his book was totally unplanned, but it was right. Now Miss Jane's story has touched, in one degree or another, more than 51 million people. Small, solitary, book choked and record strewn, this three-room apartment in a redeveloped section of San Francisco would seem to be an ordinary writer's home. Ordinary except for the severe visual prods that daily jab Ernest J. Gaines' memories of the deep South he left in the late forties. For among the portraits of great authors on his walls are moody black and white photographs he took while visiting home in Louisiana in 1968. They are of the muggy bayou country outside Baton Rouge, particularly the stark, sugar plantation where he was born in 1933 and lived for 15 years.

Most of the photographs are not of people but of ghost-like, weathered houses and lean landscapes. One is of a mammoth oak tree growing by the side of a lonely dirt road, the road Gaines' characters walk down.

His characters, Black, rural deep South peasants, had not been popular. That is, not until Gaines created Miss Jane Pittman. After 15 threadbare, relatively obscure years of writing, Gaines scored with *The Autobiography* of *Miss Jane Pittman*, a novel that took him about three years to complete. The book is a fictional account of the life of a 110-year-old ex-slave, who tells her story into the tape recorder of a history teacher/editor.

[In the first four years after] its publication in 1971, *Miss Jane . . .* sold 850,000 copies in paperback and over 26,000 in hardback, far overshadowing Gaines' first three published books. As a result of selling the book's TV rights, Gaines for the first time in his life, received a sizable amount of money and months later became famous.

His reaction to Hollywood's initial interest in the book tells a lot about Gaines' single-minded approach to his work. When his New York agent told him the Tomorrow Entertainment Company wanted the book's movie and television rights, Gaines quoted the price he'd accept and refused to see or talk to anybody until they met it.

But once Tomorrow Entertainment had the rights to the story, they had trouble finding financial backers for it. "Nobody wanted to buy the story of an old Black woman talking into a tape recorder about her past life," Gaines says. "They felt it was too episodic; they had to cover 100 years in 110 minutes and couldn't concentrate on anything very long. I couldn't have written the screen version and I had my doubts that anybody could." But CBS chanced it. The TV special, filmed in Louisiana, starred Cicely Tyson in a role as memorable as her Rebecca in *Sounder*. Forty-three million viewers saw her portrayal of Miss Jane in January of 1974. The special received rave reviews in hundreds of newspapers coast to coast, as well as in *Time*, *Newsweek*, and *The New Yorker*. It was named "outstanding special of the year" and won nine Emmys.

Credit for the prize-winning screenplay goes to Tracy Keenan Wynn, son of actor Keenan Wynn. His TV version differed from the novel in many respects, but Gaines curiously, is unperturbed.[1] "I had no control over the film. Professionally it's another man's work. I'm a struggling novelist, and once I've finished a book, you can say or do anything you want; my book is there. I hope people will credit me or damn me for the book, *not* for the film."

Gaines says most people who were familiar with the book felt the TV movie didn't measure up to it. Nonetheless some of Wynn's inventions were powerful, especially the ending. In the book, there was no march to the fountain.

"Television is a different thing," Gaines explains. "In the book you can have this little old lady saying 'I will go to the demonstration even if I can't come back here to the plantation,' and that's a dramatic enough ending. But in television you've got to punch people in the stomach. I heard Tracy was adamant[2] the march to the fountain had to be there." With a rare laugh Gaines adds, "That's what people remember more than anything, and that's what I didn't write! But you know, it doesn't matter to me one way or the other."

The oldest of eight brothers and three sisters, Gaines began working in the plantation fields outside of Baton Rouge at age nine, earning 50 cents a day picking cotton, Irish potatoes and onions. He played games with the other children but was basically a loner. Withdrawn, he often went off alone to pick blackberries along the road or to take long walks—as he still does—or to sit with his aunt Miss Augusteen Jefferson.

His mother, who was separated from her husband, worked in the fields; his grandfather was the big-house yardman. His grandmother, like Miss Jane, was the big-house cook. Many in the family were humorous storytellers and clever imitators, but they considered Ernie brilliant because, having attended

---

1. **unperturbed** undisturbed
2. **adamant** firm

a nearby church school, he could read and write. The family and their friends, which combined spanned four generations, often called on Ernie to write their letters. Once he wrote a humorous play and staged it at church. The experiences in it paralleled Jimmy's [in] *Miss Jane*.

Gaines' Aunt Augusteen, who died 21 years ago, influenced his life more than anyone. "She was crippled from birth so she never walked," he explained. "While my mother worked in the fields, Aunt Augusteen did everything—cooking, washing, and ironing. She completely ignored the wheelchair that welfare gave her (we kids played with it). She'd crawl over the floor like an infant, down the steps and into the garden to weed and hoe, then to the backyard to collect pecans and back into the house. When we misbehaved she made us cut the switch that would punish us. If it wasn't the right size, she sent us back for another one."

"My aunt never felt sorry for herself," Gaines says slowly, studying the somewhat sad, surrealistic[3] photo of her on the wall. "And the people did not feel sorry for her. She had a great moral strength. I know the kind of burden she carried trying to raise us and I feel any character I wrote about has to have a burden. The main character has to have a heavy burden, one that can knock the average person down; sometimes it does but he has to get up. This is the philosophy I have, if I have any at all, because of the struggle of my aunt, the struggle of my race, the struggle of people in general. Any person who's worth a goddamn must really struggle."

In 1948 when Gaines was 15, he joined his mother, who had remarried and moved to Vallejo, California. He hung around street corners with his buddies until his stepfather told him he would get into trouble if he didn't get off the streets. Gaines went to the library.

He wanted to read about familiar things but couldn't find any. There were no books by Black writers in Vallejo's library; the stories he found closest to American rural life were by John Steinbeck and Willa Cather. But in that same library he discovered Chekhov and Turgenev, Russians who wrote about rural peasantry[4] and outdoor life. "The peasantry of America is Black, but any peasantry touches me," he says. "I found them in foreign literature. Southerners didn't write about it. They weren't up to portraying Black peasants as humans instead of clowns."

Having attended a junior college for two years prior to joining the army, Gaines entered San Francisco State College as a junior in 1955 determined to be a writer of those experiences he hadn't found in the library. But he flunked an essay-writing course until he suggested substituting fictional work. The instructor consented and was impressed with the resulting short stories.

---

3. **surrealistic** characterized by dreamlike distortions
4. **peasantry** laborers

Gaines passed the course and one of the stories helped him win a creative-writing fellowship at Stanford University.

In the ensuing years, Gaines developed style, but his literary pursuits were not "timely." "Northern liberals and radical whites were the only people who bought the works of Black writers, and they didn't care for tales about Black peasantry. I think they were much more concerned with the Black problem than with the Black character," says Gaines. "Richard Wright's *Native Son* is a good example. It was almost a blueprint of what you had to do if you wanted to be published at all."

Gaines, however, never wanted to be anything but a writer of peasant tales. After graduation he gave himself ten years to "make it." He almost didn't, writing diligently[5] in the morning, working at jobs he didn't like in the afternoons, making inspired notes at work on paper scraps and toilet paper. He lived on $175 a month and had no phone.

"It was hand to mouth," he says, dismissing it with a wave of the hand. "But 99 percent of the people who write have gone through that. No one twisted my arm to be a writer, I chose it."

Gaines' first novel, *Catherine Carmier*, published in 1964, won the Joseph Henry Jackson Literary Prize but it didn't sell. He continued working at temporary jobs until, finally, a modest book contract in 1966 (one year before his ten-year deadline) gave him some independence that allowed him to form better working habits and not sweat the rent. *Of Love and Dust* (1967) and *Bloodline* (1968) were published but paid nothing in royalties. It was a time of militancy[6] and a literary scream came out of the ghetto. Books like *The Autobiography of Malcolm X* and *Soul on Ice* sold a bundle. When Gaines gave readings from his works at nearby colleges, crowds were sparse and few Blacks attended. If Black students didn't consider him an Uncle Tom, the best they could consider him was out of touch.

It wasn't that Gaines had no anger, but rather that his approach to anger was different. "Growing up in the South, I know the last thing in the world that whites wanted to see was humanity in Blacks," he explains. "I knew the way to show that humanity was to do something positive. Some guys get angry and go to a punching bag. As they're jabbing at it they're developing their muscles; they're getting sharper. I try to use the anger in a positive way, to create a lasting punch, one that will have a longer effect than just screaming. . . ."

Nor was Gaines' head turned by the lure of big bucks that writing *in vogue*[7] material would bring. Compromises were out of question. Fortunately

---

5. **diligently** intensely

6. **militancy** warlike or aggressive activity

7. **in vogue** popular

his determination and self-discipline prevailed. But he admits, "those first ten years of writing were hell."

The times did slowly change, "especially since the TV special. More Blacks and a new group of white intellectuals in their thirties appreciate what I'm trying to do. I don't think the book will sell any three or four million, but I think the book will be taught in schools for quite a while. It's time."

It is usually very difficult for a man to write a book narrated by a woman. Gaines read history, century-old slave narratives and books about women. He called on his aunt's voice too. "I worked her voice, plus the ex-slaves' voices, over and over until I got the one I liked. It took a while but it was no problem. I could look at my walls and remember."

Because of Gaines' concentration on peasantry in the deep South and the fact that he studied in the fifties, white writers have been a greater influence than Black writers. "Probably the only Black writer who has influenced my work is Zora Neale Hurston. But if I had read Jean Toomer's *Cane* before I developed my own way of working and writing, it probably would have influenced me as much as Faulkner, Hemingway or Turgenev."

Yet all manner of art and excellence affect the author. Excellence, itself, is a message, a challenge to emulate[8] in hard work and substance. Modest Mussorgsky's composition *Pictures at an Exhibition*—musical interpretations of pictures the composer sees, linked by a promenade theme—so inspired Gaines during the writing of *Miss Jane* that he played the album daily.

The success of *Miss Jane* doesn't seem to have changed Gaines. He does worry, however, that new demands on his time—which he guards closely—take a certain toll in daily discipline. Writing is still hard and somewhat painful. . . .

He writes longhand at a nondescript kitchen table amid the careless clutter in his tired apartment when he can now afford better. That's not important nor, in a way, is money. He's had offers to become a Hollywood writer with a handsome salary but he's completely uninterested.

Nowadays the chapters scattered in a semicircle around the table are part of *In My Father's House*, a novel he's been working on for four years. The setting is a small Louisiana town. The time is after Martin Luther King's death and it deals with young people's attitudes. It's deadline is two years old. "I hate to sound like I'm complaining, because I hate for anybody to complain to me," he says with a set jaw. "But it is giving me more hell than anything I've ever written."

Problems or no, Gaines continues listening to the whispers of his pictures and writing about the deep South.

---

8. **emulate** mimic

from

Everybody Says Freedom

Pete Seeger and Bob Reiser

The Civil Rights movement in the South in the 1960s is examined through personal accounts and protest songs compiled by songwriter Pete Seeger and writer Bob Reiser.

1960: The Sit-ins

February 1, 1960—Greensboro, North Carolina. Four black college freshmen from North Carolina Agricultural and Technical College—Joe McNeil, Frank McCain, Dave Richmond, and Ezell Blair—had spent the night before, in the college dorm, talking about how they could help the civil rights movement in their own town.

The segregation practices in Greensboro were the same as in most of the South. In movie theaters black people sat upstairs, white people sat downstairs. Whites went to white-only bathrooms, blacks to black-only bathrooms. Whites drank at white-only water fountains, black people at black-only water fountains. It was as if there were two distinct kinds of human beings inhabiting the town, and the well-kept condition of white facilities and the run-down black facilities made it clear whom the town fathers and businessmen considered the superior kind of human. Some of the most humiliating segregation practices were in dime stores, where black people could spend their money for toothbrushes and shoelaces, but could not sit down for a cup of coffee. The lunch counter was for "whites only." The four young men wondered if they could make a step toward breaking the race line at downtown lunch counters.

That morning, they go into Woolworth's. It is one of those old stores, with streaky yellow light and huge mahogany display cases. It smells of disinfectant and chewing gum. Old ladies with blue hair are moving up the aisles with their colored maids in tow. "I'd like some of those pins, Jemima, and that fabric—isn't it lovely . . ." Books under their arms, they wander around nervously. Joe McNeil buys a tube of toothpaste, Frank McCain buys a pack of notebook paper. Finally, they look toward one another—it is time. Without a word, all four sit down at the lunch counter.

At first the white waitress pays no attention to them. McCain asks for a hot dog and coffee. The confused waitress runs over to the manager. After a moment she returns, "Sorry, I can't serve you. We don't serve colored here." "But you do have hot dogs and coffee," says McNeil. He can see white customers eating that same food farther down the counter. "I can't serve you!" insists the frightened waitress, and she walks away. A black woman washing dishes walks over to them and mutters, "Why don't you boys go out and stop making trouble?"

All afternoon the students stay at the counter. A white policeman walks in from the street. "He paced up and down the aisle," McCain recalled later, "with this club in his hand, just sort of knocking it into his hand and looking mean and red and a little bit disgusted. You had this feeling he didn't know what the hell to do. See, we haven't provoked him outwardly enough for him to resort to violence. And I think it's just killing him."

A couple of older white women also come by. They pat the boys on the back. "It's a good thing I think you're doing," they say.

The school newspaper prints an account of the sit-in. Amazingly, the next day there are twenty-seven students, sitting quietly, textbooks in their hands, waiting for service. The Greensboro newspaper picks up the story. Local white toughs come in to taunt the students, but they sit quietly, refusing to move and refusing to lose their composure. By the next day, white students from North Carolina Women's College join them, occupying stools and refusing to eat until the black students are also served. When the TV cameras pick up the sight of the jeering, foul-mouthed whites, and the quiet, dignified students, something in the South stirs. "Gad!" exclaims James Kilpatrick, editor of the conservative *Richmond News Leader*. "It gives one pause!"

The story flies across the South. Other students, at other universities, see the sit-ins and decide that they want to help. Sit-ins everywhere. The police begin to break up the demonstrations, arresting the students, dragging them away with their notebooks and pencils and slide rules flying. One policeman in Orangeburg, South Carolina, picks up a dropped slide rule. He slides the center scale out at one end. He slides it out at the other. He holds up the rule. "Damnedest switchblade I ever saw," he says finally.

Nowhere else did the sit-ins create as much electricity as they did in Nashville. Fisk University, the American Baptist Seminary, Tennessee A. and I., and Meharry Medical College had an incredibly talented group of young black students, including Marion Barry, James Bevel, John Lewis,

Diane Nash, and Bernard LaFayette. For several months Rev. James Lawson, who had studied Gandhi's methods in India, had been holding workshops on nonviolence for these students. "We had begun preparing for sit-ins in Nashville in the fall of 1959," explained Diane Nash, a student at Fisk. "When word came of the North Carolina sit-ins, we began sitting in at Nashville outlets of the same chain stores."

Candie Anderson (later Candie Carawan), a white exchange student at Fisk, was another regular at Jim Lawson's workshops. "I didn't know whether, as a white person, I was just horning in on someone else's cause," she said. "But the group felt that it was important to show that this was an integrated movement. Also, we had a specific role in the sit-ins. If the stores were on the lookout for black students, white students would go in and take the seats at the lunch counter and then turn them over to blacks."

On February 18, two hundred Nashville students marched downtown and sat at the lunch counters. Miraculously, the sit-in went without incident.

Diane Nash: *The waitresses were nervous. They must have dropped two thousand dollars' worth of dishes. It was almost like a cartoon. We all worked very hard not to laugh, even though I was wall-to-wall terrified.*

Candie Carawan: *We felt like we were going to move a whole society!*

John Lewis: *I had the feeling we were involved in something like a crusade. . . . To redeem the city, like Dr. King[1] said, to redeem the soul of America. You put on your Sunday clothes, and we took our books and papers to the lunch counter, and we did our homework, trying to be as dignified as possible. I drew up these rules, like: "Show yourself friendly at the counter at all times. Sit up and face the counter. Don't strike back or curse back if attacked. Don't laugh out. Don't block entrances." And it ended with something like "Remember the teachings of Jesus, Gandhi, Martin Luther King. God bless you all."*

On Saturday, February 27, violence came.

Bernard LaFayette: *We got word from downtown that the police were going to arrest us. Also, we heard that some people were going to beat us up. On top of that it was cold and it was snowing. This was going to be a showdown. Unfortunately, there weren't many people going out on this demonstration. We debated and we debated, and finally we decided we couldn't let a threat of violence deter us. Well, we went.*

Candie Carawan: *About eighty of us went down to the lunch counter that day, fifty girls and about thirty boys. Two girls and three boys were white. I still remember how neatly we all dressed. The idea was to go just as well dressed, as dignified, as you could. The girls in their white blouses and pleated skirts, and the boys with*

---

1. **Dr. Martin Luther King Jr.** (1929–1968) clergyman and Civil Rights leader

their suits; some of them even had a Bible under their arms. There were fourteen seats at the lunch counter. Fourteen of us sat down.

Right away the toughs started throwing things over us and pouring catsup in our hair; putting out cigarette butts on our backs. I've got to say that didn't surprise me. What did surprise me was that when the police came they just watched. Finally they turned to the students at the lunch counter: "OK, you-all nigras, get up from the lunch counter or we're going to arrest you." When nobody moved, they just peeled those people, with their neat dresses and their Bibles, right off their seats and carried them to the paddy wagons. Before they were out of the store, another fourteen of us took their places at the counter. They got peeled off, and another fourteen sat down. By the end, eighty of us got arrested. Boy, it was something!

Bernard LaFayette: *I was not supposed to be arrested. My job was to help coordinate the sit-ins: if the students were being arrested in one place, my job was to let people know at another location, so they could come and help. The more the merrier in terms of being arrested.*

Well, at one place, they had some trouble, so the police asked the demonstrators to leave. The police grabbed a white student and started to pull him out. Well, the black students filed out after the policeman because they were sure they were being arrested also. But the police pushed this white fellow into the paddy wagon and locked the door behind him. They ignored the black students. Then, they locked the door to the department store so no one could go back in.

We waited around very inconspicuously. As soon as one of the customers came out of the door, the students rushed inside. But one of the young ladies pulled me inside. I wasn't supposed to go, but she pulled me. I was literally pulled into the movement. I remember her name—Angela Butler. I told one of the students to get someone else to coordinate because my role had ended.

By April, the Nashville Movement had reached into the whole community.

The movement touched the North. Bob Moses, a mathematics teacher at the Horace Mann School in the Bronx, New York, saw a picture of the Greensboro sit-inners: "The students in the picture had a certain look in their faces—determined. Before, the Negro in the South had always looked on the defensive. This time they were taking the initiative. They were kids my age, and I knew this had something to do with my life." Soon Moses would go south to join the movement.

By early spring, students all across the South were marching and protesting and sitting in. A whole new generation had entered the civil rights movement. The annual meeting of activist southern students at Highlander changed its topic to "The New Generation Fights for Equality." Eighty-two college students showed up. They came from Nashville, Knoxville, North and South Carolina. Forty-seven of them were black, thirty-five were white.

Candie Carawan: *I remember one workshop we had on tactics.*[2] *The subject worked its way around to going to jail. What good was it, what did it accomplish? Myles [Horton] was playing devil's advocate.*[3] *That's how he worked—he didn't try to push any idea, he just kept asking questions, making us clarify our thinking. By the end of the discussion we came to the conclusion that if we wanted to make jail part of our tactic, we'd have to be willing to stay in. Otherwise, we'd just be draining our resources in bail money, without tying up the opposition at all. That's the tactic the whole movement used after that. After the freedom rides, and in Mississippi—everywhere!*

The other thing I remember was the music. There was the Nashville Quartet and Bernard LaFayette and his friends and songs from all over the place. That was the first time I heard We Shall Overcome. What a perfect song—it pulled us together with such power, it had such quiet strength. We knew we were going to take it back to Nashville.

Bernard LaFayette: *Myles Horton loved to play devil's advocate. . . . He was arguing the whole question of why do black and white have to be together. He was saying things like "Why don't you do something for yourself? Why do you have to be with white people?" I had never heard a white man say those things to my face, and he was supposed to be a friend. I got madder and madder. Of course, he was trying to force us to be very clear about what we wanted. I knew what he was doing, but it made me furious. He was always pushing you further; you think you have come to some conclusion about something, and there he is, pushing out the walls, and you have to reach out and grab something. That's what a good teacher does—keeps making you rearrange the blankets to make room for broader ideas.*

---

2. **tactics** strategies
3. **devil's advocate** a person who supports a position for the sake of argument

I'm Gonna Sit at the Welcome Table

I remember, we were at a meeting and song-swap at Highlander when Ernie Martin suggested that *I'm Gonna Sit at the Welcome Table* would make a great lunch-counter song. All we had to do was change a few words. So right then and there, we all changed it. People testing out verses, throwing them in.

—*Guy Carawan*

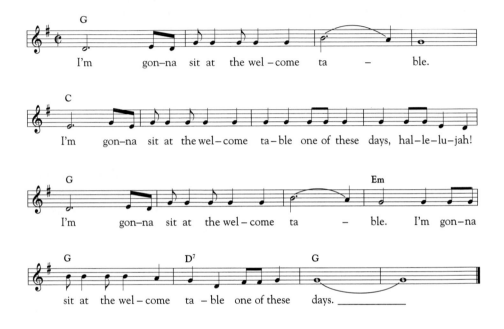

I'm gonna walk the streets of glory . . .

I'm gonna get my civil rights . . .

I'm gonna sit at the Woolworth counter . . .

Everybody Says Freedom

There were parents and grandparents bringing us sandwiches and coffee; there were high-school students marching with us; there were mass meetings, and fund raising; I had never seen a whole community come together like that. When we came to trial a crowd of 2,500 gathered around the court-house. Mostly, they were people who simply wanted to show by their presence that they were behind the students. As we waited to go inside we sang:

Everybody says Freedom, Freedom, Freedom, Free*dom*, Free*dom*,

and

Everybody says Civil Rights, Civil Rights. . . .

I looked out at the curb, where the police were patrolling, and I saw one burly cop leaning back against his car, singing away: "Civil rights! Civil rights . . ." He saw me watching him, stopped abruptly, and walked to the other side of the car.

—Candie Carawan

Martin Luther King, Jr.— The Power of Nonviolence

Diane Nash: *People think of nonviolence as something very strange and abstract and kind of wishy-washy. Nothing could be less true. Our goal was not just to gain power; it was really to heal the torn-up community around us—to rehabilitate our community. Nonviolence was a way to fight and to heal at the same time. You can't kill somebody to make a beautiful community. We never believed that ends justify means. Instead we believed that, as Mahatma Gandhi of India said, every-thing is really a series of means. . . . The way we fought was, not by hitting and hating the person who oppressed you, but by withdrawing your support from the system—in order to be oppressed you had to cooperate with the oppressor; if you stopped cooperating, the system couldn't work. Nonviolence took as much courage as hitting someone with a pipe—but the results were much deeper.*

Jim Keck, in 1966 a young seminarian[1] working with SCLC[2] in Chicago: *At first a lot of us took the attitude that Dr. King was some sort of a wind-up doll. I mean, we'd drive him around the city and hear him give the same speech over and over. . . .*

This changed one muggy night in June.

King sat in front as, one by one, the tenants of a building walked to a micro-phone to tell about the rats, roaches, lead paint—you name it—they lived with it. . . .

Then, all of a sudden, five blacks we didn't know came to the microphone. They said that this building's landlord was good for the community and that these people were lying. The last one, a woman, said she's the rent collector, and she launches into this speech about these tenants being filthy and dirty and a disgrace to Negroes. Well, a lot of people in the audience started to murmur and say things like "She's right, it is our fault. We are no good."

King expected to give, you know, sermon number 68. But now it was com-pletely on him to pull this out.

He walked calmly to the pulpit and, without any notes, . . . talked about how, after 400 years of slavery, we do have cultural problems, that a lot of testimony we have just heard is true. But we are not a people who have to be preoccupied with our problems. . . . We have a country to save, America, and we have to press on. We have to learn not to be down on one another. Then he looked at the five people who gave the testimony and said, "I understand you are trying to raise families, and we all forgive you. We've all had to do what you did today for the sake of our families."

---

1. **seminarian** someone who is studying to become a priest, minister, or rabbi
2. **SCLC** Southern Christian Leadership Conference, a Civil Rights organization cofounded by Dr. Martin Luther King Jr.

Well, lo and behold, the five each got up and admitted they'd been lying, and the last woman, in tears, asked Dr. King for forgiveness. And the whole audience was screaming, "We forgive you!" People were out of their seats, yelling "Amen!"

I have never before or since heard a person deliver a speech like that. After that, the smart-alecking about King came to an end.

Henry Aaron

The Trailblazer: Jackie Robinson

Jackie Robinson changed the face of major league baseball and was a hero to millions of Americans. Another famous African American baseball player, Henry Aaron, describes the profound effect Jackie Robinson had on his life.

I WAS 14 YEARS OLD when I first saw Jackie Robinson. It was the spring of 1948, the year after Jackie changed my life by breaking baseball's color line. His team, the Brooklyn Dodgers, made a stop in my hometown of Mobile, Ala., while barnstorming[1] its way north to start the season, and while he was there, Jackie spoke to a big crowd of black folks over on Davis Avenue. I think he talked about segregation, but I didn't hear a word that came out of his mouth. Jackie Robinson was such a hero to me that I couldn't do anything but gawk at him.

They say certain people are bigger than life, but Jackie Robinson is the only man I've known who truly was. In 1947 life in America—at least my America, and Jackie's—was segregation. It was two worlds that were afraid of each other. There were separate schools for blacks and whites, separate restaurants, separate hotels, separate drinking fountains and separate baseball leagues. Life was unkind to black people who tried to bring those worlds together. It could be hateful. But Jackie Robinson, God bless him, was bigger than all of that.

Jackie Robinson had to be bigger than life. He had to be bigger than the Brooklyn teammates who got up a petition to keep him off the ball club, bigger than the pitchers who threw at him or the base runners who dug their spikes into his shin, bigger than the bench jockeys who hollered for him to carry their bags and shine their shoes, bigger than the so-called fans who mocked him with mops on their heads and wrote him death threats.

When Branch Rickey first met with Jackie about joining the Dodgers, he told him that for three years he would have to turn the other cheek and silently suffer all the vile things that would come his way. Believe me, it

---

1. **barnstorming** touring rural areas; making brief stops

wasn't Jackie's nature to do that. He was a fighter, the proudest and most competitive person I've ever seen. This was a man who, as a lieutenant in the Army, risked a court-martial[2] by refusing to sit in the back of a military bus. But when Rickey read to him from *The Life of Christ*, Jackie understood the wisdom and the necessity of forbearance.[3]

To this day, I don't know how he withstood the things he did without lashing back. I've been through a lot in my time, and I consider myself to be a patient man, but I know I couldn't have done what Jackie did. I don't think anybody else could have done it. Somehow, though, Jackie had the strength to suppress his instincts, to sacrifice his pride for his people's. It was an incredible act of selflessness that brought the races closer together than ever before and shaped the dreams of an entire generation.

Before Jackie Robinson broke the color line, I wasn't permitted even to think about being a professional baseball player. I once mentioned something to my father about it, and he said, "Ain't no colored ballplayers." There were the Negro Leagues, of course, where the Dodgers discovered Jackie, but my mother, like most, would rather her son be a schoolteacher than a Negro Leaguer. All that changed when Jackie put on No. 42 and started stealing bases in a Brooklyn uniform.

Jackie's character was much more important than his batting average, but it certainly helped that he was a great ballplayer, a .311 career hitter whose trademark was rattling pitchers and fielders with his daring base run-ning. He wasn't the best Negro League talent at the time he was chosen, and baseball wasn't really his best sport—he had been a football and track star at UCLA—but he played the game with a ferocious[4] creativity that gave the country a good idea of what it had been missing all those years. With Jackie in the infield, the Dodgers won six National League pennants.[5]

I believe every black person in America had a piece of those pennants. There's never been another ballplayer who touched people as Jackie did. The only comparable athlete, in my experience, was Joe Louis. The difference was that Louis competed against white men; Jackie competed with them as well. He was taking us over segregation's threshold into a new land whose scenery made every black person stop and stare in reverence.[6] We were all with Jackie. We slid into every base that he swiped, ducked at every fastball that hurtled toward his head. The circulation of the Pittsburgh *Courier*, the

---

2. **court-martial** trial by a military court
3. **forebearance** self-control; restraint
4. **ferocious** fierce
5. **pennants** championships in one of the professional baseball leagues, symbolized by a flag awarded to the winning team
6. **reverence** awe; respect

leading black newspaper, increased by 100,000 when it began reporting on him regularly. All over the country, black preachers would call together their congregations just to pray for Jackie and urge them to demonstrate the same forbearance that he did.

Later in his career, when the "Great Experiment" had proved to be successful and other black players had joined him, Jackie allowed his instincts to take over in issues of race. He began striking back and speaking out. And when Jackie Robinson spoke, every black player got the message. He made it clear to us that we weren't playing just for ourselves or for our teams; we were playing for our people. I don't think it's a coincidence that the black players of the late '50s and '60s—me, Roy Campanella, Monte Irvin, Willie Mays, Ernie Banks, Frank Robinson, Bob Gibson and others—dominated the National League. If we played as if we were on a mission, it was because Jackie Robinson had sent us out on one.

Even after he retired in 1956 and was elected to the Hall of Fame in 1962, Jackie continued to chop along the path that was still a long way from being cleared. He campaigned for baseball to hire a black third-base coach, then a black manager. In 1969 he refused an invitation to play in an old-timers' game at Yankee Stadium to protest the lack of progress along those lines.

One of the great players from my generation, Frank Robinson (who was related to Jackie only in spirit), finally became the first black manager, in 1975. Jackie was gone by then. His last public appearance was at the 1972 World Series, where he showed up with white hair, carrying a cane and going blind from diabetes. He died nine days later.

Most of the black players from Jackie's day were at the funeral, but I was appalled by how few of the younger players showed up to pay him tribute. At the time, I was 41 home runs short of Babe Ruth's career record, and when Jackie died, I really felt that it was up to me to keep his dream alive. I was inspired to dedicate my home-run record to the same great cause to which Jackie dedicated his life. I'm still inspired by Jackie Robinson. Hardly a day goes by that I don't think of him.

from

I Know Why the Caged Bird Sings

Maya Angelou

This chapter from Maya Angelou's autobiography I Know Why the Caged Bird Sings *reveals that a Joe Louis fight was not just about boxing.*

T HE LAST INCH OF SPACE was filled, yet people continued to wedge themselves along the walls of the Store. Uncle Willie had turned the radio up to its last notch so that youngsters on the porch wouldn't miss a word. Women sat on kitchen chairs, dining-room chairs, stools and upturned wooden boxes. Small children and babies perched on every lap available and men leaned on the shelves or on each other.

The apprehensive[1] mood was shot through with shafts of gaiety,[2] as a black sky is streaked with lightning.

"I ain't worried 'bout this fight. Joe's gonna whip that cracker like it's open season."

"He gone whip him till that white boy call him Momma."

At last the talking was finished and the string-along songs about razor blades were over and the fight began.

"A quick jab to the head." In the Store the crowd grunted. "A left to the head and a right and another left." One of the listeners cackled like a hen and was quieted.

"They're in a clench, Louis is trying to fight his way out."

Some bitter comedian on the porch said, "That white man don't mind hugging that niggah now, I betcha."

---

1. **apprehensive** uneasy; fearful about what may happen
2. **gaiety** cheerfulness

"The referee is moving in to break them up, but Louis finally pushed the contender away and it's an uppercut to the chin. The contender is hanging on, now he's backing away. Louis catches him with a short left to the jaw."

A tide of murmuring assent[3] poured out the doors and into the yard.

"Another left and another left. Louis is saving that mighty right . . ." The mutter in the Store had grown into a baby roar and it was pierced by the clang of a bell and the announcer's "That's the bell for round three, ladies and gentlemen."

As I pushed my way into the Store I wondered if the announcer gave any thought to the fact that he was addressing as "ladies and gentlemen" all the Negroes around the world who sat sweating and praying, glued to their "master's voice."

There were only a few calls for R. C. Colas, Dr. Peppers, and Hire's root beer. The real festivities would begin after the fight. Then even the old Christian ladies who taught their children and tried themselves to practice turning the other cheek would buy soft drinks, and if the Brown Bomber's victory was a particularly bloody one they would order peanut patties and Baby Ruths also.

Bailey and I lay the coins on top of the cash register. Uncle Willie didn't allow us to ring up sales during a fight. It was too noisy and might shake up the atmosphere. When the gong rang for the next round we pushed through the near-sacred quiet to the herd of children outside.

"He's got Louis against the ropes and now it's a left to the body and a right to the ribs. Another right to the body, it looks like it was low . . . Yes, ladies and gentlemen, the referee is signaling but the contender keeps raining the blows on Louis. It's another to the body, and it looks like Louis is going down."

My race groaned. It was our people falling. It was another lynching, yet another Black man hanging on a tree. One more woman ambushed[4] and raped. A Black boy whipped and maimed. It was hounds on the trail of a man running through slimy swamps. It was a white woman slapping her maid for being forgetful.

The men in the Store stood away from the walls and at attention. Women greedily clutched the babes on their laps while on the porch the shufflings and smiles, flirtings and pinching of a few minutes before were gone. This might be the end of the world. If Joe lost we were back in slavery and beyond help. It would all be true, the accusations that we were lower types of human beings. Only a little higher than the apes. True that we were stupid and ugly and lazy and dirty and, unlucky and worst of all, that God Himself hated us

---

3. **assent** agreement
4. **ambushed** attacked by surprise

and ordained[5] us to be hewers[6] of wood and drawers of water, forever and ever, world without end.

We didn't breathe. We didn't hope. We waited.

"He's off the ropes, ladies and gentlemen. He's moving towards the center of the ring." There was no time to be relieved. The worst might still happen.

"And now it looks like Joe is mad. He's caught Carnera with a left hook to the head and a right to the head. It's a left jab to the body and another left to the head. There's a left cross and a right to the head. The contender's right eye is bleeding and he can't seem to keep his block up. Louis is penetrating every block. The referee is moving in, but Louis sends a left to the body and it's the uppercut to the chin and the contender is dropping. He's on the canvas, ladies and gentlemen."

Babies slid to the floor as women stood up and men leaned toward the radio.

"Here's the referee. He's counting. One, two, three, four, five, six, seven . . . Is the contender trying to get up again?"

All the men in the store shouted, "NO."

"—eight, nine, ten." There were a few sounds from the audience, but they seemed to be holding themselves in against tremendous pressure.

"The fight is all over, ladies and gentlemen. Let's get the microphone over to the referee . . . Here he is. He's got the Brown Bomber's hand, he's holding it up . . . Here he is . . ."

Then the voice, husky and familiar, came to wash over us—"The winnah, and still heavyweight champeen of the world . . . Joe Louis."

Champion of the world. A Black boy. Some Black mother's son. He was the strongest man in the world. People drank Coca-Colas like ambrosia[7] and ate candy bars like Christmas. Some of the men went behind the Store and poured white lightning in their soft-drink bottles, and a few of the bigger boys followed them. Those who were not chased away came back blowing their breath in front of themselves like proud smokers.

It would take an hour or more before the people would leave the Store and head for home. Those who lived too far had made arrangements to stay in town. It wouldn't do for a Black man and his family to be caught on a lonely country road on a night when Joe Louis had proved that we were the strongest people in the world.

---

5. **ordained** appointed; recommended by authority
6. **hewers** those who chop or cut
7. **ambrosia** the food of the Greek and Roman gods